Arthur Milnes Marshall

Biological Lectures and Addresses

delivered by the late Arthur Milnes Marshall

Arthur Milnes Marshall

Biological Lectures and Addresses
delivered by the late Arthur Milnes Marshall

ISBN/EAN: 9783337378103

Printed in Europe, USA, Canada, Australia, Japan

Cover: Foto ©Andreas Hilbeck / pixelio.de

More available books at **www.hansebooks.com**

BIOLOGICAL LECTURES

AND ADDRESSES

DELIVERED BY THE LATE

ARTHUR MILNES MARSHALL

M.A., M.D., D.Sc., F.R.S.

PROFESSOR OF ZOOLOGY IN OWENS COLLEGE; LATE FELLOW OF
ST. JOHN'S COLLEGE, CAMBRIDGE

EDITED BY

C. F. MARSHALL

M.D., B.Sc., F.R.C.S.

LONDON
DAVID NUTT, 270-271, STRAND
1894

PREFACE

THE majority of the lectures and addresses collected together in this volume have already been printed in the Transactions of several Societies—viz., the lecture on Animal Pedigrees, published in the *Midland Naturalist;* the Presidential address to the Biological Section of the British Association ; and several reprinted from the *Transactions of the Manchester Microscopical Society.* Of these printed addresses I have reproduced as many as possible without involving too much repetition. In the case of the British Association address however it will be found that many of the points discussed are dealt with in other addresses, especially in the lecture on Animal Pedigrees, which is indeed based on that address. It appeared however desirable to include the British Association address, even at the risk of repetition, on account of the importance of its scientific value, and for this reason I have placed it at the end of the series, the others being arranged chronologically.

With regard to the lectures in manuscript,

hitherto unpublished, I have selected a few of those which appeared to be of most interest, and in this I have of necessity been obliged to confine myself to those which were most fully written out. Where amplification was required I have endeavoured, as far as possible, to do this in words which, from my own personal knowledge, I believe would have been used.

The lectures on the Darwinian Theory, which form a distinct course by themselves, will be published as soon as possible in a separate volume, together with other series of lectures, if there appears to be a sufficient demand for them.

I must express my thanks to the Committees of the Manchester Microscopical Society, the Birmingham Natural History Society, and the British Association for permission to reproduce the addresses printed in their Transactions.

I am under great obligations to Professor G. B. Howes for his kindness in reading the proofs, and for supervising the technical points. My thanks are also due to Professor Ray Lankester for valuable suggestions, to my brother Mr. P. E. Marshall for correcting the proofs, and to Dr. C. H. Hurst for assistance on several points.

C. F. MARSHALL.

LONDON, *April* 1894.

CONTENTS

VIII. THE SHAPES AND SIZES OF ANIMALS.

IX. SOME RECENT DEVELOPMENTS OF THE CELL THEORY

X. ANIMAL PEDIGREES.

XI. SOME RECENT EMBRYOLOGICAL INVESTIGATIONS.

XII. DEATH.

XIII. THE RECAPITULATION THEORY.

I

THE MODERN STUDY OF ZOOLOGY

THE man of business knows full well—at times too well—the importance of periodical stock-taking ; of comparing his actual position with his estimated one, of ascertaining exactly how he stands, of assuring himself that his affairs are in a sound and healthy condition, and that the gain on the year's transactions is a real one.   The man who neglects such precautions is apt, sooner or later, to find himself in difficulties : his latest transaction proves a failure, and on attempting to fall back on his former position and start afresh, he finds the ground cut away from beneath him, his reserve fund mysteriously vanished, and his affairs in hopeless confusion.

As in business, so in science, it is well to have periodical stock-takings. Scientific facts accumulate rapidly, and give rise to theories with almost equal rapidity.   These theories are often wonderfully enticing, and one is apt to pass from one to another,

A

from theory to theory, without taking care to establish each before passing on to the next, without assuring oneself that the foundation on which one is building is secure.   Then comes the crash ; the last theory breaks down utterly, and on attempting to retrace our steps to firm ground and start anew, we may find too late that one of the cards, possibly at the very foundation of the pagoda, is either faultily placed or in itself defective, and that this blemish—easily remedied if detected in time—has, neglected, caused the collapse of the whole structure on whose erection so much skill and perseverance have been spent.

Thus men of science find it well occasionally to take stock, to look back for the moment instead of forward, to assure themselves that their operations since the last stock-taking have really resulted in a gain, and to define accurately the nature and extent of that gain.

Science has been aptly compared to a globe, similar to our own earth—a globe with a solid hard crust bounded by an irregular surface.   The solid crust represents ascertained facts, facts that have been confirmed and stowed away in their proper places ; the irregularity of its surface indicates the unequal accumulation of facts in the various branches of knowledge.   The atmosphere by which the whole globe is invested represents the world of speculation, of theories—an atmosphere heavily laden with germs and particles of truth, but germs as yet immature, particles whose position relative to the solid crust is not yet a fixed and determined one.

Our process of stock-taking consists in defining the boundary line between the crust and the atmosphere, between earth and air ; such a process becomes periodically necessary because the contour of the surface is constantly changing ; particles are continually being added to the crust, while those whose places are already determined are liable by reason of these additions to have their relative positions and importance altered. Thus what was at one time a lofty peak, a startling though established generalisation, may become overshadowed by the formation of a far loftier one by its side, of which the original peak becomes but an insignificant shoulder whose original importance is soon forgotten.

I propose, then, in the present paper to take stock of our zoological knowledge, to attempt to define the actual position and aims of zoological thought, the steps by which this position has been attained, and the methods by which it is hoped to achieve these ends.

Such a process is of special and peculiar interest as applied to zoology, firstly, by reason of the great and rapid accumulation of facts that has occurred of late years ; secondly, because of the far-reaching and fiercely contested theories to which these facts have given birth ; and, thirdly, because the study of zoology includes the study of man, so that generalisations concerning the rest of the animal kingdom must apply also to man himself. For these reasons, and more especially for the third one, the theories and generalisations of zoology are always subjected to rigid and jealous scrutiny, not only by those who make zoology a special study, but by the world at large.

In order to know clearly with what we are dealing we may, with Professor Huxley, define zoology as " the whole doctrine of animal life," as being in fact, if such marked alliteration may be excused, all about animals. Now, from very remote times indeed there have existed not only names for different animals, but also collective names for groups of animals agreeing with one another in certain respects but differing widely amongst themselves in others ; collective names such as fish, under which head a great number of animals are commonly included, some of which, such as the whale, are not fish at all ; or birds, including forms as diverse as a starling and a stork, a humming bird and an ostrich. The introduction of such collective names marks the earliest attempts at zoological classification.

Of such classifications we meet with examples in the Old Testament. Thus we read of Solomon that " he spake of trees, from the cedar tree that is in Lebanon even unto the hyssop that springeth out of the wall : he spake also of beasts, and of fowl, and of creeping things, and of fishes."* The object of the writer in the above passage is manifestly to bring into prominence the extent of Solomon's knowledge, and we are certainly led to believe that Solomon had made a personal study of the several groups of animals mentioned—*i.e.*, that

* 1 Kings iv. 33.

he was a zoologist. The passage quoted bears evidence in itself that the four groups named were intended to include the whole of the animal kingdom; but any doubt on this point is removed by the fact that in other parts of the Old Testament the animal kingdom is distinctly divided into these same four groups.* We are therefore justified in speaking of this as a zoological classification.

If we examine this classification more closely we see that the habits of the different animals, and more especially the media in which they live, are made the basis on which the several divisions are founded. Thus beasts include terrestrial animals, animals living on dry land; fowl are those animals that possess the power of flight and so are enabled to live as denizens of the air; fishes are animals adapted for living in water; while creeping things probably included what we now call insects, and any other small forms that could not be referred readily to either of the other groups. Such a system may be spoken of as a classification by distribution. It is one of easy application, and so far a convenient one, but inasmuch as it takes no account whatever of structural and physiological resemblances and differences between the several animals with which it deals it must be regarded as an exceedingly primitive one.

The next classification of any great importance that we meet with is that given by Aristotle, perhaps the greatest and most truly scientific man in the highest sense of the word that the world has

* *e.g.* Deuteronomy iv. 17, 18.

ever known.   Aristotle, like Solomon, is better
known in connection with other branches of knowledge than zoology; still he devoted much attention
to the study of animals, and placed zoology on a
far more scientific basis than his predecessors had
done.   It would appear that Aristotle never drew
up a formal scheme of classification; the system
commonly ascribed to him, which is in reality
compiled from his various writings and was never
given by him in its modern form, is as follows,*
the modern equivalents of the several groups being
indicated in the right hand column.

A. Animals with red blood and a
               backbone   .   .   *Vertebrata.*
    1. Provided with four legs.
        (*a*) Viviparous .   .   *Mammalia.*
        (*b*) Oviparous .   .   *Reptilia.*
    2. Provided with two legs
            and two wings .   .   *Aves.*
    3. Devoid of legs, but pro-   {*Pisces.*
            vided with fins   .   {*Cetacea.*
B. Animals without red blood and
               with no backbone .   *Invertebrata.*
    1. Soft externally   .   .   *Mollusca.*
    2. Soft internally, hard ex-   {*Crustacea.*
            ternally   .   .   .   {*Testacea.*
                                      {*Insecta.*

Such a classification is manifestly based on a

* *Vide* Claus: " Grundzuge der Zoologie " : French Translation
by Moquin-Tandon.   Note B., p. 1099.

totally different system to that of Solomon; the several groups are now characterised not by their habits or the media in which they live, but by resemblances and differences in anatomical structure. The branch of zoology that treats of the structure of animals is called Morphology; hence Aristotle's classification may be contrasted with that of Solomon as being not a classification by distribution, but a morphological classification. Inasmuch as the latter springs from a closer and more accurate acquaintance with animals than the former, it is a better and more scientific one and may be taken as marking a distinct and very important advance in the study of zoology.

The next writer on zoology of any great importance is the elder Pliny, who lost his life A.D. 79, at the celebrated eruption of Mount Vesuvius by which Pompeii and Herculaneum were destroyed. Pliny was to a far greater extent than Aristotle a professed zoologist, and left a voluminous work on natural history in thirty-seven books. He divided the animal kingdom into four main groups, which he named as follows:

1. Animalia terrestria;
2. Animalia aquatilia;
3. Volucres;
4. Animalia insecta;

i.e., he classified animals according as they lived on the ground, in the water, or in the air; dividing them into terrestrial, aquatic, and volatile, with a distinct class for those animals, such as insects, which do not belong to any element exclusively.

This is clearly a classification by distribution, and therefore differs totally from that of Aristotle, while it agrees in principle with that of Solomon. This agreement, however, is not only in principle; if the two schemes of classification be compared it will be seen that they are really identical, a point of some interest. Thus, Pliny's *Animalia terrestria* are the same as the beasts of Solomon; the *Animalia aquatilia* as the fishes; while *Volucres* are obviously equivalent to fowl, and *Animalia insecta* to creeping things. The sole difference between the two systems is in the order in which the several groups are arranged. It would, therefore, appear, that while Aristotle was a long way in advance of any of his predecessors, Pliny, who lived more than 400 years after Aristotle, not only made no advance, but even fell back on the very empirical classification that was in use in the days of Solomon, 1100 years previously, and that had probably been in use for a still longer time.

As Pliny is a writer who owed a considerable part of his reputation to his work on natural history, it may not be inappropriate here to quote the criticism passed on him many centuries after by Cuvier, in order to support my statement that Pliny, instead of placing zoology on a more scientific basis, in reality did it incalculable damage, and threw it back as a science to the condition in which it had been before Aristotle's time. Cuvier's words are as follows :*—" In general, he is only a compiler, and, indeed, for the most part, a compiler

* " Biographie Universelle," xxxv.

who has not himself any idea of the subjects on which he collects the testimony of others, and therefore cannot appreciate the truth of their testimonies, nor even always understand what they mean. In short, he is an author devoid of criticism, who, after having spent a great deal of time in making extracts, has ranged them under certain chapters, to which he has added reflections that have no reference to science properly so called, but display alternately either the most superstitious credulity or the declamations of a discontented philosophy, which finds fault continually with mankind, with nature, and with the gods themselves."

Pliny's influence on zoological thought, though most pernicious, was sufficiently great to completely outweigh his illustrious Greek predecessor; and to this must, I think, be ascribed in great part . the almost complete gap in zoological literature of any value that extends from the time of the Roman zoologist to about the sixteenth century. It was not, indeed, until nearly the middle of the eighteenth century that a system of zoological classification of any permanent value was proposed. For this we are indebted to the great Swedish naturalist Linnæus, the founder of modern natural history as he has been well called.

The system of classification proposed by Linnæus was, like that of Aristotle, a morphological one, based on resemblances and differences of structure in the several animals and groups of animals. He divided the whole animal kingdom into six classes, defined as follows :—

A.   Cor biloculare biauritum, sanguine
       calido rubro.
       1. Viviparis.   *Mammalia.*
       2. Oviparis.   *Aves.*

B.   Cor uniloculare uniauritum, san-
       guine frigido rubro.
       1. Pulmone arbitrario.   *Amphibia.*
       2. Branchiis externis.   *Pisces.*

C.   Cor uniloculare inauritum, sanie
       frigida alba.
       1. Antennatis.   *Insecta.*
       2. Tentaculatis.   *Vermes.*

Of morphological classifications there are two
principal varieties, classification by definition and
classification by type. The Linnæan classification
is a typical example of the former of these. In it
the whole animal kingdom is divided up into groups
of convenient size, each characterised by the presence or absence of some one, two or more easily
recognisable features ; stress being laid on the
differences between the several groups, rather than
on the resemblances between the several animals
included in each individual group. An illustration
will perhaps serve to give a clearer idea of what is
meant. Take a piece of paper and make a number
of dots on it in a perfectly irregular manner. We
want to classify these dots, to arrange them in
groups : if we were to classify them by definition,
we should divide the paper by means of lines passing between the dots into a number of compartments
of convenient size, to which we should give distinc-

tive names ; we should then define the position of any one dot by simply saying in which division it was. As our whole paper is divided up, every dot must fall into some one or other of these divisions, so that our classification is at any rate a simple and a convenient one.

Or, again, imagine a map of England in which the county boundaries are laid down, but all the towns and villages are left out ; such a map would give us a classification of the inhabitants of England, and a classification by definition. Stress is laid simply on the boundary lines between the several divisions, and the sole interest attaching to any particular individual consists in the question on which side of a given arbitrary line he happens to reside. It follows also that in such a scheme those individuals who reside in the centres of the several counties are subordinate in interest to those near the margins of the counties, since about these latter there may be doubt as to which division they should be referred to, while such doubt can hardly exist in the case of the former. Such a map might be very useful, and for purposes of minor importance, such as a parliamentary election or a cricket match, might contain all the information necessary, the sole interest consisting in which side of an artificially drawn line a given individual happened to live.

As the knowledge of anatomy advanced ; as zoologists became gradually acquainted with the structure of a larger and continually increasing number of animals ; as the microscope in the hands of Malpighi, Swammerdam, and their successors gradually revealed the details of minute structure and rendered possible a correct appreciation of the anatomy of animals previously too small to be investigated, it was gradually realised that the Linnæan system, with its hard and fast lines of division, no longer represented the actual state of our knowledge, and classification by definition gradually gave way to the second form of morphological classification—classification by type.

We may explain the difference between the two by means of our former illustrations : thus, to take our first case, we no longer divide our paper by artificial lines, we now look to the dots themselves ; we find that the dots are not always the same distance apart, that many of them fall naturally into groups of various sizes ; each well-marked group we give a name to, and the central member of the group round which the others seem to be arranged we call the type of the group : of the remaining dots, some are so close to our big groups that we include them with these, others form distinct smaller groups of their own, whilst some solitary ones stand quite apart and isolated from all the rest. Or we may, to take our second instance, illustrate classification by type by a map of England, in which the county boundaries are left out, but all the towns and villages marked. Here we have large centres such as London or Manchester, containing large numbers of inhabitants, and representing distinct types ; smaller centres lying immediately round them, not definitely connected with them as yet, but destined ultimately to be so, other small centres lying at a distance from the large ones, and constituting distinct types, and, finally, isolated houses representing species of animals widely separated from their fellows, and forming for the time at any rate small but distinct types of their own.

The distinguishing characteristics of classification by type, and especially the points in which it contrasts most strongly with classification by definition, have been admirably stated by the late Master of Trinity College in the following words :—" The class is steadily fixed, though not precisely limited; it is given though not circumscribed ; it is determined, not by a boundary line without, but by a central point within ; not by what it strictly excludes, but by what it eminently includes ; by an example, not by a precept ; in short, instead of a definition we have a type for our director. A type is an example of any class, for instance, a species of a genus, which is considered as eminently possessing the characters of the class. All the species which have a greater affinity with the type-species than with any others form the genus, and are ranged about it, deviating from it in various directions and different degrees."*

Such a classification represents the real affinities of animals much more truthfully than classification by definition. The sharp boundary lines, of which nature knows nothing, and which formed the main

* Whewell, " The Philosophy of the Inductive Sciences," vol. i. pp. 476-7.

feature of the older system, are here swept away; the resemblances of animals are made of more weight than their differences; and no attempt is made to define the limits of the several groups.

This doctrine of animal types was first brought forward prominently by Cuvier and Von Baer at the commencement of the present century. Cuvier, in his latest system of classification, distinguished four leading types or plans of structure in the animal kingdom, to one or other of which all animals could, according to him, be referred. Mainly owing to the weight of Cuvier's authority this doctrine of types made considerable progress during the first half of the present century; it never, however, wholly replaced classification by definition, and probably never would have done so; for, in the first place, the essence of classification is convenience, and classification by definition is far more convenient for the ordinary purpose of a zoologist than classification by type; and, secondly, although the idea of types expressed a great and important truth, yet it was but the partial expression of a still greater one, which, when fully developed, was destined to completely overthrow all former attempts, and to reveal the only true and unassailable basis of classification. The gradual rise of this new doctrine we have now to notice briefly.

About the commencement of the present century two new influences began to make themselves felt in zoology, two new branches that were afterwards to exert great influence on zoological thought began for the first time to receive serious attention. These were Palæontology and Embryology.

Palæontology, the investigation of extinct animal forms, of those animals and portions of animals known to us only through their fossil remains, was first studied systematically and raised to the rank of a science by Cuvier. Previous to his time fossils had not received serious attention ; even their animal origin was far from being commonly recognised, and the most absurd ideas were in vogue as to their nature and origin ; some supposing them to be mere freaks of nature, others that they were models used by the Creator when he was preparing to stock the earth with animals.

Cuvier did not confine himself to demonstrating that these fossil remains must have proceeded from animals that once lived on the surface of the earth; he studied the distribution of fossils in the different geological strata with great care, and was led to form generalisations of extreme value and interest. The most important of these conclusions are contained in his " Theory of the Earth,"* and are to the following effect :—In the oldest strata of all there are no fossil remains at all ; organised beings were not all created at the same time, but at different times, probably very remote from one another ; the fossil remains of the recent strata approach far

---

* First published in 1798 as the preliminary discourse to the " Recherches sur les Ossemens Fossiles ; " republished separately, with many additions, in 1825.

nearer to the existing forms of animals than do those of the older strata; finally, of the highest forms of animal life—man and the quadrumana—there are no fossil remains whatever.

From these conclusions, the importance of which it is impossible to overrate, Cuvier was led to found his doctrine of *Catastrophism*, according to which there have been periodical annihilations at long intervals of time of all the animals living on the earth at the time; each cataclysm being followed by the creation of a totally new set of animals, which though agreeing in many points with their predecessors, yet presented many marked differences from them.

Cuvier's doctrines, however, did not meet with general acceptance among geologists, and the publication of the first edition of " The Principles of Geology," by Sir Charles Lyell, in 1830, two years before Cuvier's death, may be said to mark the complete overthrow of the doctrine of catastrophism so far as the changes that have taken place in the earth's crust are concerned. A closer study of what is at present occurring on the earth's surface showed that there are now in action forces amply sufficient, given time enough, to produce changes as great as any of which we have geological record; that the elevation of great mountain chains is not due to the sudden action of immeasurably great forces but to the long continued action of apparently insignificant ones; and that there is not only no evidence whatever of the occurrence of the supposed catastrophic periods, but that all the evidence on the point tends to prove that such periods never have occurred.

Though catastrophism thus received its death-blow so far as the crust of the earth was concerned, men still hesitated to apply the same reasoning to the fossil remains of animals, and in spite of the geological evidence the doctrine of catastrophism, *i.e.*, of periodical annihilations and re-creations, continued to meet with acceptance so far as these fossil remains were concerned.

All this time there was steadily developing and gradually acquiring definite shape a doctrine des-tined ultimately to overthrow Cuvier's theories concerning fossils as completely as the geologists had done those dealing with the earth's crust. This was the doctrine of the Mutability of Species.

Cuvier, as we have seen, maintained that species were all due to separate acts of creation ; the new doctrine maintained that species were not immutable, but that one species might give rise to two or more new ones. The actual birth of this doctrine is involved in some obscurity ; it is not quite clear when it first arose, or to whom the credit of its origination is due. It was clearly recognised and advocated by the illustrious Goethe in 1796, but whether this is the date of its birth is not clear.

Its greatest advocates were Lamarck and St. Hilaire, its greatest opponent Cuvier, and long and bitter was the struggle. Though the two former, and more especially Lamarck, worked out the doctrine in the most elaborate manner, yet they were unable to point out the causes at work in the supposed transformation of species; they were unable to show why species should become modified into other species, and so, the *onus probandi* lying with them, victory in the eyes of the world rested with Cuvier. So complete was this victory considered at the time that for nearly thirty years after his death Cuvier's authority was sufficient to keep this new doctrine in abeyance.

At length came the most eventful epoch in the history of zoology, the simultaneous announcement by two independent investigators, Charles Darwin and Alfred Russel Wallace, of the doctrine of Natural Selection, at the meeting of the Linnæan Society on July 1st, 1858. This doctrine effected for the animal world exactly what the geologist had already done for the earth's crust; it showed that there are now in operation causes sufficient, given time enough, to produce all the changes requisite to convert the extinct fossil species into those now living on the earth, causes that must have been in operation since life first dawned on the earth, causes that must inevitably have led to the passage of species into species.

In this way a complete and consistent theory of the history of life on the earth was at length obtained—not only what had actually occurred, but how and why it had occurred. And now at length the true meaning of the laws of Cuvier regarding the distribution of fossil remains was seen, those laws which had led him to form his erroneous theory of catastrophism. For instance, it was seen now that the reason why the fossils of recent beds resemble existing forms more closely than do those of the older beds is simply that there has been a continuous process of evolution ; that the fossils of the recent beds are the ancestors of the now living forms, the descendants of the fossils of the older beds, and thus occupy an intermediate position genealogically ; in which case their intermediate position structurally becomes at once intelligible.

Recognising these facts, attempts were soon made to reconstruct the path of descent, to trace out the pedigree of some given species. This was first accomplished with any degree of success in the case of the horse. The horse, the zebra, and the ass stand alone among mammalia in possessing but one complete functional toe on each limb ; they must either have been specially created as such, or must have been derived from some more typical mammalian form. Owing to their large size, the fact that bones are fairly easily preserved as fossils, and the great time that must have elapsed during the gradual transformation of some typical mammal to the highly specialised horse, it is only reasonable to expect that some direct evidence of this transformation should be forthcoming. Consequently this furnishes a very good test case. Without entering into details, which would be unnecessary in what is now so familiar an instance, it will suffice to state that a series of fossil forms is now known furnishing a complete gradation from older tertiary forms with four or five toes on each foot, through newer tertiary forms to the horse with its one functional toe on each limb ; that, in other words, the pedigree of the horse has been completely and satisfactorily worked out.

Another familiar but striking example is afforded by birds. These are very highly speoialised forms, and stand apart from other vertebrates in a number of anatomical points. We are now acquainted with a large number of fossil forms serving to connect birds with reptiles, and showing the several gradations by which reptiles gradually lost their teeth, acquired wings and feathers, and became birds.

If then it is possible by the aid of fossil remains to reconstruct the pedigree of some particular form or group of forms, why should it not be possible for all animals ? As the possibility of this reconstruction gradually dawned on man, so it was slowly realised that such a reconstruction, such a pedigree, would in itself be a perfect system of classification, and the only really natural one. Such a classification may be spoken of as a genetic or genealogical classification.

The idea of such a classification is familiar to all of us through the medium of our own special genealogies : these generally take the form of a tree in which the stem represents our earliest ancestor, who, in this country at least, usually takes the form of some impoverished adventurer, whom we should probably be intensely ashamed of could we see him in the flesh, whose sole virtue lies in the fact that he "came over with the Conqueror," and whose sole possessions of any importance appear to have been a crest, a motto, and a coat of arms ; the primary branches of the stem represent the off-spring of this all-important ancestor ; the secondary branches their offspring, and so on, each branch denoting a generation. Some of the branches die off, stop, and become extinct ; others persist and thrive : the ultimate branchlets of these last bear the leaves, which are the actually living representa-tives of the family, on the topmost of which we inscribe our own name.

A genetic classification of the animal kingdom takes a similar form ; the stem represents the earliest and most primitive form of animal life, the branches the several forms derived successively from this and from one another, while the terminal leaves represent the actually existing forms. If we draw horizontal lines across our tree, these may be taken to represent the different geological ages ; then the branches cut by any one line or plane will represent the life on the earth at that period. Some of the branches never reach the top of the tree ; these represent forms of life that attained their full development in some of the earlier epochs and then became extinct.

Such a genetic classification is at once felt to be the only really natural one, to be in fact an ideal classification. It is simply an embodiment of fact, not an expression of opinion : it is therefore ab-solutely unassailable, and what is more, true for all time. The recognition of the possibility of such a classification is the distinguishing feature of modern zoology, and the determination of such genetic histories or phylogenies of the several groups of animals is the goal towards the attainment of which the efforts of zoologists are directed.

Having traced the way in which this idea arose, how increase of knowledge and perfection of methods caused classification by definition to replace the crude ideas embodied in the classifications adopted by Solomon and Pliny, and then in its turn to give way to classification by type, and having seen how finally the doctrine of natural selection rendered possible the conception of a genetic classification, it may not be out of place to devote a few words to considering the methods by which it is proposed to attain this end.   These are as follows :

1. The accumulation of anatomical facts concerning as large a number of animals as possible ; this requires no further explanation.

2. The systematic study of the geographical distribution of the different animals and groups of animals, both recent and extinct.   This, which is a comparatively new branch of zoology, has already yielded results of immense importance, and promises to yield others of even greater value in the future.

3. Palæontology, or the study of the anatomy of extinct animals and their relations to existing forms.   We have seen above that it is to palæontology that we owe the first successful attempt to reconstruct the pedigree of some one given form ; and inasmuch as the connecting links between the several groups of animals are almost necessarily extinct, it is clear that the evidence yielded by

those extinct forms must be invaluable. Still it must be borne in mind that it is only certain animals, and of these animals only certain parts, that are capable of being preserved as fossils, so that palæontology can only help us as regards certain groups of the animal kingdom, and even concerning these its evidence must necessarily be very imperfect and fragmentary. Indeed, had we only these three methods to aid us, the attempt to reconstruct the pedigree of the animal kingdom could only be successful to a very partial and limited extent. Fortunately there is another method which supplies us with evidence of the very kind we most want, and which bids fair to far outweigh in importance the other three methods. This is :

4. Embryology, or the study of the actual development of existing forms, the several changes which they undergo during their gradual evolution from the ovum. This, which is the second of the two new influences referred to in a preceding page, is, like palæontology, a young science, but one that has thriven mightily of late years. It was not till towards the middle of the present century that it began, in the hands of von Baer, to assume its modern form, and it is only of recent years that it has revealed its enormous powers as an instrument for the solution of the hard problems of phylogeny. Von Baer propounded the doctrine of animal types quite independently of Cuvier ; and he went further than his illustrious contemporary, for he showed that not only as far as structure was concerned might animals be arranged under certain definite

types, but that each type had its own mode of development, and that all the animals included in any one type agreed with one another in the fundamental features of their development. Thus the several members of the type of animals known as *Vertebrata* all develop in a fundamentally similar manner ; in their earlier stages they resemble one another so closely that it is often no easy matter to distinguish one from another, the characteristic differences not appearing till the later stages of development. A good example of this is given by von Baer himself, as follows : " In my possession are two little embryos in spirit, whose names I have omitted to attach, and at present I am quite unable to say to what class they belong. They may be lizards, or small birds, or very young mammals, so complete is the similarity in mode of formation of the head and trunk in these animals. The extremities, however, are still absent in these embryos ; but even if they had existed in the earliest stages of their development we should learn nothing, for the feet of lizards and mammals, the wings and feet of birds, no less than the hands and feet of men, all arise from the same fundamental form."

As soon as the idea of the mutability of species was fairly grasped, the reason of these embryological resemblances became apparent, and it was seen that if two species or groups of animals develop in the same way this is due to their being genetically allied to one another.

Further consideration of this question led ultimately by a series of steps, which space forbids me to notice, to the promulgation of what is known as the recapitulation hypothesis. This which is found lurking in the works of von Baer, but first received definite expression from Fritz Müller, is commonly stated thus : *The development of the individual is an epitome of the development of the species*—*i.e.*, the actual changes through which an animal passes in its development from the egg to the adult represent in a condensed form its genealogical history or pedigree.

Thus embryology provides us with a completely new and very accessible clue to the determination of animal genealogies—a clue of such extreme value that we cease to wonder at the immense importance attached to it by the modern zoologist, or at the time and perseverance that are expended in attempts to penetrate its mysteries. For the clue thus afforded is the one on which we have chiefly to rely in our efforts to unravel the knotty problems of genealogy, and it is a clue in the following up of which extreme caution is necessary. If the recapitulation hypothesis were strictly true, if the ontogenetic history of an individual were an accurate and complete reflection of its specific history or phylogeny, then our task would be a comparatively light one. But it is not so. As Fritz Müller has pointed out with admirable clearness* the ontogeny of an individual is not a simple abbreviated history of its phylogeny, but a history obscured and falsified by a variety of causes, the

* Für Darwin (English translation), chap. xi., pp. 110 *seq.*

most important of which are the tendency to shorten the processes of development, thereby causing the omission of stages which may be of extreme historical significance ; and, secondly, modifications introduced by natural selection into the ontogenetic history in consequence of the struggle for existence which free-living larvæ have, in common with adult forms, to undergo.

Thus, in spite of the powerful aid afforded us by embryology, our problem is still one of extreme difficulty, requiring for its solution great patience, great manipulative skill, and, above all, the faculty of distinguishing accurately between essentials and accidentals. A good beginning has already been made, mainly through the energy of zoologists in other countries than our own. England has not yet contributed her fair share towards the solution of a problem the conception of which was first rendered possible by the magnificent labours of one of the greatest of her children, Charles Darwin.

THE INFLUENCE OF ENVIRON-MENT ON THE STRUCTURE AND HABITS OF ANIMALS

I PROPOSE to ask your attention for a short time to the consideration of the dependence of any body, living or dead, organised or unorganised, organic or inorganic, on its environment, *i.e.*, on the external conditions surrounding and acting on it at a given time, and I propose to consider this more especially with regard to animals.

Of environment, as affecting inanimate objects, many admirable examples are afforded us by Physics. For instance, we speak of water as a definite substance having a definite existence, but we know well enough that for the existence of water as such certain definite relations of temperature and pressure are essential. At the normal pressure water will not exist as water at a temperature below $0°$ C. Similarly, if we raise the temperature beyond a certain limit, $100°$ C., the existence of water as water again becomes impossible. If we alter the pressure the relations change again, for when the pressure is increased beyond the normal amount we find that the water will remain liquid at a temperature at which it would previously have assumed the solid form of ice.

Let us take another example from Chemistry. Chemical formulæ have a very definite appearance, yet every chemist knows well that the reactions they indicate will only occur provided certain conditions of environment be fulfilled, especially those of temperature and pressure; and that a change of no great extent in environment may cause either a completely different reaction or even an actual reversal of the previous action. For instance, Mercury at 300° C. combines with oxygen to form oxide of mercury; now if the temperature is raised to 400° C. this action is reversed.

I have purposely chosen simple and familiar examples in order to illustrate with as little loss of time as possible what we mean by environment. The points to which I wish to direct attention are these: Firstly, that the actual condition of any body may be regarded as the resultant of the several forces acting on it at the time; secondly, that therefore, if we know all the conditions of environment, we can calculate with certainty the actual condition of the body; thirdly, that a change of known amount in one of the elements of the environment will produce a definite and calculable change in the conditions of the body acted on. In other words, that not only has environment a marked and definite action, but that this action is capable of exact measurement.

Now let me turn to the more immediate subject

of my paper, viz., the influence of environment on the structure and habits of animals. It will, of course, be at once conceded that changes in environment not only can but do produce changes of very great magnitude in both the structure and habits of animals—for example, domestic breeds of cattle, &c.; but in most of these cases the conditions are very complicated, and it is impossible to assign to each factor its true value. What I wish to prove to you, if possible, is that change of environment not only produces changes of structure and habit, but also produces definite and calculable changes, so that a definite change in environment is always followed by a definite change of structure, and the result can be predicted with as much certainty as a chemical reaction.

For this purpose all ordinary examples fail us because the environment is too complicated, *e.g.*, pigeon fanciers can produce at pleasure a bird with any number of feathers in the tail they wish, and with almost any variety of plumage, but as to which of the elements of a complicated and artificial environment the result is due we are completely in the dark. For this purpose it is necessary to choose our examples carefully, and the number of available ones that are not of too technical a character for general discussion is very limited.

We have seen that it is very easy to establish a general relation between changes of environment and changes of structure, and that the one series is followed at once by the other. Now this general relation is not sufficient for our proposition, much more rigid proof being necessary before we can accept it.   I wish first to ask your attention to one or two cases in which this proof appears to be present, and in which we are able to establish not only a general but a direct causal relationship between environment and structure ; as unquestionable indeed as that which holds in the case of oxide of mercury.

Now we know of at least one well authenticated case in which the structure of an animal responds in as precise a manner to simple and definite changes in one of the elements of the environment as certain chemical reactions do to alterations of temperature.

Artemia salina is a small aquatic crustacean about half an inch in length, and somewhat like a small shrimp in appearance ; its distribution is peculiar, inasmuch as it is only found in water containing from 4 to 8 per cent. of salt, a much higher proportion than is found in the sea.   It consequently can only occur in salt lakes and in such places as the salt pans of Lymington and other similar places where the sea-water is allowed to gradually concentrate by evaporation.   Another form, *Artemia Milhausenii*, is known, whose habits are still more peculiar, for it is only found in water containing at least 25 per cent. of salt ; its distribution is consequently a very limited one, since it can only occur in certain inland lakes in which, owing to special circumstances, the water attains this very high percentage of saltness.

Artemia Milhausenii differs from *Artemia salina*

in so many points of structure that the two forms have always been unhesitatingly ranked as separate species. Of these differences one will suffice for the present purpose. In *Artemia salina* the tail is split at the end into two long pointed lobes, each of which bears a large number of bristles and hairs of a peculiar structure ; the tail in the other species, *Artemia Milhausenii*, is abruptly terminated, and presents only a very slight separation into two blunt rounded lobes, which lobes are completely devoid of hairs or bristles. There are besides this many other points of difference between the two forms which need not here be noticed in detail.

Schmankewitsch has recently made the very interesting discovery that the anatomical differences between the two species depend directly and solely on the different percentages of salt in the water they inhabit. He finds if he takes *Artemia salina*, living in water containing 4 per cent. of salt, and gradually increases the percentage of salt, that the structure of the *Artemia* becomes gradually modified ; the lobes of the tail become shorter and shorter, and the hairs diminish in size and number. Ultimately, by increasing the strength of the salt up to 25 per cent., he succeeded in completely transforming *Artemia salina* into the distinct species *Artemia Milhausenii*. Not only can the transformation of one species into another be effected in the laboratory, but it can be demonstrated to actually occur in Nature. Of this fact Schmankewitsch has recorded the following very striking instance : Two lakes in the neighbourhood of the Black Sea were separated from one another by a dam ; of these the upper and larger lake contained water with about 4 per cent. of salt in which *Artemia salina* occurred in great numbers. The water of the lower lake contained about 25 per cent. of salt and had no *Artemia* living in it at all. From some cause or other the dam burst, and the water from the upper lake rushed down into the lower and smaller one, large numbers of *Artemia salina* being carried down by the flood. The dam was repaired, and the water of the lower lake, the strength of which had been reduced by the flood to about 8 per cent. of salt, began slowly and gradually to regain its former strength. Specimens of the *Artemia* were taken out and examined from time to time, and it was found that as the percentage of salt rose the tail-lobes of the *Artemia* gradually got shorter and blunter, the hairs got smaller and fewer, and the whole animal gradually became transformed from *Artemia salina* to *Artemia Milhausenii*. In about three years' time the water had regained its former strength of 25 per cent., and the *Artemiæ* had become completely transformed into *Artemia Milhausenii*.

Not satisfied with this, Schmankewitsch next tried the reverse experiment. Starting with *Artemia Milhausenii* he gradually decreased the strength of the water in which they lived by adding fresh water, and had the satisfaction of finding that as the percentage of salt diminished so the tail-lobes of his *Artemiæ* became longer and their hairs more abundant, and when the strength of the water was reduced to about 6 per cent. all the *Artemiæ* were converted to typical specimens of *Artemia salina.* Having thus satisfied himself of the causal relations between the two species of *Artemia* he determined to push his experiments still further. He therefore went on adding fresh water after he had obtained *Artemia salina,* and by this means converted *Artemia salina* into a well-known fresh-water form that had previously been considered not only a separate species but even a distinct genus—*Branchipus.*

From these very striking experiments it would appear that the relation between the structure of the animal and the degree of saltness of the water it inhabits is a perfectly definite one, so much so, that if the percentage of salt be told us, we are able to foretell with perfect confidence and certainty, not only what will be the general character of the animal inhabiting it, but such minutiæ as the size and shape of its tail-lobes, and even the number of hairs borne by these lobes.

Here then is a very striking proof of the direct action of environment on structure ; a phenomenon as definite as a chemical reaction. Nor must the case be made light of or explained away by saying that it simply shows that zoologists were at fault in describing these forms as distinct genera and species, and that the experiment showed them to be mere varieties ; for it must be noticed that the characters by which the three forms differ are characters of the very kind that are invariably employed by zoologists to distinguish the genera and species of Crustacea ; while the ultimate criterion of distinct species—fertile breeding—bears the matter out also, for no one of the three forms is capable of living in the medium dwelt in by either of the others.

We also know of several cases among butterflies in which, out of a very complex environment, we are able to put our finger on the one element which is the actual determining cause of the structural changes that we observe. One of the most important of these examples is furnished by two butterflies of widely different appearance, *Vanessa levana* and *Vanessa prorsa*.

Vanessa levana has a red ground colour, with black spots and dashes and a row of blue spots round the margin of the hind wings ; *Vanessa prorsa* is deep black, with a broad yellowish-white band across both wings and with no blue spots. These were formerly called distinct species, but have recently been shown to be varieties of one and the same species. The relation between them is a very definite one, and they are what is called seasonally dimorphic : that is, they are double brooded, and have two generations in the course of the year—a winter brood and a summer brood. In the summer or autumn Prorsa is alone met with, and the pupæ developed from the autumn brood of eggs of Prorsa hybernate during the winter and hatch in April or May of the following spring, not as Prorsa, but as Levana. This in turn produces a brood of eggs which develop into Prorsa again. This phenomenon was investigated by Weismann, who found it was to be attributed to the direct action of cold and heat. He found that if the pupæ of Levana, which would ordinarily have produced Prorsa, were put in a refrigerator for one or two months the butterflies emerged partly as Levana and partly as another form, intermediate in many respects between Levana and Prorsa. Thus the direct action of cold causes pupæ, which in the normal state of things would have produced Prorsa, to produce Levana.

The reverse process, however, is not successful, for heat does not change Levana into Prorsa. The explanation of this is, perhaps, not out of place, although it has no direct bearing on the subject in hand. Levana is the parent form, and in the glacial epoch there was only one single brooded variety and one generation in the year. The lengthening of the summer gave rise to a second generation, and the gradual action of climate caused the Prorsa form to arise. Now, Levana being the parent form, the effect of cold in causing pupæ that would normally have become Prorsa to become Levana is simply a case of reversion. The reverse action could clearly not occur. It is a long time since the glacial epoch was over, and therefore probably a long time since the two forms Levana and Prorsa were established ; hence the reconversion by cold is only partial.

A similar example is afforded by another butterfly, *Pieris napi*, the green-veined white. This is also double brooded, and occurs as two varieties, each producing the other. The winter form is rather smaller, and has more black at the bases and less at the tips of the wings than the other variety. The green veining on the under surface is also more marked. If the pupæ of the summer brood are placed in a refrigerator for three months, and then in a hothouse, they hatch in about three weeks as the winter form.

These illustrations I have cited show the direct action of cold producing a result which can be calculated on beforehand with certainty. By the long-continued application of heat the summer form has been produced, and if the environment is altered and cold substituted for heat, we reverse the action and bring back the summer form to the original winter one.

Now let me refer to an instance in which the evidence is as yet incomplete—an instance somewhat more technical than the previous ones. I choose it purposely because it is of a somewhat abstruse kind, and will therefore serve to show that some of the more intricate problems concerning the exact nature of the relation between environment and structure and habits may be well within our grasp.

Many animals possess the power of changing colours—*e.g.*, the chameleon, frog, many fish, and the cuttle-fish. This power depends on the presence of chromatophores or pigmented bodies found in the skin, which have the power of changing shape. These are of different colours and are arranged in layers, some near the surface, some deeper; the light yellow cells being most superficial, then the red and brown, and the black deepest of all. If the superficial ones contract, the deeper ones will become more apparent, and *vice versâ.* These changes of colour always bear a relation to the surface on which the animal is placed at the time, and are therefore supposed with good reason to be protective. Many attempts have been made to explain this.

Lister believed that the irritation which excites the action of the chromatophores does not act on them directly, but through the intermediation of the optic nerve. It is essential for this action that the eye and optic nerve should be present and healthy, the action ceasing if the eye is destroyed or the nerve cut. In support of this view he pointed out that blind fish are always dark. Pouchet suggested two possible paths of impulse—the spinal cord and the sympathetic system. By dividing the spinal cord the path of impulse was shown to pass along the sympathetic nerves. Again, by dividing some branches of these, he produced zebra-like markings of the skin. Dewar showed that different colours of the spectrum influence the eye differently and cause electric currents of different intensity according to the light employed. These currents are strongest with yellow light, weakest with purple, and nil with black. Semper pointed out that, though electric currents and nerve currents are far from being the same thing, we may not unfairly assume that the nerve current, like the electric current, is greatest with yellow light and nil with black. Thus a black ground, which absorbs nearly all the light, and therefore reflects little or none, will stimulate the eye to a very faint extent, and hence cause a very feeble current, if any at all, and so the chromatophores will remain unstimulated, and as in the case of the blind fish, the fish will remain dark. On the other hand, light from a red or blue object will cause a current of rather greater intensity, and will cause the brown or red chromatophores to expand, and so more or less conceal the black ones. Finally, yellow light will cause the strongest stimulation and all the chromatophores will give out processes ; the yellow ones, being most superficial, will be the most conspicuous, and will hide the deeper and darker ones to a greater or less extent.

In the foregoing remarks I have endeavoured to show, first in a general way, and afterwards by the consideration of a few selected examples, that the relation between an animal and its environment is a very definite and direct one, and in many cases a calculable one.

We have seen from certain special cases that an organism responds promptly and with certainty to certain changes in its environment. Can we not extend this and speak of the actual structure of an animal as the resultant of the various forces acting on it, both external and internal ? Small changes in environment seem to give rise to results altogether disproportionate with themselves ; but then we must remember that the bodies of animals are of very complex chemical composition and in very unstable equilibrium, and in such cases a

small force may very easily cause a very considerable rearrangement. Turning to psychology,
we see that the tendency of modern research is
to show that whatever we do or think is merely
the resultant of what we have done or thought
or suffered previously.

It is not difficult to show that, even in our own
worldly transactions, changes of environment often
produce not only direct and immediate changes
and readjustments, but also definite and calculable
ones.

Thus, as an example, let a be a merchant, and
b his purse: the combination ab will at once strike
you as a natural and stable one. Indeed there
is something about the word merchant that seems
to suggest inevitably a well-lined purse. Now
'et c be a highwayman, and d his pistol: the
combination cd is again recognised as a natural
and stable one. Now bring the compound ab
into the presence of the compound cd, and mark
how the stability of the former is shaken: ab, a
previously stable compound, becomes at once
curiously unstable; the merchant and the purse
that we were wont to view as inseparable are
split asunder at once, and the several elements
become rearranged in a manner that finds perfect
expression in the formula:

$$ab + cd = a + bcd.$$

Again to take another instance which will remind
us of the operation known in chemistry as double
decomposition: Let a be a small boy, b a penny
in his pocket, c an old woman with an apple stall,

d the apples.   The combination *ab* is a remarkably unstable one in the presence of *cd*, and the affinity between *a* and *d* is very great; an interchange takes place as follows :

$$ab + cd = ad + bc.$$

These examples are no doubt somewhat crude, yet they will serve to indicate that if we could define all the conditions we should be able to draw up an equation for a man's life and show how, given the man and the conditions acting on him, there was but one path open to him.

In conclusion let me refer to a statement by Herbert Spencer in which he discusses the influence of environment on animals; starting, however, from a standpoint that I cannot accept, viz., the Lamarckian hypothesis of animals responding by efforts of their own to changes in environment.

The more complete the correspondence between external and internal changes, the more complete the power of response to changes of environment, the higher is the grade of the animal and, as a rule, the longer is its life and the less its fertility.   In this respect man stands the highest, for instance, in the power of counterbalancing changes of temperature, and in the supply of food consequent on seasons.

Perfect correspondence to change in environment would be perfect life, eternal existence. Death, whether from natural decay, disease or accident, is simply due to failure of the organism to respond effectively to changes of environment.

III

ON EMBRYOLOGY AS AN AID
TO ANATOMY

THERE are perhaps few sciences, or branches of science, in which progress has been so rapid and whose importance has been so suddenly and unexpectedly revealed as that of embryology. When we consider the vast number of papers, memoirs, and treatises that are continually being poured forth it is difficult to realise that embryology, as we now understand it, practically commenced in 1837 with the publication of von Baer's treatise on the Development of Animals. The Study of Invertebrate Embryology is still more recent, and in its modern form is only about a dozen years old. No one who compares our text-books of biological science of the present day with those of twelve or even six years ago can fail to be struck with the great change effected by embryology in the methods of teaching this science.

At the outset men hardly knew what to do with this new branch of science; for its study the delicate methods used in histological research were necessary, and hence for a time embryology was included as a branch of physiology and taught by physiologists.   But anatomists soon saw that this science belonged by right to them, and that it was absolutely essential for them to master it.   A zoologist of the present day relies quite as much on his razor as his scalpel in his endeavour to comprehend the structure of animals.

It is not difficult to see how it is that embryology has so rapidly attained such importance, the reason being that it has afforded an altogether new and very tangible clue to many of the most interesting problems of biology which have been thereby first brought within the comprehension and grasp of man.   Thus the zoologist has in embryology obtained a very important clue to the determination of the affinities of animals ; in fact we should hesitate to definitely assign a place to some animals whose development was unknown.   To the philosophical biologist a clue is thus given to the determination of what, to him, is the problem of problems—viz., phylogeny, or the genetic connection between one animal and another and between their various classes.   While to the anatomist embryology offers an explanation of many otherwise completely unintelligible anatomical facts.   To the members of a medical society anatomy means, and perhaps I may be permitted to say rather too often means, simply human anatomy.   I therefore choose for closer consideration a problem, the main conditions of which are familiar to every one who has dissected a head and neck.   The problem to which I refer is that of the nerve supply of the muscles by which the various movements of the eyeball are effected.

Whoever has dissected the orbit cannot fail to have been struck with the large number of nerves which not only traverse it but supply parts contained therein ; and also with the additional fact that these are either distinct nerves or branches of distinct nerves, and not merely separate branches of one or two cranial nerves.   Thus, of the twelve cranial nerves no less than six are distributed wholly or in part to the contents of the orbit.   When we consider that of the remaining six, two—the olfactory and the auditory—are nerves of very special function and limited distribution, and that another one—the spinal accessory—has but slight claim to be considered a cranial nerve at all, the fact becomes still more striking.   A further and far more significant fact than the above is that of these six nerves four are exclusively distributed to the orbit, and send branches nowhere else.   Of these four nerves one is the optic nerve, while the other three supply the muscles by which the movements of the eye are effected.   I must ask your indulgence for a moment if I refer to such an exceedingly familiar fact as the arrangement and distribution of these muscles and their nerves.   I only do this because it is absolutely necessary to the argument I wish to put before you that this arrangement and distribution should be fresh in your minds.

The movements of the eyeball are effected by six muscles—four recti and two obliqui. Of these, speaking roughly, the superior rectus turns the eye upwards ; the inferior rectus turns it downwards ; the internal and external turn it inwards and outwards respectively ; the superior oblique rotates the eye outwards and downwards, the inferior oblique outwards and upwards. Of these six muscles four are supplied by the third cranial nerve, while each of the remaining two has a separate and distinct cranial nerve to itself, the fourth cranial nerve supplying the superior oblique muscle, and the sixth cranial nerve the external rectus.

Now it is a very remarkable fact that this small group of muscles should have three cranial nerves to supply them, and still more remarkable that these nerves should do little or nothing else. The third nerve, besides. supplying the muscles mentioned, also supplies the elevator muscle of the upper eyelid and sends branches which penetrate the eye and supply the ciliary muscle and iris. The fourth and sixth nerves, however, do nothing else, and form unique instances of nerves with separate origins from nerve centres distributed exclusively to single muscles, and it is very curious that these two muscles should both be connected with the eye. In order to complete the conditions of the problem it is only necessary to add that the distribution of the nerves and muscles I have just noticed is not peculiar to man but occurs throughout the whole vertebrate series almost without exception. Wherever we meet with a vertebrate having well-developed eyes, there we find this same arrangement of muscles and nerves. The exceptions to this rule that have been quoted are probably only apparent. The few exceptions that are quoted are worth noticing. In *Amphioxus* the eye is a mere spot of pigment and has no muscles at all; in *Myxinoids* the eyes are small and the eye-muscles imperfect, but all three nerves, though very small, are found to be present and with their usual distribution; in *Lepidosiren* there are no oblique muscles, and the third, fourth, and sixth nerves are said to be absent; the observations on this point are, however, imperfect. In some of the lower *Amphibia*, the newt for instance, all three nerves are present, at any rate proximally, although distally they may become closely bound up with branches of the fifth nerve. With these exceptions, in all fish, amphibia, reptiles, birds, and mammals these six muscles are all present and all have their typical nerve supply. Let me again remind you that these nerves supply nothing else; the third nerve supplies no other parts than those I have mentioned; the fourth nerve never supplies any-thing besides the superior oblique muscle; the sixth nerve invariably supplies the external rectus, but may also supply two other muscles when these are present—viz., the retractor muscle of the eye, which is found in some newts, many reptiles and most mammals, except the monkeys and ourselves, and the special muscle of the nictitating membrane, which is met with in birds and reptiles.

Such a state of things so widely spread must

have a reason for its existence, but hitherto no satisfactory or even intelligible answer has been given to the problem, and anatomy still leaves us in total ignorance as to why the external rectus muscle has a special nerve all to itself. Explanations have of course been attempted, for the problem cannot fail to strike any one who is acquainted with the anatomy of the parts in question. A common attempt is to say that the movements of the eye are so complex and have to be so extremely nicely adjusted that a complex nerve supply is necessary. This, I would submit, is no explanation at all ; it does not tell us in the least why a small group of six muscles should have three cranial nerves to supply them. For we find the same nerve supply in the lowest vertebrates, in which we cannot suppose these movements to be very complex. Nor does it suffice to say that the nerve supply is due to the two eyes having to work together, and the internal rectus of one eye having to work habitually with the external rectus of the other, for in these lowest vertebrates the eyes are situated at the sides of the head, so that they have totally distinct fields of vision and hence do not work together at all. Sir Charles Bell, the illustrious anatomist, who was keenly alive to the interest of the problem before us, attempted an explanation as follows : Observing that during sleep and also during certain involuntary acts, such as sneezing, the eyeball is turned upwards beneath the upper eyelid, and finding by experiment that the recti muscles are voluntary, he was led to regard the oblique muscles as involuntary, especially the superior oblique, whose separate nerve supply was supposed to be thus accounted for. However, as Bell himself points out, this theory involves an assumption which more recent research has failed to verify. He showed that division of the superior oblique muscle causes the upward rolling of the eyeball to be increased, and that therefore if this movement is due to an impulse transmitted along the fourth nerve this impulse must be of such a nature as to cause not contraction but relaxation of the muscle—*i.e.*, that stimulation of the fourth nerve causes relaxation of the superior oblique muscle and not contraction.

I have referred to the views of Sir Charles Bell for two very sufficient reasons : firstly, because this is, so far as I am aware, the only rational attempt that has been made to grapple with the problem before us ; secondly, because any account of such a question without reference to the opinion of the great anatomist who did so much to render it possible for us to understand problems connected with the distribution of the nerves would be a gross injustice.

So far we have failed utterly to master our problem ; anatomy and physiology have alike failed to give us the clue we require, and for my part I see no reason why, if we had nothing else to help us, this should not always be so, and the problem be ranked as insoluble. It is under circumstances such as these that the anatomist turns to embryology—that sheet-anchor of philosophical anatomy—

to which, when in difficulty, he has of late years turned so often and so rarely in vain ; and I wish now to ask your attention for a short time while I endeavour to make clear to you the evidence which embryology offers on this point.   1 must again ask your indulgence if I have to refer to matters many of which are perhaps painfully familiar to you, while others may appear at first sight to have nothing whatever to do with the matter in hand. This evidence applies only at present to Elasmobranch fishes, but the conditions of the problem are absolutely the same as in man.

You all know that there is in the trunk a space between the body walls and the alimentary canal called the pleuro-peritoneal cavity or body cavity, or, still better, the cœlom, this space or cavity being absent in the head and neck. That is, if you were to push a sharp instrument through the walls of the abdomen into the intestine the instrument would not pass through solid tissue along its whole course but would traverse a cavity—the cœlom—before reaching the intestine. While if you performed a similar operation in the neck the instrument would pass through no cavity but would penetrate solid tissue all the way until the œsophagus was reached. Now the whole body is formed from three cellular layers or strata—the epiblast, mesoblast, and hypoblast—and if we make a diagrammatic section through the body the epiblast will form the outermost layer or skin ; the hypoblast will form the lining of the alimentary canal ; all the rest will be mesoblast. The body cavity or cœlom is entirely within the substance of the mesoblast. In the earliest stage of development the mesoblast is solid and there is no cœlom. In the trunk the mesoblast very early splits into two layers which become separated from each other and so give rise to the cœlom. It was formerly assumed to be a sharp distinction between the trunk on the one hand and the head and neck on the other, that in the former the mesoblast splits in this manner and that in the latter it does not do so. This distinction is now known not to hold good, for the splitting of the mesoblast has been shown to extend to the head, but the cavities on each side do not meet in the median ventral line. Again, in the trunk the cœlomic cavity becomes divided on either side into an upper or dorsal part, and a lower or ventral part. Each of the dorsal portions becomes cut up transversely into a number of segments arranged one behind the other in series, one such segment occurring in each primary body segment or protovertebra. In the head the cœlomic cavity is first cut up transversely by the visceral clefts into a series of cavities, one in each visceral arch, and then each cavity divides again into dorsal and ventral portions. The ultimate result is the same as in the trunk, but the order of division is different.

Of these divisions of the cœlom in the head, or head cavities as they are called, we are only concerned with the three most anterior. The first head cavity—the premandibular—is in front of the mandible and immediately behind the eye ; the second—the mandibular—is situated in the mandibular arch; the third—the hyoidean—is in the hyoid arch. Now in the trunk the walls of both the dorsal and ventral divisions of the cœlom become converted into muscles, and the cavities of the dorsal division become obliterated owing to the great increase in the thickness of their walls. In the head cavities the walls of both dorsal and ventral divisions become converted into muscles in the same way, and the only difference is that both dorsal and ventral cavities become obliterated instead of the dorsal only. If we bear in mind that the transverse divisions of the dorsal portion of the cœlom into segments is obviously part of the general segmentation of the body, and that the similar division of the head cavity is manifestly of the same nature, we see that we may speak of these first three head cavities as indicating three distinct and successive segments of the head comparable to three distinct and successive body segments.

We have now accomplished by far the most difficult and tedious portion of our task, but let me direct your attention to another set of organs. The central nervous system consists at an early period in all Vertebrates of a tube closed at both ends stretching along the back of the animal from head to tail. This tube is not of uniform calibre, but its anterior part—the future brain—is from the first wider than the hinder part—the future spinal cord. The anterior part is bent in the shape of a hook, and presents along its whole length a series of alternate dilatations and constrictions which are much larger and more conspicuous in the brain than elsewhere, but occur along the whole length of the cord. The first dilatation is the fore brain, and from it the cerebral hemispheres project; the second is the mid brain; this is followed by a series of vesicles, rapidly decreasing in size, and called collectively the hind brain; behind this we have the spinal cord. In the spinal cord the dilatations, though only feebly marked, manifestly correspond to the segments, and from each one a pair of spinal nerves arises. Similarly in the brain from each well-marked vesicle a pair of nerves arises. Thus, from the mid brain the third pair of nerves arises and runs backwards to the interval between the first and second head cavities. From the first vesicle of the hind brain arises the fifth nerve, and this passes down between the second and third head cavities. From the second vesicle of the hind brain the seventh or facial nerve springs and runs down behind the third head cavity. The division of the head into segments is thus very clearly and satisfactorily shown, for all the different elements that could afford evidence—viz., brain vesicles, nerves, head cavities, and visceral clefts and arches— all point to the same divisions and agree among themselves.

We have now got all the links of our evidence nearly complete; let us fit them together and give them the finishing strokes. We have seen that the walls of the head cavities like their homologues in the body develop into muscles. Now the first head cavity lies immediately behind the eye and extends round it so as to invest it like a cup. From its walls are developed the rectus superior, rectus inferior, rectus internus and obliquus inferior muscles—*i.e.*, all the muscles supplied by the third nerve. At last we see why the third nerve supplies these and no other muscles; it does so because it is the nerve belonging to the segment in which the first head cavity lies; and therefore supplies the muscles that are formed out of the walls of that cavity. This reason is a complete and sufficient one.

Concerning the obliquus superior we are still in the dark; it does not appear to have any connection with the first head cavity, and this is sufficient reason why it should not be supplied by the third nerve. The development of the nerve that does supply it—the fourth—is at present absolutely unknown. Concerning the rectus externus muscle we are in a better position. The sixth nerve which supplies it bears the same relation to the seventh nerve that the anterior root of a spinal nerve does to the posterior root. The rectus externus has no connection with the first head cavity, but lies altogether superficially to it, and for some time behind it; it appears to be developed partly from the third head cavity and possibly in part from the second. We see now clearly why it is not supplied by the third nerve, the reason being that it does not belong to the segment which is supplied by that nerve, but to one further back.

Thus, we have not quite a complete, but quite a novel and, I think, an intelligible clue to the solution of our problem.

IV

THE THEORY OF CHANGE OF FUNCTION

WHEN asked to read the opening paper of the second session of the Owens College Biological Society, I felt that the subject most suitable for the occasion would be one gathered from the works of that great Englishman whose name it was at one time proposed that this Society should bear ; that prince of biologists who has taught us not to be satisfied with a knowledge of facts but to seek earnestly for the reason of these facts ; who has taught us both what to seek and how to seek, and who has thus rendered philosophical biology not only a possibility but an actuality.

In selecting the particular aspect of Mr. Darwin's wonderful theory, to which I should draw your attention, I have been influenced mainly by two circumstances. In the first place it appeared more profitable, and therefore more likely to prove acceptable to the Society, to select some portion to which exception has been taken rather than one which has met with general acceptance; to consider one of the numerous difficulties in the way of accepting the theory of Natural Selection, difficulties pointed out by none so clearly as Mr. Darwin himself.

The second circumstance to which I have alluded as influencing my choice was the accidental fact that some work on which I happened to be engaged some little time ago brought me into very violent, and for the time very embarrasing contact with one of these said difficulties, and thus compelled me to take its bearings and measurements very accurately in order to discover in what way it might most conveniently be circumvented or surmounted, or, if possible, removed altogether.

I purpose then asking your attention to one of the more serious of the many alleged difficulties in accepting the doctrine of Natural Selection and to a brief consideration of the means proposed for removing that difficulty. Let me first attempt to define clearly the nature of this obstacle. In the higher animals we meet with a great number of very complex organs, each with very definite functions, such as the eye, the ear, and the hand. Now, according to the Darwinian theory, the mode in which such organs have attained their present complexity and perfection is as follows:

Once upon a time the ancestors of these animals possessed eyes less perfect and less complex than those they have at present. Now no two animals of the same species have eyes absolutely identical with one another; slight differences always occur, and of these slight differences it must happen that certain ones are improvements, are changes for the better, or what we call useful modifications.   All the animals possessing these useful modifications will be slightly better off and will have a slight advantage over their companions who have not got them.   Now more animals of every species are born than can possibly live.   Hence the greater proportion of animals that are born die, and die young before they have produced any offspring.   It is clear that those animals which have this slight advantage over their brethren will by virtue of this fact have a better chance of living.   Now we know as a fact that such variations tend to be inherited—*i.e.*, to be handed down from the parents in whom they first appeared to their offspring, and not only so but also that they tend to appear in the offspring in a rather more strongly developed form.

Hence we get this state of affairs ; certain forms of a particular species, say of deer, tend to survive because they have some slight accidental modification of their eyes which gives them a slight but distinct advantage over their brethren ; they transmit this modification and with it this advantage to their offspring; certain of their offspring present the modification in a greater degree not only than their brethren but also than their parents.   These will get a slight additional advantage and will tend to survive, and so on for successive generations.   The gradual accumulation of these slight modifications will in time cause a perceptible change in the structure of the eye, and as each successive modification is preserved only because it is useful it is clear that the eye will as a whole have improved and have become more perfect. Similarly with the hand or with any other of the organs of the body; formerly less complex, it has acquired its present complexity and perfection as the result of accumulations of a long series of small but useful modifications. Each of these modifications must give some distinct advantage to its possessor or else it would not be preserved or perpetuated.

It has been objected that this explanation is not sufficient; that although it will account for the gradual perfection and increasing complexity of an organ after it has attained a certain size and after it has assumed its definite function, yet that it fails completely to explain the first origin of such organs; for in their earliest origin they must have been very minute and absolutely incapable of fulfilling or even aiding in the function which they are afterwards destined to perform.

This objection, which is the one I wish to consider to-night, must be confessed at once to be of very great weight, and is indeed freely acknowledged to be so by Darwin himself. By some writers, such as Mivart (almost the only English naturalist of any repute who at the present day rejects the doctrine of Natural Selection), it is indeed considered as absolutely fatal to the whole theory. We shall perhaps get a clearer idea of the nature and force of the objection by considering one or two examples which bring it forward prominently.

The limb of a Vertebrate in its earliest stage is a

small bud arising from the surface of the body and ·is absolutely useless for any of the purposes to which we put our arms. If this represents the primitive condition, why should such an organ have been preserved at all? Again, a more striking example and one yet not thoroughly explained is found in the wing of the bat. This is a great fold of skin connecting together the much elongated fingers, and also connecting these with the sides of the body extending downwards so as to involve the legs as well. This constitutes as we know a very efficient flying apparatus. The theory of evolution undoubtedly requires that bats should be descended from, should have had as ancestors, mammals possessing fingers of normal length and devoid of the lateral expansion of the skin. The theory of Natural Selection demands further that the various steps in the transformations of this ancestral form to the existing bat should have been slow and gradual. Now it is obvious that a very slight lengthening of the fingers, coupled with a very slight increase in the extent to which they were webbed, would in no way enable the ancestral mammal to fly; and hence that such accidental variations could never have been preserved and perpetuated because of their utility as flying organs.

Cases such as these have long been felt to offer very serious difficulty and to throw serious doubt, not on the reality of Natural Selection, but on its sufficiency. Darwin himself suggested a possible solution of the difficulty, at any rate in certain cases, by pointing out that an organ which had already attained considerable size and complexity might, owing to some change in the habits or surroundings of the animal possessing it, have not its structure but its function changed—*i.e.*, that an organ already in use for one purpose might become employed for some other purpose, might gradually lose its original function and undergo further modifications fitting it better for its adopted function.

This idea, which clearly affords us a possible mode of getting over the difficulty, is only briefly alluded to by Darwin, but was taken up and developed by Dr. Dohrn who, in a pamphlet published in 1875, discussed it at considerable length.

A very good example of the principle in question is afforded by the swimming bladder of fishes. This, in most fish, is a closed sac lying just underneath the vertebral column. In many fish it acquires a connection by a duct with some part of the alimentary canal. It then becomes an accessory breathing organ, especially in those fish which are capable of living out of water for a time— *e.g.*, the Protopterus of Africa. An interesting series of modifications exists connecting the air bladder with the lung of the higher Vertebrates, which is undoubtedly the same organ. The air bladder of fishes is in fact a very good example of change of function, inasmuch as it is used originally for purposes of flotation and afterwards it is pre- served as a lung. This example is instructive also because the evidence of embryology, on which we are accustomed to rely, fails utterly here.   The lung develops as a pit-like depression in the floor of the œsophagus.   Now this could not have been the earliest origin of the lung, for it would be utterly useless as such for the simple reason that food would always be falling into it.

In developing the theory of Change of Function Dr. Dohrn points out that it is a very common thing, if not the general rule, for an organ to have not one function alone but a number of different functions to perform, of which functions one at any given time is predominant and the rest subordinate ; but that it is quite conceivable that some slight change of circumstance might cause the relative importance to be changed, and one of the subordinate functions to become the primary one, or to put it in his own words : "Each function is a resultant of several components of which one is the principal or primary function, the other secondary.   Diminution of the primary function and increase of a secondary function alters the total function ; the secondary gradually becomes the primary, the total function is changed and the issue of the whole process is the transformation of the organ."

For instance, the primary function of the stomach is undoubtedly the secretion of gastric juice ; a secondary function is the movement of its muscular walls aiding the action of the gastric juice by bringing the contents into closer contact with it.   Now in no animal are the glands absolutely uniformly dispersed over the stomach walls, and it is readily conceivable that both glands and muscular wall might be better developed in one half of the stomach than the other, and indeed this condition actually occurs in the stomach of the rat. A continuance of this modification brings us to the condition met with in the ruminant stomach. Here the first compartment is a mere receptacle for the storing of food, and in this no digestion takes place at all. Again, from the same starting-point, we have another series. Suppose the glands to aggregate at one end of the stomach, and the muscular coat to be thickened at the other ; if we carry this far enough we get to the condition of the stomach of the bird where peptic glands are confined to one part, muscles to the other. Here the second portion has completely lost its original primary function, this having become replaced by a secondary function which has now become primary.

The modifications of the limbs of Arthropods afford numerous and admirable illustrations of the case before us. Here we have organs whose primary function is undoubtedly locomotion, but of which a certain number, greater or less, in different groups, have become modified so as to aid in the mastication of food. Naturally, those nearest the mouth are the ones so modified, and of these, those at the actual sides of the mouth are most likely to undergo the greatest modifications. Such modifications, if extreme, would unfit them for their primary locomotor function, hence we find the first post oral pair of appendages, the mandibles, in most Arthropods completely and permanently altered, both structurally and functionally, the hinder ones being altered to less extent.

Of the two divisions of the limb the inner or endopodite is the nearer to the mouth, and consequently most likely to be useful for purposes of feeding.   On the other hand, for swimming, the exopodite is of equal, if not greater, importance ; for walking the endopodite is of most use as being more directly beneath the body.   Another good example of change of function is found in the hyomandibular cleft.   This, like certain other clefts, has become saved from destruction by becoming modified into an accessory organ of hearing.

The olfactory organ furnishes another illustration of the theory, and with regard to this let us first consider what appear to be the difficulties of the case. All Vertebrates possess olfactory organs with the solitary exception of Amphioxus, that curiously exceptional Vertebrate whose anatomy seems to be made up of contradictions.   These olfactory organs have in all cases the same essential structure. Certain differences occur, but these are so slight as to leave no doubt whatever that the vertebrate olfactory organs are, wherever they occur, the same organs.   As soon, however, as we get beyond Vertebrates we meet with a difficulty.   There is no doubt that Vertebrates came into existence later than Invertebrates, therefore Vertebrates must either have inherited their olfactory organs from their invertebrate ancestors, or must have acquired them for themselves.   An olfactory organ is found in Invertebrates ; some insects almost certainly have them, but these could not have been the ancestors of the vertebrate olfactory organ.   Now if the Vertebrates did not inherit them as such they must have got them some other way, either acquired *de novo* or by change of function.   Now in its time of appearance, its mode of development, the histology of its epithelium, there is a very close resemblance between the olfactory organ and a gill. Hence there are strong reasons for regarding the olfactory organ of Vertebrates as a modified gill. It has been stated that the mode of development of the olfactory nerve as an outgrowth from the cerebral hemisphere constitutes a serious objection to this view as differing from the other cranial nerves. This objection does not now hold good, since it has been shown that the olfactory nerve develops in the same way as other cranial nerves.

In conclusion, we seem to have in this principle of change of function a real and practicable solution to the chief difficulty in the way of accepting the doctrine of Natural Selection, a solution that has long been overlooked, and whose real importance has, I believe, yet to be appreciated.

V

BUTTERFLIES

THE beauty of butterflies is partly due to their shape and proportions and to their very graceful outline, but it is in their colouring that their chief beauty lies; and concerning this colouring I wish to say a few words, even at the risk of repeating what is already familiar.

The colour of a butterfly is due to the scales which cover both surfaces of the wings and which are easily rubbed off by our fingers. These scales are of various shapes and overlap each other like the tiles on a roof, each having a short stalk for insertion into a small depression in the wing. Their variety of colour is extraordinarily great and is due partly to actual pigments; the brightest tints however, and more especially the metallic lines seen in some foreign butterflies, and perhaps best of all in humming-birds, are due to fine lines on the surface of the wings producing what are known to physicists as interference colours.

Let us consider the question. Why should

butterflies be thus gaily clothed ? The older naturalists thought it sufficient to say that butterflies were beautiful because their beauty gave us pleasure, and that it was for our enjoyment that these delicate tints and gorgeous hues existed. But this is clearly incorrect, for the most magnificent butterflies are found in parts where man but seldom visits, for instance, tropical America and the East Indies. The true explanations are varied and not the same in all cases.

Sexual Colours.—With butterflies as with birds there is often a striking difference between the sexes, the male as a rule being the more gaily coloured. Among birds, for instance, the cock bird is often most gaily coloured ; the hen bird being more soberly coloured, and indeed often plain. The peacock, drake, and bird of paradise will at once occur to our minds as illustrations. Mr. Wallace pointed out that the sober colouring of the female was explained as protective so as to escape detection when sitting on eggs on an open nest. The male usually taking no share in incubation had no special need for protective colouring. Mr. Darwin explains the specially brilliant colours of males as due to what he calls sexual selection, that is, to the fact of the female preferring a smart male to an untidy one. So with butterflies and moths ; and if we watch butterflies or birds coquetting we soon convince ourselves that the males know they are beautiful, and mean to show off their beauty to its best advantage in the hopes of gaining the affection of the female.

It has been objected that this is going too far; that the proper appreciation of the colours and tints of butterflies, birds, or flowers requires considerable training and a distinct intellectual effort on our part, and that it is absurd to suppose that what we ourselves only do imperfectly and with difficulty a butterfly can do just as well and without effort. But I do not think we ought to reject an explanation just because it happens not to be particularly flattering to ourselves. In the case of flowers it has been conclusively shown that their colours, markings and odours are developed to attract insects—bees, beetles, and butterflies—to visit them and so fertilise them; in other words, to advertise themselves. The colours of flowers are as beautiful and as varied as those of butterflies. And if, as it is acknowledged, butterflies and birds understand and appreciate the differences between the colours of gay flowers, and if those colours are developed simply to attract them, why deny them the power of appreciating similar colours in themselves and in one another? Again, the appreciation of colour in ourselves has greatly developed; for if we study the history of painting and compare the oldest pictures, whether oil or water colour, with more recent ones we note a distinct development in the power of appreciating the full effect of colour, or what is known as the colour sense.

Protective Colours.—So far we have considered the colours of the upper surface only. With regard to the colours of the under surface the case is different; here the colours are protective, and butterflies have the habit of turning up their wings when resting, so as to expose the under surface only. The under surface is coloured like the leaves, twigs, and especially the flowers on which they most love to perch, for it is then that they are most exposed to the attacks of enemies and have the most need for protection. To appreciate this it is necessary to see them in their haunts, and to watch them at home. The best marked instance is *Kallima*, which is met with in India, the Malay Archipelago and Sumatra. It is very common in these places, and is a large showy butterfly with orange and purple colouring on the upper surface, and is a rapid flier frequenting dry forests. It always settles where there is some dead and decaying foliage, for the colouring on the under surface of the wings bears a remarkable resemblance to that of a dead leaf, and when the wings are turned up and the head and body hidden between them, it is often very difficult to distinguish them from dead leaves, the resemblance being rendered even more close by the short tail which looks like the stalk of a leaf, and by the markings on the under surface which closely imitate the mid-rib and veins of a leaf. Speaking of this insect Mr. Wallace says : "The colour is very remarkable for its extreme amount of variability, from deep reddish-brown to olive or pale yellow, hardly two specimens being exactly alike, but all coming within the range of leaves in various stages of decay. Still more curious is the fact that the paler wings, which imitate leaves most decayed, are usually covered with small black dots, often gathered into circular groups, and so exactly resembling the minute fungi on decaying leaves that it is hard at first to believe that the insects themselves are not attacked by some such fungus. The concealment produced by this wonderful imitation is most complete, and in Sumatra I have often seen one enter a bush and then disappear like magic. Once I was so fortunate as to see the exact spot on which the insect settled, but even then I lost sight of it for some time, and only after a persistent search discovered that it was close before my eyes."

This example serves as an extreme case of what is really a general law among butterflies.

The mode in which this protective colouring is acquired is explained by Natural Selection. At first there is a more or less accidental resemblance. Now large numbers of butterflies are killed by birds, lizards, and other animals, and any whose markings and habits of perching rendered them less easy to see would have a better chance of escaping their enemies ; these, therefore, will survive and transmit their peculiarities to their offspring ; the survivors of these in turn transmitting the peculiarities in a more strongly marked form, and so the protective colouring becomes more marked from generation to generation and the unprotected ones perish.

Warning Colours.—These are found in specially protected individuals which are usually uneatable, or at any rate unpalatable, and whose nastiness it is desirable to advertise in order that they may not be eaten, or at any rate killed, by mistake. Their object, therefore, is not to escape notice, but to be readily seen and recognised. The best examples of these are found in three great families of butterflies—the Heliconidæ, found in South America, the Danaidæ, found in Asia and tropical regions generally, and the Acræidæ of Africa. These have large but rather weak wings and fly slowly. They are always very abundant, and all have conspicuous colours or markings and often a peculiar form of flight; characters by which they can be recognised at a glance. The colours are nearly always the same on both upper and under surfaces of the wings, and they never try to conceal themselves, but rest on the upper surfaces of leaves and flowers. Moreover, they all have juices which exhale a powerful scent; so that if they are killed by pinching the body a liquid exudes which stains the fingers yellow, and leaves an odour which can only be removed by repeated washing. This odour is not very offensive to man, but has been shown by experiment to be so to birds and other insect-eating animals.

Another example is furnished by the skunk, which, although not included in the immediate subject of this lecture, may be mentioned as an extreme case illustrating the point we are considering. Concerning this animal I cannot do better than quote Mr. Wallace again: "This animal possesses, as is well known, a most offensive secretion which it has the power of ejecting over its enemies, and which effectually protects it from attack.   The odour of this substance is so penetrating that it taints and renders useless everything it touches or in its vicinity.   Provisions near it become uneatable, and clothes saturated with it will retain the smell for several weeks even though repeatedly washed and dried.   A drop of the liquid in the eyes will cause blindness, and Indians are said sometimes to lose their sight from this cause.   Owing to this remarkable power of offence the skunk is rarely attacked by other animals, and its black and white fur and the bushy white tail carried erect when disturbed, form the danger signals by which it is easily distinguished in the twilight or moonlight from unprotected animals. Its consciousness that it needs only to be seen to be avoided gives it that slowness of motion and fearlessness of aspect which are, as we shall see, characteristic of most creatures so protected."

Recognition Colours. — A good instance of this class of colouring is seen in the upturned white tail of the rabbit which, although making it conspicuous to its enemies as well as friends, is probably a signal of danger to other rabbits ; and when feeding together, in accordance with their social habits, soon after sunset or on moonlight nights, the upturned tails of those in front serve as guides to those behind to run home on the appearance of an enemy.   Many birds, antelopes, and other animals have markings believed to serve a similar purpose, and probably the principle of distinctive colouring for recognition has something to do with the great diversity of colour met with in butterflies.

Mimicry.—Many butterflies escape destruction through mimicking the appearance of uneatable or venomous forms ; for instance, *Leptalis*, a form allied to the common garden white, mimics the *Heliconidæ*, a widely distinct family, in the shape of its body and wings, in its colour, and even in its habits and mode of flight, so much so that they are difficult to distinguish. They are much rarer than the forms they mimic, and may aptly be compared to the Ass in the Lion's Skin. It is often only the female which mimics, for this has greater need for protection. The deception is indeed often so good that it may deceive not merely an expert naturalist but even the insects themselves, and Fritz Müller says : " I have repeatedly seen the male pursuing the mimicked species till after closely approaching and becoming aware of his error he suddenly returned." Other examples of mimicry are found in the beehawk moth, which mimics the humble bee ; in the clearwing moths, which receive names such as apiforme, vespiforme, from the insects they mimic ; and, among other animals, the harmless snakes mimic the venomous ones. Again, the " devil's coach horse," the beetle with the habit of turning its tail over its back and pretending to have a sting, certainly deceives children and perhaps grown-up people as well. Many other instances of mimicry could be cited ; a certain spider simulates the droppings of birds for instance, and a blue butterfly was actually seen by Wallace resting on what was apparently dung but in reality a spider. Nor is the advantage of the power of mimicry confined to animals, for among ourselves the power of pretending to be other than what we really are is often of the greatest possible service to us. For example, the success of a detective largely depends on his being able to pass himself off as something else and to entirely conceal his real calling.

There is an old view which holds that colours are due to the direct action of the sun, but this will not explain the constancy of colouring in most species, or the bright colours of butterflies in climates such as our own. There are some cases, however, in which differences in temperature, at any rate in the season of the year, appear to have had a distinct influence on colour, the best known examples being the common continental butterflies *Vanessa levana* and *Vanessa prorsa* and the English butterfly *Pieris napi.**

Colour is perhaps in part a matter of indifference, and a part may be red because there is no reason why it should be otherwise. The red colour of blood, the red colour of many deep sea animals, the blue colour of the sky, and perhaps the green colour of the grass and vegetation generally, may, for all we know, be indifferent.

The Senses of Butterflies.—Our knowledge of this very interesting subject is at present very imperfect. We know that the sense of smell must, at any rate in some forms which have a liking for dead and decaying animal matter, be very acute. The eyes

---

* For a full account of these see paper on "Environment," p. 34.—ED.

are compound and their facets extraordinarily numerous, as many as 12,000 being present in the eye of the death's-head moth, and 17,000 in the swallow-tailed butterfly. The range of vision in butterflies is unknown. Of the sense of hearing in butterflies we know very little, but in moths and other insects the antennæ are often fringed; and some most interesting experiments have been made with the antennæ of the male mosquito, special hairs of which were found to vibrate to particular notes, those hairs being most affected which were at right angles to the direction from which the sound came. The sound is thus most intense if directly in front of the head; if one antenna is affected more than the other the head is turned till both are equally affected, and so the mosquito is enabled to direct its flight directly towards the point from which the sound originates; this power being specially used to aid it in finding the female.

The Life-History of Butterflies.—A butterfly is not always a butterfly, but goes through several phases—viz., the egg, the larva or caterpillar, the pupa or chrysalis, and the adult form or imago. The caterpillar phase is the nutritive one; the adult phase is reproductive and usually short-lived, often not more than a few days, and sometimes limited to a few hours. The *eggs* are usually protectively coloured, and often show very beautiful markings under the microscope. It has been shown that while at least nine-tenths of the eggs and larvæ of North American butterflies are destroyed by parasites or disease, such parasites never attack the eggs of the Danaidæ, and it is possible that these are distasteful to their foes at all stages of their existence. The eggs of butterflies are always laid in safe places and as near as possible to the proper food for the young; the butterfly never sees her young and can have no clear idea as to the respective merits of cabbages, carrots, and oak-leaves, yet she makes no mistake.

The *larva*, or caterpillar, is soft and fleshy and is very easily injured. It is furnished with a biting mouth, soft fleshy fore-legs, and a terminal sucker. It has three pairs of harder jointed legs corresponding to the legs of a butterfly and which are sometimes very long, as in the lobster moth. The great and only work of caterpillars is to eat, and this they do all night, many of them all day as well. They feed on the leaves of plants by means of their powerful jaws, and have no need even to stop to take breath, for their breathing is carried on by means of spiracles or pores along the sides of the body which lead to the tracheal tubes by which the respiration of insects is effected. Their rapid growth soon renders their skin too tight and the outer layer, or cuticle, is thrown off like that of a crab or lobster; after this they eat more ravenously than ever to make up for lost time, often commencing with their cast-off clothes. As a rule there are several of these castings before the caterpillar attains its full size. Their gain in weight is prodigious, the caterpillar of one of the hawk moths for instance, *Acherontia*, weighing about one-eighth of a grain on leaving the egg, in thirty days increases its weight 10,000 times. Even this is not the limit, for some caterpillars live three years ; for instance, the goat moth, which grows to 72,000 times its weight on hatching.

The shapes and colours of caterpillars follow the same laws as those concerning the adult insect, the colour being generally protective because the caterpillar is soft and fleshy and good eating for birds. The colour for this reason is usually green, and those feeding on grass are striped longitudinally, those on larger leaves obliquely, this forming a very effective protection. Others are brown, and so like twigs in shape that even the most experienced may be deceived. Mr. Jenner Weir writes : "After being thirty years an entomologist I was deceived myself. I took out my pruning knife to cut from a plum tree a spur which I thought I had overlooked. This turned out to be a larva of a geometer two inches long. I showed it to several members of my family and defined a space of four inches in which it was to be seen, but none of them could perceive that it was a caterpillar."

Warning colours are well seen in caterpillars. All green and brown ones are readily and greedily eaten by birds, lizards, and frogs, but many are conspicuously coloured and do not attempt to conceal themselves, and these are usually nauseous to the taste. For instance, the gooseberry moth caterpillar was given to frogs to eat, whereupon they "sprang forward and licked them eagerly into their mouths ; no sooner had they done so than they seemed to become aware of the mistake they had made, and sat with gaping mouths rolling their tongues about until they had got quit of the nauseous caterpillars, which seemed perfectly un-injured and walked off as briskly as ever."

Terrifying colours are also met with ; in the caterpillars of the puss moth and hawk moth the eye spots are of this nature, and the caterpillar of *Bombyx regia*, the " hickory horned devil " of the Southern States of North America, is ornamented with an immense crown of orange-red tubercles which if disturbed it erects and shakes from side to side in a very alarming manner, the negroes believing it to be as deadly as the rattlesnake, whereas it is really perfectly harmless.

The *pupa*, or chrysalis, is the last stage of existence of the caterpillar. The change from caterpillar to butterfly is an enormous one, not merely as regards the possession of wings, but as regards the whole organisation ; the mouth, the digestive system, the nerves, the eye and all parts being most profoundly modified. The chry-salis period is the stage of rest, and constitutes a protected condition in which these changes can be effected. This stage sometimes lasts a few weeks or even days only, sometimes months or during a whole winter. In the case of the small eggar moth, insects of the same brood appear a few at a time each year up to fourteen or fifteen years. Now the time of appearance of the moth being February, it is obvious that in a severe winter the whole brood might be killed off if they all appeared at the same time, hence the advantage of appearing a few at a time in successive years.

Pupæ are of various forms: (1) *Underground pupæ*, which are found in crevices in walls and the roots of trees, the holes in which they lie being often carefully lined. These pupæ have some power of motion, and work their way to the surface before the imago emerges from the pupa. (2) *Suspended pupæ*. A good example of these is found in the pupa of the common tortoiseshell butterfly. The larva having chosen a suitable place, by means of the glands which open on the under lip, spins a little button of silk strong enough to support its weight; it then thrusts its tail into the button and swings head downwards. It has now to get out of its skin without letting go its hold, and this it does by gradually working out of its skin, which has previously been split along the back, and pushing it towards its tail. Before completely escaping, it gets the tip of its tail free while the part in front of the tail is still fixed, the lining of the trachea and intestine helping to suspend it; it then stretches its tail up to the button of silk, fixes itself and spins round several times to secure a firm hold, finally casting away its larval skin. Other larvæ sling themselves up by a girth of silk, and some are flexible enough to attach the thread on one side, carry it over and fix it on the other side, repeating this process several times. Others again spin the girth of silk first and then slip their heads under it; some, such as the swallow-tail, hold the silk in their claws till it is strong enough, and then slip it over their heads.

Many other interesting points could be mentioned in connection with butterflies, but those I have briefly touched upon will serve to indicate what interesting questions arise from the study of butterflies and other insects, and what good examples they afford us of many of the problems of Natural History.

FRESH-WATER ANIMALS

I PROPOSE to speak this evening about the fauna of fresh-water ponds and streams, a subject of very special interest to the members of the Society, many of whom have a far more intimate and accurate acquaintance with special groups than I can either claim or reasonably hope to possess. Still, there are some points of general interest which may have escaped the observation of those who have chiefly concerned themselves with one or two particular groups ; and it is with regard to these more general conclusions that I propose to speak to-night.

As regards geographical distribution the entire animal kingdom may conveniently be divided into terrestrial and aquatic forms, and the latter again subdivided into those that live in the sea, and those inhabiting fresh water. The marine fauna is infinitely more abundant, and includes a far greater number of species than that found in fresh water ; and we can hardly be surprised at this. A glance at a map of the world will show that the area covered by the ocean is much greater than that occupied by land—the proportion being about three to one. Moreover, only a very small portion of the land is taken up by rivers and ponds; so that the area over which fresh-water forms can exist is necessarily much more restricted than that inhabited by marine animals.

Again, geologists show us that the land is subject to constant change in level and in extent, owing to upheaval or depression ; and these oscillations, especially those of depression, must cause great disturbance, or even local annihilation, of the fresh-water fauna. By upheaval on the other hand, shallow water marine areas may be cut off from the sea, and converted into brackish marshes, and ultimately into fresh-water ponds ; the animals inhabiting them being either killed off, or else adapting themselves to the altered environment, and becoming converted into fresh-water forms.

From these and other similar considerations it may be concluded that fresh-water animals must, with few exceptions, have been derived from marine forms, and my chief object this evening is to consider the various modifications, either in structure or life-texture, which marine animals undergo in consequence of becoming adapted to fresh-water life.

Why should marine animals strive to work their way up rivers ? Why should they not stop in the sea ? The reason is not far to seek, and is to be found in that struggle for existence we hear so much about, but the full extent of which we too often fail to realise. Very large numbers of every species of animal perish before reaching maturity. If we reflect for a moment on the really enormous number of eggs which fish and other marine animals lay, it is clear that if all these eggs, in the case of any single species, were to come to maturity, there would very soon be little room in the sea for anything else. A mackerel of a pound weight, for instance, will lay eighty thousand or ninety thousand eggs, a cod may produce five millions, and a conger-eel no less than fifteen millions. However, the vast majority in every species never come to maturity, but are devoured while young by other animals, as food ; while a very small minority, favoured by the possession of some slight accidental advantage, escape destruction, survive, and perpetuate the species. So keen is the struggle for existence in the sea, especially in the shallow waters round the coasts, where life is far more abundant and competition more severe than at greater depths, that many forms, belonging to different groups, have, to escape it, worked their way up the rivers, and adapted themselves to fresh-water life.

Let us now see what these fresh-water animals are like, to what groups they belong, and what are their most important characteristics. The first of the eight large groups into which the animal kingdom is usually divided is that of the Protozoa. These include the simplest unicellular forms of animal life, and occur very abundantly in fresh water, though certain important subdivisions—*e.g.*, the

Radiolaria, are almost exclusively marine. Of the next group, or Sponges, some thirty-nine or forty families are recognised, of which one only occurs in fresh water, the rest being exclusively marine. Among the Cœlenterata, to which the polypes, sea anemones and corals belong, much the same state of things occurs, for of about seventy families only three have fresh-water representatives; whilst of the next group, the Echinodermata or starfish, sea-urchins, etc., not a single species inhabits fresh water. In the remaining groups we find the fresh-water forms rather more abundant. The Vermes, or "worms," using the term in its widest sense, have a large number of fresh-water representatives, such as the river worms, Rotifera ; but here also the greater number of families of worms have no fresh-water members. Among the Mollusca we find that several of the best marked groups never get into fresh water, while other groups, as the snails and bivalves, have a large number of fresh-water representatives. The seventh group, or Arthropoda, tells much the same tale ; for though the lower forms, such as the Entomostraca, occur abundantly in fresh water, the higher families are very poorly represented. Turning to the last group, that of the Vertebrates, we find that there are a very large number of fresh-water fish ; yet even here, out of 137 families of fish recognised by Dr. Günther and other leading authorities, there are only thirty-five that get into fresh water, and many of these are only represented by single species. On the other hand the Amphibians, such as newts and frogs, form perhaps the most purely fresh-water group of animals known. They are, with very few exceptions, aquatic, at any rate in their earlier or tadpole stages ; and yet no single Amphibian is found in salt water.

The general conclusion we arrive at is that only a very small proportion of the families of marine animals have made their way into fresh water. Of the eight large groups into which the animal kingdom is divided, one is exclusively marine, two others have an exceedingly small number of fresh-water representatives, whilst in the remainder, fresh-water forms, though more abundant, are con-fined to certain families.

It becomes now of interest to enquire why it is that the bulk of marine animals do not make their way up the rivers, and thereby escape from the enemies that devour them in such enormous numbers. For a long time it was supposed that the real and sufficient reason was that marine animals are unable to live in fresh water ; but it is now known that though this may apply to some cases, it certainly will not to all. A. series of remarkable experiments were made some years ago, at Marseilles, by Beudant. He took a large number of specimens of different species of marine snails and bivalves, and by gradually adding fresh water to the salt water in which they were origin-ally living he succeeded in gradually converting them into fresh-water animals. During the experi-ments only 37 per cent. of the animals died, 63 per cent. surviving the change from sea water to fresh water. This result is rendered still more remarkable by a check experiment performed at the same time, in which an equal number of individuals of the same species as before were taken, and kept in salt-water tanks, when it was found that 34 per cent. died ; so that the difference in mortality between those living in their natural medium, and those constrained to change from marine to fresh-water habitat, was but 3 per cent.

A still more remarkable case is that of the two Entomostracan genera, Artemia and Branchipus, of which the former is marine, the latter fresh-water. Of Artemia two species are known, the differences between which are very well marked. *Artemia salina* lives in water containing from 4 to 6 per cent. of salt, and is found in the brine pans of salt works, and in other similar places. The other species, *Artemia Milhausenii*, requires water containing not less than 25 per cent. of salt. By direct experiment it has been shown that the differences between the two species depend simply on the percentage of salt in the water in which they live ; and that by gradually adding salt, or adding water, *Artemia salina* may be converted into *Artemia Milhausenii*, or *vice versâ*. This experiment has been performed not merely in the laboratory, but also by Nature herself.*

The reverse experiment also succeeded, and by gradually adding fresh water, and so reducing the strength of the solution, *Artemia Milhausenii* has been converted into *Artemia salina*. The ex-

* *Vide* Lecture on " Environment," p. 31.—Ed.

periments have been pushed still further : and by addition of fresh water *Artemia salina* has been converted into the fresh-water genus *Branchipus*, which is of larger size, and in many respects very different.

A number of other cases could readily be quoted illustrating the same point, namely, that many marine animals which never do make their way into rivers, are quite capable of living in fresh water, if the change is made sufficiently gradually. If therefore it is not the difference between sea water and fresh water that prevents marine animals from entering rivers, there must be some other cause or causes at work. One of these is, undoubtedly, the severity of the climatic conditions to which fresh-water animals are exposed, as compared with the practically uniform temperature of the sea. Further, the variation in the amount of water in rivers at times of drought and flood respectively, the changes in the strength of the current and modifications in the character of the water from sewage and other contamination, all conspire to render the environment a very shifting one and at times a very harmful one, as compared with the much greater uniformity of external conditions under which the marine fauna exists.

But even these causes, potent as they undoubtedly are, will not suffice to account for so few marine families getting into fresh water. Some further explanation is required, and this is, I believe, to be found in a suggestion made originally by Professor Sollas, of Dublin, who has pointed out that though the adult animal might be thoroughly well adapted to fresh-water life, yet it would by no means follow that the early stages of development would be equally well suited to the change. Professor Sollas also shows that the early larval stages of most of the marine animals are forms peculiarly ill-adapted to living in fresh-water streams, forms indeed which could not hold their own under such conditions. Thus, in the *Echinodermata*, which we have already seen are exclusively marine, the young hatch as very minute larvæ swimming freely in the water by means of cilia ; and larvæ similarly occur in almost all the other groups of marine invertebrates. Now such small ciliated larvæ are altogether unsuited to fresh-water streams, and could never hold their own in them. They are quite incapable of swimming against even weak currents, and the inevitable consequence is that each succeeding generation would be carried further and further down stream, and ultimately the whole species carried out to sea. This is a very important point, and as it is one that has not yet received general attention I think it will be well that we should enquire into it more fully, taking the several groups one by one and seeing how far it will serve to explain the special characters in the distribution of fresh-water animals.

Before doing so, there is one further point of a preliminary nature that will require attention. It is a very familiar fact that the eggs of different animals vary greatly in size. Thus, the egg of a herring is about the size of a pin's head, that of a salmon is as big as a pea, while that of a dog-fish, or of a hen is very much larger still.   Every egg contains two chief kinds of matter, germ-yolk and food-yolk, the former of which develops directly into the embryo, while the latter is simply a store of food material generally in the form of minute granules dispersed through the germ-yolk, which can be drawn upon as required and at the expense of which the embryo is able to develop.   The difference in size between one egg and another concerns almost exclusively the amount of food-yolk, which is very abundant in large eggs, but comparatively scanty in small ones.   Until the food-yolk is used up there is no need for the embryo to hatch : consequently embryos developed from large eggs will be of much larger size and greater strength at the time of hatching than those developed from smaller eggs.   This is well illustrated in the development of frogs.   In the ordinary frog the egg has but a comparatively small amount of food-yolk and the embryo hatches as a tadpole, an animal of small size and of much simpler organisation than the frog.   In the little West Indian frog Hylodes however, the eggs are of larger size—*i.e.*, they contain more food-yolk— and the embryo consequently hatches, not as a tadpole, but as a fully-formed frog.

As small free-swimming larvæ are as a rule unable to hold their own in fresh water it follows that any increase in the size of egg—*i.e.*, in the amount of food-yolk—will be a direct advantage to a fresh-

water animal, enabling it to hatch of greater size
and strength and consequently better able to resist
the currents of the river.   Hence we find that in
fresh-water animals the eggs are usually larger
than in their marine allies.   A crayfish, for example, though only a third the length of a lobster
lays actually bigger eggs.   Having thus seen
what are the special conditions under which fresh-
water animals exist, we may now proceed with our
inquiry and consider in what way the fresh-water
representatives of the several groups of animals
meet these conditions.

Concerning the Protozoa I am not aware of any
points, either in structure or life-history, that
would distinguish the fresh-water from the marine
forms.   The mode of life is apparently the same in
the two cases; though it is very possible that
closer examination would show that differences do
exist, at any rate in certain cases.   From this point
of view a careful study of the fresh-water Protozoa
might very possibly yield results of interest and
importance.   Among Sponges Spongilla is the most
familiar one occurring in fresh water. Spongilla
reproduces sexually, like the marine sponges ; but,
unlike the latter, it can also reproduce by means of
special buds or " gemmules."   Each gemmule
consists of a little spherical group of cells, formed
in the deeper part of the sponge, of which the
superficially placed cells become specially modified
so as to form a thick projecting capsule strengthened
by peculiarly formed silicious spicules.   Such gemmules are formed usually in the autumn.   Owing

to their protective capsules they are enabled to survive the cold, and other adverse conditions of the winter months, which are often fatal to the parent sponge; and in the spring the capsule ruptures, and the contained cells crawling out commence to develop into little sponges. Such gemmules, or clusters of specially protected cells, are unknown among marine sponges, and there can be no doubt that their occurrence in Spongilla is to be regarded as a special adaptation to the fresh-water habits of this genus.

Among Cœlenterates the production of small free swimming ciliated embryos is almost universal, and this is almost certainly the reason why so very few fresh-water members of the group are found. Of those that do occur, the best known is the fresh-water Hydra, whose marvellous powers of recovery from injury have been so admirably investigated and described by Mr. Dunkerley.* As regards its life-history Hydra exhibits several peculiarities, which I believe, are to be associated with its fresh-water habits. In the first place, un-like its marine allies, it not only does not give rise to free-swimming reproductive zooids or jelly-fish, but does not even show the slightest tendency to form such zooids. Secondly, only a single ovum, and this of very large size, is found in the ovary, a point in which Hydra is unique among Cœlenterates, and a point the special advantage of which, in fresh-water forms, has already been fully

* " Hydra : its Anatomy and Development," by J. W. Dun-kerley, F.R.M.S.

discussed. Furthermore, this single egg has a special protective capsule formed around it, and the young at the time of hatching has the form of the parent and adopts at once its mode of life.

Although jelly-fish, which are weak swimmers, are apparently altogether unsuited to fresh-water life, yet it is of interest to note that one truly fresh-water form, Limnocodium, is known, while several others occur in brackish water.* Limnocodium has however only been found as yet in ponds, not in streams, and the mode of its development is not known. It was discovered a few years ago in large numbers in an artificially heated pond of the Regent's Park Botanical Gardens, and may possibly have been introduced with the Victoria regia or other plants living in the pond.

Concerning "worms," few worms are more familiar to microscopists than the Rotifers; active little animals, sometimes swimming freely, sometimes attached and living in tubes, and sometimes massed together into colonies. Nothing is more remarkable concerning them than their extraordinary power of resisting desiccation. Mr. Sykes has recently sent me some dust he collected more than a year ago from a gutter on a house-top, and containing some of these dried-up Rotifers. On placing a little of the dust in warm water for about half an hour, a number of the Rotifers came out and swam about actively. Rotifers have been known to exist in this dried-up condition for many

* A second genus of fresh-water Medusæ (*Limnocnida*) has since been found in Lake Tanganyika.—ED.

years, and there is no doubt that their geographical distribution, and their persistence as fresh-water forms is largely dependent on this power, for while in the desiccated condition they can withstand the action of cold or drought, and can also be blown by the wind for very considerable distances from pond to pond, or stream to stream.

Polyzoa again, of which some of the most beautiful and interesting forms are fresh-water, exhibit special modifications in accordance with their habitat. Almost all the fresh-water Polyzoa give rise to specially protected buds or " statoblasts," which are collections of cells very similar to the gemmules of Spongilla,* and like these, enclosed in hard protective capsules. These statoblasts survive the winter, which is usually fatal to the parent, and in the spring a young fully formed Polyzoon emerges from each, and at once adopts the mode of life of the parent.

Among the Entomostraca, such as Daphnia and Cyclops, we meet with what seem at first sight to be striking exceptions to the rules we have laid down concerning fresh-water animals ; for while some, such as Daphnia, produce large and specially protected eggs which hatch in the full form of the parent, yet a very large number of others, such as Cyclops and Cypris, produce very small eggs, from which small free-swimming embryos arise. We may note however that in

---

* These have since been shown (*Ephydatia Mülleri*) to retain the power of giving rise to free embryos after two years desiccation.—ED.

these cases the small free-swimming larva, or nauplius, though very unlike the parent, is provided with very powerful swimming appendages, and is therefore able to hold its own against streams which would be fatal to those small larvæ which depend for locomotion on the action of cilia. In fact in these Entomostraca the mode of life of larva and adult is the same, and hence if the adult can hold its own, there is little reason why the larva should not do so also. Still it is a point that requires further investigation, how it comes about that Daphnia should lay large eggs, while the allied genera, Cyclops and Cypris, living under the same conditions, and in the same ponds and streams, produce very small eggs.

Concerning these fresh-water Entomostraca there is another point of much interest, that would well repay further examination. In the sea there are marked differences between the shore and shallow-water animals living near to the land, and on the other hand the oceanic or pelagic forms that are met with in the open sea hundreds of miles from land. The same distribution applies to the large fresh-water lakes, in which shallow-water and pelagic fauna may also be recognised.

The pelagic forms are very generally character-ised by the possession of eyes of unusual and often of gigantic size, and by their habit of remaining down at some depth during the daytime and only coming to the surface at night. Professor Weis-mann has suggested that these two peculiarities may be associated together, in this way. Ordinary daylight only penetrates to a limited depth in water, and it has been shown that below 25 fathoms photographic paper is not acted on by daylight. It is also found that 25 fathoms is about the depth to which the pelagic Entomostraca descend during bright sunshine. The object of so descending is apparently to utilise the light, so as to range during the four and twenty hours over their whole hunting ground for food. Were they to remain at the surface in the daytime they would lose their sole chance of obtaining food from the greater depths. It is for this reason again that the eyes are of such great size, for it is clear that forms with larger and more perfect eyes would have a better chance in the pursuit of food than those less well equipped ; and hence by the action of natural selection, the large-eyed forms would survive, and any further improvement of the eyes would be preserved and transmitted to their descendants.

Turning now to the Mollusca, one of the best known and interesting fresh-water forms is the common river mussel, *Anodonta cygnea*. Like bivalves in general, Anodonta produces eggs of small size ; however, these are not immediately passed from the body of the parent, but are transferred to the outer gills where they remain for some time, and where they pass through all the early stages of their development.

The gill consists of a couple of laminæ fused together along their ventral edges ; each lamina is not a continuous membrane, but a trellis-work composed of very numerous vertical bars, crossed and connected together by a smaller number of horizontal bars. The two laminæ are further bolted together at intervals by cross bars. The eggs, which are exceedingly numerous, form a bulky mass lying between the two laminæ. Owing to the cilia which clothe the outer surface of the bars, streams of water are constantly passing through the meshes of the trellis-work ; and in this way the embryos not merely obtain perfect protection during the early stages of development, but are also abundantly supplied both with oxygen for respiration, and with food in the shape of minute particles of vegetable or animal matter suspended in the water. The outgoing stream will also serve to carry away any excretory or fæcal matter passed out by the embryos.

At the time of leaving the parent the young Anodonta is a fully formed bivalve, but is still very unlike the parent, and of too small size, and too weak to hold its own against the currents of the streams in which the adult lives. The young at this period have bivalved shells, the two halves of which are triangular, with the apices incurved so as to form sharp serrated projections, which, when the valves are closed, form a very efficient pair of pincers ; they have a very rudimentary foot and gills, and in other respects differ markedly from the adult.

On passing out from the gills of the parent into the water, they swim by snapping movements of the valves, like a Pecten, but very speedily attach themselves by the pincer-like processes of their shells to fish, such as the stickleback, or else to the legs of water birds. The skin either of the fish or bird, irritated by the pincers, swells up and forms a capsule within which the young Anodonta completes its development. When it has attained the adult form it leaves its host, drops down to the bottom of the stream, and henceforth leads the life of the adult, half buried in the mud at the bottom of the stream, along which it slowly ploughs its way by means of its powerful muscular foot.

No better illustration could possibly be given of the special modifications acquired by fresh-water animals as regards their life-history. Marine bivalves, such as the oyster or cockle, all give rise to small ciliated embryos, adapted to a free swimming existence. So also does Anodonta, but the embryos are not set free in the streams, where as we have seen they would be entirely unable to hold their own, but are retained within the gills of the parent until they have attained sufficient size and strength to look after themselves. The second phase in their life-history, during which they are attached to fish or birds, has probably been acquired rather as a means of ensuring wider distribution than as a precaution against the strength of the currents. The adult Anodonta leads a very sedentary life, while through the stickleback or bird, new colonies may be started miles further up stream, or even in other streams some distance off.

Among fish very numerous examples are met with of marine animals that have taken partly or completely to fresh-water life. In many cases, as in the salmon, the fish live normally in the sea, and run up rivers merely for the sake of laying eggs in places where they are exposed to less danger than in the sea. It is the species and not the individual that here benefits, for while the salmon on running up the rivers in the winter months is fat and in good condition, on its return journey, after laying eggs, it is in wretched condition, and very many die on their way back to the sea. Many other fish, such as lampreys and sturgeons, have similar habits, ascending rivers during the spawning season. On the other hand many characteristically fresh-water fish, as the stickleback, frequently descend the rivers to the sea, in which they are perfectly at home.

The large size of the eggs of fresh-water fish, as the trout, or such fish as breed in fresh water, as the salmon, is worthy of notice. In consequence of the larger supply of food contained in the eggs, as compared with those of marine fish, the young hatch of larger size and greater strength, and are therefore better able to cope from the time of their birth with the downward currents of the streams and rivers.

The Amphibians may be briefly alluded to in conclusion. They are a characteristically fresh-water group of animals, the chief interest about which is that during their development, at least in the higher forms, such as the frogs, they pass from a gill-breathing aquatic fish-like stage, to a lung-breathing terrestrial condition, and show us very clearly steps by which air breathing vertebrates have been evolved from the more primitive water-breathing forms.

Summarising the results arrived at, we may say that fresh-water animals have almost certainly descended from marine animals which have become habituated to fresh-water life : that very little modification, if any, is required in the adult structure to fit an animal for the change in habitat; and that many purely marine animals will live readily in fresh-water, if the change from one to another is sufficiently gradual.   We have further seen that the reasons why so few groups of marine animals have given rise to fresh-water representatives, concern not so much the adult condition as the earlier larval stages ; and that it is the inability of small free-swimming ciliated larvæ to hold their own against the currents in the streams and rivers that is probably the main cause of this paucity of fresh-water species.

An examination of the life-history of those forms that have established themselves in fresh-water, has shown that in many cases there are very special devices of a curiously interesting kind to enable the animals to get over these difficulties. We have only had time to notice a few of the more striking instances, and very much yet remains to be done before we can explain fully all the peculiarities of the fresh-water fauna.

The aspect of the question which I have touched on this evening, has only very recently attracted notice ; the subject is one of great importance and interest, and I would venture to commend it very earnestly to the attention of members of the Society, as one the further and more systematic investigation of which would, beyond doubt, yield results of high scientific value.

VII

INHERITANCE

THE members of a Microscopical Society may find very legitimate cause of congratulation in the progress that is being daily made in the use and application of their favourite instrument. As regards natural history—the history of nature—it may rightly be said that the microscope has effected a veritable revolution ; and this not in one branch only, but in all. In Zoology, it has rendered possible the detailed examination of forms barely perceptible, or even invisible, to the naked eye : witness the five huge volumes lately published in the reports of the *Challenger* Expedition, in which are recorded Professor Haeckel's researches on the Radiolaria, and those of Professor Brady on the Foraminifera. It has also revealed to us numberless facts of the utmost importance concerning the minute structure of animals whose general anatomy was previously well known : facts which in many cases have shown that our earlier ideas as to the affinities of these forms were defective or erroneous.   But far more than all this, it has opened up to us the science of Embryology—the most fascinating study a man can pursue—which not merely teaches us the several stages through which the complexities of adult structure are reached, but also enables us to reconstruct the pedigrees, the genealogical histories of the various groups of animals, and proves to us that morphological resemblances are no mere accidents, but are indications of true blood relationship between one form and another.

In Botany, results of similar nature have been attained ; and the amount of space accorded in our more recent text-books to the lower orders of plants is cogent evidence of the importance attached to the results of microscopical examination by those best qualified to pass judgment upon them.   Nor has the benefit been confined to the student of biological science.   To the geologist, the microscope is rapidly becoming as important, and indispensable as it has long been to the zoologist or botanist.   Like his biological brethren, the modern geologist is no longer content with a knowledge, however accurate and minute, of the structure and present condition of the rock he is examining, but recognises that in the microscope he has a means which, used aright, will enable him to unravel the pedigree of the rocks, to reconstruct their past history, and to determine through what series of changes, in what order, and by what agencies, their present condition has been brought about.

The limits of time and space forbid that I should

refer, save in the briefest manner, to the ever-widening applications of the microscope in other branches of knowledge, and the benefits which it is conferring on mankind. In trade and commerce the microscope is employed more frequently and relied on more fully than is generally appreciated; and in such matters as the adulteration of food, and in criminal enquiries, it often yields evidence of the most material and convincing character. There is perhaps no direction in which microscopical enquiry has advanced more rapidly of late years than its employment as a means of detecting disease, or even of determining its true nature and causation. Pathology is one of the most actively growing of modern sciences; and though its fulness of time has not yet come we may feel well assured, from the results already attained, that the scientific, and especially the microscopical, investigation of disease, will in the immediate future afford us most powerful and welcome assistance in the alleviation of human suffering. It is in considerations of this kind—presented here, I am but too well aware, in the crudest possible form—that we find the justification for the high position to which a Microscopical Society may rightly aspire. In the microscope we have perhaps the most potent instrument of research that mankind has ever possessed; and in the ever-widening circle of its influences, in its far-reaching applications, we may see opportunity for enrolling amongst our numbers men of the most varied interests and pursuits, and so gaining that free interchange of independent opinion which is one of the highest privileges and delights of civilised humanity.

One sometimes hears it said that a microscopist, being occupied with small things, is usually, perhaps of necessity, a man of small ideas. This may possibly be true in individual cases, but as a general statement I believe it to be utterly false. No better justification of this belief could be found than is afforded by the present state of our knowledge with regard to the subject I have chosen for my address.

The real nature and *modus operandi* of Inheritance are problems of the widest possible interest and importance, problems which have baffled many in the past, and which are at this moment being attacked by different observers, working from different sides, and along different lines of attack, but all relying for their evidence on microscopical observation. In dealing with the subject of Inheritance it is well to bear in mind that the problem is as yet unsolved, the question still an open one. Neither can I myself make any material contribution towards its solution : all I propose to do here is to indicate the main conditions of the problem, and to point out what appear, in the light of recent investigation, to be the most promising lines of attack. The problem itself is familiar enough, and may be expressed in its simplest form by the question—Why is a child like its father ? Why is it ; how does it come about that a young animal resembles and grows into the likeness of its parent ? Stated thus, the problem seems definite enough. However, it is really much more complicated than appears at first sight, and it will be well to consider briefly certain preliminary matters before dealing with the more serious attempts that have been made to grapple with its difficulties.

In the first place it should be remembered that reproduction, whether of animals or plants, is effected in two principal ways; asexual and sexual; and that the phenomena of inheritance are seen in both cases. Thus, to take a familiar case, the common fresh-water Hydra reproduces either by budding, or by the formation of eggs. The former is an asexual process, the bud appearing as a hollow outgrowth from the body wall of the parent, which acquires mouth and tentacles at its distal end, and after a longer or shorter time detaches itself and becomes an independent Hydra. An egg, on the other hand, is a specialised cell of the ectoderm, or outer layer of cells of the parent, which is incapable of development of any sort until it has been fertilised by a spermatozoon, from the same or another animal. After fertilisation the egg segments, *i.e.*, divides repeatedly so as to give rise to a number of cells from which, by further growth and differentiation, an embryo and ultimately an adult Hydra is produced. The two modes of reproduction, sexual and asexual, are absolutely unlike, and yet the final results are the same ; for so far as we are aware, there are no points of difference that will distinguish with certainty a Hydra produced by budding from one

produced from a fertilised egg. Inasmuch as these
two forms are not only similar to each other, but
similar also to their parents, it follows that a
Theory of Inheritance, to be of any real value,
must apply equally to sexual and asexual processes of reproduction. I lay stress on this point
as it is one which appears to me to have
been very frequently overlooked, especially of late
years.

The power of repairing mutilation, that is
possessed in so marked a degree by many animals,
is another phenomenon of which account must be
taken in any Theory as to the real nature and
mode of action of Inheritance. A Hydra may be
cut into many pieces, and each piece will regenerate
the missing portions and give rise to a perfect
animal. One or more of the arms of a starfish
may be removed, the whole of the viscera of an
Antedon may be turned out, the leg of a crab or
the limb or tail of a newt may be cut off, and the
loss will in each case be made good. Spallanzani
cut off the tail of a salamander six times in succession, and Bonnet eight times ; while the eye-
bearing tentacle of a snail has been removed
twenty times ; and yet after each mutilation the
missing organ has been reproduced. In the more
highly organised animals, such as birds and
mammals, this power of repairing mutilation is
much restricted : removal of parts of the epidermis
is, however, readily made good ; while such
operations as skin-grafting, and transfusion of
blood from one animal to another, show that

isolated parts of even the highest animals may retain their vitality and special properties when placed under favourable conditions. More striking examples are afforded by such cases as those quoted by Mr. Darwin: in one instance, the spur of a cock inserted into the ear of an ox lived for eight years, and grew to a length of nine inches; while in another, the tail of a pig removed from its natural position and grafted into the middle of the animal's back lived for a time and recovered sensibility.

The phenomena of Reversion are again of great importance in reference to the problem of Inheritance. It is well known that animals may transmit to their offspring characters which are not manifested in themselves: the tendency of gout and some other diseases to appear in alternate generations is perhaps the most familiar instance. In such cases we must regard the disease, or other peculiarity, as present in a latent form in the generations which it apparently skips, for how otherwise could we understand its reappearance in a later generation? The tendency of domestic animals, and more especially of cultivated flowers and fruits, to revert—either in form, colour, or other characteristics—to the ancestral wild condition, is another good illustration of what may well be termed Latent Inheritance. Readers of Mr. Darwin's works will call to mind his famous experiments on pigeons; more especially that crucial one in which he first paired a black Barb with a red Spot; then another black Barb with a white Fantail; and then paired the mongrel Barb-Spot with the mongrel Barb-Fantail, the result being that he obtained a family of birds which in colour and markings were almost identical with the blue Rock pigeon, the common ancestor of all domestic pigeons.

The tendency of cultivated and domesticated plants and animals to revert to a former ancestral condition may perhaps be illustrated mechanically in this way. Take a pack of cards, and lay it on the table ; the cards will all lie on their sides, and be in a condition of stable equilibrium, so that the table may be struck or shaken without materially affecting their position : this represents the normal, *i.e.*, the wild or ancestral condition of the race. Now arrange the cards on their edges, resting them against one another, and so building them up into a pagoda: the resulting structure is a far more imposing one than the pack of cards when laid flat on the table, but it is also an eminently unstable one, its instability being directly proportional to the extent to which it departs from the initial condition : a very slight shake or push of the table will cause the whole structure to collapse, and revert to its condition of initial stability, the cards all falling flat on their sides as at first. So the Pouter or the Fantail are much more impressive and remarkable birds than the blue Rock, but the former are artificial productions, in a condition of great instability, and very readily revert to the ancestral condition. These are but a few of the considerations which must be kept in mind when dealing with Inheritance. Let us now consider in what way the problem may best be attacked.

Of Theories of Inheritance there are two which have attracted special attention, and which demand careful consideration. These are, first, Mr. Darwin's " Provisional Hypothesis of Pangenesis ; " and secondly, the view more recently advanced by Professor Weismann, of Freiburg.

Mr. Darwin's Theory is stated by himself as follows : " It is universally admitted that the cells or units of the body increase by self-division or proliferation, retaining the same nature, and that they ultimately become converted into the various tissues and substances of the body. But besides this means of increase, I assume that the units throw off minute granules, which are dispersed throughout the whole system ; that these when supplied with proper nutriment, multiply by self-division, and are ultimately developed into units like those from which they were originally derived. These granules may be called *gemmules*. They are collected from all parts of the system to constitute the sexual elements, and their development in the next generation forms a new being ; but they are likewise capable of transmission in a dormant state to future generations, and may then be developed. Their development depends on their union with other partially developed or nascent cells, which precede them in the regular course of growth. Why I use the term union, will be seen when we discuss the direct action of pollen on the tissues of the mother-plant. Gemmules are supposed to be thrown off by every unit, not only during the adult state, but during each stage of development of every organism ; but not necessarily during the continued existence of the same unit. Lastly, I assume that the gemmules in their dormant state have a mutual affinity for each other, leading to their aggregation into buds or into the sexual elements. Hence, it is not the reproductive organs or buds which generate new organisms, but the units of which each individual is composed. These assumptions constitute the provisional hypothesis which I have called Pangenesis. Views in many respects similar have been propounded by various authors."

It will be seen that Pangenesis is a mechanical theory of Inheritance ; and that it recognises and faces fully the difficulties of Reversion and of Repair of Mutilations, and explains how organs may become abnormally multiplied and transposed through the gemmules developing accidentally in wrong places, as in the case of supernumerary fingers or toes, or the development of hairs or teeth in unusual situations.

Pangenesis, in spite of the ready explanation it gives of many difficulties, has never met with anything like general acceptance. Its illustrious author, however, while careful to speak of it always as a Provisional Hypothesis, regarded it with much affection ; and alludes to it almost pathetically as his neglected child, for which he predicts confidently a future career of greatness. Such an opinion claims the highest respect, and compels the utmost caution in criticising the theory : yet it cannot be denied that it involves certain difficulties which seem of great weight, and which have not yet been satisfactorily met. In the first place, there is the mechanical difficulty of the extraordinary numbers of these gemmules which must be present. Gemmules must be derived from every component cell of the body : for Mr. Darwin lays much stress on the independence of these cells, quoting Virchow to the effect that "Every single epithelial and muscular fibre cell leads a sort of parasitical existence in relation to the rest of the body . . . . every single bone corpuscle really possesses conditions of nutrition peculiar to itself." Again, Sir James Paget speaks of each cell as living its appointed time, and then dying and being cast off or absorbed ; while further on Mr. Darwin continues, "I presume that no physiologist doubts that, for instance, each bone-corpuscle of the finger differs from the corresponding corpuscle in the corresponding joint of the toe ; and there can hardly be a doubt that even those on the two sides of the body differ, though almost identical in nature."

Again, these gemmules must not only be formed from every cell, but must be present in enormous numbers from every cell, and at every period of life : for it is well known that a portion of a leaf of Begonia or Asplenium can reproduce the whole plant ; and to do this there must, on the theory of Pangenesis, be present in this portion of the leaf gemmules from every part of the plant. So again, the repair of mutilations can only be possible through the presence of a great reserve stock of gemmules of every kind, from all parts, Moreover, it must be borne in mind that the component cells of the body are not simple, homogeneous structures, but that, as is daily becoming more and more evident, some at any rate of them have an exceedingly complex structure, consisting of parts of very different composition, and discharging very different functions. Hence it must follow that many kinds of gemmules, each in enormous numbers, must be required from a single cell in many cases. Inasmuch as the body structure of the young and of the adult animal are different, there must also be different sets of gemmules for the several stages of existence : and it becomes a matter of the utmost difficulty to form the slightest conception of how these different sets take up the running in successive stages of development. If we remember that gemmules from all parts, from each component cell of the body, have not only to be formed in great numbers, but have also to find their way about the body to be collected together from the most remote parts, and planted in due proportion in each of the ova or spermatozoa of the parent, we become fairly staggered at the magnitude of the operations we are asked to believe that each animal performs with such apparent ease.

It must also be remembered that Pangenesis requires that besides the active gemmules there must be enormous numbers of latent gemmules, corresponding to ancestral characters, present in each egg and spermatozoon : for Pangenesis explains such instances of Reversion as the production of a pigeon practically identical with the blue Rock from a Barb-Fantail and a Barb-Spot as due to the development of ancestral blue Rock gemmules, which must be supposed to be present in all pigeons in sufficient numbers to produce fully formed offspring, though they usually remain in a latent condition. Considering the enormous number of generations that must have intervened between the original ancestral blue Rock and the present Barb or Fantail, and that each member of each of these generations must be supposed to have possessed these ancestral germs in sufficient numbers to cause Reversion if an opportunity occurred, the magnitude of the operation and the numbers of such germs originally present become simply inconceivable.

A further difficulty is found in the consideration that Pangenesis, involving as we have seen the presence of gemmules corresponding to the different periods of life of the parent, fails altogether to explain the inheritance of the characters of old age, or of any period beyond that at which the ova or spermatozoa were discharged from the parent. It is hardly sufficient to say in answer to this that " in all the changes of structure which regularly super-vene in old age, we probably see the effects of deteriorated growth, and not of true development," for the objection may apply not merely to the period of old age, but to three-fourths or more of the entire life of the animal.

One further objection may be alluded to: On

the theory of Pangenesis we should certainly expect that the removal of a part, such as the tail of a sheep or horse, especially when effected in early life before the breeding period has been reached, would lead at any rate to diminution of size of the part in the offspring: for surely the removal at an early age of the source from which the gemmules arise ought to have at least some effect on the transmission, through the gemmules, of this part to the offspring; yet it is well known that such mutilations do not tend to be inherited.

Considerations such as these show clearly that whatever may be the ultimate fate of the Theory of Pangenesis, it is not yet in a position to command acceptance: indeed, some of the objections seem of so important and fundamental a nature as to compel us to regard them as fatal to the Theory, at any rate in its present form. Quite recently, Mr. Francis Galton has published the results of a series of most laborious statistical enquiries, undertaken with the view of ascertaining whether inheritance takes place according to definite laws, and if so to determine as accurately as possible what these laws are. His researches, which are of the greatest possible interest and importance, and must exercise great influence on future speculations, lead him to a view which he refers to as Particulate Inheritance, and which may be described as an aggravated form of the Theory of Pangenesis, propounded by his illustrious kinsman. Mr. Galton states his view thus: "All living beings are individuals in one aspect, and composite in another. They are

stable fabrics of an inconceivably large number of
cells, each of which has in some sense a separate
life of its own, and which have combined under
influences that are the subjects of much speculation,
but are as yet little understood. We seem to inherit, bit by bit, this element from one progenitor,
that from another, under conditions that will be
more clearly expressed as we proceed, while the
several bits are themselves liable to some little
change during the process of transmission.
Inheritance may therefore be described as largely,
if not wholly, particulate." Farther on, he compares
the process of inheritance to the construction of a
modern building out of the corresponding parts of
the ruined edifices of former days. "This simile,"
he says, "gives a rude though true idea of the
exact meaning of Particulate Inheritance, namely,
that each piece of the new structure is derived from
a corresponding piece of some older one, as a lintel
was derived from a lintel, a column from a column,
a piece of wall from a piece of wall. We appear
then to be severally built up out of a host of
minute particles of whose nature we know nothing,
any one of which may be derived from any one
progenitor, but which are usually transmitted in
aggregates, considerable groups being derived from
the same progenitor. It would seem that while the
embryo is developing itself, the particles more
or less qualified for each new post wait as it were
in competition to obtain it. Also, that the
particle that succeeds must owe its success
partly to accident of position, and partly to

being better qualified than any equally well placed competitor to gain a lodgment. Thus the step by step development of the embryo cannot fail to be influenced by an incalculable number of small and most unknown circumstances."

These views are boldly expressed but they are also distinctly crude, and the metaphor, which Mr. Galton is dangerously fond of using, rather confuses than aids the explanation. Of more real value are his attempts to determine the numerical ratio in which characters, such as height, colour of eyes, etc., tend to be transmitted to successive generations. On this point Mr. Galton comes to the following very definite and important conclusions: "The average contributions of each separate ancestor to the heritage of the child were determined apparently within narrow limits, for a couple of generations at least. The results proved to be very simple; they assign an average of one quarter from each parent, and one-sixteenth from each grandparent. According to this geometrical scale continued indefinitely backwards, the total heritage of the child would be accounted for." Results of this kind are of the greatest possible value, and open up a most promising field for further enquiry.

I turn now to a consideration of the important series of researches by Professor Weismann, which have of late years attracted so much attention. These are of especial interest to microscopists, because the data on which Prof. Weismann bases his arguments are obtained from a careful study, with the most refined histological methods, of the minute structure of the egg, and of the changes which it undergoes during development. This is a perfectly philosophical standpoint to adopt ; for the egg, say of a hen, has the power of developing into a chick without any further assistance from the parent, provided only that certain conditions of temperature and moisture are fulfilled : and it follows that the problem of heredity is centred in the egg, and that it is therefore reasonable to hope that patient investigation of the egg-structure may throw some light on the question.

Weismann in the first instance lays special stress on the fundamental difference between the unicellular animals, or Protozoa, on the one hand, and the Metazoa, or multicellular animals, on the other. In Protozoa there is no distinction between body cell and germ cell : the entire animal is but one single cell. Reproduction is effected by simple division of this cell, and every individual peculiarity in the parent must therefore be transmitted directly to the offspring. Heredity therefore in Protozoa is no problem at all, but a simple and direct consequence of the mode of reproduction. In the Metazoa however the case is different : here the adult animal consists not of a single cell, but of many cells arranged variously so as to form the epithelial, muscular, nervous, and other component tissues of the animal. Of these cells certain ones are early distinguished as genital cells, and to these the power of reproduction, at any rate sexual reproduction, is confined, and in them are centred the hereditary tendencies of the whole organism.

The problem is to explain how it is that in the Metazoa, one particular cell, the ovum, should have acquired and retained this special power of transmitting the characters of the entire animal. This problem Weismann proceeds to attack. He calls special attention to the general agreement among competent observers, that the part of the cell directly concerned in the transmission of hereditary features is the nucleus ; and he brings forward observations of his own in support of this view. He assumes the presence in the nucleus of a special substance to which he gives the name *germ-plasma*, and to which he supposes the power of hereditary transmission to be confined. He maintains that this germ-plasma is of exceedingly complex structure, and that it has the power of indefinite growth without loss of its essential characters. He further supposes that the germ-plasma of an egg is not wholly employed in building up the body of the embryo, or young animal, but that a certain portion of it remains unchanged, and produces the germ cells of the succeeding generation. In this way the germ-plasma is supposed to pass unchanged from one generation to another, and this *continuity of the germ-plasma* is regarded by Weismann as the fundamental cause of heredity. It cannot be said that this explanation is a satisfactory one. In the first place it is not really an explanation of inheritance at all ; for unlike Darwin's theory of Pangenesis, it does not attempt to explain the actual *modus operandi* of inheritance, but merely localises the power of transmitting hereditary characters to the germ-plasma ; and asserts that the power is due to the special and utterly unknown molecular constitution of this germ-plasma, the very existence of which is altogether hypothetical.

A more valuable part of Weismann's work concerns the share which sexual reproduction takes, in his opinion, as the direct cause of specific variation. Inasmuch as the germ-plasma is supposed to be of constant composition, and to be transmitted unchanged from generation to generation, it follows that characters acquired by the parent cannot be transmitted to the offspring. This statement, that acquired characters are not inherited, is one that has attracted much attention, and that at the present time is being most keenly debated. Should it prove to be true, it becomes necessary to look elsewhere for the cause of specific variation in animals : and this, Weismann maintains, is to be found in the mingling of germ-plasma from two separate animals in the act of fertilisation of the ovum by a spermatozoon.

Limits, both of time and space, forbid that I should follow these arguments further. We are at present very ignorant concerning the nature, properties, and reactions of living things, while life itself remains as great a mystery as ever. Perhaps it will not be until we have gained some clue to the mystery that we shall be able to understand what is the real nature of inheritance : in the meantime we may heartily welcome all earnest efforts towards the solution of the problem.

VIII

THE SHAPES AND SIZES OF ANIMALS

IT may, I believe, be laid down as a general rule, that when a man deliberately selects a particular subject for conversation or for more serious consideration, his choice is made, consciously or unconsciously, for one of the following reasons. Either it is because he has himself paid attention to the subject, and has something to say about it which he thinks will be novel or at any rate interesting to his hearers; or it is because he is addressing others better instructed in the subject than himself, whose opinions he is desirous to obtain; or finally, it may be that he introduces the subject with the express though probably unavowed purpose of finding out what his own opinions are about it.

I confess at once that it is this last motive that has determined my choice of a theme for the Presidential Address, and I make no apology for this. It must have happened many times to each of us, that ideas have occurred unexpectedly on subjects to which we had previously paid but little attention ; ideas, which though recognised at once as crude and disjointed, are yet felt instinctively to contain germs of interest, worthy of future development.   Such ideas should not be let slip : it is well to docket them, and without attempting too soon to frame a consistent notion of their real bearing, or of the conclusions to which they may lead, it is well also to keep a look-out for any additional facts or ideas bearing on the subject, to take due note of them, and after a time to turn out one's box, go over one's notes, and take stock of one's material.   At this stage conversation and discussion with others will probably afford material assistance : and in bringing before you this evening a subject concerning which my state of mind is exactly expressed by saying that I want to find out what I think about it, I believe I am utilising in a very proper and legitimate manner the advantages which such a Society as ours confers upon its members.

The problem that I desire to deal with, that of the forms and dimensions, or in more popular language, the shapes and sizes of animals, may be stated thus : Is it a mere matter of chance that animals, say butterflies and birds, have certain characteristic shapes ?   Clearly it is not altogether so : it is plain to every one that the shapes of animals are correlated with their habits, and that if it were a purely haphazard business there would be no reason why butterflies should so much resemble one another, or why birds should be constructed on one common plan. If then it is not mere matter of chance, can we determine in any way what are the causes which govern the shapes of animals, and what are the laws in accordance with with which their effects are produced ?

So with size : for each animal we have a certain standard of size, which is rarely very greatly departed from.   Such names as cat, pigeon, cockroach, convey to our minds not merely impressions of animals of certain shape, structure, and habits, but also of tolerably fixed dimensions. A cockroach as big as a cat would at once arrest our attention as unusual.   The problem we have to deal with is to find out, if possible, the causes which regulate the dimensions of animals, and determine that there shall be for each kind of animal a certain average size.   These are most elementary considerations, but they will serve to show us what our subject is, and that it is one well worthy of attention.

With regard to the shapes of animals, we find that among the simplest animals, or Protozoa, it is characteristic of the more primitive genera that there should be no definite or consistent shape. This is well seen in Amœba, which consists of a minute speck of protoplasm equally contractile in all directions ; protrusions of the protoplasm, known as pseudopodia, being put out from any part of the surface, and in any direction.   In Amœba and in all forms which exhibit similar " amœboid " movements, there is no distinction of ends, sides, and surfaces, such as we are familiar with in the higher animals. Anterior and posterior ends, right and left sides, dorsal and ventral surfaces, are terms which have no meaning in reference to an Amœba, for any part of the animal may go first in locomotion, and when crawling the animal moves along on whatever part of its surface happens to be in contact with foreign bodies. The only distinction in such an animal is between inside and outside, and even this is not permanent in all cases. In the higher Protozoa the body presents a clear distinction between its outer or superficial layer, which is clearer, firmer, and more contractile ; and the inner or central part, which is more fluid, less contractile, and usually less transparent ; the former being named ectosarc, the latter endosarc. In the simpler forms however as may be seen in many Amœbæ, this distinction between ectosarc and endosarc is not a constant or permanent one ; the protoplasm of the whole body exhibits constant flowing movements, by which parts that at one time are at the surface, at another are carried into the interior : in such cases the ectosarc is merely the layer of protoplasm that at any one moment is at the surface ; and if this differs in appearance from the more deeply placed protoplasm, such difference is perhaps due to the effects of contact with the water in which the animal dwells, rather than to any fundamental distinction in structure or composition of the protoplasm itself.

Even amongst the Amœboid Protozoa it is however possible to speak of a distinct shape, for when perfectly at rest they all tend to withdraw their processes, and to assume more or less definitely a spherical form. This spherical shape is very characteristic either of the normal condition or of the resting state of a large number of Protozoa, and deserves further notice. When widely departed from, such departure is commonly associated with induration of part of the surface either as a mere thickening of the ectosarc, or in the form of a definite shell; a condition which is clearly a more modified one, and usually involves and is associated with further differentiation, such as the presence of a definite mouth, and usually of distinct oral and aboral ends to the body.

Concerning the spherical forms, it may be noted that they are all aquatic and free swimming: aquatic, because in the case of animals with soft body-substance, it is only in water that the body of the animal can be sufficiently supported on all sides to enable the spherical shape to be retained : free swimming, because a habit of crawling leads, as we shall see directly, to definite modification of external shape, involving a distinction between dorsal and ventral surfaces, and almost invariably a further distinction between anterior and posterior ends. In the typically spherical animal, all parts of the surface are equidistant from the centre, and are alike in all respects ; and such an animal will float suspended in the water with any part of the surface uppermost, or any part undermost.

There is much reason for thinking that the

spherical shape is not merely the simplest which an animal can offer, but is also the most primitive. In evidence of this we may quote the spherical shape of the ovum, which is characteristic of all the higher animals as regards the earliest stage of its formation, and of most as regards its fully matured condition.   If we are right in regarding the embryological development of an animal as a re-capitulation of its ancestral history, then the earliest developmental condition—*i.e.*, the ovum, or egg— must represent the most primitive ancestral phase, and the significance of the spherical shape so characteristic of the earliest condition becomes at once apparent.

A further argument in favour of the primitive nature of the spherical form may be drawn from the development of the more modified forms of cells, even in adult animals.   Thus, the shapes of the epithelial cells vary greatly, according to the part from which they are taken.   Cells from the surface-layer of the epidermis, such as those lining the mouth or covering the hand, are thin scales fitted together edge to edge, and with their flat surfaces parallel to the surface which they cover. Cells from the epithelial lining of the stomach or intestine on the other hand, are columnar or rod-like in form, being placed side by side with their long axes vertical to the surface they clothe. Yet a section through the epidermis shows that its deepest layer consists of spherical cells, which gradually approach the surface as those lying over them get rubbed away, and which, as they move towards the surface, get flattened more and more until ultimately they become converted into the scale-like cells. Thus, each scale-like or pavement epithelial cell is in the first instance, in its earliest stage of existence, a spherical cell. So also with the columnar cells of the stomach or intestine. Each such cell is formed in the deeper layers of the epithelium as a spherical cell, and gradually becomes elongated into a columnar cell as it approaches the surface. The spherical cell is therefore the link connecting the scale-like and the columnar cells; an indifferent or primitve form, from which either of the more modified forms may be derived, and which is really the earliest stage in the developmental history of both. It would be easy to multiply instances of this kind, but I have said enough to show that there is really strong ground for holding that the spherical form is to be regarded as a primitive one ; perhaps as the most primitive form met with amongst animals.

The truly spherical shape, in which all parts of the surface are alike and of equal value, is only seen in the unicellular animals, or Protozoa, and in the individual cells of higher animals. The early embryonic phases of many of the higher animals, known as Morula and Blastula, are also spherical, the former being a solid heap of spherical and polygonal cells resulting from the repeated division of the fertilised ovum ; while the blastula is a later stage, having the form of a hollow ball with a wall composed of a single layer of cells surrounding a cavity filled with fluid. Neither morula nor

blastula however is absolutely spherical in the
sense in which I have used the word above,
for the boundary lines between the individual cells
must be of different value to the cells themselves,
so that all parts of the surface cannot be identical.
Moreover, the component cells very usually, perhaps
always, present differences of size or structure by
which upper and lower hemispheres may be
marked off from each other, and by which the true
spherical symmetry becomes still further disturbed.
Volvox and Pandorina may be quoted as examples
of permanent blastulæ in which the component
cells present no such differences, but they are
forms the animal nature of which is still extremely
doubtful.

Leaving the spherical forms, the next characteristic shape we meet with among animals is that
known as radially symmetrical, of which the most
typical instances are met with in the group of
Cœlenterates ; an ordinary jelly-fish affording as
excellent an example as one could wish to find.
A sphere is said to have an infinite number of
axes, all equal to one another ; but a jelly-fish may
be described, if the mathematicians will pardon the
phrase, as having of axes a number that can only
be expressed as being one more than infinity, for
its bell-shaped body, besides having an infinite
number of transverse equal axes, has one definite
longitudinal axis round which all the parts are
symmetrically arranged.   Watch a jelly-fish swimming in still water, and you will note that while
locomotion is always effected in the direction of the

main or longitudinal axis of the animal, the rounded end of the bell going first, the open mouth of the bell last, yet that it is a matter of indifference which part of the rim of the bell is uppermost. The animal, in fact, may be said to have anterior and posterior ends, but no distinction between dorsal and ventral surfaces, or between right and left sides ; and this is the characteristic arrangement in a radially symmetrical animal.

If the spherical form is primitive, then the radially symmetrical form must be derived from it, and of this we have direct evidence in the fact that every radially symmetrical animal is developed directly or indirectly from a spherical egg. Concerning the actual historical mode of derivation of the radial from the spherical form however there has been much discussion, and the question cannot yet be regarded as settled. The chief difficulty arises from the fact that in actual development there are at least two quite different ways in which the spherical ovum may give rise to a radial larva, and it has not yet been determined which of these modes is the more primitive, and in what way one of them could have been derived from the other.

The more usual mode of development is as follows : The ovum, after fertilisation, divides into two cells ; each of these again divides, giving four in all ; the process is repeated until a solid heap of cells, the morula, is produced ; then this becomes converted into a blastula by the cells moving away from the centre and becoming arranged so as to form a spherical ball, consisting of a single layer of cells enclosing a central space filled with fluid. The blastula now becomes flattened on one side and the flattened side becomes doubled up within the rounded part, so that the larva now assumes the form of a hemispherical cup, the walls of which consist of two layers of cells, outer and inner, between which is a narrow chink-like space containing fluid, which is really the last disappearing remnant of the blastula cavity of the earlier stage. The cup-shaped larva is spoken of as a gastrula. A gastrula developing in this fashion is said to be formed by invagination. Such an invaginate gastrula is of very wide occurrence, occurring as an early larval stage in members of all the large groups of the animal kingdom above the *Protozoa*— *i.e.*, in *Sponges, Cœlenterates, Echinoderms, Worms, Molluscs, Arthropods*, and *Vertebrates*.

The second mode, referred to above, in which a gastrula is formed is by what is called delamination. The starting-point, the egg, is the same as before, and so also is the gastrula itself, for the delaminate and invaginate gastrulæ, though formed in entirely different ways, cannot always be distinguished from each other. In the development of the delaminate gastrula the egg segments, giving rise to a solid heap of cells, the morula ; and this becomes a blastula as before. Each cell of the blastula now divides into inner and outer parts, so that the blastula wall becomes double, consisting of outer and inner layers of cells, surrounding a central cavity filled with fluid. By perforation of one pole the cavity is placed in communication with the exterior, and the embryo becomes a gastrula.

It is by no means easy to determine which of these two forms is the more primitive. The invaginate gastrula is much more widely distributed in the animal kingdom, occurring, as we have seen, in all the large groups, while the delaminate gastrula is much more restricted. On the other hand it is not easy to see how the invaginate gastrula first came into existence, for it is by no means clear what advantage a spherical blastula-like animal gets by becoming flattened on one side, or what further advantage is conferred by a very slight depression or cupping of this flattened surface. Such a depression is useful enough after it has reached such proportions as to give rise to a sac-like cavity suitable for the reception and digestion of food, but the early stages of its formation are useless, and could not have been preserved for such purpose. In the case of the delaminate' gastrula however there is no such difficulty, and it is possible to construct a hypothetical series of forms which may well represent the ancestral series in the pedigree of the gastrula, each step marking a distinct advance in organisation, and being a sufficiently definite improvement to justify its perpetuation ; and the whole series corresponding to the successive stages of development of the delaminate gastrula of the present day.

Starting with the blastula stage, a hollow ball whose wall is but one cell thick, we note that the inner and outer ends of each of the cells are exposed to very different environment. The outer ends being on the surface of the blastula can come in contact with and gain cognisance of the outer world, while the inner ends facing towards the blastula cavity can have no direct contact or concern, except with bodies that have passed inwards through the outer parts of the cells. Hence merely as a consequence of this arrangement, physiological differentiation will be set up between the outer and inner ends of each cell ; the outer parts of the cells will become the seats of sensation and of locomotive activity, while the inner ends, freed from these functions, apply themselves to other purposes and become specially nutritive or digestive in function. The next stage is a simple one. The differences between the outer and inner ends of each cell once established will tend to increase as each part of the cell learns to discharge its special functions more efficiently : a mechanical separation of the two parts of the cell is but a slight further differentiation ; each cell dividing into two— an outer cell, sensitive and locomotive and probably respiratory in function, and an inner cell specially digestive in purpose.

So far we have supposed the food to consist of small particles captured by the outer parts of the cell, or the surface cells where two layers are established, and passed inwards to the inner parts, or the inner cells, to be digested. The act of digestion is still intra-cellular—*i.e.*, is effected entirely within the substance of the cells just as in an Amœba. If now we suppose particles of larger size to be taken in as food, we can well imagine how these might be passed on by the inner cells into the central cavity, which will then become a digestive cavity; the inner cells pouring out into this cavity the secretions which dissolve the food, and which it is their special purpose to manufacture. The formation of a mouth by thinning away of the wall at one point, will be a manifest advantage, as it will avoid the necessity of the food particles having to pass through both layers of cells in order to reach the digestive cavity ; and on its appearance the gastrula is completed.

The Theory of Natural Selection requires that each stage in the gradual evolution of a complex organ or system should be a distinct, if slight, advance on the stage immediately preceding it ; an advance so distinct as to confer on its possessor an appreciable advantage in the struggle for existence. This condition is often overlooked ; we are apt to assume, though most erroneously, that if it can be shown that the ultimate stage is more advantageous than the initial or earlier condition, then the whole problem of the evolution of the organ in question is solved. It is indeed seldom that we are able to refer to so complete a series of intermediate stages as that given above in the case of the delaminate gastrula, each step being but a very slight advance beyond the previous condition, and yet each step conferring on its possessor a distinct and tangible advantage. The fact that such a series of forms can be pointed out, every one of which is repeated in the life-history of certain jelly-fish, is a strong argument in favour of the primitive nature of the delaminate gastrula ; while, as already noticed, it tells strongly against the claims of its rival, the invaginate gastrula, that it is at present not possible to point out the progressive advantage gained by the successive stages of gradual flattening and gradual invagination through which the gastrula stage is acquired.   Indeed, we seem here driven to suppose a much more rapid change to have occurred than is commonly recognised as possible.   Perhaps the real explanation may be that the delaminate gastrula is the older form historically, and that the formation of a gastrula by invagination is merely an embryological device to save time and facilitate the course of individual development.

The formation of the mouth, which in the delaminate gastrula is the final stage of development, is an event of first-rate importance, both from the morphological and physiological standpoints. Now in the invaginate gastrula a mouth is, by the very mode of development, present from the first commencement of the process of invagination, and it may be that the advantage gained by the early formation of this important organ, which at once obviates the necessity of the food having to traverse the ectoderm cells in order to reach the digestive layer or endoderm, it may be that this advantage has led to the substitution in actual or individual development of the invaginate for the historically delaminate older type of gastrula formation.

Turning from this somewhat lengthy digression to our more immediate subject, we find that radial symmetry, seen in its most typical form in the gastrula, is confined to aquatic forms. The reason for this is the same as in the case of the still more primitive spherical form—*i.e.*, that it is only in the case of animals, whether young or adult, which live immersed in fluid, that the relations between the animal and the surrounding medium are such as to allow of the animal having identical relations to the environment, whichever part of its circumference happens to be uppermost or undermost. It is also a matter of common observation that radially symmetrical animals are not merely all aquatic, but are almost entirely marine. The reason for the paucity of radially symmetrical forms in the fresh-water fauna appears to be that they are weak swimmers, depending for locomotion on the action of cilia when the animals are of small size, and having no special locomotive organs when of larger dimensions. Fresh-water animals, at any rate such as dwell in rivers and streams, have to be able to hold their own against the currents in which they live ; nay more, they must not merely be able to hold their own but also to make their way up stream as well as down, or else in the long run they will be carried slowly but steadily lower and lower down the river, until ultimately they become swept out to sea. For this reason weakly swimming animals cannot, unless under exceptional circumstances, establish themselves in fresh water.

While the typically radial animal is a free swimming form, there are a large number that in the adult condition are attached either temporarily or permanently. Of these the common fresh-water Hydra, and the whole of the great group of Hydrozoa, known popularly as zoophytes, are familiar examples. The majority of these attached radial animals reproduce by budding, the buds usually remaining attached to their parent, and so giving rise to plant-like colonies. In many of these, and especially in the higher group of Cœlenterates, the Actinozoa, of which sea anemones and corals are instances, a curious modification of the typical radial symmetry is manifested, to which the term biradiate symmetry is commonly applied. In a biradiate animal, while the radial symmetry is well preserved, there is superadded to it a further change in the shape and arrangement of certain of the internal organs, whereby a definite plane of symmetry is established, on either side of which the organs are perfectly similarly and symmetrically arranged, but which is the only plane by which the animal can be so divided.

The simplest case of biradiate symmetry would be of this kind : Imagine a Hydra with the body, as usual, cylindrical, *i.e.*, circular in transverse section, and with the mouth also circular in outline; and, for the sake of simplicity, imagine the tentacles to be absent. Such an animal has any number of planes of symmetry, for any plane of division passing along the whole length of the animal and along its axis will divide the Hydra into two perfectly symmetrical halves. Now, imagine the mouth of our Hydra to become oval or elliptical in outline instead of circular; there will now be only two planes of symmetry, which will divide the animal into exactly similar and corresponding halves; one of these planes passing along the longer diameter of the elliptical mouth, the other along its shorter diameter. Next imagine the mouth, instead of being elliptical, to be ovoid or egg-shaped in outline, with a larger and a smaller end. There is now only one single plane of symmetry possible, namely, that passing along the longer diameter of the mouth opening, for any other plane will divide the mouth, and therefore the animal, into two unlike halves.

The origin of this biradiate symmetry is a little obscure. There are reasons for thinking that it first arose in colonial forms, such as Alcyonium or Pennatula, inasmuch as in these colonial forms it is very well marked, and furthermore the plane of symmetry of the individual polypes always has a definite relation to the axis of the entire colony, and the differences between the two sides of the animal on which the biradiate symmetry depends seems to be associated with a special provision for securing a rapid and efficient circulation of water, not merely through the individual polypes themselves, but throughout the whole colony. This explanation seems fairly satisfactory in most cases. It must be noted however that it involves the descent of solitary forms, such as Cerianthus and many other Anemones in which biradiate symmetry is well marked, from colonial ancestors, a line of ancestry for which there is but little independent evidence.   Much greater difficulty is offered by the Ctenophora, in which biradiate symmetry is usually well established, and by some Medusæ, in which the number of tentacles arising from the margin of the bell may be reduced to two, or even to a single one; in these latter cases however the biradiate symmetry is probably independently acquired, as theoretically it might readily be by any radiate animal.

We have next to consider the type of animal shape spoken of as bilaterally symmetrical, which must be carefully distinguished from the biradiate symmetry we have just been describing.   In biradiate symmetry, as in a sea anemone, there is one divisional plane or plane of symmetry, by which the animal can be divided into identical halves; this plane however concerns the internal organs only, and has no constant relation to the movements of the animal.   In cases of bilateral symmetry on the other hand, the animal, as in a worm, a lobster, or a frog, is divided by a median vertical plane into symmetrical right and left halves, while furthermore a distinction may be readily made between dorsal and ventral surfaces and between anterior and posterior ends.

Just as the radiate and biradiate shapes are associated with free-swimming habits, or else with an attached condition, so is the presence of bilateral symmetry similarly connected in its earlier phases with the habit of crawling along the sea-bottom.   A most instructive series of gradations is shown by the simpler Turbellarian worms, commencing with such forms as Anonymus, in which the body is greatly flattened and almost circular in outline, and in which the mouth is almost in the centre of the ventral or oral surface, while a row of eye spots occurs all round the edge of the animal, though more thickly set at the two extremities. Starting from such a form as Anonymus, which may be compared to a very flat jelly-fish, like Aurelia, which instead of swimming freely in the water, has taken to crawling about on the sea-bottom mouth downwards, we find two diverging series in both of which the body gradually becomes more and more elongated and vermiform in shape, while the sense organs tend to become concentrated at the anterior end. In one series, that of the Turbellaria Acotylea, the mouth gradually moves backwards as the shape of the body becomes more markedly oval and elongated; in the other series, the Turbellaria Cotylea, which receive their name from the presence of a muscular sucker on the ventral surface, the mouth, starting as in the Acotylea from a central position, gradually shifts further and further forwards until it ultimately, in the genus Prosthiostomum, becomes placed quite at the anterior end of the body.

There is little room for doubt that, just as among epithelial cells the spherical form is the primitive one from which both the columnar and the squamous forms have been derived, so also in the series of Turbellarian worms, those with the body approximately circular in outline and with a centrally placed mouth are really the primitive ones from which the more modified Cotylea and Acotylea have alike sprung. It is very significant that these more primitive Turbellarians should present many points of affinity with the radiate animals, such as Cœlenterates, not merely in general shape but in the position of the mouth and central gastral chamber, the radial arrangement of the diverticula of the gastral chamber by which nutriment is distributed to all parts of the animal, the disposition of the sense organs all round the margin of the animal, and the position and relations of the nervous system and reproductive organs. These resemblances are too close and too fundamental to be accidental, and they lend much support to the view hinted at above, that bilateral animals are descended from radiate ancestors, that bilateral symmetry is something additional to and imposed on the radiate symmetry, and that this further modification is a direct consequence of the animals having exchanged their pelagic free-swimming habits for crawling ones ; a change that would at once lead to the establishment of a difference, both structural and physiological, between the ventral or oral surface along which locomotion is effected, and the opposite or dorsal surface; while the further differentiation between anterior and posterior ends would very soon follow as a necessary consequence of this same crawling habit. It is very possible also that the Turbellarians are themselves the simplest group in which the crawling habit has been acquired, and are directly descended from Cœlenterate ancestors, a view that finds favour with many zoologists, but which can at present hardly be regarded as more than an hypothesis.

With regard to the mechanical origin of bilateral symmetry suggested above, Herbert Spencer, whose writings on the fundamental laws governing animal form and structure are of the greatest possible interest, speaks as follows: " Where the movements subject the body to different forces at its two ends, different forces on its under and upper surfaces, and like forces along its two sides, there arises a corresponding form, unlike at its extremities, unlike above and below, but having its two sides alike."

We have seen above that there are reasons of very great weight for regarding the radiate type as more primitive than the bilaterally symmetrical one, and further than this, for regarding the latter as directly descended from the former. The group of Echinodermata, including the starfish, brittle stars, sea urchins, and their allies, warn us however that we must not generalise too hastily. About the radiate symmetry of an Echinoderm there can be no possible doubt; a starfish is as markedly, as conspicuously, radiate as any animal in existence, indeed it has been by older writers taken as the type of radiate animals. Take one of the ordinary five-fingered starfish for instance: note its shape; the central disc-like body produced into five equal and symmetrically arranged arms, the mouth placed centrally on the lower, or oral surface, the anus subcentrally on the dorsal surface. As regards internal structure, the radiate symmetry is

equally well marked ; the muscular, skeletal, digestive, circulatory, nervous, and reproductive systems
all extend radially and symmetrically along the
arms.   There are no anterior or posterior ends,
right or left sides to the animal, for in its dilatory
ramblings a starfish moves indifferently in any
direction, any one of its five arms leading.

Bearing in mind what has been said above as to
the primitive nature of radiate symmetry, and of
the relation between it and bilateral symmetry,
bearing in mind also that Echinodermata are not
merely all aquatic, but are exclusively marine, and
that there are the most cogent reasons for regarding the marine fauna as the primitive one, from
which both the fresh-water and terrestrial have
sprung, we should I think naturally conclude that
the radiate symmetry of Echinodermata is primitive,
and that a starfish is a radiate animal, which has
adopted crawling rather than pelagic habits, presumably for convenience in obtaining food, and in
which consequently a distinction between ventral
and dorsal surfaces has been established ; but that
the further structural modification by which anterior
and posterior ends, right and left sides, become
differentiated, has not yet appeared in it.   If we
want further evidence in support of this primitive
character of Echinodermata, we may obtain it from
the past history of the group, for Echinoderms are,
geologically considered, a group of extreme antiquity,
and a group in which the characteristic radiate symmetry is as marked in the older as in the more
recent members.   If however we consider the

actual embryological development of a starfish or other Echinoderm, we find difficulties in the way of the view sketched out above, difficulties which have not yet been overcome and which may not improbably prove fatal.

A starfish lays small eggs, from which a radially symmetrical larva, a gastrula, is developed. This larva however soon acquires a very marked and unmistakable bilateral symmetry ; ventral and dorsal surfaces, anterior and posterior ends, right and left sides may readily be distinguished in it, and the internal organisation shows the bilateral symmetry as clearly as does the external shape. This bilateral symmetry is not confined to starfish, but is present in the larval stages of all other Echinoderms as well. The importance of the point is at once apparent: it shows us that the radiate symmetry of the adult Echinoderm is not directly continuous with, and may indeed not be the same thing as, the radiate symmetry of the early larva, for between the two radiately symmetrical stages a bilaterally symmetrical stage is intercalated. If the developmental history of an Echinoderm is a true recapitulation of the pedigree of the race, then the history can only be interpreted as meaning that Echinoderms are descended from bilaterally symmetrical ancestors, and that the radiate symmetry of the adult Echinoderm is secondary, and of later origin. The matter is one of great interest, especially when we bear in mind that the relations of Echinoderms with other groups of animals are at present entirely unknown to us, and that consequently any light that can be obtained from a study of embryology would be peculiarly welcome.

It is impossible to discuss the question at all adequately here, but it is perhaps worth while pointing out that though the adult starfish is an animal showing radiate symmetry in a marked manner, yet that the radiate symmetry of a starfish, or indeed of any other Echinoderm, differs in some important respects from the radiate symmetry of the Cœlenterate. Thus, in the first place, the symmetry of an Echinoderm is pentamerous, the typical number of arms in a starfish being five, and five being the typical number of corresponding parts met with in the other groups of Echinoderms also. This may seem an unimportant point, but it becomes significant when we note that though the actual number of corresponding parts in a Cœlenterate varies very greatly in different forms, yet that it is almost invariably either four or six, or some multiple of these numbers, while five or any multiple of five is unknown. Then again, in the actual development of an Echinoderm the radial symmetry of the adult is first shown by a set of organs, the ambulacral system, which is absolutely and entirely unrepresented in Cœlenterates ; and it is apparently on this radially arranged ambulacral system that the radial symmetry of other parts and systems is based. When further we bear in mind that the whole structure of an Echinoderm is altogether different to that of a Cœlenterate, and in many respects very much more complex, any real comparison between the two groups becomes very nearly impossible, and we find it less anomalous than it at first appeared to regard the adult symmetry of an Echinoderm as something quite distinct from, and acquired perfectly independently of, that of a Cœlenterate.

Limits both of space and time forbid that I should pursue further the discussion of the shapes of animals. Where once bilateral symmetry is established however the further modifications seen in the higher forms become comparatively easy to follow. The development of a head, with accompanying concentration of the nervous system and sense organs, are merely further developments of processes and tendencies which we have seen already established in the Turbellarian worms, while the formation of limbs, perhaps shadowed forth in the parapodia of Chætopods, is the most important step in the upward progress to the highest groups of animals.

Bilateral symmetry is characteristic of all the higher groups, though it may be masked or modified by further development, as the twisting of the body of a snail or other gastropod, the asymmetrical form of the tail of a hermit crab, or the shifting of the eye in a sole. Speaking generally we may say that the forms of the higher animals are derived from those of the lower bilaterally symmetrical worms, by exaggerating the differences between one part of the body and another already present in these latter. Thus the differences between the dorsal and ventral surfaces or rather halves of the body, and between the anterior and posterior ends of the body, gradually become intensified, attaining their maximum in birds and mammals, the two highest groups of animals.

I can hardly conclude this part of my address more fittingly than by the following quotation from Herbert Spencer who, in his "Principles of Biology," has discussed in most philosophical fashion, and with far greater thoroughness than I can pretend to here, the laws regulating the shapes of animals. "The one ultimate principle," says Spencer, " that in any organism equal amounts of growth take place in those directions in which the incident forces are equal, serves as a key to the phenomena of morphological differentiation. By it we are furnished with interpretations of those likenesses and un-likenesses of parts which are exhibited in the several kinds of symmetry; and when we take into account inherited effects wrought under ancestral conditions, contrasted in various ways with present conditions, we are enabled to comprehend, in a general way, the actions by which animals have been moulded into the shapes they possess."

Passing from the consideration of the shapes to that of the sizes of animals, is very like turning from a well-made road into a ploughed field, across which progression becomes not only slow but difficult and irregular. Hitherto the problems concerned with the sizes or magnitudes of animals have received but very scant attention, and we are not only ignorant of the principles and laws that govern them but of the directions in which to seek for these principles. Indeed we have at present but a very limited number or range of facts on which to base our arguments. Still the questions are of much interest, and it is certainly worth while enquiring into them, even though we may not be able to make much progress to-night.

In the natural or wild state the size of each kind of animal in the adult condition is fairly well defined, and often very sharply so. The words cat, rabbit, sparrow, convey to our minds the impression of animals, not merely of certain appearances, habits, and structure, but also of a certain well understood and fairly constant size. The limits of variability are much wider in some cases than in others. Speaking generally they are much wider in the case of aquatic, and especially of marine, than of terrestrial animals. If we say of an animal that it is as large as a fox, we know fairly exactly what is meant; but to speak of anything being as large as a salmon, would convey a very vague notion of magnitude. As a standard of size, the salmon is indeed but little better than the traditional "lump of chalk." The same is true of most other fish, and indeed is characteristic of aquatic animals in general. The explanation seems to be that in terrestrial animals the period of growth is practically limited to the earlier stages of existence; while aquatic animals continue to grow for a much longer period, or indeed throughout their entire lives. Why an animal should stop growing on reaching a given size is a very difficult question to answer, but one that, if time permits, I will return to later on.

As regards the actual dimensions attained, here

again the aquatic animals lead the way. Of all animals now existing, whales are incomparably the largest ; next to the aquatic come the terrestrial forms, with the elephant in the forefront ; while last and smallest of all, come the aerial, or flying animals. The actual size seems here to be associated with the density of the medium in which the animal lives. In water an animal has to support but a very small part of its weight by its own muscular effort, for more than half the weight of a fish or whale is water, and of the solid components the fats are lighter than water, so that the specific gravity of such an animal is not much in excess of the water in which it dwells. Flying animals live under very different circumstances, for here every part of the body is considerably heavier than the air and great muscular efforts are necessary to sustain the animal during flight. Large size or great weight of the body becomes therefore impossible.

Again, we may lay it down as a general rule that the largest animals belong to the higher, or even the highest groups, *i.e.*, that great size is associated with great complexity of organisation. Exceptions are readily met with, but on the whole the statement is correct. Vertebrates are clearly on the whole of much larger size than any group of Invertebrates. Amongst Vertebrates, mammals rank as the highest group and to them belong the largest animals now living, both aquatic and terrestrial. So also amongst Invertebrates ; in the important group of Mollusca, the highest forms are undoubtedly the Cephalopoda, and it is amongst these that the largest members of the group occur.

It has been suggested recently that the rule is a stricter one than has been hitherto recognised ; and evidence has been quoted in support of the further statement that the ancestral forms or progenitors of the higher groups, such as mammals or birds, were of distinctly small size, *i.e.*, much below the average stature attained by their descendants—the present members of the groups in question.. The direct influence of size on structure has as yet been but very imperfectly investigated, but there are many cases known in which among animals of the same zoological group the larger forms are distinctly of more complicated structure than their smaller allies, and in which there are very valid grounds for holding that the greater complication of structure is connected casually with the increased dimensions.

We shall perhaps best deal with the several points just mentioned by taking the large groups into which the animal kingdom is divided one by one, and noticing with regard to each, the principal facts concerning the sizes of the several members of the group.

Protozoa, the simplest of all animals, are defined as those forms which, not merely in the earliest phases of their existence, but throughout their entire lives, remain in the condition of single cells. This unicellular nature is associated with great simplicity of organisation and with extremely small size.   The differentiation of parts or organs within a single cell can only proceed up to certain limits, and if of great bulk parts of the cell would be too far removed from the surface to obtain nourishment or to get rid of excretory matter. What the actual limits of size are among unicellular animals we perhaps do not know accurately. Stentor, which may attain a length of $\frac{1}{20}$ inch, is usually regarded as one of the largest.   Individual cells in higher animals may however attain much larger dimensions : thus, if histologists are right in regarding a single muscle fibre as formed by differentiation within a single cell, then we must grant that a cell may be some inches in length ; while, if the statement be true that a nerve fibre is merely a process of a single cell, it will follow that a single cell may in a man extend from the spinal cord, perhaps from the brain itself, to the extremity of the fingers or toes—*i.e.*, may attain a length of some feet, or in an animal the size of a whale as much as 60 feet or more.   Such nerve fibres are however exceedingly slender.

Among the largest cells known to us are the eggs of reptiles, of Elasmobranch fishes, and, largest of all, those of birds.   Embryology shows us that the yolk of a bird's egg, which is the only part from which the embryo is directly developed, is morphologically a single cell, and is indeed in the earlier stages of its formation indistinguishable from the ordinary epithelial cells covering the surface of the ovary.   The largest eggs are those laid by the Struthious birds, and the yolk of the egg of an ostrich is perhaps the largest individual cell known to us, though it was very greatly exceeded in recent geological times by that of the gigantic Æpyornis. It must however be remembered that the large size of the yolk of an egg is due mainly to its distension by the granules of food-yolk imbedded in it, which cannot properly be regarded as part of the living substance of the cell.

In the next group—that of the Sponges—it is difficult to speak of the size of the individual animals, owing to the very general habit of forming colonies by continuous gemmation, in which colonies the outlines of the component individuals are impossible to determine. The solitary sponges are usually of small size, not exceeding an inch or two in height, but some forms, as the beautiful Euplectella, attain a height of a foot or more.

Among Cœlenterates the same habit of colony formation prevails, but the boundaries and hence the size of the component members of the colony can almost always be determined. The majority of Cœlenterates are of small size: the individual zooids of a hydroid colony are commonly but a fraction of an inch, rarely much over an inch in length, though occasionally attaining a larger size. The entire colonies often reach great dimensions; the branching zooids may form brush-like masses some feet across, while the reef-building corals reach a far larger size.

Speaking generally the Anthozoa, which are the higher group of the two, are of larger size than the

Hydrozoa ; and it is also among the more highly organised groups that the largest individuals, the giant Cœlenterates, are met with. Thus, of the two groups of jelly-fish, the Hydromedusæ, which belong to the Hydrozoa, are small, while the Scyphomedusæ, which in many points of structure and also in some peculiarities of development are more nearly allied to the Anthozoa, are of much greater average size and occasionally reach extraordinary dimensions, individuals measuring as much as seven feet in diameter with tentacles nearly fifty feet in length having been met with. Sea anemones again, the typical Anthozoa, are much larger than the hydroids ; a height of three or four inches with a diameter of one or two inches is not at all uncommon, while from tropical seas anemones have been described over three feet in diameter.

The Echinodermata are as a rule of small size and are measured by inches. The vermiform Holothurians are sometimes greatly elongated, some species of Synapta measuring five feet or more in length, while the extinct Crinoids had stems up to seventy feet long.

Among the heterogeneous and in many respects unnatural assemblage of animals grouped together by zoologists under the name Vermes, the average dimensions are distinctly small. Turbellarian worms, perhaps the most primitive members of the group, average less than an inch in length, though some forms may measure four to six inches. Trematodes are similarly small ; and the great length attained by some Tapeworms, thirty feet or more, is due rather to their peculiar mode of a sexual reproduction than to increase in individual dimensions.

Nemertines may attain an enormous length, fifteen or twenty feet being not uncommonly exceeded. Amongst Annelids the average length is certainly below six inches ; but individual genera, as Halla, often exceed three feet, and the giant earthworm of Australia measures six feet or more.

Rotifers are a very interesting group ; invariably of small size, and often actually microscopic, they yet exhibit very great complexity of organisation. A Rotifer may be actually smaller than a Stentor, and yet while the latter is but a single cell exhibiting but very slight differentiation of parts, the former is an animal with well developed cutaneous and muscular systems, a large body cavity, an alimentary canal in which the various regions are modified in special manner for special purposes, a definite system of excretory organs, a very perfect nervous system, with well developed and sometimes highly specialised sense organs ; and all these various parts formed of specially differentiated cells. Comparison of a Rotifer with a Protozoon shows us very forcibly that although it may be true that larger animals are, on the whole, more highly organised than smaller ones, yet it is not magnitude alone that determines structure.

Arthropoda, though an extraordinarily numerous group, far exceeding in number of species all the other groups put together, yet do not present any unusually great diversity of size.   The majority of arthropods are small, and a length of four inches is a long way above the average, while many large and very numerous groups such as Entomostraca are minute, indeed almost microscopic, in. their dimensions.   Crabs may reach a large size, but this is almost entirely due to great elongation of their legs.

Amongst Mollusca a much larger size may be attained.   Of Lamellibranchs the genus Tridacna affords the giants, shells of these huge clams having been found measuring two feet across and weighing upwards of five hundred pounds, the animal itself exceeding twenty pounds in weight.   Gastropods also reach a large size, but are far exceeded by the Cephalopods, or cuttle-fish, which group yields the largest invertebrates known to exist.

From time to time the bodies of enormous cuttle-fish are cast up on the shores in various parts of the world.   Two or three very large specimens have occurred on the West Coast of Ireland, others are described from New Zealand, but by far the largest and also the most numerous cases are from the East Coast of North America, more especially the Coast of Newfoundland.   Some of the specimens are of really gigantic proportions, a length of body of as much as twenty feet having been measured, while the long arms, or tentacles as they are often named, were thirty or even forty feet in length.

The Gastropods yield some very instructive series of forms, illustrating in a remarkable way the influence of size on structure. Of these one of the most interesting is that afforded by the genera Aplysia, Doris, Eolis, and Pontolimax, all four of which belong to the group of Opisthobranchiate Gastropods, or sea slugs. Aplysia, the sea hare, is an animal of some size, four or five inches in length, and has a very well-developed gill covered over and protected by a thin uncalcified shield-like shell. Doris is of smaller size, has no shell, and has its gill processes less developed than in Aplysia, but still grouped together in a tuft on the hinder part of its back. In Eolis, there are a number of elongated papillæ covering the back of the animal, some of which, at any rate, act as respiratory organs. Pontolimax, finally, is a very small slug-like animal only a twelfth of an inch in length, and having a perfectly smooth dorsal surface devoid of respiratory processes of any kind.

Herbert Spencer has pointed out very clearly how in two animals of the same zoological type, but of markedly different size, the smaller one may be able to do without respiratory organs, while to the larger one, merely in consequence of its larger size, such organs are absolutely essential. Suppose you have two animals of identical shape, but of different size: for the sake of simplicity let us suppose the animals to be spherical, and let the diameter of the smaller animal be one inch, that of the larger two inches. The extent of surface in the two will be proportionate to the squares of their linear dimensions—*i.e.*, in this case, the larger animal will have a surface four times as extensive as the smaller one.   But the mass of bulk of the animals will be proportionate to the cubes of their linear dimensions—*i.e.*, the larger animal will be eight times the bulk of the smaller one.   Hence the larger animal, with a bulk or mass eight times that of the smaller one, will have a surface only four times as extensive.   This fact, that as animals increase in size their bulk or mass increases at a much faster ratio than their surface, explains how it is that a small animal, such as Pontolimax, may find its body surface sufficient for the interchange of gases that constitutes respiration, while in a larger animal Doris, of similar shape and constitution, the body surface may be altogether insufficient and special respiratory organs may become necessary.   Again, in a small animal no part of the body is very far removed from either the surface or from the digestive organs, hence each part is able to effect its respiratory interchange of gases and to obtain its due supply of nutriment directly, without the intermediation of a system of circulatory organs or blood-vessels.   In a larger animal however such blood-vessels are absolutely necessary, for without them the more deeply lying parts would be unable to obtain the oxygen which is necessary for their vital activity, or to get rid of the carbonic acid and other poisonous products of that activity ; while the nutrition of the surface and more remote parts of the body could not be properly kept up unless there were direct communication between the digestive organs and these parts.   Such considerations must suffice to illustrate in what way mere increase of size may involve and necessitate greater complexity of structure.

Amongst Vertebrates we have already noticed the extreme individual variability of size seen amongst fish, in which apparently growth continues throughout the whole period of life. The actual limits of size of fish are probably only imperfectly known to us. The blue shark, Carcharias, attains a length of twenty-five feet; specimens of Carcharadon have been measured over forty feet in length, while of the genus Rhinodon examples of fifty, sixty, or even seventy feet in length have been described. This is very probably the limit of size reached by fish at the present day, but judging from the fossil teeth of Carcharodon, Cestracion, and other forms, sharks of these genera must have existed in tertiary times more than twice the dimensions of any now living.

It is difficult to speak with any certainty about the size of Amphibians, but the existing genera are all small. Some of the Salamanders attain a length of four feet or more, but the majority of recent Amphibians are of much smaller size. Fossil forms occur of much larger dimensions, some, such as the Labyrinthodonts, being veritable giants. It is however impossible in most cases to speak with certainty as to the Amphibian character of these fossils, but we are probably right in regarding recent Amphibians as diminutive and pigmy representatives of a group formerly of much larger size.

Reptiles are in much the same position, many

of the largest groups being now extinct.   Of these the Plesiosauri and Ichthyosauri attained lengths up to twenty feet, while the flying Pterodactyls were also of large size, some measuring as much as twenty feet in expanse of wing; but these dimensions were greatly exceeded by other forms. It has been estimated that Mosasaurus was as much as seventy feet in length, while in the genus Brontosaurus, Professor Marsh believes we have a truly terrestrial reptile eighty feet in length, thirty feet high, and estimated to have weighed not less than twenty tons.   Of recent reptiles the Crocodiles and some of the Chelonians attain large dimensions, while snakes are described up to thirty feet in length and as thick as a man's body.

It is however amongst Mammals that we find as already noticed the real giants, and it is interesting to note, that in different geological periods different groups of Mammals have worked up to a maximum of size and then disappeared.   Thus the Edentates at one time gave rise to giant forms culminating in the huge Glyptodon and still larger Megatherium, but the existing Edentates like existing Amphibians are a very puny race compared to their forefathers.   Ungulates seem in past times to have had a greater number of large forms than at present, though even now they are among terrestrial animals second only to the Elephants. It is interesting also to note that there seems to be an actual limit to the size of a terrestrial mammal, which has been approached more than once by separate groups.   It can hardly be an accident that the Megatherium attained dimensions very closely comparable to those of an elephant, while the biggest fossil Ungulates were not far short of this size.

It has been suggested that the limits of size are due to the nature of the materials of which animals are constructed, and that the difficulty in increasing that size is a mechanical one; that just as it would be impossible to construct a Forth Bridge of stone, for in order to get sufficient strength it would be necessary to employ so great a quantity of material that the structure would be crushed by its own weight, so the bones, ligaments, and muscles of which the animal frame is constructed will permit of size up to that of an elephant but not beyond. It is not hard to find points in the anatomy of the elephant that support this view. The several joints of each limb, which in smaller quadrupeds are in the natural standing position bent on one another, often at considerable angles, are in the elephant placed vertically one above another, an arrangement that enables them to support with less muscular effort the enormous weight of the body and head. The massive pillar-like form of the legs, which take up the greater part of the space below the body, are also indications that the limits of size are being approached, and when we find that though approached closely time after time, the size of the elephant has not been exceeded in past times by terrestrial animals, save by a few members of its own group, and with the possible but as yet doubtful exception of Brontosaurus and some other reptiles, we are probably not far wrong in assuming that this size is somewhere near the mechanical limit imposed by the strength of the materials of which the animal frame is composed.

With aquatic animals in which the body is supported on all sides, and the specific gravity of the entire animal is not greatly in excess of that of the water in which it lives, the case is very different ; and among the whales we meet with genera which attain the length of ninety feet, and whose weight is estimated at upwards of one hundred tons, figures which according to some authorities may in exceptional cases be considerably exceeded.   Whales are not merely the biggest animals that live, they are probably also the biggest that ever have lived, for we have no satisfactory evidence of larger forms at any period in the world's history.

It is worth while also to note that the giants, whether aquatic or terrestrial, are doomed to extinction.   Elephants have been tolerated because of the readiness with which they can be tamed and made to place their great strength at the service of man ; but it is many centuries since the African elephant was so employed, and no one of the African tribes at the present day makes the slightest attempt to so use him ; while with regard to the Indian elephant, though large numbers are still employed, experts are becoming more and more doubtful as to the profitable nature of this mode of labour.   Elephants require much attention, they consume enormous quantities of food, and they are subject to a variety of ailments, which more or less incapacitate them for their work, so that the elephant seems in real danger of being shouldered out of existence by the steam engine and hydraulic jack, which are more reliable, easier to apply, and on the whole less costly.   Enormous numbers of elephants, both African and Indian, are killed each year for the sake of the ivory of which their tusks consist ; it is difficult to form anything like a correct estimate of the actual number, but competent authorities state that it cannot be less than 100,000 annually.   This terrible destruction is admittedly thinning their numbers, and elephants are on all hands recognised as doomed to destruction ; and with the whales, which are yearly becoming scarcer, to form the last and greatest victims of a ruthlessly advancing civilization.

A final problem, that time only permits me to hint at but which has been keenly discussed by many writers, is this.   Why is it, how does it come about, that some animals are so much bigger than others ?   To take a concrete case : why is a cow bigger than a sheep ?   The two animals belong to closely allied groups ; we see them side by side in our fields, eating the same food and digesting it in the same characteristic fashion ; why then should there be so great and constant a difference in size ?   Herbert Spencer, who discusses the problem at some length, is inclined to explain it by the size of the animal at birth, and attempts to establish the position that those animals which are larger at the time of birth or of hatching are those which are larger also when adult.   It is true that an ostrich lays a bigger egg than a hen, and a hen than a sparrow; but it is very easy to show that the relation is not a general one, and that size at birth has no necessary relation to size in the adult condition.   For example, a crayfish and a lobster are two closely allied animals, and yet the crayfish lays the larger egg of the two, though the adult is not more than a quarter the length of a lobster.   Or again, were Spencer's contention right, then an eight months' child, being born of smaller size than the average, should not attain to average stature.   It is more probable that the real explanation is a much more complicated one, and that there is for each animal a certain average size which is most advantageous to the animal when living wild in its natural condition.   Natural Selection will then tend to preserve this average size by placing at a disadvantage those individuals which depart from it conspicuously, whether in the way of excess or diminution.

In connection with this point, reference must be made to Mr. Galton's law of Regression, enunciated in his recently published and most important book on Natural Inheritance.   It is impossible to discuss the subject further on the present occasion, and I will conclude by giving the Law in Mr. Galton's own words, referring my readers for further details to his most fascinating and suggestive work.   " If the word 'peculiarity' be used to signify the difference between the amount of any faculty possessed by a man, and the average of that possessed by the population at large, then the Law of Regression may be described as follows : Each peculiarity in a man is shared by his kinsmen, but *on the average* in a less degree. It is reduced to a definite fraction of its amount, quite independently of what its amount might be. The fraction differs in different orders of kinship, becoming smaller as they are more remote." In other words, according to Mr. Galton's Law of Regression, any tendency to individual deviation—say, from the normal stature—whether in the way of excess or of diminution, is counteracted by an inexorable law, which acting to a definite degree in each succeeding generation, constrains return to the normal height.

IX

SOME RECENT DEVELOPMENTS OF THE CELL THEORY

My address last year was concerned with big rather than with little animals, and might perhaps with greater propriety have been delivered to a macroscopical rather than to a microscopical society. For this however I propose to make amends to-night ; and to the subject-matter of my address the most ardent microscopist could hardly take exception, however legitimate may be his dissatisfaction at the mode of its presentation. For these more recent developments of the cell theory not merely depend absolutely on the use of the microscope, but require for their elucidation the very highest powers obtainable, and the most refined methods of modern histological research. In what I have to say to-night I can make no claim to originality : my aim is rather to give a summary of recent progress along certain important lines of investigation, and a statement of the present position of problems recognised by all as of the highest interest and importance.

A few words concerning the origin and the earlier phases of the cell theory may fitly preface my remarks. Like all great theories it is impossible to date precisely its first enunciation. Commonly stated to have been founded in 1839, first for plants by Schleiden, and almost directly afterwards extended to animals by Schwann, the cell theory in its main outlines is to be found lurking in an incomplete unformed condition, rather hinted at than clearly expressed, in the earlier writings of Robert Brown, Dutrochet, Von Mohl, and others. These earlier and less precise attempts were however confined to vegetable tissues. As regards animals, to which I propose to limit myself this evening—from no desire to minimise the importance of the sister science of Botany, but merely because I am unfortunately less familiar with it and unable to speak from my own knowledge and observation—as regards animal tissues, Schwann is rightly regarded as the founder of the cell theory.

By the cell theory, Schwann meant that the bodies of all animals, as also of all plants, are formed of cells : that it is by evolution of, and changes in these cells, that the tissues of which the various parts of the body consist are formed, and further, " that the differences in the properties of the different tissues and organs of animals and plants depend on differences in the chemical and physical activities of the constituent cells." Concerning the mode of formation of cells, Schwann held that they might arise independently in a

surrounding matrix or blastema.   In 1845 however Goodsir first promulgated the doctrine that
cells never originate without pre-existing cells, from
which they arise by fission ; a view strongly
supported by Remak, Kölliker, and Virchow, and
soon universally accepted.   The next great step
was von Baer's discovery of the mammalian egg or
ovum, and his recognition of the fact that it was a
single nucleated cell ; a discovery that threw an
entirely new light on Harvey's dictum, *omne vivum ex
ovo.*

The cell theory was now firmly established.
Histology, or the microscopical study of the
animal body, showed that all its parts and tissues
were really built up of cells, as a wall is of bricks ;
while embryology furnished even more cogent proof,
showing that the ovum or egg of all animals is one
single cell, and that from this single cell by
repeated division all the component cells of the
adult animal are derived.   Thus expressed the
theory is the grandest generalisation and the
most firmly established fact in all morphology ;
and the division of the animal kingdom into Protozoa and Metazoa—*i.e.*, into animals which on the
one hand remain single cells all their lives, and
on the other hand commence as single cells or
ova but speedily become multicellular, takes rank
as the most fundamental and most natural of all
zoological distinctions.

The cell theory early gained acceptance as
regards its main conclusions, but concerning the
detailed structure of the unit or cell discussions

quickly arose, which the progress of knowledge has served rather to widen than to restrict. Schwann's idea of a cell was " a vesicle closed by a solid membrane, containing a liquid in which floats a nucleus enclosing a nucleolus, and in which also one may find small granular bodies." This definition was soon challenged. The cell wall was first attacked, and shown by Nägeli in 1845 to be not essential to a cell. Others speedily confirmed Nägeli on this point, and in 1857 we find Leydig defining a cell as " a soft substance containing a nucleus." Next the nucleus received attention. Max Schultze, one of the most careful of observers, denied its existence in Amœba porrecta ; other investigators quickly followed on the same line, and by Haeckel a distinct sub-kingdom, the Protista, was proposed for the reception of forms such as Protamœba, Protomyxa, and Protomonas, which were supposed to be devoid of nucleus and were regarded as possibly representing the parent forms from which animals and plants have alike descended. Further research has however tended to check rather than to confirm these statements; and the use of special reagents and more refined histological methods has shown that nuclei are present in many forms, such as the Foraminifera, in which their existence was at first denied.

The more recent investigations have also shown that the nucleus is not as was at first supposed a structure always presenting the same characters, but that it may vary greatly in form, structure, and relations, even amongst the simplest animals, or

Protozoa. In the young of many forms no nucleus can be detected, while the adult possesses a conspicuous one. Some forms, as Amœba, have a single nucleus ; others, as Opalina, or Arcella, have many nuclei. In Paramœcium there are two nuclear structures, the nucleus proper and the paranucleus, which have different properties and very different functions. Then as to shape, the nucleus is in most cases spherical or approximately so ; in Vorticella it is greatly elongated ; in Stentor it is elongated, and furthermore constricted in a moniliform manner ; and in such forms as Dendrosoma it presents an extraordinarily branched and extremely complex condition. A still more curious state is seen in Opalinopsis, an Infusorian living parasitically in the liver of the squid. Here the nucleus appears at times as a much branched reticular structure extending the whole length of the animal ; at other times the reticular nucleus breaks up or becomes " pulverised " into an immense number of extremely minute particles, which become diffused through the protoplasm of the animal, and would most certainly escape detection but for a knowledge of their previous condition. These few illustrations will serve to show how extraordinarily variable the nucleus may be even amongst the Protozoa. I shall return later on to the condition of the nucleus in higher animals, but propose first to deal with the cell-body itself.

The cell-body or cell contents—*i.e.*, the whole cell except the cell membrane and the nucleus—were spoken of by Dujardin as consisting of " sarcode," which he defined as "a kind of mucus endowed with spontaneous movement and contractility." His idea of the physiological activity of the cell-body was very early recognised as important, and Schwann himself expressed the conviction that the study of the cell-body or cell-substance was essential to a true knowledge of the processes of life. The term "protoplasm" that has since come into general use for the cell-substance was first applied to the cell-contents of plants, and was adopted by Max Schultze for animals as well, when in 1861 he maintained the fundamental identity of the living matter of animals and plants, however high or however low in grade they might be.

In 1868 Huxley, in his celebrated lecture at Edinburgh on "The Physical Basis of Life," laid great stress on the fundamental unity of the living matter of animals and plants, maintaining that it is right to speak of life as a property of protoplasm ; and that just as the properties of water—*e.g.*, convertibility under given conditions of temperature and pressure into steam—result from the nature and disposition of its component molecules, so do the properties of protoplasm result from the nature and disposition of its molecules. This idea, really originating with Schwann himself, that the riddle, the mystery of life, was to be solved by study of the molecular constitution of living matter or protoplasm was a great conception and in all probability a correct one. However for the moment it checked rather than aided the progress of biological science ; it was too big a jump. Our knowledge of molecular physics is far too incomplete to enable us to tackle the problem of life from this side, with even the remotest prospect of success ; while the habit which this conception almost necessarily engendered, of speaking of protoplasm as a substance of a certain chemical constitution, containing so much carbon, hydrogen, nitrogen, oxygen, phosphorus, and so on, as a substance allied to the albumens, perhaps most akin to white of egg, by diverting attention from other and more promising lines of enquiry, threatened to hamper rather than to further real progress.

The reaction soon came. Physiologists reminded themselves that it is the essence of protoplasm that it should be alive, and that their wisest course was to study directly the phenomena of life as manifested by it. The more conspicuous of these phenomena, contractility and irritability, the powers of movement and of sensation, first attracted attention. More recently attention has been specially directed to a further problem, resulting from the consideration that protoplasm is never idle, never at rest, but is always wearing itself away, incessantly wasting. Every living animal or plant wastes—*i.e.*, loses weight ; and this in all its parts and at all times, though at unequal rates. The loss of weight must mean loss of actual matter, and this loss is due to the breaking down of the body substance into simpler chemical bodies or excretory matters, of which carbonic acid and urea are the most important and the most characteristic.

But this is not all. A dead body also wastes

away, and the products of its wasting are much the same as the excretory matters formed by a living animal. The difference is that the living animal or plant has the power of repair, renewal, or regeneration of its living substance, while the dead body has no such power. This renewal is effected at the expense of the food. Food is essential, or we starve and die; and it has been well said that hunger is the essential and diagnostic character of living things. This power of building up living from non-living matter is peculiar to protoplasm, of which we have seen that the cell-bodies, whether of animals or plants, consist. The process is partly a chemical one, a building up of simpler into more complex bodies; but in part it is something more, something peculiar, the true nature of which we do not understand. The final touch, the conversion of the dead food into living brain, muscle, etc., is effected by a process which we name assimilation, but of which the *modus operandi* is at present absolutely unknown.

This conception of protoplasm or the living matter of animals and plants, as undergoing incessant change or metabolism as it is termed, is one of much importance. Living protoplasm has been compared to a fountain in which the form remains constant though each component particle of water is in constant movement. In protoplasm as in the fountain, we distinguish two main processes, an uphill or anabolic process, as the water rises to the crest of the wave, or the food is being built up into the living tissues; and a downhill or katabolic process, as the water falls from the crest back into the basin, or as the living brain, muscle, etc., become broken down into the various excretory products. The up-hill or anabolic processes are synthetic and require or absorb energy. The water of the fountain will not rise of itself, but must be forced above the level of the water of the basin ; and similarly the digestion and assimilation of food, the building-up of protoplasm, demand an expenditure of energy on the part of the animal.

On the other hand, the downhill or katabolic processes are analytic and are sources of energy ; and just as the falling water of the fountain may be used to drive a wheel or other machine, so in the living body the katabolic changes, like a series of explosions, give out energy which as muscular movement or mental activity or in other ways may be employed to do the work of the body. And just as in a fountain, the energy required to raise the water a given height is equal to the energy liberated by the water in falling from the same height ; and if work is to be done by the fountain, the water must be allowed to fall to a lower level than that from which it was raised ; so also in the living protoplasm of an animal, if work, muscular, mental, or of other kind is to be performed, the katabolic fall must be greater than the synthetic rise ; or in other words the excretory matters must be of simpler constitution than the food taken in.

Considerations of this kind which form the basis

of modern physiology, lead us to regard the protoplasm of which the cell-bodies consist, in rather a
different manner, and from a new standpoint.
Protoplasm may, to adopt the simile given above,
be regarded as the topmost point, the crest of the
physiological wave, consisting of matter in a condition of extremely unstable equilibrium, and varying
greatly in structure and in composition in different
cells, or even in the same cell at different times.
The essential character however of protoplasm is
that it is alive; and although we are unable to
formulate precisely what we mean by life, there is
at any rate one very definite idea which we asso-
ciate with living matter and with it alone, and this
is the power which living matter possesses of
building itself up, renewing itself from the dead
matter which is taken in as food. To define
protoplasm is difficult, perhaps impossible, but the
one essential thing to remember about it is that
it is alive. To speak of dead protoplasm is a
misnomer.

Starting from this new position attempts were
soon made to determine whether the protoplasm of
which cell-bodies consist possesses any structure,
and more especially whether there are any structural
changes which occur normally in cell-bodies, in
association with vital acts. It was soon found that
the cell-body or cell-substance is not necessarily
homogeneous. In many, perhaps in most cases, a
more or less pronounced reticular structure is
present; the protoplasm consisting of a network of
firmer strands, the meshes of which are filled with

a fluid or gelatinous substance in which are often present minute particles or granules.

Furthermore the action of reagents of various kinds shows that the network or reticulum is of different character, presumably of different composition, to the substance filling the meshes, and that in some cases the network itself may vary in different parts. Examples of such reticular protoplasm are frequent among Protozoa—as for example in the genera Noctiluca, Trachelius, and many other Infusoria ; while extreme cases of reticulation or vacuolation are seen among the Heliozoa, Radiolaria, and many of the Foraminifera—*e.g.*, Globigerina, in which the protoplasm has a characteristic bubbly or frothy appearance from the great number and size of the vacuoles. The contents of the meshes are usually fluid, or semi-fluid, and a study of their behaviour under various conditions, with a comparison of the mode of formation of fat cells, suggests strongly that the reticulum or network is the active part of the protoplasm, and that the substance filling the meshes is of secondary importance to it. Of this view, a most suggestive application has been made with regard to the structure of striated muscular fibre, which appears to consist of a reticulum, the strands of which are arranged in regular geometric pattern, and the meshes filled with a more fluid sarcous substance. It has been suggested that the reticulum is the active agent by contraction of which shortening of the muscle is produced ; and that the reticulum of a striated muscle fibre cell is equivalent to the reticulum of a Protozoan or of any ordinary cell, differing mainly in its more regular arrangement.

The changes that actually go on within the protoplasm of the cell-body in different phases of its activity have been studied most closely, and with the most definite results in secreting cells, either from special glands, such as the pancreas or salivary gland, or with still greater success in the epithelial cells lining the digestive stomach of certain insects. These secreting cells have their outer ends bathed in lymph, which diffuses from the neighbouring blood-vessels, while their inner ends form the bounding surface either of the gland or of the alimentary canal itself. The cells separate from the lymph certain products which they modify in various ways, and finally discharge at their free surface as the special secretion of the gland. Careful histological examination has shown that during rest the gland-cell enlarges, the special secretions accumulating in the meshes of the reticulum as a fluid or semi-fluid substance, often granular in appearance. During digestion, this secreted matter is discharged from the cells at their free surface, the meshes of the network becoming more or less completely emptied. As to the part played by the network itself the evidence is incomplete, but there is some reason to think that the secreted substance is formed in part at the expense of the reticulum. The discharge of the secretion does not necessarily involve the death of the cell, which may fill up again, time after time, with the secreted matter.

This very brief and imperfect account must suffice to indicate the lines along which investigation is at present advancing, in the attempt to determine the nature of the processes which go on within active living protoplasm.

Turning now to the nucleus, we find that an extraordinary number of minute researches have been made of late years, more especially with a view to determine as far as possible the part played by the nucleus in the acts of fertilisation and reproduction, in the hope of obtaining some clue to the attractive but bewildering problem of heredity. The important part played by the nucleus in initiating, indeed determining, the act of cell-division, was first definitely established by F. E. Schulze, in Amœba polypodia. He describes the successive changes as follows : The nucleus first elongates, then becomes dumb-bell shaped ; then the bridge between the two knobs becomes thinner and thinner, and finally breaks, so that there are now two separate nuclei, formed by division of the single original one. Next, the body of the Amœba begins to elongate in the same direction as the nucleus did previously ; then follow constriction, and finally the division of the Amœba into two parts, each containing one of the two nuclei already formed. The entire process occupied ten minutes ; division of the nucleus taking about a minute and a half, and the remaining eight and a half minutes being occupied by division of the body of the Amœba. A similar process of direct nuclear division, as it is called, has been described by Ranvier in the leucocytes of the Axolotl, in which case the process occupied an hour and a half; by Waldeyer in Infusoria; and since then by many other writers.

Of recent years attention has been more specially directed to a far more complicated series of changes, which have been seen by many observers to occur in the nucleus during division, and which are spoken of as karyokinesis or mitosis, or indirect nuclear division, in contrast with the former or direct mode. To understand these more complicated processes, we must first describe the structure of the nucleus as determined by more recent and more detailed investigations. It now appears that in the cell-nucleus there may normally be distinguished four elements : the network or reticulum, the nucleoli, the nuclear membrane, and the nucleoplasm.

The network or reticulum consists of finer or coarser threads, which differ in their arrangement in different cells. In epithelial cells from a Chironomus larva, Balbiani found the nuclear reticulum to be one single complexly coiled thread. In a large number of other cases it has been found by Rabl and others that the typical arrangement is as follows : Two kinds of threads may be distinguished ; thicker primary threads and thinner secondary ones. The primary threads may be twenty or more in number : each is folded on itself so as to form a loop, and the several looped threads are placed in a symmetrical manner in the nucleus ; the loops being arranged around one pole of the nucleus, and the free ends of the threads interlacing at the other pole. The secondary threads form a fine network, connecting together the primary threads, and may be so numerous as to conceal more or less completely the definite arrangement of these latter. The nucleoli are spherical bodies of various size, which stain deeply with the ordinary colouring reagents. It is not certain whether they are in all cases corresponding structures. Sometimes they are merely nodes or local thickenings of the network of threads, while at other times they appear to be quite independent of the network. The general tendency at present is to regard them as non-essential, or at any rate secondary structures ; and it is held by many that their purpose is to serve as a store of reserve matter for the nutrition of the other constituents of the nucleus.

The nuclear membrane has recently attracted renewed attention. By many it is regarded merely as a denser and superficial part of the nuclear reticulum ; while by others it is held that it is, at any rate in certain cases, a continuous membrane, though authorities are not agreed as to whether it belongs really to the nucleus itself, or is rather to be regarded as a limiting layer of the cell protoplasm, immediately surrounding the nucleus.

The nucleoplasm or nuclear sap, which fills up the whole of the rest of the nucleus, is an albuminous coagulable liquid. A fine reticulum has been described in some cases as traversing the nucleoplasm, and apparently independent of the main nuclear reticulum.

As regards the chemical constitution of the various parts of the nucleus, very little is as yet known. The network and the nucleoli take up stains more readily than the rest of the nucleus : the substance of which they consist is hence contrasted as chromatin with the non-staining nucleoplasm. In some cases the threads of the reticulum appear to consist of rows of minute chromatin granules arranged in an achromatin basis.

We are now in a position to consider the changes which occur in the nucleus during the process of indirect nuclear division or mitosis. The first change is that the secondary threads of the reticulum disappear, apparently through being absorbed into the primary threads. The primary threads thus become much more conspicuous, and their arrangement in loops is clearly seen. The threads forming the loops next become somewhat shorter and thicker ; they may also by transverse division become more numerous. There is some reason for thinking that in cells of the same kind from the same animal, the number of threads is constant, but this has not yet been proved to be a general rule. In the epidermal cells of the Salamander twenty-four loops are said to be constantly present. The next stage is an extremely important one, for the discovery of which we are indebted to Flemming. Each of the looped threads splits longitudinally along its whole length into two parallel threads. The pair of threads formed by the splitting of a single primary thread are spoken of as " sister-threads." As they are of exactly equal size, and as each of the primary threads becomes divided into a pair in this way, the upshot of the process is that the whole of the chromatin becomes divided into two precisely equal portions, a process the full significance of which will become apparent immediately. About or shortly after the time of the splitting of the primary threads into sister-threads, a structure known as the nuclear spindle appears. This is a fusiform figure, bounded by a number of exceedingly fine and feebly staining threads. It is said to be formed not from the nucleus, but from the cell protoplasm immediately surrounding the nucleus. At the time of its first appearance it has no clear relation to the looped threads of the nucleus, but very soon the two structures take up definite positions with regard to each other, the looped threads being grouped in a ring round the equator of the spindle, with the loops directed inwards towards the centre and the free ends outwards. At the same time the spindle itself becomes more clearly marked; at its poles are two rounded bodies, the " pole-bodies " of van Beneden, from which fine threads radiate outwards in all directions through the protoplasm of the cell-body. The nuclear membrane disappears about this time, though what exactly happens to it is unknown. It was formerly supposed to give rise, at any rate in part, to the nuclear spindle, but it is now generally agreed that the spindle is extra-nuclear and a product of the cell protoplasm alone. The chromatin loops now begin to move from the equator along the threads of the spindle, towards its poles. This takes place in a perfectly regular manner, the sister-threads of each pair moving towards opposite poles. As the two sister-threads of each pair are precisely equal, the two groups of threads around the two poles of the spindle will contain precisely equal quantities of chromatin. The two groups separate completely from each other, and each group becomes arranged in a manner corresponding to that of the primary threads in the original nucleus. In this way two daughter-nuclei are formed by division of the mother-nucleus : each daughter-nucleus containing half the chromatin of the mother-nucleus. After completion of the daughter-nuclei, the protoplasm of the cell-body divides, precisely as in the process of direct division, and the division of the mother-cell into two daughter-cells is complete.

The above description of the phenomena of mitosis or indirect nuclear division, represents the generally accepted view as to the sequence of events, but several points in it are still very imperfectly understood. One of the most important of these is the origin of the nuclear spindle and its pole-bodies. Van Beneden, whose long-continued and extraordinarily careful observations entitle him to speak with great authority, maintains that the pole-bodies are of primary importance. He says that the pole-bodies appear before the spindle ; that they arise distinctly in the cell protoplasm, quite independently of the nucleus ;

and that they appear to be centres from which the spindle threads diverge : the spindle threads themselves he describes as " apparently muscular," and as governing the movements of the chromatin threads. Van Beneden would therefore regard the pole-bodies as the most important structures, and as really determining cell division rather than the nuclei. Other observers however are not yet prepared to accept this view, but regard the nuclei as the determining agents in all cases of cell division.

A still more important problem is as to whether the direct and indirect processes of nuclear division are entirely independent, or whether they are not really related to each other, and if so in what manner. On this point very keen discussion has been and is still being carried on. As regards the relative frequency of the two processes, direct nuclear division has only been seen in comparatively few cases : in leucocytes by Rabl and Flemming ; in the intestinal epithelium of Crustacea by Frenzel ; in regenerating tissues by Fraisse ; in the Infusorian Euplotes by Möbius ; in the early stage of spermatozoon formation in Amphibia, and in a few other cases. On the other hand indirect nuclear division, or mitosis, has been seen in both animal and vegetable cells of almost every kind, and in processes both normal and pathological, and would certainly appear to be by far the more usual method.

With reference to a possible relation between the two methods, Waldeyer has strenuously maintained that there is one fundamental form of nuclear division, presenting a series of gradations from the simple direct method described by Remak up to the extreme complication seen in typical cases of mitosis ; and in favour of this view there is a considerable amount of evidence already accumulated. Thus Waldeyer himself has shown that if a frog's epidermis, in which mitosis usually occurs, be treated with silver nitrate, direct nuclear division can alone be demonstrated, from which he argues with great justice that the distinction between the two methods may in other cases also be only apparent, and due to the particular mode of histological treatment adopted.   Pfitzner has succeeded in staining both the nucleoplasm and chromatin simultaneously, and maintains that mitosis concerns not merely the chromatin but the entire nucleus ; and further that the cell protoplasm takes no part in the process.   Bütschli, Hertwig, Schewiakoff, and others have shown that in Protozoa, in which all the phenomena of mitosis occur, the nuclear membrane may remain complete the whole time until the final division of the nucleus into the two daughter-nuclei ; while Boveri and others have found that in segmenting eggs of various animals the various stages of mitosis may sometimes be very clear, and at others very obscure.   Finally, Carnoy asserts that mitosis, so far from being a uniform process in all cases, presents so many varieties that no one series can be viewed as essential ; he even denies that the longitudinal splitting of the chromatin threads into sister-threads is universal : a point on which Waldeyer differs from him emphatically.

On the whole it would appear that the balance of evidence is against the existence of a sharp distinction between the direct and indirect methods of nuclear division ; and in favour of there being one common form, subject to considerable variation in detail.   Much however yet remains to be done before the question can be regarded as settled. We are at present absolutely in the dark as to the real meaning and significance of the chromatin threads ; and it is especially important that the true relation of van Beneden's pole-bodies and of the nuclear spindle should be clearly determined, for until this is done, no theory of nuclear division can be held to be definitely established.   Perhaps the most striking points brought to light by the recent researches on nuclear division are the extreme complication of a process formerly regarded as a perfectly simple one, and the mathematical precision with which the division of the chromatin into equal halves is effected in typical cases.

One of the most interesting problems arising from the advance of our knowledge concerning the minute changes that occur during nuclear division, is the relation of the phenomena of mitosis to the act of fertilisation of the egg.   By the older writers it was supposed that either prior to, or as a consequence of the act of fertilisation, the nucleus of the egg, or germinal vesicle as it is commonly termed, disappears completely.   It is now however known that part of the egg-nucleus persists and fuses with part of the spermatozoon, this fusion constituting the act of fertilisation.   Auerbach was the first to show, in 1874, that in the egg of Ascaris two nuclei may be seen shortly after the spermatozoa reach the egg, and that these two nuclei fuse together.   In 1875 Oscar Hertwig stated, as the result of a careful series of observations on the eggs of Echini, that one of the two nuclei seen by Auerbach is the head of the spermatozoon, and that the other is part of the nucleus or germinal vesicle of the egg, probably the nucleolus or germinal spot.   In 1875 and 1876 van Beneden saw the fusion of two nuclei, or pronuclei as he named them, in the ovum of the rabbit, as a result of fertilisation ; one of these pronuclei he found to arise from the egg nucleus, though not as Hertwig had supposed from the nucleolus; the other, or male pronucleus, van Beneden recognised as in some way connected with the spermatozoon, though he failed to trace it directly to the head of the spermatozoon as Hertwig had done in the sea urchins.   These discoveries naturally attracted great attention, as they for the first time rendered possible a theory of fertilisation based on the changes actually known to occur during the process.   A number of other investigators, prominent among them being Fol, Greeff, Selenka, Flemming, Hensen, and Boveri, studied the phenomena in various groups of animals and definitely established the fact that the essence of the act of fertilisation consists in fusion of part of the egg nucleus with the head or nucleus of the spermatozoon—*i.e.,*

fusion of the male and female pronuclei.   Concerning the details of this fusion, and especially
its relations to the processes of mitosis or karyokinesis described above, many elaborate and careful
investigations have been made of late years which
have brought to light points of extraordinary
interest.

Before describing these in detail it is necessary
to say a few words concerning a phenomenon
closely connected with fertilisation, though no part
of the actual process itself; I mean the extrusion
from the egg, prior to fertilisation and independent
of it, of the so-called polar bodies.   Carus first
noticed, in 1828, minute globules on the surface of
an egg which took no part in the formation of the
embryo.   These were described carefully by
Friedrich Müller in 1848 as seen by him in the
snail's egg, and were called by him directive corpuscles because of the constant relation they
appeared to have to the first plane of segmentation ;
he showed clearly that they were derived from the
egg itself.   Hensen was the first to show that the
extrusion of the directive corpuscles or polar bodies
occurred independently of fertilisation, for he found
that in the rabbit and guinea-pig the polar bodies
were formed while the eggs were still in the
Graafian follicles, before their discharge from the
ovary.   This has been confirmed by many other
investigators, who have shown that as a rule two
polar bodies are extruded in succession ; that both
are usually extruded previous to fertilisation ; but
that in some cases as in the lamprey and the

frog, the first polar body may be extruded prior to fertilisation, and the second after or during the process; while in some cases, as in Ascaris, according to van Beneden, both polar bodies are extruded after the entrance of the spermatozoon. In 1875 Bütschli showed that in Nematodes the extrusion of polar bodies is accompanied by the formation of a nuclear spindle, and by other changes similar to those seen in indirect nuclear division.   He in consequence suggested the view that the formation of a polar body is really a division of the egg cell into two very unequal portions, and is accompanied by the ordinary nuclear changes seen in typical cases of mitosis. This view has since been widely adopted, though authorities are not yet agreed as to whether any part of the protoplasm of the egg is extruded with the daughter nucleus in the polar body. The point is of considerable interest, for on one view the whole process would be one of cell division, on the other merely nuclear division with extrusion of one of the daughter nuclei. The balance of opinion inclines strongly towards the former of these views, but the point cannot be considered definitely settled as yet.

The changes that occur in the egg nucleus during the formation of polar bodies have been recently studied with great care by many observers. In the frog's egg Oscar Schultze has shown that at the time of ripening of the egg the nucleus undergoes important changes. Previous to this time it has been of very large size, as much as a third the diameter of the egg itself, and consists of a well-marked nuclear membrane enclosing fluid nucleoplasm in which float a number of chromatin globules of varying size and apparently unconnected with one another. At the time of ripening of the egg, shortly before it leaves the ovary, the nuclear membrane becomes crumpled and indistinct; the whole nucleus shrivels very greatly, its fluid contents being diffused through the egg; the majority of the chromatin globules disappear, but a group of very small ones near the centre persist; these unite together to form a convoluted varicose chromatin thread which soon breaks up into loops; then a nuclear spindle appears with which the loops soon become connected as in ordinary mitosis. The spindle with the associated loops, which together are of exceedingly small size, move to the surface of the ovum; the loops and the spindle now divide in the ordinary way into two equal halves which become the daughter nuclei. One of the daughter nuclei is extruded as the first polar body, while the other retreats into the interior of the egg. The formation of the second polar body is a repetition of the process by which the first was formed. As the amount of chromatin is halved at each nuclear division, the female pronucleus, which is the portion of the egg nucleus left after the formation of the seccnd polar body, will contain exactly one-fourth of the amount of chromatin present in the egg nucleus at the formation of the nuclear spindle. Van Beneden's account of the process in Ascaris agrees exactly with this. At each division of the nucleus to form a polar body the chromatin, which is present rather in the form of spherules than of threads, is exactly halved in amount.

Concerning the fusion of the male and female pronuclei in the act of fertilisation some points of great interest have recently been brought to light. In some cases, as shown by Nussbaum in Ascaris, a direct fusion of the two pronuclei is described as occurring, while in other forms and by other observers the process is said to be of a more complicated character. In the Nematodes, genus Leptodera, Nussbaum says that the two pronuclei, male and female, take up a position parallel to the long axis of the egg, which is ovoid in shape, and then fuse together lengthways. The first segmentation plane is a longitudinal one and passes along the axis of the fused pronuclei, so that each of the two cells formed by the first cleft contains one-half of the male pronucleus and one-half of the female pronucleus. Inasmuch as all the cells of the body of the adult animal are derived by division from the two primary ones, it follows, as Nussbaum points out, that if this equal division of male and female nuclear elements obtains in the later stages of cell division, each cell of the adult animal will possess a nucleus, one half of which is derived from the father and the other half from the mother.

This suggestion, the bearing of which on theories of heredity is of the greatest importance, has received most striking confirmation from the extraordinarily minute observations of van Beneden on the eggs of Ascaris. These investigations, made in the years 1883 and 1884, rank deservedly among the most remarkable of microscopical triumphs. Van Beneden finds that after extrusion of the polar bodies, and entrance of the spermatozoon into the egg, the two pronuclei, male and female, which are precisely equal in all respects, come very close together but do not fuse directly. Each pronucleus bears at first a single much convoluted and varicose thread of chromatin, which soon divides transversely into two, each of which becomes bent into a U-shaped loop. There are then four loops in all, two male and two female. Each loop now splits longitudinally into two sister threads. A spindle figure with pole-bodies and polar rays at its apices now appears, and the outlines of the pronuclei, previously distinct, disappear. The chromatin loops, of which owing to the longitudinal splitting there are now eight, four male and four female, take up a position at the equator of the spindle. The two sister threads of each pair now separate, one moving towards one pole of the spindle the other towards the opposite pole; so that at each pole of the spindle there is a group consisting of two male threads and two female threads. Each group now forms a daughter nucleus, and then the entire egg divides into the first two segmentation cells. This account agrees with Nussbaum's as regards the equal division of male and female threads between the first two segmentation cells; but differs inasmuch as according to Nussbaum, the two pronuclei fuse directly, while, according to van Beneden, there is no fusion of the pronuclei, but merely a re-arrangement of the chromatin threads. Zacharias and Hertwig have suggested that fusion really does occur but may have been overlooked, but for the present the point cannot be considered settled. It is possible indeed that the details are not the same in all cases.

The equal division of male and female elements in the first segmentation, a point in which Nussbaum and van Beneden agree and which has been confirmed by others, is of the highest possible interest and importance. If it should prove to occur in the later as well as in the earliest stages of development, then, as pointed out above, it will follow that the nucleus of each cell in the body of the adult animal will contain male and female elements derived from the male and female pronuclei—*i.e.*, from the father and mother—in precisely equal amounts. In other words, each cell of the adult body may be spoken of as hermaphrodite. If this is true, then the egg, which is merely an epithelial cell indistinguishable in its early stages from the surrounding cells, must itself be hermaphrodite. The further suggestion at once presents itself: Is not the extrusion of the polar bodies a casting out of the male elements of the egg ?

This is a view which in one form or another has commended itself to many embryologists. Balfour first suggested that the extrusion of the polar bodies was a device for ridding the egg of its male elements, and so ensuring that cross fertilisation must occur, the advantage of which as regards vigour of offspring is well known. Minot has independently suggested and strongly supported the same view. A serious difficulty however has been raised to this view by Weismann, who points out that if the male element in the egg is got rid of completely by extrusion of the polar bodies, then it becomes very difficult to understand the transmission of male ancestral characters through the mother. It is well known that children may inherit peculiarities of their grandfather on the mother's side, and this, according to Weismann, should not be possible if the extrusion of the polar bodies removes all male elements from the egg. We must suppose that a small remnant is or may be left behind ; but then, asks Weismann, why should any be eliminated at all if it is not necesary that all should be got rid of ?

The matter is very far from a simple one. Weismann himself has shown that in various parthenogenetic crustacea, Polyphemus, Moina, Daphnia, and others, only one polar body is extruded ; and Blochmann in 1887 announced that in Aphis the parthenogenetic eggs extrude one polar body only, while those that require fertilisation extrude two. This seems to indicate that the two polar bodies may have very different value in spite of the close similarity in their modes of formation ; for the extrusion of one polar body seems to leave the egg still capable of developing without fertilisation ; while after two polar bodies are extruded, fertilisation is necessary for development to occur.

Weismann's explanation of the process is a complicated one. Regarding the nucleus as specially concerned with heredity, he distinguishes in the nuclear substance two kinds of matter, which he names histogenic plasma and ancestral plasma respectively. The former or histogenic plasma he regards as specially concerned with the growth, nutrition, and shaping of cells ; while the second or ancestral plasma is supposed to be specially concerned with reproduction and heredity. He then assumes that the histogenic plasma having completed its work when the egg has reached maturity, it is convenient to get rid of it, which is done by extruding it bodily from the egg as the first polar body. The remaining half of the nuclear substance is the ancestral plasma ; and with regard to the second polar body, Weismann argues that if the whole of the ancestral plasma of the egg were retained, and were to fuse with the whole of the ancestral plasma of the spermatozoon, then the total amount of ancestral plasma would be doubled at each generation. This he argues would cause inconvenience, and so the device is adopted of getting rid of half of this ancestral plasma in the form of the second polar body.

Apart from its extreme complexity, this theory of Weismann's is open to grave objection. In the first place the supposed difference between histogenic plasma and ancestral plasma is a pure assumption, in support of which no direct evidence has been advanced. Secondly, it is very difficult to understand why, on Weismann's view, the histogenic plasma should be exactly half the nucleus. Thirdly, it cannot be overlooked that the modes of formation of the first and of the second polar bodies are precisely similar to each other, and also that they agree precisely with the changes that occur in the nucleus of an ordinary epithelial cell during indirect division, similarities which become very difficult to understand if, as Weismann supposes, the two polar bodies are of totally different nature, and do not correspond to the halves of the nucleus of a dividing epithelial cell. Lastly, it may be noted that cases have been described in which more than two polar bodies have been extruded.

On the whole therefore, while acknowledging the extreme ingenuity of Weismann's theory and the service which its publication has rendered by stimulating investigation and discussion, it cannot be said that the theory is in accordance with all the facts it seeks to explain, or that it helps us very materially towards an understanding of these facts. So far direct observation has failed to show any difference in structure or in mode of formation of the two polar bodies, or any important respects in which their development differs from the phenomena of ordinary mitosis. These processes are so complicated and require such extraordinary care and patience for their successful investigation, that it is but natural to assume that they have some deep and far-reaching significance ; and it is well therefore to remember that they are in no way specially concerned with the processes of sexual reproduction, but occur as characteristically in the act of division of an ordinary epithelial cell as in the formation of a polar body by a ripe ovum.

It is well also to bear in mind that although the arrangements and divisions of the chromatin threads naturally attract special attention, it is by no means certain that these threads are the main factors in the act of nuclear division. Indeed the comparison of the direct method of division with the indirect method which we have discussed above, rather suggests that the nucleoplasm or nuclear substance itself is the really essential element, and that the chromatin threads need not even be present, at any rate in a form capable of being brought into view by the reagents at present in use.

And so it would appear from these more recent researches, of which time has only permitted me to give a brief and most imperfect summary, that the cell theory, great and important as it is most undoubtedly, is rather the commencement of a great movement, a fresh starting-point from which to begin investigations anew, than a complete scheme or final explanation; and the one great lesson for us to learn is that processes of apparently the simplest kind are really of an extremely complicated nature, and will well repay the most minute and attentive study: for a right understanding of the changes that occur during the act of division of an ordinary epithelial cell, and of the causes determining those changes, would throw most welcome light on the more complicated processes accompanying the ripening and fertilisation of the egg, which microscopists of all nationalities are at present studying with such intense earnestness.

X

ANIMAL PEDIGREES

There are few things in which men take greater pride or from which they derive more solid enjoyment, than in tracing out and publishing to the world their pedigrees; and we must acknowledge that the proceeding itself, and the satisfaction obtained from it, are entirely legitimate. For we all have pedigrees; for two or three generations each one of us could give his descent, trace his pedigree, offhand; and if we fail in attempting to go further back we know that this is from lack of knowledge, not of facts.

Would we learn these facts, we know that there are those whose profession it is to supplement our deficiencies of memory or of information on these points, and who are prepared for a sum of half-a-crown, to provide the enquirer with a duly attested pedigree dating from the time of the Conquest. For a guinea a Roman emperor can.be obtained; while the avaricious in such matters, who are prepared to spend a five-pound note, may satisfy themselves, and for all we know, truthfully, of their descent from a Pharaoh of the 19th dynasty.

The mode of construction of such pedigrees, or genealogical trees, is familiar to us all from our school days. We begin by ruling a series of horizontal lines, which we agree shall represent successive generations. Then, assuming that we

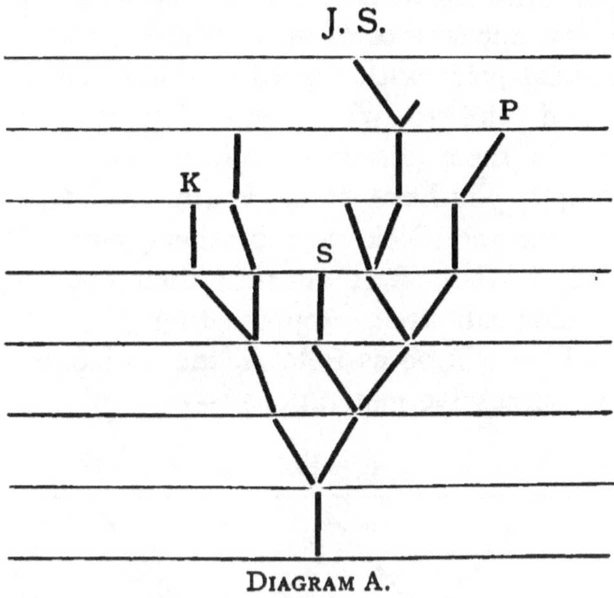

DIAGRAM A.

are of those whose aspirations are satisfied by a two-and-sixpenny ancestry, we commence with the dawn of respectability in the year 1066, and gradually trace upwards from this date the line representing our descent from the selected progenitor.

We indicate in capitals, or in italics, any kings, or statesmen, or poets, or other eminent people whose memories we like to think derive renewed lustre from association with ourselves; and to include a sufficient number of these we trace the side branches of our tree for some distance. Finally, on the topmost twig, and in largest letters, we write—John Smith.

We all have such pedigrees, whether we can declare them or not ; and for the prince and the pauper they are of equal length, dating back not merely to the Norman Invasion of England, but to the first appearance of man on the earth.

A special point with regard to these genealogical trees, and one to which attention may well be directed, is their absolute truthfulness. Suppose for example, you have three young friends, two of whom, Tom and Dick, are brothers, while Harry, the third, is their first cousin ; then the diagram, or genealogical tree, representing their mutual relationships will be as follows, the horizontal lines marking successive generations :—

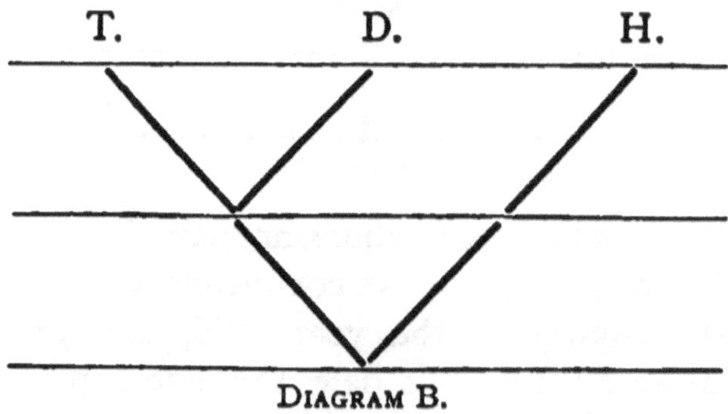

DIAGRAM B.

Go back one generation, and Tom and Dick's lines meet, for they are sons of one father. Before Harry's line joins in it is necessary to go back one generation further—*i.e.*, to the grandfather of our young friends, who was one and the same person for all three, and who forms the true link or bond of union between them. If once these relationships are determined correctly, and the diagram constructed aright, then it expresses facts, and facts only, and can never be disturbed. It matters not what the occupations or residences of the three may be; they may never see one another, never even suspect one another's existence. It makes no difference how many people may be living contemporaneously, how many may have preceded, how many may be born in after ages; this little bit of history remains untouched and absolutely true for all time. It is for this reason that genealogy or blood relationship affords the only satisfactory basis for a classification of men; and we shall find that the same considerations apply to the lower animals as well.

One further matter of a preliminary nature requires mention. It is customary in preparing genealogical tables to construct them as is done above, starting from some one more or less remote ancestor, and following upwards the branches representing his descendants, so that the whole diagram takes the form of an upright tree. It should be noted however that in a certain sense the diagram would be more correct if it were inverted. In tracing back human pedigrees there is a marked tendency to follow out one special line of descent, and to concentrate attention on one particular ancestor from whom we desire to make our line arise, ignoring the fact that there were many other contemporary ancestors from any of whom our path might with equal truth have commenced.

A man has two parents, four grandparents, eight great-grandparents—*i.e.*, in tracing back his pedigree from the present time the number of his ancestors in each generation is double those of the generation that succeeded it in time. This is graphically expressed in the following diagram:

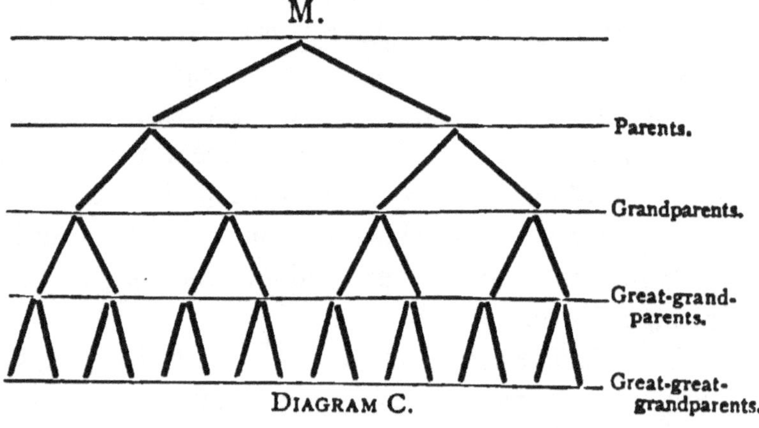

DIAGRAM C.

which takes, as noted above, the form of an inverted, not an erect, tree. If we allow three generations to a century there will have been twenty-five generations between the Norman Invasion and the present time: so that a man now living may be descended not merely from one ancestor who came over to England in 1066, but directly and equally from over sixteen million ancestors who lived at or about that date. I say advisedly "*may* be descended;" for unless we assume that many of these ancestors were identical individuals, we shall find that the existence of a single man to-day involves the existence, a thousand years ago, of over a thousand millions of ancestors; and at the commencement of the Christian era of nearly seventy thousand millions of millions of ancestors : a state of things which would involve serious reconsideration of the dimensions of the earth.

Genealogical trees, such as I have described, we are all familiar with. Furthermore we know that the principles employed in constructing them are not confined to Smith and Jones and the kings and queens of England, but apply to the lower animals as well. The pedigrees of racehorses, and of other artificially bred animals, such as cattle, sheep, pigs, dogs, pigeons, poultry, etc., have for many years past been kept with the most scrupulous care; and there are men who could tell you in detail the pedigree of the winner of last year's Derby or Leger, who would be sorely perplexed if asked for their own, and would perhaps prefer that the results of researches on this point should not be made too public.

We all recognise that the cats and rabbits and dogs of to-day did not come into existence spontaneously, but are descended from the cats, rabbits, and dogs of preceding generations, decades, or centuries ; and that the same applies to birds, to butterflies, to sea anemones, or to any other animals we like to think of. We have now merely to enlarge our sphere of action, to widen our boundaries with regard to such genealogies, and we find ourselves face to face with the great problem with which naturalists are confronted, and which they are attacking on every side and by all means in their power.

We recognise that Diagram A represents correctly the relation between man and man: and we admit that it is equally true when applied to horses, to cows, to dogs, or to canaries. In other words, we acknowledge that the principle on which the diagram is constructed is true in all cases in which historical or documentary evidence is forthcoming.

Can we not go further than this ? Is this written testimony essential ? Would the facts be in any way altered if no documentary evidence were forthcoming ? Do we not agree that all animals have had pedigrees of this kind ; and is it not worth enquiring whether we cannot reconstruct, unravel these pedigrees, even in cases where of necessity documentary evidence cannot be obtained ?

Again, to return for a moment to the human argument. So far our horizontal lines have been used to indicate successive generations, and the relation, admitted by all, has been that each generation has sprung from the preceding generation, and has in its turn given birth to the next succeeding one.

Supposing now that we widen our boundaries, and agree that the intervals between successive horizontal lines shall indicate, not generations but longer intervals, say centuries, the relations will remain unaltered.

	XIX Century.
	XVIII Century.
	XVII Century.
* * * *	XVI Century.
	XV Century.
	XIV Century.

If for example we fix our attention on the sixteenth century, we find that the men of that century did not arise spontaneously, but were the direct descendants of those of the preceding or fifteenth century ; furthermore we all admit that from the men of the sixteenth century those of the seventeenth, eighteenth, and nineteenth centuries have all directly sprung. And what holds good with regard to the men of the sixteenth century applies equally well to the horses, the cats, the dogs, the birds, the butterflies, the starfishes of that time. Now widen the intervals still further : let them represent not merely centuries but thousands, tens of thousands, of years ; let them finally indicate the great geologic periods, and the argument will still hold :

	Quaternary and Recent.
	Pliocene.
* * * *	Miocene.

Eocene.

Cretaceous.

The animals, and for that matter the plants too, of the Miocene age, did not come into existence irrespective of pre-existing animals and plants, but were the direct lineal descendants of the Eocene animals and plants ; and the forefathers of those of Pliocene and Recent times.

Kainozoic.

*   *   *   *   Mesozoic.

Palæozoic.

So also were the animals of Mesozoic times the children of those of the Palæozoic age, and the parents of the Kainozoic fauna. And so this idea of continuity of life from its earliest dawn on the earth, through age after age, down to the present time, forces itself upon us : an idea involving the further conception of the evolution of existing animals from unlike ancestors of former times : an idea constraining us to admit that animals, like men, have pedigrees, and that between the animals of all ages a kinship, a blood relationship, exists.

The recognition of this kinship is the determining feature of the Natural History of to-day. The reconstruction of these pedigrees is the great work of the future : the rewriting of the past histories, not merely of one or two groups for a limited

number of generations, but of all animals and for
all time :—a formidable, but an entrancing problem ;
and whatever misgivings I may have as to my
power of presenting it aright, no apology is needed
for asking your attention to a consideration of the
means at our disposal for attacking it, of the evidence on which we rely in our attempts to reconstruct the past histories, to determine the pedigrees
of animals.

On the present occasion, it is not with the
whole evidence, but with one special side of it, that
we shall be concerned, that namely which is
derived from a study of the development of existing
animals.   Every one knows that animals in the
earlier stages of their existence differ greatly in
form, in structure, and in habits from the adult
condition ;   a lung-breathing frog for example
commences its life as a gill-breathing tadpole ; and
a butterfly passes its infancy and youth as a
caterpillar.   It is clear that these developmental
stages, and the order of their occurrence, can be no
mere accidents ; for all the individuals of any
particular species of frog, or of butterfly, pass
through the same series of changes.   It is not
however until recent years that naturalists have
realised that each animal is constrained to develop
along definitely determined lines ; and that the successive stages in its life-history are forced on an
animal in accordance with a law, the determination
of which ranks as one of the greatest achievements
of biological science.

The doctrine of Descent, or of Evolution, teaches

us that as individual animals arise, not spontaneously, but by direct descent from pre-existing
animals, so also is it with species, with families,
and with larger groups of animals, and so also has
it been for all time; that as the animals of
succeeding generations are related together, so also
are those of successive geologic periods; that all
animals living or that have lived are united
together by blood relationship of varying nearness
or remoteness; and that every animal now in
existence has a pedigree stretching back, not
merely for ten or a hundred generations, but
through all geologic time since the dawn of life on
this globe.

The study of Development, in its turn, has
revealed to us that each animal bears the mark of
its ancestry, and is compelled to discover its
parentage in its own development; that the phases
through which an animal passes in its progress
from the egg to the adult are no accidental freaks,
no mere matters of developmental convenience, but
represent more or less closely, in more or less
modified manner, the successive ancestral stages
through which the present condition has been
acquired. Evolution tells us that each animal has
had a pedigree in the past. Embryology reveals to
us this ancestry, because every animal in its own
development repeats its history, climbs up its own
genealogical tree. Such is the Recapitulation
Theory, hinted at by Agassiz, and suggested more
directly in the writings of Von Baer, but first
clearly enunciated by Fritz Müller, and since

elaborated by many, notably by Balfour and Ernst Haeckel.

A few illustrations from different groups of animals will best explain the practical bearings of the theory, and the aid which it affords to the zoologist in his attempts to reconstruct the pedigrees of animals ; while these will also serve to illustrate certain of the difficulties which have arisen in the attempt to interpret individual development by the light of past history ; difficulties which I propose to consider at greater length.

A very simple example of recapitulation is afforded by the eyes of the sole, flounder, plaice, turbot, and their allies. These " flat fish " have their bodies greatly compressed laterally, and the two surfaces, really the right and left sides of the animal, unlike, one being white or nearly so, and the other coloured. The flat fish has two eyes, but these, in place of being situated as in other fish one on each side of the head, are both on the coloured side. The advantage to the fish is clear, for a flat fish when at rest lies on the sea bottom, with its white surface downwards and the coloured one upwards. In such a position an eye situated on the white surface could be of no use to the fish, and might even become a source of danger, owing to its liability to injury from stones or other hard bodies on the sea bottom.

No one would maintain that flat fish were specially created as such. The totality of their organisation shows clearly enough that they are true fish, akin to others in which the eyes are symmetrically placed one on each side of the head, in the position they normally hold among vertebrates. We must therefore suppose that flat fish are descended from other fish in which the eyes are normally situated.

The Recapitulation Theory supplies a ready test; and on employing it—*i.e.*, on studying the development of the flat fish—we obtain a conclusive answer. A young flounder or other fish, on leaving the egg, is shaped just as any ordinary fish, and has the two eyes placed symmetrically on the right and left sides of the head. As the young fish increases in size, the shape gradually approaches that of the adult; the body increases in height and becomes flattened laterally, the median, dorsal, and ventral fins becoming greatly developed at the same time; and the fish now begins to adopt the habit of the adult of lying on one side on the sea bottom. Another change occurs: the eye of the side on which the fish lies, usually the left side in a flounder, becomes shifted slightly forwards, then rotated on to the top of the head, and finally twisted completely over to the opposite or right side.

Crabs differ markedly from their allies, the lobsters, in the small size and rudimentary condition of their abdomen or "tail." Development however affords abundant evidence of the descent of crabs from macrurous ancestors. A crab leaves the egg in what is termed the zoea condition, possessing a long and clearly jointed abdomen; and throughout all the earlier stages of existence the abdomen remains at least as long as the body.

At the megalopa stage the shape and proportions are very similar to those of a lobster or other macrurous decapod. It is only in the last stages of development when the shape, though not the size, of the adult crab is attained, that the abdomen becomes relatively smaller, and is turned forwards out of sight beneath the hinder part of the thorax.

Molluscs afford excellent illustrations of recapitulation. The typical gasteropod has a large spirally coiled shell; the limpet however has a large conical shell, which in the adult gives no sign of spiral twisting, although the structure of the animal shows clearly its affinity to forms with spiral shells. Development solves the riddle at once, telling us that in its early stages the limpet embryo has a spiral shell, which is lost on the formation subsequently of the conical shell of the adult.

Recapitulation is not confined to the higher groups of animals, and the Protozoa themselves yield most instructive examples. A very striking case is that of Orbitolites, one of the most complex of the porcellanous Foraminifera, in which each individual during its own growth and development passes through the series of stages by which the cyclical or discoidal type of shell was derived from the simpler spiral form.

The fully formed Orbitolite shell is a thin calcareous disc. It is hollow, and the central cavity is divided into chambers by concentric partitions or septa. These chambers are further subdivided by incomplete radial partitions. The concentric partitions are perforated by numerous holes, which place the chambers in communication with one another; and the outermost or marginal chamber communicates with the outer world through a series of holes round the edge or rim of the disc. During life all the cavities are filled with a slimy protoplasm, very similar to that of which an Amœba consists; through the perforations in the septa the protoplasm of one chamber communicates freely with that of the neighbouring chambers; and through the marginal apertures at the rim of the shell pseudopodia can be protruded and food captured and digested.

An Orbitolite grows by addition of new chambers round the margin of the shell. The protoplasm, becoming too abundant to be contained within the cavities of the shell, protrudes as a rim all round the margin of the shell, and by deposition of calcareous matter gives rise to successive new chambers to the shell.

The discoidal shape of shell, so characteristic of Orbitolites, is very unusual amongst Foraminifera, and it is a matter of great interest to determine in what way it has been acquired. Bearing in mind what has just been said as to the mode of growth of the shell, it is clear that the oldest part—*i.e.*, that which alone was present in the young animal—is the central portion, and that the successive concentric rings are younger and younger as we pass outwards towards the circumference, the marginal chamber being the youngest and latest formed of the whole series. Now if we look at the central or oldest part of an Orbitolite we find that it has not the concentric arrangement of the peripheral part, but is coiled spirally like the majority of Foraminifera. The central or oldest turns of this spiral are not chambered; the outer turns are divided by partitions into chambers, and these chambers, as we follow the spiral round, become wider and wider, so as to overlap and wrap round the older part of the shell, at first partially but ultimately completely; the first chamber that completely surrounds the shell marking the transition from the spiral to the discoidal type.

We thus find that the discoidal Orbitolite shell commences its development as a spiral shell, and acquires the discoidal character merely through an exaggerated mode of growth on the part of the spiral. The Recapitulation Theory tells us that this is to be interpreted as meaning that the discoidal shells are descended from spiral ancestors, and the close agreement between a young Orbitolite and an adult Peneroplis suggests that either Peneroplis itself, or forms closely allied to it, were the actual ancestors.

The Orbitolite is peculiarly instructive, owing to the fact that the addition of new chambers during growth takes place in such a way as to leave the older parts of the shell unaltered and fully exposed to view, so that simple inspection of an adult shell reveals the whole course of development, and shows us not merely the anatomy but the embryology as well. It is as though a kitten were to develop into a cat, not by interstitial growth in all its parts, but by the addition of successive lengths to its nose, its ears, its legs, and its tail; the additions being cleverly effected so as to leave the original kitten unaltered in the middle, and fully exposed to view the whole time.

The above examples, selected almost haphazard, will suffice to illustrate the Theory of Recapitulation. The proof of the theory depends chiefly on its universal applicability to all animals, whether high or low in the zoological scale, and to all their parts and organs. It derives also strong support from the ready explanation which it gives of many otherwise unintelligible points.

Of these latter, familiar and most instructive instances are afforded by rudimentary organs—*i.e.*, structures which, like the outer digits of the horse's leg, or the intrinsic muscles of the ear of a man, are present in the adult in an incompletely developed form, and in a condition in which they can be of no use to their possessors; or else structures which are present in the embryo, but disappear completely before the adult condition is attained; for example, the teeth of whalebone whales or the gill-slits present in the neck during the embryonic phases of all higher vertebrates.

Natural selection explains the preservation of useful variations, but will not account for the formation and perpetuation of useless organs, and rudiments such as those mentioned above would be unintelligible but for Recapitulation, which solves the problem at once, showing that these organs, though now useless, must have been of functional value to the ancestors of their present possessors, and that their appearance in the ontogeny of existing forms is due to repetition of ancestral characters.

Rudimentary organs are extremely common, especially among the higher groups of animals, and their presence and significance are now well understood. Man himself affords numerous and excellent examples, not merely in his bodily structure, but by his speech, dress, and customs. For the silent letter *b* in the word "doubt," the *g* in "reign," or the *w* of "answer," or the buttons on his elastic-side boots are as true examples of rudiments, unintelligible but for their past history, as are the ear muscles he possesses but cannot use; or the gill-clefts, which are functional in fishes and tadpoles, and are present, though useless, in the embryos of all higher vertebrates; which in their early stages the hare and the tortoise alike possess, and which are shared with them by cats and by kings.

The fossil remains of animals and of plants yield results of the greatest importance when studied in the light of the Recapitulation Theory. I have thought it well to ask special attention to these, even at the risk of repeating what has been said elsewhere and by others, for it seems to me that zoologists are too apt nowadays to neglect palæontology, while palæontologists have a tendency to regard embryology as something beyond their own ken, and concerning them but little. Moreover there are certain points arising from a study of fossils which, I venture to think, may possibly commend themselves to some of our members as suitable subjects for practical investigation.

The elder Agassiz was the first to point out, in 1858, the remarkable agreement between the embryonic growth of animals and their palæontological history. He called attention to the resemblance between certain stages in the growth of young fish and their fossil representatives, and attempted to establish, with regard to fish, a correspondence between their palæontological sequence and the successive stages of embryonic development. He then extended his observations to other groups of animals, and stated his conclusions in these words : "It may therefore be considered as a general fact, very likely to be more fully illustrated as investigations cover a wider ground, that the phases of development of all living animals correspond to the order of succession of their extinct representatives in past geological times."

This point of view is of great importance. If the development of an animal is really a repetition or recapitulation of its ancestral history, then it is clear that the agreement or parallelism which Agassiz insists on between the embryological and palæontological records must hold good, and a most important field of work is thus opened up to us. It is sometimes urged however that such work is necessarily unfruitful and inconclusive, because of the scantiness of our knowledge concerning life in the earlier geologic periods, or as it is commonly termed, the imperfection of the geological record. I have elsewhere protested against this objection, and would repeat my protest here. The actual number of fossils already obtained, especially from the more recent formations, is prodigious; and what we have to do is to make the most of the material already accumulated, rather than to fold our hands and idly lament the absence of forms that perhaps never existed.

It is true that with all groups the chances are not equal. But by judicious selection of groups in which long series of specimens can be obtained, and in which the hard skeletal parts, which alone can be suitably preserved as fossils, afford reliable indications of zoological affinity, it is possible to test directly this alleged correspondence between the palæontological and embryological histories; while in some instances a single lucky specimen may afford us, on a particular point, all the evidence we require. Many serious attempts have already been made to work out in detail this comparison between fossils and the developmental stages of living forms, and the results obtained are most promising.

Following the lines laid down by his father, Alexander Agassiz has made a detailed comparison between the fossil series and the embryonic phases of recent forms in the case of the Echinoids or Sea Urchins, a group peculiarly well adapted for such an investigation, as the fossil representatives are extremely numerous and well preserved, and the existing members well known and comparatively few in number. Agassiz shows that the two records in this case agree remarkably closely; more especially in the independent evidence they give of the origin of the asymmetrical forms from

more regular ancestors. The young Clypeastroid
for example has an ovoid test, a small number of
coronal plates, few and large primary tubercles and
spines, simple straight ambulacral areas, and no
petaloid ambulacra ; in fact has none of the
characteristic features of the adult Clypeastroid,
while the characters it does possess are those of
geologically older and preceding forms. So again,
in the group of Echinidæ, the members of the comparatively recent polyporous group, in which each
ambulacral plate bears more than three pairs of
ambulacral pores, commence their existence in the
older and more primitive oligoporous condition, and
become polyporous through fusion of originally distinct ambulacral plates.

Agassiz gives many other examples, and from
a careful consideration of the entire group, arrives
at the conclusion that " comparing the embryonic
development with the palæontological one, we find
a remarkable similarity ; " and again, " the comparison of the Echini which have appeared since
the Lias with the young stages of growth of the
principal families of recent Echini, shows a most
striking coincidence, amounting almost to identity,
between the successive fossil genera and the various
stages of growth."

In this connection Agassiz makes a suggestion of
much interest. We are apt he says to assume,
and perhaps rightly, that enormous periods of time
have elapsed during the conversion of genus into
genus, but the fact that these very changes can be
repeated before our eyes in a few days' or even

hours' time, during the development of the individual animal, may perhaps afford us a hint that such enormous periods are not really necessary in historical development, and that transformation of one form to a widely different one may, under favourable circumstances, be effected with considerable rapidity.

The Echinoids, and other groups of Echinoderms as well, have been worked at from the same standpoint and with the same results by Neumayr, in whom we have recently lost one of the most gifted and painstaking of palæontologists.

As an example of the extreme value in certain cases of a single fossil specimen, the singular fossil bird Archæopteryx may be referred to. In recent birds the metacarpal bones of the wing are firmly fused with one another and with the distal row of carpal or wrist bones, but in development the metacarpals are at first and for some time distinct. The first specimen of Archæopteryx discovered, which is now in the British Museum, showed that in it this distinctness was preserved in the adult— *i.e.*, that what is now an embryonic character in recent birds was formerly an adult one.

Another very excellent illustration of the parallelism between the palæontological and the developmental series is afforded by the antlers of deer, which as is well known are shed annually, and grow again of increased size and complexity in each succeeding year. In the case of the red deer, *Cervus elaphus*, the antlers are shed in the spring, usually between the months of February and April;

during the summer the new antlers sprout out, and growing rapidly attain their full size at the pairing season in August or September: they persist throughout the winter, and are shed in the following spring. The antlers of the first year are small and unbranched; those of the second year are larger and branched; in the antlers of the third year three tynes or points are present; in the fourth year four points, and so on until the full size of the antler and the full number of points are attained.

The geological history of antlers has been worked out by Professor Gaudry and by Professor Boyd Dawkins, and is of great interest. In the Lower Miocene and earlier deposits no antlers have been found. In the genus Procervulus from the Middle Miocene, a pair of small, erect, branched, but non-deciduous antlers were present, intermediate in many respects between the antlers of deer and the horns of antelopes. From slightly later deposits a stag has been found with forked deciduous antlers, which however do not appear to have had more than two points. In Upper Miocene times antlered ruminants were more abundant, and the antlers themselves larger and more complex: while from Pliocene deposits very numerous fossils have been obtained showing a gradual increase in the size of the antlers and the number of their branches down to the present time.

Antlers are therefore, geologically considered, very recent acquisitions: at their first appearance they were small, and either simple or branched once only; while in succeeding ages they gradually increased in size and in complexity. The palæontological series thus agrees with the developmental series of stages through which the antlers of a stag pass at the present day before attaining their full dimensions.

There is another point of view from which fossils acquire special interest in connection with the Recapitulation Theory. If the theory is correct, it must apply not merely to the animals now living on the earth, but to all animals that ever have lived; and it becomes a matter of considerable interest to enquire whether we have any evidence whereby we can test this point, and determine whether or not the fossil animals in their own individual development repeated the characters of their ancestors.

At first sight the enquiry does not seem a promising one, for it may well be asked what possibility there is of determining the embryology or mode of development of animals which are only known to us through the chance preservation of their bones or shells as fossils. In most cases it is true that such determination is impossible, but in some groups as for example the Trilobites, great numbers of well preserved specimens have been obtained, not merely of adults, but of young forms in various stages of growth; and the study of these young forms has already yielded results of considerable interest. According to Barrande, to whom our knowledge of these early stages is mainly due, four chief types of development may be recognised, differing from one another much as existing Crustaceans do in the relative size and perfection of the three regions, head, thorax, and tail, into which the body is divided.

Evidence of a very different kind, and often of far greater value, is afforded by the study of shells, whether of Mollusca or of Foraminifera. Such shells, like those of Orbitolites already noticed, have no power of interstitial growth, and increase in size can only be effected by the addition of new shelly matter to the part already in existence. In most instances these additions take place in such manner that the older parts of the shell are retained unaltered in the adult ; and examination of the adult or fully formed shell will then reveal the several stages through which the shell passed in its development. In such a shell for instance as Nautilus or Ammonites, the central chamber is the oldest or first formed one, to which the remaining chambers are added in succession. If therefore the development of the shell is a repetition of ancestral history, the central chamber should represent the palæontologically oldest form, and the remaining chambers, in succession, forms of more and more recent origin.

Ammonite shells present, more especially in their sutures and in the markings and sculpturing of their surface, characters that are easily recognised. Upwards of four thousand species are known to us, of many of which large numbers of specimens can be obtained, in excellent preservation. The group consequently is a very suitable one to study from our present standpoint; and the enquiry gains additional interest from the fact that Ammonites are an entirely extinct group of animals, no single species having survived the cretaceous period, so that our only chance of learning anything about their embryology is to study the fossil shells themselves.

Würtenberger, who has made a special study of the Jurassic Ammonites, has shown that there is the same correspondence between historic and embryonic development that obtains among living animals. In the middle Jurassic deposits, for instance, the older Ammonites are flattened and disc-like, with numerous ribs; in later forms the shell bears rows of tubercles near the outer side of the spiral, and later still a second inner row of tubercles as well, while the ribs gradually become less conspicuous and ultimately disappear. In forms from more recent deposits the outer row of tubercles disappears, and then the inner row, the shell becoming smooth, swollen, and almost spherical. On taking one of these smooth spherical shells, such as Aspidoceras cyclotum, and breaking away the outer turns of the spiral so as to expose the more central and older turns, Würtenberger found first an inner and then an outer row of tubercles appearing, which nearer the centre disappeared, and in the oldest part of the shell were replaced by the ribs characteristic of the earlier, and presumably ancestral forms. Results such as these open up to us a new field of inquiry, which if energetically worked must yield results of great interest and importance.

In order to understand fossils aright, and to derive from them the full amount of information they are capable of yielding us, it is necessary that we should have a thorough knowledge of the development of their living descendants ; and more especially that we should be fully acquainted with the several stages of formation of the shells or other hard parts of the recent forms, which in their fossil representatives are, with rare exceptions, the only parts sufficiently well preserved to give trustworthy evidence.

Embryologists have too often confined themselves to the earlier stages of development, and have unduly neglected the later stages, and more especially the later stages of the skeletal structures. By so doing they have failed to afford to palæontologists the aid which they are peculiarly qualified to give, and which to the palæontologist would be of the utmost value. Fortunately the mistake is now recognised, and serious efforts are being made to remove the reproach.

We must now turn to another side of the question. Although it is undoubtedly true that development is to be regarded as a recapitulation of ancestral phases, and that the embryonic history of an animal presents to us a record of the race history ; yet it is also an undoubted fact, recognised by all writers on embryology, that the record so obtained is neither a complete nor a straightforward one. It is indeed a history, but a history of which entire chapters are lost, while in those that remain many pages are misplaced and others are so blurred as to be illegible ; words, sentences, or entire paragraphs are omitted, and worse still alterations or spurious additions have been freely introduced by later hands, and at times so cunningly as to defy detection.

Very slight consideration will show that development cannot in all cases be strictly a recapitulation of ancestral stages. It is well known that closely allied animals may differ markedly in their mode of development. The common frog is at first a tadpole, breathing by gills, a stage which is entirely omitted by the West Indian Hylodes. A crayfish, a lobster, and a prawn are allied animals, yet they leave the egg in totally different forms. Some developmental stages, as the pupa condition of insects, or the stage in the development of a dogfish in which the œsophagus is imperforate, cannot possibly be ancestral stages. Or again, a chick embryo of, say the fourth day, is clearly not an animal capable of independent existence and therefore cannot correctly represent any ancestral condition, an objection which applies to the developmental history of many, perhaps of most, animals.

Haeckel long ago urged the necessity of distinguishing in actual development between those characters which are really historical and inherited and those which are acquired or spurious additions to the record. The former he termed palingenetic or ancestral characters, the latter cenogenetic or acquired. The distinction is undoubtedly a true one, but an exceedingly difficult one to draw in practice. The causes which prevent development from being a strict recapitulation of ancestral characters, the modes in which these came about, and the influence which they respectively exert, are matters which are greatly exercising embryologists ; and the attempt to determine them has as yet met with only partial success.

The most potent and the most widely spread of these disturbing causes arise from the necessity of supplying the embryo with nutriment. This acts in two ways. If the amount of nutritive matter with the egg is small, then the young animal must hatch early, and in a condition in which it is able to obtain food for itself. In such cases there is of necessity a long period of larval life, during which natural selection may act so as to introduce modifications of the ancestral history, spurious additions to the text.

If on the other hand the egg contain within itself a considerable quantity of nutrient matter, then the period of hatching can be postponed until this nutrient matter has been used up. The consequence is that the embryo hatches at a much later stage of its development, and if the amount of food material is sufficient may even leave the egg in the form of the parent. In such cases the earlier developmental phases are often greatly condensed and abbreviated ; and as the embryo does not lead a free existence, and has no need to exert itself to obtain food, it commonly happens that these stages are passed through in a very modified form, the embryo being, as in a four-day chick, in a condition in which it is clearly incapable of independent existence.

The nutrition of the embryo prior to hatching is most usually effected by granules of nutrient matter, known as food yolk, and embedded in the protoplasm of the egg itself; and it is on the relative abundance of these granules that the size of the egg chiefly depends.

Large size of eggs implies diminution of their number, and hence in that of the offspring; and it can be well understood, that while some species derive advantage in the struggle for existence by producing the maximum number of young, to others it is of greater importance that the young on hatching should be of considerable size and strength, and so better able to begin the world on their own account. In other words, some animals may gain by producing a large number of small eggs, others by producing a smaller number of eggs of larger size—*i.e.*, provided with more food yolk.

The immediate effect of a large amount of food yolk is to mechanically retard the processes of development; the ultimate result is to greatly shorten the time occupied by development. This apparent paradox is readily explained. A small egg, such as that of Amphioxus, starts its development rapidly, and in about eighteen hours gives rise to a free-swimming larva, capable of independent existence, with a digestive cavity and nervous system already formed; while a large egg, like that of the hen, hampered by the great mass of food yolk with which it is distended, has in the same time made but very slight progress. From this time however other considerations begin to tell. Amphioxus has been able to make this rapid start owing to its relative freedom from food yolk. This freedom now becomes a retarding influence, for the larva, containing within itself but a very scanty supply of nutriment, must devote much of its energies to hunting for and to digesting its food, and hence its further development will proceed more slowly.

The chick embryo on the other hand has an abundant supply of food in the egg itself; it has no occasion to spend time in searching for food, but can devote its whole energies to the further stages of its development. Hence, except in the earliest stages, the chick develops more rapidly than Amphioxus, and attains its adult form in a much shorter time.

The tendency of abundant food yolk to lead to shortening or abbreviation of the ancestral history, and even to the entire omission of important stages, is well known. The embryo of forms well provided with yolk takes short cuts in its development, jumps from branch to branch of its genealogical tree, instead of climbing steadily upwards.

An excellent illustration of the influence of food yolk on development is afforded by the life histories of frogs. The common frog, *Rana temporaria*, lays as is well known eggs of small size, about $\frac{1}{10}$ inch in diameter. A small egg can only contain a limited amount of food yolk, and hence the young frog can only accomplish a small part of its developmental history within the egg, and must then hatch in order to obtain food from without. Consequently a frog hatches not as a frog but as a tadpole—*i.e.*, at the fish stage in the ancestral history of frogs. At the time of hatching there are no limbs and no lungs; the heart, the alimentary canal, and the nervous system are in an extremely imperfect condition; while other organs of the adult frog, such as the kidneys, have not yet commenced to appear. The frog has therefore to effect the greater part of its development after the time of hatching.

In the little West Indian frog, Hylodes, the course of events is very different. This frog which is of small size—less than a couple of inches in length—lays its eggs not in water but on the leaves of plants. The eggs are large, having a diameter of about $\frac{1}{4}$ inch—*i.e.*, are about three times the diameter and twenty-seven times the bulk of the eggs of the common English frog. The large size of the egg is caused as we have seen by great abundance of food yolk; and the consequence of this large supply of food yolk in the egg of Hylodes is that the frog is enabled to complete the whole of its development before hatching, and emerges from the egg capsule in a form differing from the adult merely in the possession of a rudimentary stump of a tail; and even this disappears before the close of the first day of its existence.

A further and direct consequence of this development within the egg is that the successive stages are hurried over, and are at best but imperfectly recapitulated.   Thus although Hylodes passes through what may be called a tadpole stage, it never develops gills ; so that were Hylodes the only frog known to us, it is very likely that we should have arrived at other conclusions concerning the pedigree of frogs.

The influence of food yolk on the development of animals is closely analogous to that of capital in human undertakings. A new industry, for example that of pen-making, has often been started by a man working by hand and alone, making and selling his own wares; if he succeed in the struggle for existence, it soon becomes necessary for him to call in others to assist him, and to subdivide the work ; hand labour is soon superseded by machines, involving further differentiation of labour ; the earlier machines are replaced by more perfect and more costly ones ; factories are built, agents engaged, and in the end a whole army of workpeople employed.   In later times a man commencing the same business with very limited means will start at the same level as the original founder, and will have to work his way upwards through much the same stages—*i.e.*, will repeat the pedigree of the industry.   The capitalist on the other hand is enabled, like Hylodes, to omit these earlier stages, and after a brief period of incubation, to start business with large factories equipped with the most recent appliances, and with a complete staff of workpeople—*i.e.*, to spring into existence fully fledged.

There is no doubt that abundance of food yolk is a direct and very frequent cause of the omission of ancestral stages from individual development ; but it must not be viewed as the sole cause. It is quite impossible that any animal, except perhaps in the lowest zoological groups, should repeat all the ancestral stages in the history of the race ; the limits of time available for individual development will not permit this. There is a tendency in all animals towards condensation of the ancestral history, towards striking a direct path from the egg to the adult. This tendency is best marked in the higher, the more complicated members of a group— i.e., in those which have a longer and more tortuous pedigree ; and, although greatly strengthened by the presence of food yolk in the egg, is apparently not due to this in the first instance.

Thus the simpler forms of Orbitolites, such as *O. tenuissima*, repeat in their development all the stages leading from a spiral to a discoidal shell ; but in the more complicated species, as Dr. Carpenter has pointed out, there is a tendency towards precocious development of the adult characters, the earlier stages being hurried over in a modified form ; while in the most complex examples, as in *O. complanata*, the earlier spiral stages may be entirely omitted, the shell acquiring almost from its earliest commencement the discoidal mode of growth. There is no question here of relative abundance of food yolk, but merely of early or precocious appearance of adult characters.

Of causes other than food yolk, or only indirectly connected with it, which tend to falsify the ancestral history, many are now known, but time will only permit me to notice the more important. These are distortion, whether in time or space ; sudden or violent metamorphosis ; a series of modifications, due chiefly to mechanical causes, and which may be spoken of as developmental conveniences ; the important question of variability in development ; and finally the great problem of degeneration.

Concerning distortion in time, all embryologists have noticed the tendency to anticipation or precocious development of characters which really belong to a later stage in the pedigree. The early attainment of the discoidal form in the shell of *Orbitolites complanata* is a case in point ; and Würtenberger has specially noticed this tendency in Ammonites. Many early larvæ show it markedly, the explanation in this case being that it is essential for them to hatch in a condition capable of independent existence—*i.e.*, capable at any rate of obtaining and digesting their own food. Anachronisms, or actual reversal of the historical order of development of organs or parts, occur frequently. Thus the joint surfaces of bones acquire their characteristic curvatures before movement of one part on another is effected, and before even the joint cavities are formed.

Another good example is afforded by the development of the mesenterial filaments in Alcyonarians. Wilson has shown, in the case of Renilla, that in the development of an embryo from the egg the six endodermal filaments appear first, and the two long ectodermal filaments at a later period; but that in the formation of a bud this order of development is reversed, the ectodermal filaments being the first formed. He suggests in explanation, that as the endodermal filaments are the digestive organs, it is of primary importance to the free embryo that they should be formed quickly. The long ectodermal filaments are chiefly concerned with maintaining currents of water through the colony; in bud-development they appear before the endodermal filaments, because they enable the bud during its early stages to draw nutrient matter from the body fluid of the parent; while the endodermal filaments cannot come into use until the bud has acquired its own mouth and tentacles.

The completion of the ventricular septum in the heart of higher vertebrates before the auricular septum is an often quoted anachronism, and every embryologist could readily furnish many other cases. A curious instance is afforded by the development of the teeth in mammals, if recent suggestions as to the origin of the milk dentition are confirmed, and the milk dentition prove to be a more recent acquisition than the permanent one.*

Distortion of a curious kind is seen in cases of abrupt metamorphosis where, as in the case of many Echinoderms, of Phoronis, and of the metabolic insects, the larva and the adult differ greatly in form, habits, mode of life, and very usually in the nature of their food and the mode of obtaining it; and the transition from the one stage

* This has since been disproved.—ED.

to the other is not a gradual but an abrupt one, at
any rate so far as external characters are concerned.
Sudden changes of this kind, as from the free
swimming Pluteus to the creeping Echinus, or from .
the sluggish leaf-eating caterpillar to the dainty
butterfly, cannot possibly be recapitulatory, for
even if small jumps are permissible in nature, there
is no room for bounds forward of this magnitude.
Cases of abrupt metamorphosis may always be
viewed as due to secondary modifications, and
rarely if ever have any significance beyond the
particular group of animals concerned.   For
example, a Pluteus larva may be recognised as
belonging to the group of Echinoidea before the
adult urchin has commenced to be formed within it,
and the Lepidopteran caterpillar is already an unmistakable insect.   Hence, for the explanation of
the metamorphoses in these cases it is useless to
look outside the groups of Echinoidea and Insecta
respectively.

Abrupt metamorphosis is always associated with
great change in external form and appearance, in
manner of life, and very usually in mode of
nutrition.   A gradual transition in such cases is
inadmissible, because in the intermediate stages the
animal would be adapted to neither the larval nor
the adult condition ; a gradual conversion of the
biting mouth of the caterpillar to the sucking
proboscis of a moth would inevitably lead to
starvation.   This difficulty is evaded by retaining
the external form and habits of one particular stage
for an unduly long period, so that the relations of

the animal to the surrounding environment remain unchanged, while internally preparations for the later stages are in progress.

Cinderella and the princess are equally possible entities, each being well adapted to her environment. The exigencies of the situation do not permit however of a gradual change from one to the other : the transformation, at least as regards external appearance, must be abrupt.

Embryology supplies us with many unsolved problems, and it is not to be wondered at that this should be the case. Some of these may fairly be spoken of as mere curiosities of development, while others are clearly of greater moment. I do not propose to catalogue these, but will merely mention one which I happen to have recently run my head against, and remember vividly.

The solid condition of the œsophagus in dogfish embryos, first noticed by Balfour, is a very curious point. The œsophagus has at first a well-developed lumen, like the rest of the alimentary canal ; but at an early period, stage K of Balfour's nomenclature, the part of the œsophagus overlying the heart, and immediately behind the branchial region, becomes solid and remains solid for a long time, the exact date of reappearance of the lumen not being yet ascertained. A similar solidification of the œsophagus occurs in tadpoles of the common frog. In young free swimming tadpoles the œsophagus is perforate, but in tadpoles of about $\frac{1}{3}$ inch length it becomes solid and remains so until a length of about $\frac{1}{2}$ inch has been attained. The solidification occurs at a stage closely corresponding with that in which it first appears in the dogfish, and a curious point about it is that in the frog the œsophagus becomes solid just before the mouth opening is formed, and remains solid for some little time after this important event. This closing of the œsophagus clearly cannot be recapitulation, but the fact that it occurs at corresponding periods in the frog and the dogfish suggests that it may possibly, as Balfour hinted, "turn out to have some unsuspected morphological bearing."

A matter which at present is attracting much attention is the question of degeneration. Natural selection, though consistent with and capable of leading to steady upward progress and improvement, by no means involves such progress as a necessary consequence. All it says is that those animals will in each generation have the best chance of survival which are most in harmony with their environment, and such animals will not necessarily be those which are ideally the best or most perfect.

If you go into a shop to purchase an umbrella the one you select is by no means necessarily that which most nearly approaches ideal perfection, but the one which best hits off the mean between your idea of what an umbrella should be and the amount of money you are prepared to give for it; the one in fact that is on the whole best suited to the circumstances of the case, or the environment for the time being. It might well happen that you had a violent antipathy to a crooked handle, or else were determined to have a catch of a particular kind to secure the ribs, and this might lead to the selection—*i.e.*, the survival, of an article that in other and even in more important respects was manifestly inferior to the average.

So is it also with animals: the survival of a form that is ideally inferior is very possible. To animals living in profound darkness the possession of eyes is of no advantage, and forms devoid of eyes would not merely lose nothing thereby, but would actually gain, inasmuch as they would escape the dangers that might arise from injury to a delicate and complicated organ. In extreme cases, as in animals leading a parasitic existence, the conditions of life may be such as to render locomotor, digestive, sensory, and other organs entirely useless ; and in such cases those forms will be most in harmony with their surroundings which avoid the waste of energy resulting from the formation and maintenance of these organs.

An excellent illustration of this downhill progress is afforded by the Rhizocephala, a curious group of parasitic Crustaceans, of which the genus Sacculina is perhaps the best known member. The adult Sacculina is found as a soft shapeless bag, an inch or so in length, attached to the under surface of the tail of a crab by a fleshy stalk which, passing through the skin of the crab, spreads out within it into a complicated system of branching tubular roots by which the parasite sucks up the juices of the crab, on which it depends for food. As regards structure, the Sacculina in its fully developed form is little more than a bag of eggs enclosed in a loosely fitting outer skin, with a single orifice through which the young escape. A nervous system is present, but there are no traces of limbs, digestive system, heart, breathing organs, or sense organs. Indeed, examination however careful of an adult Sacculina would fail to afford any clue as to its real zoological affinities.

Development however in obedience to the potent law of recapitulation, shows us at once that Sacculina is a Crustacean, more closely allied to the Barnacles than to any other of the more familiar members of the group. From each of the exceedingly numerous eggs which a Sacculina produces, there emerges a minute, free swimming larva of the type known as a Nauplius, characterised by possessing a somewhat pyriform body, a single median eye, and three pairs of swimming appendages or legs. Nauplius larvæ are widely spread amongst Crustaceans. All Entomostraca, except the Cladocera, hatch in this form, and Nauplius larvæ are found in individual members in nearly all the higher groups as well. The only special peculiarity about the Sacculina Nauplius is that it has neither mouth nor digestive organs of any kind, these being unnecessary by the presence of a considerable quantity of food yolk. The Sacculina larva continues its free existence for a time; it casts its skin, or rather its cuticle many times, emerging each time rather more complicated in structure though actually smaller in size, for it cannot yet take in food. Ultimately it reaches the condition spoken of as the pupa stage. The pupa is enclosed in a bivalved carapace, very similar to that of a Cypris. It possesses a pair of well-developed antennules in front and six pairs of swimming-legs behind. The Nauplius eye is still present, a little way behind the basal joints of the antennules.

Now comes the great change. The pupa meeting with a crab fastens itself to the under surface of the crab's tail by its antennules, and then goes to the bad with startling rapidity. Within three hours of the time of fixing itself to the crab, the six pairs of swimming legs, with the muscles moving them, and the whole posterior part of the body disintegrate and are cast off. The antennules become modified into a tube, piercing the skin of the crab ; the head of the Sacculina remains as a bottle-shaped mass in connection with the modified antennules, but the bivalved carapace, with all the other organs including the eye, are cast off and lost. The Sacculina now passes for a time completely into the interior of the crab : later on, after increasing in size, it comes once more to the surface and becomes the bag-like mass which we have found to be the adult condition.

This is a typical instance of degeneration or retrograde development, the animal being more highly organised, and standing at a higher morphological level in its early stages than when adult. Yet inasmuch as the organs that are lost, such as the limbs and eye, would be of no use to it in its changed conditions of life, there is nothing in the whole history that is in any way inconsistent with natural selection. This principle of degeneration, recognised by Darwin as a possible, and under certain conditions a necessary consequence of his theory, has been since advocated strongly by Dohrn, and later by Lankester, in an evening discourse delivered before the British Association at the Sheffield meeting, in 1879. Both Dohrn and Lankester have suggested that degeneration may occur much more widely than is commonly supposed.

In animals which are parasitic when adult, but free swimming in their early stages, as in the case of Sacculina, degeneration is clear enough ; so also is it in the case of the solitary Ascidians, in which the larva is a free swimming animal with a notochord, an elongated tubular nervous system, and sense organs, while the adult is fixed, devoid of the swimming tail, with no notochord, and with a greatly reduced nervous system and aborted sense organs.   In such cases the animal, when adult, is, as regards the totality of its organisation, at a distinctly lower morphological level, is less highly differentiated than it is when young, and during individual development there is actual retrograde development of important systems and organs.

About such cases there is no doubt ; but we are asked to extend the idea of degeneration much more widely. It is urged that we ought not to demand direct embryological evidence before accepting a group as degenerate. We are reminded of the tendency to abbreviation or to complete omission of ancestral stages of which we have quoted examples above ; and it is suggested that if such larval stages were omitted in all the members of a group, we should have no direct evidence of degeneration in a group that might really be in an extremely degenerate condition. Supposing for instance the free larval stages of the solitary Ascidians were suppressed, say through the acquisition of food yolk, then it is urged that the degenerate condition of the group might easily escape detection. The supposition is by no means extravagant. Food yolk varies greatly in amount in allied animals, and cases like Hylodes, or amongst Ascidians, Pyrosoma, show how readily a mere increase in the amount of food yolk in the egg may lead to the omission of important ancestral stages.

The question then arises whether it is not possible, or even probable, that animals which now show no indication of degeneration in their development are in reality highly degenerate, and whether it is not legitimate to suppose such degeneration to have occurred in the case of animals whose affinities are obscure or difficult to determine. It is more especially with regard to the lower vertebrates that this argument has been employed; and at the present day zoologists of authority, relying on it, do not hesitate to speak of such forms as Amphioxus and the Cyclostomes as degenerate animals, as wolves in sheep's clothing, animals whose simplicity is acquired and deceptive rather than real and ancestral.

I cannot but think that cases such as these should be regarded with some jealousy; there is at present a tendency to invoke degeneration rather freely as a talisman to extricate us from morphological difficulties ; and an inclination to accept such suggestions, at any rate provisionally, without requiring satisfactory evidence in their support.

Degeneration of which there is direct embryological evidence stands on a very different footing from suspected degeneration, for which no direct evidence is forthcoming ; and in the latter case the burden of proof undoubtedly rests with those who assume its existence.   The alleged instances among the lower vertebrates must be regarded particularly closely, because in their case the suggestion of degeneration is admittedly put forward as a means of escape from difficulties arising through theoretical views concerning the relation between vertebrates and invertebrates.

Amphioxus itself, so far as I can see, shows in its development no sign of degeneration, except possibly with regard to the anterior gut diverticula, whose ultimate fate is not altogether clear.   With regard to the earlier stages of development, concerning which, thanks to the patient investigations of Kowalevsky and Hatschek, our knowledge is precise, there is no animal known to us in which the sequence of events is simpler or more straightforward.   Its various organs and systems are formed in what is recognised as a primitive manner ; and the development of each is a steady upward progress towards the adult condition.   Food yolk, the great cause of distortion in development, is almost absent, and there is not the slightest indication of the former possession of a larger quantity. Concerning the later stages our knowledge is incomplete, but so much as has been ascertained gives no support to the suggestion of general degeneration.

Our knowledge of the conditions leading to degeneration is undoubtedly incomplete, but it must be noticed that the conditions usually associated with degeneration do not occur. Amphioxus is not parasitic, is not attached when adult, and shows no evidence of having formerly possessed food yolk in quantity sufficient to have led to the omission of important ancestral stages. Its small size, as compared with other vertebrates, is one of the very few points that can be referred to as possibly indicating degeneration, but by no means proving its occurrence.

A consideration of much less importance, but deserving of mention, is that in its mode of life Amphioxus not merely differs, as already noticed, from those groups of animals which we know to be degenerate, but agrees with some, at any rate, of those which there is reason to regard as primitive or persistent types. Amphioxus, like Balanoglossus, Lingula, Dentalium, and Limulus, is marine, and occurs in shallow water, usually with a sandy bottom, and like the three smaller of these genera it lives habitually buried almost completely in the sand, into which it burrows with great rapidity.

I do not wish to speak dogmatically. I merely wish to protest against a too ready assumption of degeneration ; and to repeat that, so far as I can see, Amphioxus has not yet, either in its development, in its structure, or in its habits, been shown to present characters that suggest, still less that prove, the occurrence in it of general or extensive degeneration. In a sense all the higher animals are degenerate ; that is, they can be shown to possess certain organs in a less highly developed condition than their ancestors, or even in a rudimentary state. Thus a crab as compared with a lobster is degenerate in the matter of its tail, a horse as compared with Hipparion in regard to its outer toes ; but it is neither customary nor advisable to speak of a crab as a degenerate animal compared to a lobster ; to do so would be misleading. An animal should only be spoken of as degenerate when the retrograde development is well marked, and has affected not one or two organs only, but the totality of its organisation.

It is impossible to draw a sharp line in such cases, and to limit precisely the use of the term degeneration. It must be borne in mind that no animal is at the top of the tree in all respects. Man himself is primitive as regards the number of his toes, and degenerate in respect to his ear muscles ; and between two animals even of the same group it may be impossible to decide which of the two is to be called the higher and which the lower form. Thus, to compare an oyster with a mussel. The oyster is more primitive than the mussel as regards the position of the ventricle of the heart and its relations to the alimentary canal ; but is more modified in having but a single adductor muscle ; and almost certainly degenerate in being devoid of a foot.

Care must also be taken to avoid speaking of an animal as degenerate in regard to a particular organ merely because that organ is less fully developed than in allied animals. An organ is not degenerate unless its present possessor has it in a less perfect condition than its ancestors had. A man is not degenerate in the matter of the length of his neck as compared with a giraffe, . nor as compared with an elephant in respect of the size of his front teeth, for neither elephant nor giraffe enters into the pedigree of man. A man is however degenerate, whoever his ancestors may have been, in regard to his ear muscles ; for he possesses these in a rudimentary and functionless condition, which can only be explained by descent from some better equipped progenitor.

We have now considered some of the more important of the influences which are recognised as affecting developmental history in such a way as to render the recapitulation of ancestral stages less complete than it might otherwise be ; which tend to prevent ontogeny from correctly repeating the phylogenetic history. It may at this point reasonably be asked whether there is any test by which we can determine whether a given larval character is or is not ancestral. Most assuredly there is no one rule, no single test, that will apply in all cases ; but there are certain considerations which will help us, and which should be kept in view. A character that is of general occurrence among the members of a group, both high and low, may reasonably be regarded as having strong claims to ancestral rank; claims that are greatly strengthened if it occurs at corresponding developmental periods in all cases; and still more if it occurs equally in forms that hatch early as free larvæ, and in forms with large eggs, which develop directly into the adult. As examples of such characters may be cited the mode of formation and relations of the notochord, and of the gill-clefts of vertebrates, which satisfy all the conditions mentioned. Characters that are transitory in certain groups, but retained throughout life in allied groups, may with tolerable certainty be regarded as ancestral for the former; for instance, the symmetrical position of the eyes in young flat-fish, the spiral shell of the young limpet, the superficial position of the madreporite in Elasipodous Holothurians, or the suckerless condition of the ambulacral feet in many Echinoderms.

A more important consideration is that if the developmental changes are to be interpreted as a correct record of ancestral history, then the several stages must be possible ones, the history must be one that could actually have occurred—*i.e.*, the several steps of the history as reconstructed must form a series, all the stages of which are practicable ones. Natural selection explains the actual structure of a complex organ as having been acquired by the preservation of a series of stages, each a distinct, if slight, advance on the stage immediately preceding it, an advance so distinct as to confer on its possessor an appreciable advantage in the struggle for existence. It is not enough that the ultimate stage should be more advantageous than the initial or earlier condition, but each intermediate stage must also be a distinct advance. If then the development of an organ is strictly recapitulatory, it should present to us a series of stages, each of which is not merely functional, but a distinct advance on the stage immediately preceding it. Intermediate stages—*e.g.*, the solid œsophagus of the tadpole, which are not and could not be functional—can form no part of an ancestral series; a consideration well expressed by Sedgwick thus: "Any phylogenetic hypothesis which presents difficulties from a physiological standpoint must be regarded as very provisional indeed."

A good example of an embryological series fulfilling these conditions is afforded by the development of the eye in the higher Cephalopoda. The earliest stage consists in the depression of a slightly modified patch of skin; round the edge of the patch the epidermis becomes raised up as a rim; this gradually grows inwards from all sides, so that the depressed patch now forms a pit, communicating with the exterior through a small hole or mouth. By further growth the mouth of the pit becomes still more narrowed, and ultimately completely closed, so that the pit becomes converted into a closed sac or vesicle; at the point at which final closure occurs formation of cuticle takes place, which projects as a small transparent drop into the cavity of the sac; by the formation of concentric layers of cuticle this drop becomes enlarged into the spherical transparent lens of the eye; and the development is completed by histological changes in the inner wall of the vesicle, which convert it into the retina, and by the formation of folds of skin around the eye, which become the iris and the eyelids respectively. Each stage of this developmental history is a distinct advance, physiologically, on the preceding stage, and furthermore, each stage is retained at the present day as the permanent condition of the eye in some member of the group Mollusca. The earliest stage, in which the eye is merely a slightly depressed and slightly modified patch of skin, represents the simplest condition of the Molluscan eye, and is retained throughout life in Solen. The stage in which the eye is a pit with widely open mouth, is retained in the limpet; it is a distinct advance on the former, as through the greater depression the sensory cells are less exposed to accidental injury. The narrowing of the mouth of the pit in the next stage is a simple change, but a very important step forward. Up to this point the eye has served to distinguish light from darkness, but the formation of an image has been impossible. Now, owing to the smallness of the aperture, and the pigmentation of the walls of the pit which accompanies the change, light from any one part of an object can only fall on one particular part of the inner wall of the pit or retina, and so an image, though a dim one, is formed. This type of eye is permanently retained in the Nautilus. The closing of the mouth of the pit by a transparent membrane will not affect the optical properties of the eye, and will be a gain, as it will prevent the entrance of foreign bodies into the cavity of the eye. The formation of the lens by deposit of cuticle is the next step. The gain here is increased distinctness and increased brightness of the image, for the lens will focus the rays of light more sharply on the retina, and will allow a greater quantity of light, a larger pencil of rays from each part of the object, to reach the corresponding part of the retina. The eye is now in the condition in which it remains throughout life in the snail and other gastropods. Finally the formation of the folds of skin known as iris and eyelids provides for the better protection of the eye, and is a clear advance on the somewhat clumsy method of withdrawal seen in the snail.

It is not always possible to point out so clearly as in the above instance the particular advantage gained at each step, even when a complete developmental series is known to us ; but in such cases, as for instance in Orbitolites, our difficulties may be largely ascribed to ignorance of the particular conditions that confer advantage in the struggle for existence, in the case of the forms we are dealing with. That ontogeny really is a repetition of phylogeny must I think be admitted, in spite of the numerous and various ways in which the ancestral history may be distorted during the actual development.

Before leaving the subject, it is worth while inquiring whether any explanation can be found of recapitulation. A complete answer can certainly not be given at present, but a partial one may perhaps be obtained. Darwin himself suggested that the clue might be found in the consideration that at whatever age a variation first appears in the parent, it tends to reappear at a corresponding age in the offspring; but this must be regarded rather as a statement of the fundamental fact of embryology than as an explanation of it. It is probably safe to assume that animals would not recapitulate unless they were compelled to do so: that there must be some constraining influence at work, forcing them to repeat more or less closely the ancestral stages. It is impossible, for instance, to conceive what advantage it can be to a reptilian or mammalian embryo to develop gill-clefts which are never used, and which disappear at a slightly later stage; or how it can benefit a whale, that in its embryonic condition it should possess teeth which never cut the gum, and which are lost before birth. Moreover, the history of development in different animals or groups of animals offers to us, as we have seen, a series of ingenious, determined, varied, but more or less unsuccessful efforts to escape from the necessity of recapitulating, and to substitute for the ancestral process a more direct method.

A further consideration of importance is that recapitulation is not seen in all forms of development, but only in sexual development; or at least only in development from the egg. In the several forms of asexual development, of which budding is the most frequent and most familiar, there is no repetition of ancestral phases; neither is there in cases of regeneration of lost parts, such as the tentacle of a snail, the arm of a starfish, or the tail of a lizard. In such regeneration it is not a larval tentacle, or arm, or tail, that is produced, but an adult one.

The most striking point about the development of the higher animals is that they all alike commence as eggs. Looking more closely at the egg and the conditions of its development, two facts impress us as of special importance. First, the egg is a single cell, and therefore represents morphologically the Protozoon, or earliest ancestral phase; secondly, the egg, before it can develop, must be fertilised by a spermatozoon, just as the stimulus of fertilisation by the pollen grain is necessary before the ovum of a plant will commence to develop into the plant-embryo.

The advantage of cross-fertilisation in increasing the vigour of the offspring is well known, and in plants devices of the most varied and even extraordinary kind are adopted to ensure that such cross-fertilisation occurs. The essence of the act of cross-fertilisation, which is already established among Protozoa, consists in combination of the nuclei of two cells, male and female, derived from different individuals. The nature of the process is of such a kind that two individual cells are alone concerned in it; and it may I think be reasonably argued that the reason why animals commence their existence as eggs—*i.e.*, as single cells—is because it is in this way only that the advantage of cross-fertilisation can be secured, an advantage admittedly of the greatest importance, and to secure which natural selection would operate powerfully.

The occurrence of parthenogenesis, either occasionally or normally, in certain groups is not I think a serious objection to this view. There are very strong reasons for holding that parthenogenetic development is a modified form, derived from the sexual method. Moreover, the view advanced above does not require that cross-fertilisation should be essential to individual development, but merely that it should be in the highest degree advantageous to the species ; and hence leaves room for the occurrence, exceptionally, of parthenogenetic development.

If it be objected that this is laying too much stress on sexual reproduction, and on the advantage of cross-fertilisation, then it may be pointed out in reply that sexual reproduction is the characteristic and essential mode of multiplication among Metazoa: that it occurs in all Metazoa, and that when asexual reproduction, as by budding, occurs, this merely alternates with the sexual process which, sooner or later, becomes essential.

If the fundamental importance of sexual reproduction to the welfare of the species be granted, and if it be further admitted that Metazoa are descended from Protozoa, then we see that there is really a constraining force of a most powerful nature compelling every animal to commence its life-history in the unicellular condition, the only condition in which the advantage of cross-fertilisation can be obtained—*i.e.*, constraining every animal to begin its development at its earliest ancestral stage, at the very bottom of its genealogical tree.

On this view the actual development of any animal is strictly limited at both ends: it must commence as an egg, and it must end in the likeness of the parent. The problem of recapitulation becomes thereby greatly narrowed; all that remains being to explain why the intermediate stages in the actual development should repeat the intermediate stages of the ancestral history.

Although narrowed in this way, the problem still remains one of extreme difficulty. It is a consequence of the theory of Natural Selection that identity of structure involves community of descent; a given result can only be arrived at through a given sequence of events: the same morphological goal cannot be reached by two independent paths. A negro and a white man have had common ancestors in the past; and it is through the long-continued action of selection and environment that the two types have been gradually evolved. You cannot turn a white man into a negro merely by sending him to live in Africa: to create a negro the whole ancestral history would have to be repeated; and it may be that it is for the same reason that the embryo must repeat or recapitulate its ancestral history in order to reach the adult goal.

I am not sure that we can get much further than this at present. However, be the explanation what it may, there can I think be no doubt as to the general truth of the Recapitulation Theory, and the wonderful assistance which it gives us in reconstructing the pedigrees of animals. Yet it must not be supposed that all we have to do in order to determine the past history of a species is to study the actual development of the existing members of that species.

Embryology is not to be regarded as a master key that will open the gates of knowledge, and remove all obstacles from our path without further trouble on our part; it is rather to be viewed and treated as a delicate and complicated instrument, the proper handling of which requires the utmost nicety of balance and adjustment, and which unless employed with the greatest skill and judgment may yield false instead of true results. We are indeed only just beginning to understand the real power of our weapons and the right way of employing them; and in the future embryology, especially when studied as it should be in conjunction with palæontology, may be confidently relied on to afford a far clearer insight than we have yet obtained into the history of life on the earth.

XI

SOME RECENT EMBRYOLOGICAL INVESTIGATIONS

THE close resemblance between the embryos of animals which, when adult, are widely different in form, in size, and even in structure, greatly impressed the earlier embryologists, and was often insisted on by them. A reptile, a bird, and a mammal are in their early stages of development so closely similar that v. Baer himself was unable to decide to which of these groups three unnamed embryos in his collection were to be referred.

A still more striking illustration is afforded by the controversy which raged for many years over Krause's famous embryo. In 1875 Krause described an early human embryo which appeared to differ from all known human embryos in having a large vesicular allantois like that of a chick or reptile, instead of the thick allantoid stalk by which the human embryo is normally connected with the chorion. This peculiarity with regard to the allantois was so marked that doubts were at once raised as to the embryo being really a human one ; and Professor His, one of the most expert of embryologists, asserted roundly that Krause must have made a mistake, and that his specimen was a chick embryo and not a human one at all. An ardent, almost furious, discussion arose, and continued for many years : it is indeed only within the last twelve months that the points at issue have been finally put at rest, and it has been shown that while Krause was right in describing his embryo as a human one, he was mistaken in regard to the supposed peculiarity in the allantois, the bladder-like vesicle which he took for the allantois being merely a pathological dilatation of the allantoic stalk.

Among Invertebrates the resemblances between the early larval forms of allied groups are equally striking : the veliger and trochophore larvæ, for example, or the nauplius larva of Crustacea, having not merely very wide zoological distribution, but presenting marked constancy in essential, or even in minor characters in the groups in which they occur.

That the early larval stages of a prawn, a cyclops, and a barnacle ; or of a reptile, a chick, and a man, should be so closely similar that it is possible to mistake one for the other, is undoubtedly a very remarkable thing ; and it was perhaps inevitable that there should be at first a tendency to over-estimate the exactness of this resemblance. Embryologists have indeed too often overrun their facts ; and, misled by the undoubtedly striking similarity between embryos of forms zoologically akin, have not hesitated to fill the gaps in their knowledge of the developmental history of certain animals, by reference to the known processes in allied forms.   More especially is this the case with regard to man himself : material for direct observation is difficult to obtain, and it is only too common to find that descriptions purporting to be of human embryos are really founded on observations derived from the study of pigs and rabbits, or even of animals so remote zoologically as chicken, lizards, or dog-fish.   Of late years however there has been a marked reaction in this respect, and the pendulum has shown a tendency to swing over to the opposite side.   More exact observations on many groups of animals have proved that even in allied forms the course of development may be markedly different ; in some cases indeed not only genera and species, but even the eggs of the same brood, may develop in ways curiously unlike one another.

This inconstancy in the mode of development, more especially in the earliest stages, is one of the most striking results of recent embryological investigation, and may well claim attention on the present occasion.   If at first sight it appear bewildering or even unwelcome to those who, from the study of development of existing animals, would seek to unravel the past history of the race, it is to be remembered that facts must always be accepted ; and it may even be that in this variability, by which his labours are so greatly extended, the embryologist will find the clue he has so long waited for, which will enable him to distinguish the real from the spurious, the ancestral from the acquired characters.

The earliest stage of development in every Metazoon is the act of cell-division, or segmentation as it is commonly termed, by which the single cell, or egg, becomes divided into a number of cells or blastomeres. The details of the process vary greatly in the eggs of different animals, and are affected more particularly by the amount of food yolk, or deutoplasm, present in the egg; this food yolk offering mechanical hindrance to the division of the egg. In each species or genus, or even in larger groups, the mode of segmentation was formerly assumed to be constant, but the more recent researches have shown that this is by no means always the case.

In 1878, Kleinenberg noticed that the eggs of an earth-worm, *Lumbricus trapezoides*, which he was investigating, showed considerable individual differences in the mode and order in which the successive cell-divisions were effected; an observation which was afterwards confirmed by Wilson, and extended to other species of earthworms. In 1884, while studying the development of Renilla, one of the Pennatulida or Sea-Pens, Wilson found an extraordinary range of variation in the mode of segmentation of eggs, even of the same brood. In some cases the egg divided into two blastomeres in the normal manner, each of these in its turn again dividing; in other cases however the egg divided at once into eight, sixteen, or even thirty-two blastomeres, which in different specimens were approximately equal or markedly unequal in size. Sometimes a preliminary change of form occurred without any further result, the egg returning to its spherical shape, and pausing for a time before recommencing the attempt to segment. Segmentation sometimes commenced at one pole, as in the telolecithal eggs of birds or reptiles, with the formation of four or five small segments, the rest of the egg breaking up later, either simultaneously or progressively, into segments about equal in size to those first formed ; while lastly, in some instances segmentation was very irregular, following no apparent law. Similar modifications in the segmentation of the egg have been described in the oyster by Brooks, in Anodonta and in other Mollusca, and in Hydra. In the different species of Peripatus there appear also to be considerable variations in the details of segmentation.

It has long been known that the eggs of Amphibia may vary greatly in the mode in which the early stages of segmentation are effected ; and recently Jordan and Eycleshymer have described these variations in detail. The first cleft usually corresponds with the median sagittal plane, dividing the egg into two blastomeres, which give rise respectively to the right and left halves of the embryo. The cleft may however be oblique, or even transverse to this plane. The two first blastomeres are usually equal, but may be very unequal, one being sometimes twice the size of the other.

The second cleft is usually at right angles to the first, and divides the egg into anterior and posterior halves; but it may cut the egg obliquely. The third and fourth clefts also present considerable variability in their position and relations to the earlier clefts. In all the cases described above the variability was confined to the earliest phases of segmentation: the earlier stages of development were the same, whatever the mode in which segmentation was effected; and apparently identical, and certainly normal embryos, resulted in all cases.

Some recent observations of Loeb give a possible clue to these phenomena. He found by experimenting on the eggs of sea urchins that the process of segmentation could be retarded, or modified, by varying the proportion of sodium chloride present in the sea-water in which the eggs were laid. A slight increase in the normal proportion of sodium chloride delayed the occurrence of segmentation; but on the return of the eggs to normal sea-water they very quickly divided, often simultaneously, into a number of blastomeres. He states his results thus: "If we bring impregnated eggs into sea-water of a certain higher concentration, no segmentation takes place; but if we bring them back into normal sea-water, they divide in about twenty minutes directly into nearly, but not quite so many, cleavage spheres as they would contain by that time if they had remained in normal sea-water all the time." Further investigation showed that, although when placed in water containing more than the normal proportion of sodium chloride, the eggs did not segment, yet that division of the nucleus occurred : unsegmented eggs were in this way obtained with from four to as many as thirty nuclei.

It is at least possible that some of the variations in the normal process of segmentation mentioned above as observed in other animals may be due to changes in the composition, or perhaps of the temperature of the water in which the eggs were developing. Herbst's interesting experiments on the modifications in the development of Echinoderm larvæ produced by the addition of potassium or lithium salts to the sea-water in which they were contained, led him to conclude that the influence on the developing ova was not directly chemical, but was due to the altered osmotic pressure of the sea-water. The field of enquiry thus opened up is a most promising one, and is certain to receive the attention of embryologists in the immediate future. We are at present ignorant of the causes which determine the division of a cell, or the segmentation of an egg ; but we shall have made an appreciable step towards a right understanding of the phenomena when we have determined with precision in what way they can be modified by slight, but known, alterations in the environment.

Variations occur in the later as well as in the earlier stages of development ; and the differences between allied genera or species, or even between closely related individuals, may be very marked. Among Cœlenterates, for example, the mode of formation of the inner germinal layer, or hypoblast, presents most perplexing modifications: it may arise as a true gastrula invagination; as cells budded off from one pole of the blastula into its cavity; as cells budded off from various parts of the wall of the blastula; by delamination, or actual division of each cell of the blastula wall into outer or epiblastic, and inner or hypoblastic elements; or it may be present from the first as a solid mass of cells enclosed by the epiblast cells. Another good illustration is afforded by the extraordinary modifications in the position, and in every detail of formation of the middle germinal layer, or mesoblast, in different and often in closely allied forms of the higher Metazoa: differences which have given rise to ardent discussion, and have led to the proposal of theory after theory, each rejected in its turn as affording only a partial explanation, and finally culminating in Kleinenberg's protest against the use of the term mesoblast at all, at any rate in a sense implying any possibility of comparison with the primary cellular layers, epiblast and hypoblast, of Cœlenterata. Amongst Vertebrates the frog and the newt differ greatly in important developmental points. The stages immediately following segmentation of the egg are very unlike in the two cases. The epiblast is but one cell thick in the newt, while in the frog it consists of two distinct layers from the first; the ear of the newt develops as a pit-like depression of the skin, while in the frog it is from the first a closed sac; and many other differences will readily occur to embryologists. In the common English frog, *Rana temporaria*, and in the closely allied *Rana esculenta*, the branchial blood-vessels develop in very different manner, although ultimately reaching the same condition.

But the most remarkable series of facts with regard to variation in the later stages of development is afforded by the recently published observations of Professor Brooks and Mr. Herrick on the metamorphoses of certain small decapod Crustacea of the genus Alpheus. These are essentially tropical forms, not unlike small crayfish in appearance, and about an inch or so in length. They are brilliantly coloured and occur most abundantly in shallow water, more especially amongst coral reefs. A few species live freely, but the majority are found inhabiting the tubes of sponges, or dwelling in holes and crannies in the porous coral limestone. The development of thirteen species was carefully studied by Messrs. Brooks and Herrick, and the remarkable conclusion was arrived at that "individuals of a single species sometimes differ more from each other as regards their metamorphoses than do the individuals of two very distinct species." It is not merely that different individuals hatch at different stages of development: one individual may appear with characters, *e.g.*, the number and form of the legs, which occur at no stage in the development of other individuals of the same species. In some cases the differences in developmental history were associated with differences in the locality from which the specimens were obtained. Thus individuals of a given species observed at

Key West, in Florida, differed constantly from individuals of the same species from N. Carolina, and these again from individuals living at the Bahamas. In other instances the differences in development appeared to be related to the conditions of life. At the Bahamas a species of Alpheus was observed dwelling in the chambers of sponges. Two kinds of sponge were employed by the prawn, one sponge being green, the other brown. The prawns living in the green sponge produced considerable numbers of small eggs ; while the individuals of the same species which dwelt in the brown sponge gave rise to a few eggs of large size, from which the young prawns were hatched at a stage corresponding to that reached at the third moult by the young developed from the smaller eggs in the green sponge.

Another very curious series of facts has been made known to us by the careful researches of the Russian embryologist, Salensky, on the early development of certain Ascidians. The normal course of development in a Metazoon, as is well known, is that the fertilised egg segments, *i.e.*, divides into a number of nucleated cells from which, by further division, and accompanying differentiation, all the various parts and tissues of the embryo, and finally of the adult animal, are produced. Every individual cell of the adult, whether an epithelial cell, a nerve cell, a muscle cell, or a bone cell, owes its origin to direct descent from the original egg-cell or ovum. The most striking fact in the whole range of embryology is that all animals above Protozoa commence their existence as eggs—*i.e.*, as single cells—from which all parts of the adult body are ultimately derived. The purpose of this arrangement appears to be to secure the advantage to be derived from cross fertilisation, a process which concerns two cells only, male and female respectively; and which necessitates a unicellular stage as the initial one in individual development. The eggs of Metazoa, while still in the ovary, are very commonly enclosed in follicles. These consist of one or more layers of cells which are of epithelial origin, and which are of the same order as the ova themselves, and in their earlier stages indistinguishable from these. The follicle cells play an important part in the nourishment of the egg which they surround; but they are left behind in the ovary, or are rubbed off after the egg has ripened and discharged from the ovary, and they have nothing to do with the formation of the embryo.

In the genus *Pyrosoma* however, a well-known colonial and pelagic Ascidian, Salensky discovered a very peculiar condition of things. Each Pyrosoma individual produces one very large egg, which is closely invested by a follicle or capsule. The egg is meroblastic; and as in the hen's egg, segmentation is confined to one pole, and results in the formation of a small cap of cells or blastoderm, lying on the top of the mass of unsegmented yolk formed by the rest of the egg. As segmentation proceeds, certain of the follicle cells investing the egg grow in between the segmentation cells or blastomeres. These follicle cells, or kalymmocytes as they are called by Salensky, are at first very distinct in appearance from the blastomeres, and easily recognised from these; but as development proceeds the differences become less and less marked, and finally cease to be evident. These ingrowing follicle cells, or kalymmocytes, enter directly into the formation of the embryo, which is thus built up partly from cells derived, as in other Metazoa, from division of the fertilised egg or ovum; and partly from cells of independent origin, the kalymmocytes, which are unfertilised, and have grown into the egg from the surrounding follicle. In the genus *Salpa* a similar condition of things has been described by Salensky; the only difference, as compared with Pyrosoma, being that in Salpa the kalymmocytes are actually more numerous and more bulky than the blastomeres formed by segmentation of the ovum, so that the major part of the embryo is composed of unfertilised cells.

These observations are of the greatest possible interest, and we wait anxiously to learn whether this curious mode of development is confined to the groups of Ascidians, or whether it occurs in other animals as well. It is perhaps worth while suggesting that if the process were carried one stage further than it actually is in Salpa, we should arrive at a condition of things curiously resembling the mode of formation of gemmules in Sponges, or of statoblasts in Polyzoa. In Pyrosoma, the follicle cells or kalymmocytes form part, but the smaller part, of the embryo. In Salpa, the kalymmocytes are more abundant than the blastomeres, so that the greater part of the embryo is formed from the unfertilised kalymmocytes or follicle cells. If now we imagine this carried one step further, if we suppose the blastomeres, or fertilised elements, to be completely absent, then the whole embryo would be formed by an aggregation of unfertilised cells, and the process would become most suggestively similar to that by which a Sponge gemmule is formed.

The last series of phenomena to which I wish to refer are those resulting from the natural or artificial division of an egg, in the early stages of its development, into two or more fragments. In 1869, Haeckel, while studying the development of *Crystallodes*, a genus of Siphonophora or pelagic Hydroids, was struck with the fact that the polyhedral cells of which the egg consisted at the close of segmentation exhibited active amœboid changes of shape, and appeared to possess a certain amount of independence. The idea occurred to him to test this power of independent existence by breaking up the embryo into fragments, and following their fate. By means of needles, eggs at the close of segmentation on the second day of development were broken into two, three, or four pieces, and it was found that these not only lived for eight or ten days, but developed and gave rise, in almost normal manner, to rudimentary Siphonophoran colonies. These observations of Haeckel's are the earliest experiments on lines which have recently led to remarkable results.

Kleinenberg, in 1878, published an account of the early stages of development of an earthworm, *Lumbricus trapezoides*, which he obtained abundantly in the gardens of the island of Ischia. The worms lay their eggs in capsules : each capsule is from one to eight millimetres in length, and is filled with an albuminous mass in which are contained bundles of ripe spermatozoa, and from three to eight eggs. Of the eggs only one develops as a rule, the remainder gradually disappearing. At an early stage in development, as soon as the germinal layers are established, and before the appearance of any of the organs or parts of the embryo, the ovum divides into two parts which are usually equal and similar. Each of these parts develops into an embryo, and subsequently into an adult worm ; the two remaining for a time connected together like Siamese twins, but ultimately separating.

The upshot of the process is that what Haeckel effected artificially for *Crystallodes*—*i.e.*, the division of the segmented egg into two parts each of which develops into an embryo—is found to be a natural or even normal occurrence in *Lumbricus trapezoides*. Kleinenberg supposed that the tendency to form twins, which is so marked a feature in *Lumbricus trapezoides*, was due to a process of double fertilisation, two spermatozoa instead of one being concerned in the act. Vejdovsky however suggested that the twinning was perhaps influenced by warmth, for it occurred most frequently in warm weather ; a suggestion which receives much support from some experiments made by Driesch on Echinoid eggs, which when artificially warmed were found to have a marked tendency to develop twin-embryos.

Another line of research was initiated independently by Chabry and by Roux, who investigated the effects of injuring or destroying one of the two or four blastomeres resulting from the first or second cleavage of the egg. Chabry, whose results were published in 1887, used for his experiments the egg of an Ascidian, *Ascidia aspersa.* Taking eggs in which segmentation had just commenced, and division into two cells had been effected, he destroyed one of the two cells by pricking with a needle. Under such circumstances he found that the surviving cell developed into a half-embryo. By experimenting in similar manner on eggs which had divided into four cells or blastomeres, he was able to produce either quarter, half, or three-quarter embryos. Chabry concluded from his results that each blastomere, at any rate in the early stages of development, has a determined destiny and represents a definite part of the larva. This view was first propounded by Professor His who, in 1874, maintained the existence of "special regions in the germ, which give rise to special organs," and held that each organ of the embryo is represented by a definite part of the body of the egg.

This view is closely similar to the old doctrine of "Evolution" or "Preformation," according to which it was held that all the organs and parts of the embryo were already present in the egg when laid; and that development consisted in an unfolding and perfecting of these parts, much as the flower is formed by the expansion of parts already present in the bud. This doctrine of Preformation, in its original form, was overthrown in 1759 by Wolff, who substituted for it the doctrine of Epigenesis—*i.e.*, that there is no trace of the embryo or of any of its parts in the egg, and that the formation of the embryo is an entirely new process. It is not a little curious to find the older doctrine, which embryologists thought disposed of for ever, coming up again in somewhat modified form, as a result of more recent investigations.

Almost simultaneously with Chabry, Roux investigated in similar manner, but in more detail, the results of localised injuries to frog embryos at early stages of development. His method consisted in destroying one or more of the cells of a segmenting egg by puncturing them with a hot needle. He took a frog's egg at the completion of the first cleft— *i.e.*, an egg which had just divided into the first two cells or blastomeres—and destroyed one of the two cells. The surviving cell developed into a half-embryo, from which by a process of regeneration the missing half was gradually formed, a whole embryo ultimately resulting. A more satisfactory method of experimenting, inasmuch as it does not involve the destruction of any of the cells, consists in shaking apart the blastomeres at an early stage, and then following their subsequent fate. This was first done, in 1877, by Chun, and has since been repeated by other observers. Chun experimented with the eggs of Ctenophora, and found that if the two first segmentation cells, or blastomeres, were separated by shaking, each developed into a half-larva, which actually became sexual, and which ultimately regenerated the missing half by a process of budding.

Driesch, in 1891, carried out a similar but more complete series of experiments at Trieste, employing for the purpose the eggs of sea-urchins, chiefly *Echinus microtuberculatus* and *Sphærechinus granularis.* Selecting eggs which had just completed the first division, into two segmentation cells or blastomeres, he put from fifty to a hundred in a small quantity of sea-water in a glass tube about an inch and a half long and a quarter of an inch in diameter. By vigorously shaking the tube for five minutes or longer he succeeded in rupturing the egg membranes, and isolating the blastomeres. The contents of the tube were then poured into a shallow vessel, and the isolated blastomeres picked out with a fine pipette, and placed in separate watch-glasses, in which their further development could be followed. Each blastomere so treated developed at first into a half-embryo. By the evening of the first day a hemi-blastula was formed. During the night a change took place, and by the following morning each hemi-blastula had become a complete blastula or sphere, but of half the normal size. By the end of the second day invagination commenced. Each blastula became a gastrula in the normal manner; and the formation of the various organs, mouth, arms, cœlom, and ambulacral system was effected in the typical fashion. In some cases the shaking had effected imperfect separation of the two blastomeres, without rupturing the egg membrane.   From these eggs either twins or double embryos were produced, a result which suggests that the twinning which occurs so commonly in *Lumbricus trapezoides* may not after all be a result of double fertilisation as was supposed by Kleinenberg.

The most recent and the most complete of the experiments on the results of shaking apart the blastomeres of segmenting eggs are those performed by Wilson on Amphioxus eggs in 1892.   The eggs of Amphioxus are very minute, about 0·1 mm. in diameter ; and their early stages of development are extremely simple.   The egg divides by a vertical cleft into two equal blastomeres : by a second vertical cleft, at right angles to the first, each of the two blastomeres is bisected, and four blastomeres of equal size result.   The third cleft is a horizontal one, and is rather nearer the upper pole than the lower : by it each of the four blastomeres is divided into an upper and rather smaller cell, and a lower and rather larger one. In the later stages the number of cells is rapidly increased ; a blastula, and then by invagination a gastrula is formed, and the several organs of the embryo quickly appear.   In the early stages the blastomeres hang together very loosely, and are easily separated by shaking.   Commencing with the stage at which two blastomeres are present, Wilson isolated them by shaking, and found that each developed as though it were a complete egg, segmenting in the normal fashion, giving rise to a blastula, and then a gastrula, and ultimately becoming a larva, which differed from a normal one merely in being half the usual size.

Wilson next took the stage with four blastomeres, and found that each of the four, if isolated, developed into a larva of typical form, but one-fourth the usual size: if two or three of the blastomeres held together a larva resulted which was half or three-quarters the normal size. It appears therefore that at the stage with four blastomeres, either one, two, three, or all four of the blastomeres have the power of developing into an embryo which will be normal in all respects, saving only as regards size. Anxious to determine the limits to which this extraordinary process could be continued, Wilson tried the next stage, that in which eight blastomeres are present, of which four are rather smaller, and four rather larger in size. Each blastomere when isolated commenced to develop, but never became a complete embryo. Flat plates, curved plates, even blastulas one-eighth the normal size were formed, which swam about freely by means of cilia, but which underwent no further development.

These results are of very great interest. They must I think be regarded as fatal to the doctrine of " Evolution " in its new form, as maintained by His and Weismann ; for if any one of the first four blastomeres is able by itself to develop directly into an embryo, it seems impossible to hold that each blastomere has a predestined part to play in the formation of the embryo.

Another very interesting result is the precise point at which the power of developing an embryo from a single blastomere ceases. Discussion has taken place as to whether the failure is due to quantitative or to qualitative considerations; to an insufficiency in amount of living matter, or to incompleteness in its structure or composition. Wilson is of opinion that the difficulty is mainly a qualitative one, and has advanced arguments in support of his view. Perhaps the most important consideration in its favour is that so long as the blastomeres are precisely alike—*i.e.*, up to the stage with four blastomeres—each one possesses the power when isolated of developing into an embryo; while as soon as a distinction between smaller and larger blastomeres appears—*i.e.*, at the third cleavage—this power ceases.

This last consideration becomes still more significant if we regard a Metazoon as comparable to a colony of Protozoa, in which differentiation between the component units, and consequent mutual dependence, and the necessity for holding together have become established; and if further we view the early development of a Metazoon as a shadowing of the process by which this condition was originally attained. So long as the cell units or blastomeres remain identical, so long does each one retain the power of independent existence and development; but as soon as differentiation is established between one and another this power of separate life ceases. This view, though extremely suggestive, must however be regarded as entirely provisional, until we gain more complete and exact knowledge concerning the conditions under which the power of independent development can be exerted, not only in Amphioxus, but in other animals as well.

The present paper is merely a record of some recent investigations, and has no pretence to completeness.   These researches however all tend in one direction, namely to emphasise the fact that the development of animals takes place in far more varied manner than is generally supposed, and that marked differences may occur both in the earlier and the later stages of the embryological history, not merely in allied genera and species, but even between individual members of the same brood.   I will conclude with a brief summary of the principal modes in which the development of a Metazoon may be effected.   It should be noted that the adult structure as a rule gives no indication of the particular mode in which development has occurred: a sponge developed from a gemmule is, so far as we know, indistinguishable in its adult form from one developed from a fertilised egg.

AN ADULT METAZOON MAY BE DEVELOPED.

   1. From a group of (mesoblast ?) cells, which are originally independent of one another, and of which none are fertilised. *Examples:* The gemmules of Sponges, or the statoblasts of Polyzoa.

2. Partly from a fertilised ovum, and partly from unfertilised follicle cells. *Examples:* Salpa and Pyrosoma.

3. From a single fertilised ovum, together with a greater or less number of yolk cells, which are at first independent cells, but which ultimately become absorbed into the ovum. *Examples:* Fasciola, Pisidium.

4. From a single fertilised ovum, aided by nutrient matter derived from the surrounding follicle cells. *Examples:* Cephalopoda, and most Vertebrates.

5. From a single fertilised ovum, without the aid of follicle cells. *Example:* Amphioxus.

6. From an unfertilised cell, or ovum. *Examples:* The parthenogenetic ova of Entomostraca or of Rotifera.

7. From one or more of the blastomeres resulting from the segmentation of a fertilised ovum. *Examples:* Echinus, Amphioxus.

8. From a portion, large or small, of the body of the parent. *Examples:* Hydra, Sponge.

9. By local proliferation of the cellular elements of the parent, forming an external or internal bud. *Examples:* Sporocyst, Hydra.

XII

DEATH

THE subject of my address is I admit open to objection from more than one standpoint. It is commonly regarded as dull and uninviting; and although in the long run it must concern us all, there would seem to be little reason for urging its consideration prematurely. Then again it may be objected that having, from the nature of the case, no personal experience of the phenomenon, I am not in a position to speak about it with authority.

I can only reply that a matter which concerns vitally all living things, animal or vegetable, cannot be devoid of interest. The problems of life are the most fascinating of all scientific enquiries; and surely death, the cessation of life, must have something to teach us, must throw some light on the nature of life itself. The beginnings of life are at present hidden from us; the other end of the series, the termination of life, we have daily opportunities of studying. With regard to the second objection, it is true that from personal experience I can say nothing on the subject of death; but this is a disqualification which I share with all members of our Society, and with all living men. If nobody is to be allowed to talk about death until he has qualified by personal acquaintance with the " fell sergeant," it is clear that any knowledge to be derived, any lessons to be learnt from its study, are lost to us for ever.

My choice of the subject has been determined mainly by the consideration that of recent years it has attracted considerable attention, and has given rise to interesting speculations, many of which are based on facts made known to us by those extraordinarily minute investigations into the structure of the lower animals, which the modern improvements in microscopical methods and appliances have rendered possible. My purpose this evening is to give a summary of these more recent contributions to our knowledge of the nature and causation of death, and an indication of the paths along which it seems probable that advances will be made in the future.

In a scientific enquiry it is above all things desirable to have clear ideas as to the nature of the subject we are dealing with. Unfortunately it is not easy to define with any degree of precision what it is that we understand by death. Götte regards death as something inherent in life itself, a view which is held more or less explicitly by the majority of mankind. This is however disputed by Weismann, whose contributions to the subject are of importance. Weismann defines death as "an arrest of life, from which no lengthened revival, either of the whole or any of its parts, can take place ; or to put it concisely, as a *definite arrest of life*." "The real proof of death," according to Weismann, "is that the organised substance which previously gave rise to the phenomena of life, for ever ceases to originate such phenomena." He adds to this the corollary that death involves the presence of something dead—*i.e.*, a corpse. Weismann next challenges the statement that death is a necessity, inseparable from the idea or existence of life. He calls attention to the conditions which obtain among animals such as Protozoa, in which reproduction is normally effected by fission ; and points out that in the life-history of such animals natural death does not occur. An Amœba for example reproduces by simply dividing into two. In such an act of fission the parent generation disappears, but nothing has died. If the original Amœba be called Tom, and the products of fission Dick and Harry, the upshot of the process may be expressed by saying that Tom has disappeared without having died, while Dick and Harry have come into existence without having been born. Nothing has died, there is no corpse to bury, and our ordinary ideas with regard to individuality and identity fail altogether to afford answer to the question——Where is Tom at the end of the process ?

Hence arises the idea of the immortality of the Protozoa. An Amœba or other Protozoon reproducing by simple fission can indeed be killed, as by boiling the water in which it is contained; but it does not, in the ordinary course of events, die. The production of one generation involves the disappearance but not the death of the parent generation. From the first Amœba to the present day there has been direct continuity of living matter. Death may occur through violence, but it is not a necessary accompaniment or consequence of life. Moreover death, when it does happen in the case of an Amœba, causes a final interruption, an absolute break in the chain. No Amœba that has died has left offspring, for such offspring can only arise by the division of the living body of the parent. "No Amœba," it has been well expressed, "has ever lost an ancestor by death."

The above considerations, which clearly apply not only to Protozoa but to any other animals which reproduce by fission, form the basis on which Weismann has built up his theory of the origin of death. This theory may be briefly summarised as follows: Protozoa, reproducing by fission, are immortal in the sense that death does not occur as a necessary or natural termination of the life-cycle. Natural death must therefore be limited to Metazoa, or multicellular animals. In Metazoa a distinction is always found between somatic cells and reproductive cells; the former being the component elements of which the body of the individual is constructed, while the latter are the units from which the individuals of the next succeeding generation will be developed. The somatic cells are concerned with the existence and welfare of the individual;

the reproductive cells with the perpetuation of the species.

The normal life-cycle of a Metazoon is as follows : The fertilised egg, or reproductive cell, by repeated division gives rise to a number of cells, of which some become the somatic cells—*i.e.*, the body of the individual animal—while others remain as its reproductive cells ; from these latter, in due course and in similar manner, the individuals of the next generation are formed. Of the two kinds of cells, the somatic cells alone are liable to natural death : the reproductive cells survive as the individuals of the succeeding generation. The reproductive cells of Metazoa are therefore immortal, in exactly the same sense as are Amœbæ. The reproductive cells, like the Amœbæ, can be destroyed, but they do not die naturally. Each reproductive cell is derived by fission from a corresponding cell of the preceding generation ; and in Metazoa, as in Protozoa, there has been from generation to generation direct continuity of living matter. We are apt to think of the somatic cells—*i.e.*, the body of the individual animal—as the essential part, by reason of its greater bulk and impressiveness ; and to regard the reproductive cells as structures whose purpose it is to give rise to the somatic cells—*i.e.*, the individuals of the next generation. In doing so however we lose sight of the true relation between the two groups of cells. The reproductive cells are the really essential elements, and the part of the somatic cells is a subordinate one ; their purpose being to nourish and protect the reproductive cells in such way as to afford them the best chance of completing their special duty, the perpetuation of the species.

The above considerations bring us to the final point in Weismann's argument. If natural death affects the somatic cells only, and is a character acquired by them, it remains to inquire why such natural death should occur, and what determines the time of its occurrence. Weismann answers these questions by saying that death occurs because it is advantageous to the species that it should do so ; and that the normal time for such death to occur is the end of the reproductive period of the individual. Both these points require further consideration. With regard to the former it is of great importance to distinguish clearly between what is for the good of the individual on the one hand, and on the other hand what is advantageous for the species. A good illustration is afforded by the elaborate provision which insects make for their offspring, which they will never see. Certain wasps have the habit of stinging the larvæ of beetles in their nerve centres in such manner as to paralyse their victims without killing them. On the body of the paralysed larva a single egg is laid by the wasp, and then left to its fate. From the egg a grub is hatched in due time, which at once begins to suck the juices of the larva ; the victim supplying it with food sufficient for the whole period of its development. The grub changes to a pupa on the skin of its victim, and passing through the winter in the pupa state, emerges in the spring as a wasp with the same instincts and habits as its parent. Difficulty is sometimes felt in accounting for such instincts. The individual wasp, it is true, derives no advantage whatever from its ingenuity ; but the gain to the species is enormous ; and the preservation of the habit is due to the fact that those individuals which took the greatest care to make provision for their young would be most likely to give rise to offspring which would survive in the struggle for existence. Natural selection would tend to preserve the instinct because it is advantageous to the species, though of no benefit whatever to the individual.

So with regard to death; Weismann argues that the origin thereof is to be found in the consideration that it is advantageous to the species that individuals should die. The argument is perhaps best stated in his own words. "Let us imagine," he says, "that one of the higher animals became immortal ; it then becomes perfectly obvious that it would cease to be of value to the species to which it belonged. Suppose that such an immortal individual could escape all fatal accidents through infinite time,—a supposition which is of course hardly conceivable. The individual would nevertheless be unable to avoid from time to time slight injuries to one or another part of its body. The injured parts could not regain their former integrity, and thus the longer the individual lived the more defective and crippled it would become, and the less perfectly would it fulfil the purpose of its species. Individuals are injured by the operation of external forces, and for this reason alone it is necessary that new and perfect individuals should continually arise and take their place, and this necessity would remain even if the individuals possessed the power of living eternally." "From this follows, on the one hand the necessity of reproduction, and on the other the utility of death. Worn-out individuals are not only valueless to the species, but they are even harmful, for they take the place of those which are sound. Hence by the operation of natural selection the life of our hypothetically immortal individual would be shortened by the amount which was useless to the species. It would be reduced to a length which would afford the most favourable conditions for the existence of as large a number as possible of vigorous individuals at the same time."

The passage just quoted is extremely ingenious, but is hardly convincing, for it does not attempt to explain the real nature of death, nor how it came about in the first instance. The distinction between somatic and reproductive cells is a real one in Metazoa. The actual steps by which it was established have yet to be traced: but it would seem probable that in the earliest Metazoa all the cells originally retained their reproductive power, and that the process by which this power became restricted to particular groups of cells was a gradual one. The gemmules of sponges, or the statoblasts of Polyzoa, are perhaps to be interpreted as examples of the retention of reproductive power by groups of cells which in allied animals have become exclusively somatic in character ; and similar instances could be quoted from the vegetable kingdom.

Weismann's contention that the reproductive cells of Metazoa are immortal in the same sense as an Amœba, must also be admitted to be established. He however leaves altogether undecided the question of the way in which death of the somatic cells arose in the first instance ; and we shall find later on that there are strong grounds for holding that natural death appeared first, not as Weismann supposed among Metazoa, but in the Protozoa themselves.

Before considering these more recent aspects of the problem it will be well to refer briefly to Weismann's views, which have already been mentioned, in regard to the causes determining the duration of life in different animals. According to Weismann the duration of life in a given case is that which is most advantageous for the species. In the simpler cases death occurs at the close of the reproductive period. In the silkworm moth, or the May fly, the adult existence is only of a few hours' duration ; the insect laying all its eggs simultaneously, and then dying. In other insects, as in many of the hawkmoths, and in most butterflies, the eggs are laid at intervals and in different places ; in such cases the life of the adult is prolonged until a sufficient number of eggs have been laid to ensure the perpetuation of the species, and then the insect dies. In birds, owing to the small number of the eggs that are produced at any one time, and the great destruction to which the eggs are liable from the attacks of enemies, several years may elapse before enough eggs are produced to ensure survival of the species ; and the life of the adult is consequently prolonged for many years. A further lengthening of life takes place in mammals and other animals which tend or rear their young, either by retaining the eggs or embryos within their bodies for a longer or shorter portion of their development, or by protecting and feeding the young after birth.

The whole subject thus opened up is of extreme interest, but it would be impossible to treat it adequately on the present occasion. Weismann himself has accumulated a large number of statistics with regard to different groups of animals, which lead him to the conclusion that "the end of the reproductive period is usually more or less coincident with death ;" while in cases in which the duration of life is prolonged, owing to the parent tending or nursing the young after birth, he concludes that " as a general rule the increase in length of life is exactly proportional to the time which is demanded by the care of the young."

With regard to the actual cause of death in Metazoa, Weismann suggested in his earlier essay published in 1881, that death may be due to the somatic cells losing the power of reproduction by cell-division after a certain number of generations. In 1883 in a further essay on life and death, he repeated this suggestion and developed it more fully. After referring to his former view that the varying duration of life in the animal kingdom " is determined in different species by the varying number of somatic cell-generations," he frankly admits that he is quite unable to indicate the changes in the physical constitution of protoplasm upon which the variations in the capacity for cell-division depend, or the causes which determine the greater or smaller number of cell-generations ; but he urges that if we must wait until we understand the molecular structure of cells before advancing views concerning the nature and limits of their activities we shall probably never solve the problem. " Therefore," he continues, " it is in my opinion an advance if we may assume that length of life is dependent upon the number of generations of somatic cells which can succeed one another in the course of a single life ; and furthermore that this number, as well as the duration of each single cell-generation, is predestined in the germ itself. This view seems to me to derive support from the obvious fact that the duration of each cell-generation, and also the number of generations, undergo considerable increase as we pass from the lowest to the highest Metazoa."

This bold suggestion, based entirely on theoretical considerations, received striking confirmation a couple of years later, from the results of Maupas' famous researches into the reproduction of Infusoria. The normal mode of reproduction among the ciliated Infusoria is by means of fission, essentially similar to the fission of Amœbæ. In addition to this a process of conjugation has long been known to occur in Infusoria, though its real nature has been much disputed. Balbiani described the process in great detail as long ago as 1858, and was led to the conclusion that it was a true sexual act, comparable to fertilisation in the higher animals. Balbiani's views were for a long time discredited, mainly through the unwillingness of zoologists to admit the possibility of sexual reproduction occurring in unicellular animals. More recent researches however and in particular those of Maupas, have shown that while Balbiani was not absolutely right with regard to all the details of the process, yet that he was correct in his interpretation of the conjunction of Infusoria as a true sexual act.

The problem which Maupas set himself to solve was to determine the relation between the two modes of reproduction in Infusoria, to ascertain the conditions under which asexual and sexual reproduction respectively occur, and to find out what causes lead to the substitution at particular times of one process for the other. To do this it was necessary to isolate an individual Infusorian, to place it under known conditions as to temperature and food supply, and then to follow the fate of the successive generations of offspring to which it gave rise by fission.

The investigation was an extraordinarily laborious one. Continuous observations for over five months were necessary; the production and fate of from 200 to 300 successive generations had to be followed accurately, and in some cases the observations extended over more than 600 generations. The most suitable temperature at which to conduct the experiments, and the kind of food best suited to the particular Infusorian under observation, had in each case to be determined. No less than twenty different species were experimented upon, and the whole research, both as regards the extreme patience necessary for its proper conduct, and the great importance of the results obtained, justly ranks among the most famous of its kind.

The general results of Maupas' investigation, which deserve to be followed in detail by all microscopists, were to this effect: In conjugation the paranucleus of each of the conjugating individuals acts as a hermaphrodite sexual element: it undergoes successive divisions, and parts are extruded and lost completely. The remaining parts of each paranucleus become differentiated into male and female pronuclei; interchange of the male pronuclei takes place between the conjugating individuals, and the male pronuclei then fuse with the female pronuclei of the individuals to which they have been transferred. The entire nuclear apparatus of each of the conjugating individuals is now reconstituted, and the two Infusoria separate and become independent once more. The purpose of conjugation appears to be to stimulate the asexual act of fission. Individuals which previous to conjugation showed no tendency to divide, begin to do so actively as soon as conjugation has been completed. In order however for conjugation to be effective, Maupas finds that it must take place between individuals which are not closely related to each other. Members of the same family show no tendency to conjugate with each other, and appear indeed to be incapable of doing so, for attempts at such conjugation have been found to prove abortive.

By his method of isolating Infusoria and following the fate of the successive generations produced by fission, Maupas was enabled to prove that there are natural and definite limits to the continuance of asexual reproduction. An Infusorian, *Stylonychia pustulata*, was isolated in November 1885, and the successive generations followed until March 1886. By that time there had been 215 generations produced by successive acts of fission. Conjugation had not occurred, since nearly related individuals will not conjugate, and unrelated forms were excluded by the conditions of the experiment. Towards the close of the experiment the tendency to multiply by fission became less manifest, and the individuals themselves were in a condition well described as senescent; they were of reduced size, often distorted in shape, or actually malformed; their nuclear apparatus was in a degenerate condition, and they no longer had the power, which all the younger generations possessed, of conjugating effectively with unrelated individuals when transferred to water containing such. Finally the nutritive powers of these senescent members failed and death of these exhausted forms brought the experiment to an end. The same results were obtained from experiments conducted in a similar way with other Infusorians. The general conclusions arrived at were: (i.) That in those Protozoa which reproduce both by fission and by a sexual process of conjugation there are definite limits to the number of generations which can be produced asexually; (ii.) that conjugation only occurs between individuals which are not nearly related to each other; (iii.) that if conjugation with unrelated forms be prevented, senescence, and finally death occur.

These results are of the utmost interest in connection with Weismann's views regarding the nature and origin of death. They show that Weismann was wrong in supposing that death occurred first amongst Metazoa. Natural death occurs among Protozoa; and the tendency to it and inability to escape from it, are probably inherited by Metazoa from their Protozoon ancestors. On the other hand, Maupas' results confirm in the fullest manner Weismann's bold suggestions, (i.) that the original occurrence of death is intimately connected with sexual reproduction, if not indeed an actual consequence of it; (ii.) that the number of generations of somatic cells which can succeed one another in the course of a single life may be strictly limited. Maupas' experiments seem to me to afford the very evidence of which Weismann was in search. They prove that amongst Infusoria asexual reproduction by cell division cannot be continued indefinitely, but that it leads in time to senescence and ultimately to death.

If we apply these results to Metazoa the conclusions become very striking. In Metazoa, as in Infusoria, there is alternation of sexual and asexual modes of reproduction. The fusion of male and female pronuclei in the act of fertilisation of the egg is the sexual process, and is equivalent to the similar fusion of male and female pronuclei of unrelated cells, seen in the conjugation of Infusoria. On the other hand the successive acts of cell division, by which the fertilised egg gives rise to the embryo and the embryo becomes converted into the adult, are asexual processes, equivalent to the repeated acts of cell division by which the successive generations of the Infusorian are produced. In the Infusorian the number of such asexually produced generations that can succeed one another is limited; so also is it in the Metazoon; and the gradual failure of the power to divide further leads in both cases alike first to senescence or old age, and ultimately to death.

This comparison between Protozoa and Metazoa in regard to the modes in which reproduction is effected appears to be a just one. The striking difference, that in the Protozoon the products of the asexual process of cell division become independent and similar unicellular animals, while in the Metazoon they are component and differentiated units in the body of a multicellular animal, does not affect the comparison so far as concerns the essential point— *i.e.*, the mode in which successive cell generations come into existence in the two cases alike. A further point of difference is·found in the consideration that in the Infusoria all the asexually produced cells retain, at any rate for a number of generations, the power of conjugating with other cells; while in

Metazoa the power appears to be lost very early by the majority of the cells, and retained only by the reproductive cells. This however does not in any way invalidate the comparison, and is merely an example of that structural and physiological differentiation which distinguishes Metazoa from colonial Protozoa, and which affords the key to all Metazoon structure.

Moreover, it is at present entirely unknown to us at what period or to what extent somatic cells of a Metazoon lose their power of conjugating. From this standpoint it would be of the greatest interest to know precisely what happens in cases of introduction of cells from without into a living Metazoon; for example, in vaccination or in other methods of inoculation; or in cases of transfusion of blood on a large scale. Theoretically it seems possible that rejuvenescence of the somatic, as of the reproductive cells of a Metazoon might be effected, and a new lease of life obtained for these cells and their descendants. This however is a matter of mere speculation, and not to be lightly entered upon. The general conclusions to which these recent investigations have led us may be briefly summarised as follows :—

> i. Death is not an intrinsic necessity, either of life or of organisation.
> ii. Natural death first appeared, so far as we know at present, among the higher Protozoa.
> iii. Death is closely associated with the occurrence of conjugation, and the consequent

alternation of sexual and asexual modes of reproduction.

iv. The asexual mode of reproduction, by fission, is the more primitive one. Conjugation, or sexual reproduction, gives an advantage in the struggle for existence; and at first a luxury, has through the action of natural selection become a necessity.

v. The normal duration of life of a given species is that which is most advantageous to the species—*i.e.*, an animal dies when it has produced sufficient young to ensure the perpetuation of the species under existing conditions.

vi. In Metazoa, as in Protozoa, there is direct continuity of living matter by cell division from generation to generation.

vii. The statement that "no Protozoon has ever lost an ancestor by death" may now be extended thus : *There is not a single component cell in the body of a Metazoon that has ever lost an ancestor by death.* For each component cell in the body of a Metazoon is descended by direct fission from the egg. The egg was a body cell of the parent, and in its turn was derived by cell division from the egg cell from which the parent was developed ; and so on, generation behind generation, there has been unbroken continuity of living matter.

XIII

THE RECAPITULATION THEORY

As my theme for this morning's address I have selected the Development of Animals. I have made this choice from no desire to extol one particular branch of biological study at the expense of others, nor through failure to appreciate or at least admire the work done and the results achieved in recent years by those who are attacking the great problems of life from other sides and with other weapons. My choice is determined by the necessity that is laid upon me, through the wide range of sciences whose encouragement and advancement are the peculiar privilege of this Section, to keep within reasonable limits the direction and scope of my remarks ; and is confirmed by the thought that, in addressing those specially interested in and conversant with biological study, your President acts wisely in selecting as the subject-matter of his discourse some branch with which his own studies and inclinations have brought him into close relation.

Embryology, referred to by the greatest of naturalists as " one of the most important subjects in the whole round of Natural History," is still in its youth, but has of late years thriven so mightily that fear has been expressed lest it should absorb unduly the attention of zoologists, or even check the progress of science by diverting interest from other and equally important branches.   Nor is the reason of this phenomenal success hard to find. The actual study of the processes of development ; the gradual building up of the embryo, and then of the young animal, within the egg ; the fashioning of its various parts and organs ; the devices for supplying it with food, and for ensuring that the respiratory and other interchanges are duly performed at all stages : all these are matters of absorbing interest.   Add to these the extraordinary changes which may take place after leaving the egg, the conversion, for instance, of the aquatic gill-breathing tadpole—a true fish as regards all essential points of its anatomy—into a four-legged frog, devoid of tail, and breathing by lungs ; or the history of the metamorphosis by which the sea-urchin is gradually built up within the body of its pelagic larva, or the butterfly derived from its grub.   Add to these again the far wider interest aroused by comparing the life-histories of allied animals, or by tracing the mode of development of a complicated organ—*e.g.*, the eye or the brain—in the various animal groups, from its simplest commencement, through gradually increasing grades of efficiency, up to its most perfect form as seen in the highest animals. Consider this, and it becomes easy to understand the fascination which embryology exercises over those who study it.

But all this is of trifling moment compared with the great generalisation which tells us that the development of animals has a far higher meaning ; that the several embryological stages and the order of their occurrence are no mere accidents, but are forced on an animal in accordance with a law, the determination of which ranks as one of the greatest achievements of biological science. The doctrine of descent, or of Evolution, teaches us that as individual animals arise, not spontaneously, but by direct descent from pre-existing animals, so also is it with species, with families, and with larger groups of animals, and so also has it been for all time ; that as the animals of succeeding generations are related together, so also are those of successive geologic periods ; that all animals, living or that have lived, are united together by blood relationship of varying nearness or remoteness ; and that every animal now in existence has a pedigree stretching back, not merely for ten or a hundred generations, but through all geologic time since the dawn of life on this globe.

The study of Development, in its turn, has revealed to us that each animal bears the mark of its ancestry, and is compelled to discover its parentage in its own development ; that the phases through which an animal passes in its progress from the egg to the adult are no accidental freaks, no mere matters of developmental convenience, but represent more or less closely, in more or less modified manner, the successive ancestral stages through which the present condition has been acquired. Evolution tells us that each animal has had a pedigree in the past. Embryology reveals to us this ancestry, because every animal in its own development repeats this history, climbs up its own genealogical tree. Such is the Recapitulation Theory, hinted at by Agassiz, and suggested more directly in the writings of von Baer, but first clearly enunciated by Fritz Müller, and since elaborated by many, notably by Balfour, and by Ernst Haeckel. It is concerning this theory, which forms the basis of the science of Embryology, and which alone justifies the extraordinary attention this science has received, that I venture to address you this morning. A few illustrations from different groups of animals will best explain the practical bearings of the theory, and the aid which it affords to the zoologist of to-day, while these will also serve to illustrate certain of the difficulties which have arisen in the attempt to interpret individual development by the light of past history—difficulties which I propose to consider at greater length.

A very simple example of recapitulation is afforded by the eyes of the sole, plaice, turbot, and their allies. These " flat fish " have their bodies greatly compressed laterally ; and the two surfaces, really the right and left sides of the animal are, unlike, one being white, or nearly so, and the other coloured. The flat fish has two eyes, but these in place of being situated, as in other fish, one on each side of the head, are both on the coloured side. The advantage to the fish is clear, for the natural position of rest of a flat fish is lying on the sea bottom; with the white surface downwards and the coloured one upwards. In such a position an eye situated on the white surface could be of no use to the fish, and might even become a source of danger, owing to its liability to injury from stones or other hard bodies on the sea bottom. No one would maintain that flat fish were specially created as such. The totality of their organisation shows clearly enough that they are true fish, akin to others in which the eyes are symmetrically placed one on each side of the head, in the position they normally hold among vertebrates. We must therefore suppose that flat fish are descended from other fish in which the eyes are normally situated.

The Recapitulation Theory supplies a ready test. On employing it—*i.e.*, on studying the development of the flat fish—we obtain a conclusive answer. The young sole on leaving the egg is shaped just as any ordinary fish, and has the two eyes placed symmetrically on the two sides of the head. It is only after the young fish has reached some size, and has begun to approach the adult in shape, and to adopt its habit of resting on one side on the sea bottom, that the eye of the side on which it rests becomes shifted forwards, then rotated on to the top of the head, and finally twisted completely over to the opposite side.

The brain of a bird differs from that of other

vertebrates in the position of the optic lobes, these being situated at the sides instead of on the dorsal surface. Development shows that this lateral position is a secondarily acquired one, for throughout all the earlier stages the optic lobes are, as in other vertebrates, on the dorsal surface, and only shift down to the sides shortly before the time of hatching.

Crabs differ markedly from their allies, the lobsters, in the small size and rudimentary condition of their abdomen or "tail." Development however affords abundant evidence of the descent of crabs from macrurous ancestors, for a young crab at what is termed the Megalopa stage has the abdomen as large as a lobster or prawn at the same stage.

Molluscs afford excellent illustrations of recapitulation. The typical gasteropod has a large spirally coiled shell; the limpet however has a large conical shell, which in the adult gives no sign of spiral twisting, although the structure of the animal shows clearly its affinity to forms with spiral shells. Development solves the riddle at once, telling us that in its early stages the limpet embryo has a spiral shell, which is lost on the formation subsequently of the conical shell of the adult.

Recapitulation is not confined to the higher groups of animals, and the Protozoa themselves yield most instructive examples. A very striking case is that of Orbitolites, one of the most complex of the procellanous Foraminifera, in which each individual during its own growth and development passes through the series of stages by which the cyclical or discoidal type of shell was derived from the simpler spiral form.

In *Orbitolites tenuissima*, as Dr. Carpenter has shown,* "the whole transition is actually presented during the successive stages of its growth. For it begins life as a Cornuspira, ... its shell forming a continuous spiral tube, with slight interruptions at the points at which its successive extensions commence; while its sarcodic body consists of a continuous coil with slight constrictions at intervals. The second stage consists in the opening out of its spire, and the division of its cavity at regular intervals by transverse septa, traversed by separate pores, exactly as in Peneroplis. The third stage is marked by the subdivision of the 'peneropline' chambers into chamberlets, as in the early forms of Orbiculina. And the fourth consists in the exchange of the spiral for the cyclical plan of growth, which is characteristic of Orbitolites; a circular disc of progressively increasing diameter being formed by the addition of successive annular zones around the entire periphery."

The shells both of Foraminifera and of Mollusca afford peculiarly instructive examples for the study of recapitulation. As growth of the shell is effected by the addition of new shelly matter to the part already existing, the older parts of the shell are retained, often unaltered, in the adult; and in favourable cases, as in *Orbitolites tenuissima*, all the

* W. B. Carpenter, "On an Abyssal Type of the Genus Orbitolites," *Phil. Trans.* 1883, part ii. p. 553.

stages of development can be determined by simple inspection of the adult shell.

It is important to remember that the Recapitulation Theory, if valid, must apply not merely in a general way to the development of the animal body, but must hold good with regard to the formation of each organ or system, and with regard to the later equally with the earlier phases of development. Of individual organs, the brain of birds has been already cited. The formation of the vertebrate liver as a diverticulum from the alimentary canal, which is at first simple, but by the folding of its walls becomes greatly complicated, is another good example ; as is also the development of the vomer in Amphibians as a series of toothed plates, equivalent morphologically to the placoid scales of fishes, which are at first separate, but later on fuse together and lose the greater number of their teeth.

Concerning recapitulation in the later phases of development and in the adult animal, the mode of renewal of the nails or of the epidermis generally is a good example, each cell commencing its existence in an indifferent form in the deeper layers of the epidermis, and gradually acquiring the adult peculiarities as it approaches the surface, through removal of the cells lying above it.

The above examples, selected almost haphazard, will suffice to illustrate the Theory of Recapitulation. The proof of the theory depends chiefly on its universal applicability to all animals, whether high or low in the zoological scale, and to all their parts and organs.   It derives also strong support from the ready explanation which it gives of many otherwise unintelligible points.

Of these latter a familiar and most instructive instance is afforded by rudimentary organs—*i.e.*, structures which, like the outer digits of the horse's leg, or the intrinsic muscles of the ear of a man, are present in the adult in an incompletely developed form, and in a condition in which they can be of no use to their possessors—or else structures which are present in the embryo, but disappear completely before the adult condition is attained, for example the teeth of whalebone whales, or the branchial clefts of all higher vertebrates.

Natural Selection explains the preservation of useful variations, but will not account for the formation and perpetuation of useless organs ; and rudiments such as those mentioned above would be unintelligible but for Recapitulation, which solves the problem at once, showing that these organs, though now useless, must have been of functional value to the ancestors of their present possessors, and that their appearance in the ontogeny of existing forms is due to repetition of ancestral characters. Such rudimentary organs are, as Darwin pointed out, of larger relative or even absolute size in the embryo than in the adult, because the embryo represents the stage in the pedigree in which they were functionally active.

Rudimentary organs are extremely common, especially among the higher groups of animals, and their presence and significance are now well understood. Man himself affords numerous and excellent examples, not merely in his bodily structure, but by his speech, dress, and customs. For the silent letter *b* in the word doubt, or the *w* of answer, or the buttons on his elastic side boots are as true examples of rudiments, unintelligible but for their past history, as are the ear muscles he possesses but cannot use, or the gill-clefts, which are functional in fishes and tadpoles, and are present though useless in the embryos of all higher vertebrates, which in their early stages the hare and the tortoise alike possess, and which are shared with them by cats and by kings.

Another consideration of the greatest importance arises from the study of the fossil remains of the animals that formerly inhabited the earth. It was the elder Agassiz who first directed attention to the remarkable agreement between the embryonic growth of animals and their palæontological history. He pointed out the resemblance between certain stages in the growth of young fish and their fossil representatives, and attempted to establish, with regard to fish, a correspondence between their palæontological sequence and the successive stages of embryonic development. He then extended his observations to other groups, and stated his conclusions in these words : * " It may therefore be considered as a general fact, very likely to be more fully illustrated as investigations cover a wider ground, that the phases of development of all living animals correspond to the order of succession

* L. Agassiz, " Essay on Classification," 1859, p. 115.

of their extinct representatives in past geological times."

This point of view is of the utmost importance. If the development of an animal is really a repetition of its ancestral history, then it is clear that the agreement or parallelism which Agassiz insists on between the embryological and palæontological records must hold good. Owing to the attitude which Agassiz subsequently adopted with regard to the theory of Natural Selection, there is some fear of his services in this respect failing to receive full recognition, and it must not be forgotten that the sentence I have quoted was written prior to the clear enunciation of the Recapitulation Theory by Fritz Müller.

The imperfection of the geological record has been often referred to and lamented. It is very true that our museums afford us but fragmentary pictures of life in past ages ; that the earliest volumes of the history are lost, and that of others but a few torn pages remain to us ; but the later records are in far more satisfactory condition. The actual number of specimens accumulated from the more recent formations is prodigious ; facilities for consulting them are far greater than they were ; the international brotherhood of science is now fully established, and the fault will be ours if the material and opportunities now forthcoming are not rightly and fully utilised.

By judicious selection of groups in which long series of specimens can be obtained, and in which the hard skeletal parts, which alone can be suitably preserved as fossils, afford reliable indications of zoological affinity, it is possible to test directly this correspondence between palæontological and embryological histories, while in some instances a single lucky specimen will afford us, on a particular point, all the evidence we require.

Great progress has already been made in this direction, and the results obtained are of the most encouraging description. By Alexander Agassiz a detailed comparison was made between the fossil series and the developmental stages of recent forms in the case of the Echinoids, a group peculiarly well adapted for such an investigation. The two records agree remarkably in many respects, more especially in the independent evidence they give as to the origin of the asymmetrical forms from more regular ancestors. The gradually increasing compilation in some of the historic series is found to be repeated very closely in the development of their existing representatives ; and with regard to the whole group, Agassiz concludes that,* " comparing the embryonic development with the palæontological one, we find a remarkable similarity in both, and in a general way there seems to be a parallelism in the appearance of the fossil genera and the successive stages of the development of the Echini." Neumayr has followed similar lines, and by him, as by other authorities on the group, there seems to be general agreement as to the

* A. Agassiz, " Palæontological and Embryological Development," an Address before the American Association for the Advancement of Science, 1880.

parallelism between the embryological and palæontological records, not merely for Echini, but for other groups of Echinodermata as well.

The Tetrabranchiate Cephalopoda are an excellent group in which to study the problem, for though no opportunity has yet occurred for studying the embryology of the only surviving member of the group, the pearly nautilus, yet owing to the fact that growth of the shell is effected by addition of shelly matter to the part already present, and to the additions being made in such manner that the older part of the shell persists unaltered, it is possible, from examination of a single shell—and in the case of fossils the shells are the only part of which we have exact knowledge—to determine all the phases of its growth; just as in the shell of Orbitolites all the stages of development are manifest on inspection of an adult specimen. In such a shell as Nautilus or Ammonites the central chamber is the oldest or first formed one, to which the remaining chambers are added in succession. If therefore the development of the shell is a repetition of ancestral history, the central chamber should represent the palæontologically oldest form, and the remaining chambers in succession, forms of more and more recent origin. Ammonite shells present, more especially in their sutures, and in the markings and sculpturing of their surface, characters that are easily recognised, and readily preserved in fossils; and the group consequently is a very suitable one for investigation from this standpoint. Würtenberger's admirable and well-known researches* have shown that in the Ammonites such a correspondence between historic and embryonic development does really exist; that, for example, in Aspidoceras the shape and markings of the shells in young specimens differ greatly from those of adults, and that the characters of the young shells are those of palæontologically older forms. Another striking illustration of the correspondence between palæontological and developmental records is afforded by the antlers of deer, in which the gradually increasing complication of the antler in successive years agrees singularly closely with the progressive increase in size and complexity shown by the fossil series from the Miocene age to recent times.

Of cases where a single specimen has sufficed to prove the palæontological significance of a developmental character, Archæopteryx affords a typical example. In recent birds the metacarpals are firmly fused with one another, and with the distal series of carpals; but in development the metacarpals are at first, and for some time, distinct. In Archæopteryx this distinctness is retained in the adult, showing that what is now an embryonic character in recent birds, was formerly an adult one. Other examples might easily be quoted, but these will suffice to show that the relation between Palæontology and Embryology, first enunciated by Agassiz, and required by the Recapitulation

* L. Würtenberger, " Studien über die Stammesgeschichte der Ammoniten. Ein geologischer Beweis für die Darwin'sche Theorie." Leipzig, 1880.

Theory, <u>does in reality exist</u>.   There is much yet
to be done in this direction.   A commencement, a
most promising commencement, has been made,
but as yet only a few groups have been seriously
studied from this standpoint.

It is a great misfortune that palæontology is not
more generally and more seriously studied by men
versed in embryology, and that those who have so
greatly advanced our knowledge of the early
development of animals should so seldom have
tested their conclusions as to the affinities of the
groups they are concerned with by direct reference
to the ancestors themselves, as known to us
through their fossil remains.   I cannot but feel
that for instance the determination of the affinities
of fossil Mammalia, of which such an extraordinary
number and variety of forms are now known to us,
would be greatly facilitated by a thorough and
exact knowledge of the development, and especially
the later development, of the skeleton in their
existing descendants, and I regard it as a reproach
that such exact descriptions of the later stages of
development should not exist even in the case of
our commonest domestic animals.

The pedigree of the horse has attracted great
attention and has been worked at most assiduously,
and we are now, largely owing to the labours of
American palæontologists, able to refer to a series
of fossil forms commencing in the lowest Eocene
beds, and extending upwards to the most recent
deposits, which show a complete gradation from a
more generalised mammalian type to the highly

specialised condition characteristic of the horse and its allies, and which may reasonably be regarded as indicating the actual line of descent of the horse. In this particular case, more frequently cited than any other, the evidence is entirely palæontological. The actual development of the horse has yet to be studied, and it is greatly to be desired that it should be undertaken speedily. Klever's * recent work on the development of the teeth in the horse may be referred to as showing that important and unexpected evidence is to be obtained in this way.

A brilliant exception to the statement just made as to the want of exact knowledge of the later development of the more highly organised animals is afforded by the splendid labours of Professor W. K. Parker, whose recent death has deprived zoology of one of her most earnest and single-minded students, and zoologists, young and old alike, of a true and sincere friend. Professor Parker's extraordinarily minute and painstaking investigations into the development of the vertebrate skull rank among the most remarkable of zootomical achievements and afford a rich mine of carefully recorded facts, the full value and bearing of which we are hardly yet able to appreciate.

If further evidence as to the value and importance of the Recapitulation Theory were needed, it would suffice to refer to the influence which it has had on the classification of the animal kingdom. Ascidians and Cirripedes may be quoted as

* Klever, " Zur Kenntniss der Morphogenese des Equidengebisses," *Morphologisches Jahrbuch*, xv. 1889, p. 308.

important groups, the true affinities of which were first revealed by embryology ; and in the case of parasitic animals the structural modifications of the adult are often so great that, but for the evidence yielded by development, their zoological position could not be determined. It is now indeed generally recognised that in doubtful cases embryology affords the safest of all clues, and that the zoological position of such forms can hardly be regarded as definitely established unless their development, as well as their adult anatomy, is ascertained.

It is owing to this Recapitulation Theory that Embryology has exercised so marked an influence on zoological speculation. Thus the formation in most, if not in all, animals of the nervous system and of the sense organs from the epidermal layer of the skin, acquired a new significance when it was recognised that this mode of development was to be regarded as a repetition of the primitive mode of formation of such organs ; while the vertebral theory of the skull affords a good example of a view, once stoutly maintained, which received its death-blow through the failure of embryology to supply the evidence requisite in its behalf. The necessary limits of time and space forbid that I should attempt to refer to even the more important of the numerous recent discoveries in embryology, but mention may be very properly made here of Sedgwick's determination of the mode of development of the body cavity in Peripatus, a discovery which has thrown most welcome light on what was previously a great morphological puzzle.

We must now turn to another side of the question. Although it is undoubtedly true that development is to be regarded as a recapitulation of ancestral phases, and that the embryonic history of an animal presents to us a record of the race-history, yet it is also an undoubted fact, recognised by all writers on embryology, that the record so obtained is neither a complete nor a straightforward one. It is indeed a history, but a history of which entire chapters are lost, while in those that remain many pages are misplaced and others are so blurred as to be illegible ; words, sentences, or entire paragraphs are omitted, and, worse still, alterations or spurious additions have been freely introduced by later hands, and at times so cunningly as to defy detection.

Very slight consideration will show that development cannot in all cases be strictly a recapitulation of ancestral stages. It is well known that closely allied animals may differ markedly in their mode of development. The common frog is at first a tadpole, breathing by gills, a stage which is entirely omitted by the West Indian Hylodes. A crayfish, a lobster, and a prawn are allied animals, yet they leave the egg in totally different forms. Some developmental stages, as the pupa condition of insects, or the stage in the development of a dog-fish in which the œsophagus is imperforate, cannot possibly be ancestral stages. Or again, a chick embryo of say the fourth day is clearly not an animal capable of independent existence, and therefore cannot correctly represent any ancestral condition, an objection which applies to the developmental history of many, perhaps of most animals.

Haeckel long ago urged the necessity of distinguishing in actual development between those characters which are really historical and inherited, and those which are acquired or spurious additions to the record. The former he termed palingenetic or ancestral characters, the latter cenogenetic or acquired. The distinction is undoubtedly a true one, but an exceedingly difficult one to draw in practice. The causes which prevent development from being a strict recapitulation of ancestral characters, the mode in which these came about, and the influence which they respectively exert, are matters which are greatly exercising embryologists, and the attempt to determine which has as yet met with only partial success.

The most potent and the most widely spread of these disturbing causes arise from the necessity of supplying the embryo with nutriment. This acts in two ways. If the amount of nutritive matter within the egg is small, then the young animal must hatch early, and in a condition in which it is able to obtain food for itself. In such cases there is of necessity a long period of larval life, during which natural selection may act so as to introduce modifications of the ancestral history, spurious additions to the text.

If on the other hand, the egg contain within

itself a considerable quantity of nutrient matter, then the period of hatching can be postponed until this nutrient matter has been used up. The consequence is that the embryo hatches at a much later stage of its development, and if the amount of food material is sufficient may even leave the egg in the form of the parent. In such cases the earlier developmental phases are often greatly condensed and abbreviated ; and as the embryo does not lead a free existence, and has no need to exert itself to obtain food, it commonly happens that these stages are passed through in a very modified form, the embryo being, as in a four-day chick, in a condition in which it is clearly incapable of independent existence.

The nutrition of the embryo prior to hatching is most usually effected by granules of nutrient matter, known as food yolk, and embedded in the protoplasm of the egg itself ; and it is on the relative abundance of these granules that the size of the egg chiefly depends. Large size of eggs implies diminution of number of the eggs, and hence of the offspring ; and it can be well understood that while some species derive advantage in the struggle for existence by producing the maximum number of young, to others it is of greater importance that the young on hatching should be of considerable size and strength, and able to begin the world on their own account. In other words, some animals may gain by producing a large number of small eggs, others by producing a smaller number of eggs of larger size—*i.e.*, provided with more food yolk.

The immediate effect of a large amount of food yolk is to mechanically retard the processes of development; the ultimate result is to greatly shorten the time occupied by development. This apparent paradox is readily explained. A small egg, such as that of Amphioxus, starts its development rapidly, and in about eighteen hours gives rise to a free swimming larva, capable of independent existence, with a digestive cavity and nervous system already formed; while a large egg like that of the hen, hampered by the great mass of food yolk by which it is distended, has in the same time made but very slight progress. From this time however other considerations begin to tell. Amphioxus has been able to make this rapid start owing to its relative freedom from food yolk. This freedom now becomes a retarding influence, for the larva, containing within itself but a very scanty supply of nutriment, must devote much of its energies to hunting for and to digesting its food, and hence its further development will proceed more slowly.

The chick embryo, on the other hand, has an abundant supply of food in the egg itself; it has no occasion to spend time searching for food, but can devote its whole energies to the further stages of its development. Hence, except in the earliest stages, the chick develops more rapidly than Amphioxus, and attains its adult form in a much shorter time.

The tendency of abundant food yolk to lead to shortening or abbreviation of the ancestral history, and even to the entire omission of important stages, is well known. The embryo of forms well provided with yolk takes short cuts in its development, jumps from branch to branch of its genealogical tree, instead of climbing steadily upwards. Thus the little West Indian frog, Hylodes, produces eggs which contain a larger amount of food yolk than those of the common English frog. The young Hylodes is consequently enabled to pass through the tadpole stage before hatching, to attain the form of a frog before leaving the egg; and the tadpole stage is only imperfectly recapitulated, the formation of gills for instance being entirely omitted.

The influence of food yolk on the development of animals is closely analogous to that of capital in human undertakings. A new industry, for example that of pen-making, has often been started by a man working by hand and alone, making and selling his own wares; if he succeed in the struggle for existence, it soon becomes necessary for him to call in others to assist him, and to subdivide the work; hand labour is soon superseded by machines, involving further differentiation of labour; the earlier machines are replaced by more perfect and more costly ones; factories are built, agents engaged, and in the end a whole army of work-people employed. In later times a man commencing business with very limited means will start at the same level as the original founder, and will have to work his way upwards through much the same stages—*i.e.*, will repeat the pedigree of the industry.

The capitalist on the other hand, is enabled like Hylodes, to omit these earlier stages, and after a brief period of incubation, to start business with large factories equipped with the most recent appliances, and with a complete staff of workpeople—*i.e.*, to spring into existence fully fledged.

There is no doubt that abundance of food yolk is a direct and very frequent cause of the omission of ancestral stages from individual development; but it must not be viewed as the sole cause. It is quite impossible that any animal, except perhaps in the lowest zoological groups, should repeat all the ancestral stages in the history of the race; the limits of time available for individual development will not permit this. There is a tendency in all animals towards condensation of the ancestral history, towards striking a direct path from the egg to the adult. This tendency is best marked in the higher, the more complicated members of a group—*i.e.*, in those which have a longer and more tortuous pedigree—and, though greatly strengthened by the presence of food yolk in the egg, is apparently not due to this in the first instance.

Thus the simpler forms of Orbitolites, as *O. tenuissima*, repeat in their development all the stages leading from a spiral to a cyclical shell; but in the more complicated species, as Dr. Carpenter has pointed out, there is a tendency towards precocious development of the adult characters, the earlier stages being hurried over in a modified form; while in the most complex examples, as in *O. complanata*, the earlier spiral stages may be entirely omitted, the shell acquiring almost from its earliest commencement the cyclical mode of growth. There is no question here of relative abundance of food yolk, but merely of early or precocious appearance of adult characters.

The question of the relations and influence of food yolk, involving as it does the larger or smaller size of the egg, is however merely a special side of the much wider question of the nutrition of the embryo, one of the most potent of the disturbing elements affecting development. Speaking generally, we may say that large eggs are more often met with in the higher than the lower groups of animals. Birds and Reptiles are cases in point, and if Mammals do not now produce large eggs, it is because a more direct and more efficient mode of nourishing the young by the placenta has been acquired by the higher forms, and has replaced the food yolk that was formerly present, and is now retained in quantity by Monotremes alone. Molluscs afford another good example, the eggs of Cephalopoda being of larger size than those of the less highly organised groups. The large size of the eggs of Elasmobranchs, and perhaps that of Cephalopods also, may possibly be associated with the carnivorous habits of the animals; for it is of importance that forms which prey on other animals should hatch of considerable size and strength.

The influence of habitat must also be considered. It has long been noticed as a general rule that marine animals lay small eggs, while their fresh-water allies have eggs of much larger size. The eggs of the salmon or trout are much larger than those of the cod or herring ; and the crayfish, though only a quarter the length of a lobster, lays eggs of actually larger size. This larger size of the eggs of fresh-water forms appears to be dependent on the nature of the environment to which they are exposed. Considering the geological instability of the land as compared with the ocean, there can be no doubt that fresh-water fauna are, speaking generally, derived from the marine fauna ; and the great problem with regard to fresh-water life is to explain why it is that so many groups of animals which flourish abundantly in the sea should have failed to establish themselves in fresh water. Sponges and Cœlenterates abound in the sea, but their fresh-water representatives are extremely few in number ; Echinoderms are exclusively marine ; there are no fresh-water Cephalopods, and no Ascidians ; and of the smaller groups of Worms, Molluscs, and Crustaceans, there are many that do not occur in fresh water.

Direct experiment has shown that in many cases this distribution is not due to inability of the adult animals to live in fresh water ; and the real explanation appears to be that the early larval stages are unable to establish themselves under such conditions. This interesting suggestion, which has been worked out in detail by Professor Sollas,* undoubtedly affords an important clue. To

* W. J. Sollas, "On the Origin of Freshwater Fauna," *Scientific Transactions of the Royal Dublin Society*, vol. iii. Ser. ii., 1886.

establish itself permanently in fresh water an animal must either be fixed, or else be strong enough to withstand and make headway against the currents of the streams or rivers it inhabits, for otherwise it will in the long run be swept out to sea, and this consideration applies to larval forms equally with adults.

The majority of marine Invertebrates leave the egg as minute ciliated larvæ, and such larvæ are quite incapable of holding their own in currents of any strength. Hence it is only forms which have got rid of the free swimming ciliated larval stage, and which leave the egg of considerable size and strength, that can establish themselves as fresh-water animals. This is effected most readily by the acquisition of food yolk—hence the large size of the eggs of fresh-water animals—and is often supplemented, as Sollas has shown, by special protective devices of a most interesting nature. For this reason fresh-water forms are not so well adapted as their marine allies for the study of ancestral history as revealed in larval or embryonic development.

Before leaving the question of food yolk, reference must be made to the proposal of the brothers Sarasin, to regard the yolk cells as forming a distinct embryonic layer, the lecithoblast,* distinct from the blastoderm. I do not desire to speak dogmatically on a point the full bearings of which are not yet apparent, but I venture to think that

* P. and F. Sarasin, "Ergebnisse naturwissenschaftlicher Forschungen auf Ceylon," Bd. ii. Heft iii. 1889.

this suggestion will not commend itself to embryologists. The distinction between the yolk granules and the cells in which they are embedded is a real and fundamental one; but I see no reason for regarding the yolk cells as other than originally functional endoderm cells in which yolk granules have accumulated to such an extent that they have in extreme cases become devoted solely to the storing of food for the embryo.*

Of all the causes tending to modify development, tending to obscure or falsify the ancestral record, food yolk is the most frequent and the most important; its position in the egg determines the mode of segmentation, and its relative abundance affects profoundly the entire embryonic history, and decides at what particular stage, and of what size and form, the embryo shall hatch.

The loss of food yolk is another disturbing element, the full influence of which is as yet imperfectly understood, but the possibility of which must be always kept in mind. It is best known in the case of mammals, where it has led to apparent, though very deceptive, simplification of development; and it will probably not be until the embryology of the large-yolked monotremes is at length described, that we shall fully understand the formation of the germinal layers in the higher placental mammals. Amongst invertebrates we know but little as yet concerning the effects of loss of food yolk. It has been suggested that the

* *Cf.* E. B. Wilson, "The Development of Renilla," *Phil. Trans.* 1883, p. 755.

extraordinary nature of the segmentation of the egg of *Peripatus capensis*, made known to us through Mr. Sedgwick's admirable researches, may be due to loss of food yolk : a suggestion which receives support from the long duration of uterine development in this case. Our knowledge is very imperfect as to the ease with which food yolk may be acquired or lost ; but until our information is more precise on this point it seems unwise to lay much stress on suggested pedigrees which involve great and frequent alternations in the amount of food yolk present.

Of causes other than food yolk, or only indirectly connected with it, which tend to falsify the ancestral history, many are now known, but time will only permit me to notice the more important. These are distortion, whether in time or space ; sudden or violent metamorphosis ; a series of modifications, due chiefly to mechanical causes, and which may be spoken of as developmental conveniences ; the important question of variability in development ; and finally the great problem of degeneration.

Concerning distortions in time, all embryologists have noticed the tendency to anticipation or precocious development of characters which really belong to a later stage in the pedigree. The early attainment of the cyclical form in the shell of *Orbitolites complanata* is a case in point ; and Würtenberger has specially noticed this tendency in Ammonites. Many early larvæ show it markedly, the explanation in this case being that it is essential for them to hatch in a condition capable of independent existence—*i.e.*, capable at any rate of obtaining and digesting their own food.

Anachronisms, or actual reversal of the historical order of development of organs, or parts, occur frequently. Thus the joint surfaces of bones acquire their characteristic curvatures before movement of one part or another is effected, and before even the joint cavities are formed. Another good example is afforded by the development of the mesenterial filaments in Alcyonarians. Wilson has shown in the case of Renilla that in the development of an embryo from the egg the six endodermal filaments appear first, and the two long ectodermal filaments at a later period ; but that in the formation of a bud this order of development is reversed, the ectodermal filaments being the first formed. He suggests in explanation, that as the endodermal filaments are the digestive organs, it is of primary importance to the free embryo that they should be formed quickly. The long ectodermal filaments are chiefly concerned with maintaining currents of water through the colony; in bud-development they appear before the endodermal filaments, because they enable the bud during its early stages to draw nutrient matter from the body fluid of the parent ; while the endodermal filaments cannot come into use until the bud has acquired both mouth and tentacles. The completion of the ventricular septum in the heart of higher vertebrates before the auricular septum is a well-known anachronism, and every embryologist could readily furnish many other cases. A curious instance is afforded by the development of the teeth in mammals, if recent suggestions as to the origin of the milk dentition are confirmed, and the milk dentition prove to be a more recent acquisition than the permanent one.*

But the most important case in reference to distortion in time concerns the reproductive organs. If development were a strict and correct recapitulation of ancestral history, then each stage would possess reproductive organs in a mature condition. This is not the case, and it is clearly of the greatest importance that it should not be. It is true that the first commencement of the reproductive organs may occur at a very early stage, or even that the very first step in development may be a division of the egg into somatic and reproductive cells ; and it is possible that, as maintained by Weismann, this latter condition is a primitive one. Still even in these cases the reproductive organs merely commence their development at these early stages, and do not become functional until the animal is adult.

Exceptionally in certain animals, and as a normal occurrence in others, precocious maturation of the reproductive organs takes place, and a larval form becomes capable of sexual reproduction. This may lead to arrest of development, either at a late larval period as in the Axolotl, or at successively

* *Cf.* Thomas Oldfield, " On the Homologies and Succession of the Teeth in the Dasyuridæ, with an attempt to trace the history of the evolution of the Mammal and Teeth in general," *Phil. Trans.* 1887.

earlier and earlier stages, as in the gonophores of the Hydromedusæ, until finally the extreme condition seen in Hydra is produced. We do not know the causes that determine the period, whether late or early, at which the reproductive organs ripen, but the question is one of great interest and importance, and deserves careful attention. The suggestion has been made that entire groups of animals, such as the Mesozoa, are merely larvæ, arrested through such precocious acquiring of reproductive power, and it is conceivable that this may be the case. Mesozoa are a puzzling group in which the life history, though known with tolerable completeness, has as yet given us no reliable clue concerning their affinities to other animals, a tantalising distinction that is shared with them by Rotifers and Polyzoa.

Distortion of a curious kind is seen in cases of abrupt metamorphosis, where, as in the case of many Echinoderms, of Phoronis, and of the metabolic insects, the larva and the adult differ greatly in form, habits, mode of life, and very usually in the nature of their food and the mode of obtaining it ; and the transition from one stage to the other is not a gradual but an abrupt one, at any rate so far as external characters are concerned. Sudden changes of this kind, as from the free swimming Pluteus to the creeping Echinus, or from the sluggish leaf-eating caterpillar to the dainty butterfly, cannot possibly be recapitulatory, for even if small jumps are permissible in nature, there is no room for bounds forward of this magnitude. Cases of abrupt metamorphosis may always be viewed as due to secondary modifications, and rarely, if ever, have any significance beyond the particular group of animals concerned. For example, a Pluteus larva may be recognised as belonging to the group of Echinoidea before the adult urchin has commenced to be formed within it, and the Lepidopteran caterpillar is already an unmistakable insect. Hence, for the explanation of the metamorphoses in these cases it is useless to look outside the groups of Echinoidea and Insecta respectively.

Abrupt metamorphosis is always associated with great change in external form and appearance, and in mode of life, and very usually in mode of nutrition. A gradual transition in such cases is inadmissible, because in the intermediate stages the animal would be adapted to neither the larval nor the adult condition ; a gradual conversion of the biting mouth parts of the caterpillar to the sucking proboscis of a moth would inevitably lead to starvation. The difficulty is evaded by retaining the external form and habits of one particular stage for an unduly long period, so that the relations of the animal to the surrounding environment remain unchanged, while internally preparations for the later stages are in progress. Cinderella and the princess are equally possible entities, each being well adapted to her environment. The exigences of the situation do not permit however of a gradual change from one to the other : the transformation, at least as regards external appearance, must be abrupt.

Kleinenberg has recently directed attention to cases in which the larval and adult organs develop independently—the larval nervous system for instance, aborting completely and forming no part of that of the adult. I am not sure that I fully understand Kleinenberg's argument, but it seems very possible that such cases, which are probably far more numerous than is yet admitted, may be due to what may be termed the telescoping of ancestral stages one within another, which takes place in actual development, and may accordingly be grouped under the head of developmental convenience. Undue prolongation of an early ancestral stage, as in cases of abrupt metamorphosis, must involve modification, especially in the muscular and nervous systems; in such cases a telescoping of ancestral stages takes place as we have seen, the adult being developed within the larva. Such telescoping must distort the recapitulatory history, and as the shape of the larva and adult may differ widely, an independent origin of organs, especially the muscular and nervous systems, may be acquired secondarily.

The stage in the development of Squilla, in which the three posterior maxillipedes disappear completely, to reappear at a later stage in a totally different form, is not to be interpreted as meaning that the adult maxillipedes are entirely new structures unconnected historically with those of the larva. Neither is the annual shedding of the antlers of deer to be regarded as the repetition of an ancestral hornless condition intercalated historically between successive stages provided with antlers. In both cases the explanation is afforded by convenience, whether of the embryo or adult.

Many embryological modifications or distortions may be attributed to mechanical causes, and may fairly be considered under the head of developmental conveniences. The amnion of higher vertebrates is a case in point, and is probably rightly explained as due in the first instance to sinking or depression of the embryo into the yolk, in order to avoid distortion through pressure against a hard unyielding eggshell. A similar device is employed, presumably for the same reason, in the early development of many insect embryos ; and the depression of the Tænia head within the cyst is a phenomenon of very similar nature.

Restriction of the space within which development occurs often causes displacement or distortion of organs whose growth, restricted in its normal direction, takes place along the lines of least resistance. The telescoping of the limbs and other organs within the body of an insect larva is a simple case of such distortion ; and a more complicated example, closely comparable in many ways to the invagination of the Tænia head, is afforded by the remarkable inversion of the germinal layers in Rodents, first described by Bischoff in the guinea pig, and long believed to be peculiar to that animal, but subsequently and simultaneously discovered by three independent observers, Kupffer, Selenka, and Fraser, to occur in varying degrees in rats, mice, and in other rodents.

One of the most recent attempts to explain developmental peculiarities as due to mechanical causes is Mr. Dendy's suggestion with regard to the pseudogastrula stage in the development of calcareous sponges. It is well known that while the larva is in the amphiblastula stage, and still imbedded in the tissues of the parent, the granular cells become invaginated within the ciliated cells, giving rise to the pseudogastrula stage. At a slightly later stage, when the larva becomes free, the invaginated granular cells become again everted, and the larva spherical in shape; while still later invagination occurs once more, the ciliated cells being this time invaginated within the granular cells. The significance of the pseudogastrula stage has hitherto been undetermined, but Mr. Dendy points out that the larva always occupies a definite position with reference to the parental tissues ; that the ciliated half of the larva is covered by a soft and yielding wall, while the opposite half, composed of the granular cells, is covered by a layer stiffened with rigid spicules ; and his observations on the growth of the larva lead him to think that the pseudogastrula stage is brought about mechanically by flattening of the granular cells through pressure against this rigid wall of spicules.

Embryology supplies us with many unsolved problems, and it is not to be wondered at that this should be the case. Some of these may fairly be spoken of as mere curiosities of development, while others are clearly of greater moment. I do not propose to catalogue these, but will merely mention two or three which I happen to have recently run my head against and remember vividly.   The solid condition of the œsophagus, in Elasmobranch embryos, first noticed by Balfour, is a very curious point.   The œsophagus has at first a well-developed lumen, like the rest of the alimentary canal ; but at an early period, stage K of Balfour's nomenclature, the part of the œsophagus overlying the heart, and immediately behind the branchial region, becomes solid, and remains solid for a long time, the exact date of reappearance of the lumen not being yet ascertained.   Mr. Bles and myself have recently noticed that a similar solidification of the œsophagus occurs in tadpoles of the common frog.   In young free swimming tadpoles the œsophagus is perforate, but in tadpoles of about $7\frac{1}{2}$ mm. length it becomes solid and remains so until a length of about $10\frac{1}{2}$ mm. has been attained.   The solidification occurs at a stage closely corresponding with that in which it first appears in the dogfish, and a curious point about it is that in the frog the œsophagus becomes solid just before the mouth-opening is formed, and remains solid for some little time after this important event.   This closing of the œsophagus clearly cannot be recapitulation, but the fact that it occurs at corresponding periods in the frog and dogfish suggests that it may possibly, as Balfour hinted, " turn out to have some unsuspected morphological bearing."

Another developmental curiosity is the duplication of the gill slits by growth downwards of tongues from their dorsal margins ; a duplication which is described as occurring in Amphioxus and in Balano-glossus, but in no other animal ; and the occurrence of which, in apparently closely similar fashion, is one of the strongest arguments in favour of a real affinity between these two forms. It is hardly possible that such a modification should have been acquired independently twice over.

A much more litigious question is the significance of the neurenteric canal of vertebrates, that curious tubular communication between the central canal of the nervous system and the hinder end of the alimentary canal that is conspicuously present in the embryos of lower vertebrates, and retained in a more or less disguised condition in the higher groups as well. The neurenteric canal was discovered by that famous embryologist Kowalevsky in Ascidians and in Amphioxus. He drew special attention to the occurrence of a stage in both Ascidians and in Amphioxus in which the larva is free swimming and in which the sole communication between the alimentary cavity and the exterior is through the neurenteric canal and the central canal of the nervous system ; and suggested * that animals may have existed or may still exist in which the nerve tube fulfilled a non-nervous function, and possibly acted as part of the alimentary canal ; a suggestion that has recently been revived in a somewhat extravagant form. A passage of food particles into the alimentary cavity through the neural tube has not

---

* A. Kowalevsky, " Weitere Studien über die Entwickelungsgeschichte des Amphioxus lanceolatus," *Archiv. für mikroskopisch Anatomie*, Bd. xiii. 1877, p. 201.

yet been seen, and probably does not occur, as the larva still possesses sufficient food yolk to carry it on in its development. It is therefore permissible to hold that the neurenteric canal may be a mere embryological device, and devoid of any deep morphological significance.

The question of variation in development is one of very great importance, and has perhaps not yet received the attention it deserves. We are in some danger of assuming tacitly that the mode of development of allied animals will necessarily agree in all important respects or even in details, and that if the development of one member of a group be known, that of the others may be assumed to be similar. The more recent progress of embryology is showing us that such inferences are not safe, and that in allied genera or species, or even in different individuals of the same species, variations of development may occur affecting important organs and at almost any stage in their formation.

Great individual variations in the earliest processes of development—*i.e.*, the segmentation of the egg—have been described by different writers. In Renilla, Wilson found an extraordinary range of variation in the segmentation of eggs from which apparently identical embryos were produced. In some cases the egg divided into two in the normal manner ; in other cases it divided at once into eight, sixteen, or thirty-two segments, which in different specimens were approximately equal or markedly unequal in size. Sometimes a preliminary change of form occurred without any further result, the egg returning to its spherical shape, and pausing for a time before recommencing the attempt to segment. Segmentation sometimes commenced at one pole, as in telolecithal eggs, with the formation of four or five small segments, the rest of the egg breaking up later, either simultaneously or progressively, into segments about equal in size to those first formed; while lastly, in some instances segmentation was very irregular, following no apparent law. It is noteworthy that the variability in the case of Renilla is apparently confined to the earliest stages, for whatever the mode of segmentation, the embryos in their later stages were indistinguishable from one another. Similar modifications in the segmentation of the egg have been described in the oyster by Brooks, in Anodon and other Mollusca, in Hydra, and in Lumbricus, in which last Wilson has recently shown that marked differences occur in the eggs even of the same individual animal. In the different species of Peripatus there appear also to be considerable variations in the details of segmentation.

In the early embryonic stages after the completion of segmentation very considerable variation may occur in allied species or genera. Among Cœlenterates for instance the mode of formation of the hypoblast presents most perplexing modifications: it may arise as a true gastrula invagination; as cells budded off from one pole of the blastula into its cavity; as cells budded off from various parts of the wall of the blastula; by delamination or actual division of each cell of the blastula wall; or it may be present from the first as a solid mass of cells enclosed by the epiblast cells.   It is in connection with these variations that controversy has arisen as to the primitive mode of development of the gastrula, a point to which I shall return later on.

Among the higher Metazoa or Cœlomata the extraordinary modifications in the position and in every conceivable detail of formation of the mesoblast in different and often in closely allied forms have given rise to ardent discussion, and have led to the proposal of theory after theory, each rejected in turn as only affording a partial explanation, and now culminating in Kleinenberg's protest against the use of the term mesoblast at all, at any rate in a sense implying any possibility of comparison with the primary layers, epiblast and hypoblast, of Cœlenterata.

This is not the place to attempt to decide so difficult and technical a point, even were I capable of so doing; but we may well take warning from this extraordinary diversity of development, the full extent of which I believe we as yet realise most imperfectly, that in our attempts to reconstruct ancestral history from ontogenetic development we have taken in hand no light task.   To reconstruct Latin from modern European languages would in comparison be but child's play.

Of the readiness with which special developmental characters are acquired by allied animals the brothers Sarasin* have given us evidence in

* P. and F. Sarasin, "Ergebnisse naturwissenschaftlicher Forschungen auf Ceylon," vol. ii. chap. i. pp. 24–38.

the extraordinary modifications presented by the embryonic and larval respiratory organs of Amphibians. Confining ourselves to those forms which do not lay their eggs in water, and in which consequently development takes place within the egg, we find that Ichthyophis and Salamandra have three pairs of specially modified external gills. Nototrema has two pairs ; Alytes and Typhlonectes have only a single pair, which in the latter genus take the form of enormous leaf-like outgrowths from the sides of the neck. In Hylodes and Pipa there are no gills, the tail acting as the larval respiratory organ ; and in *Rana opisthodon*, according to Boulenger, larval respiration is effected by nine pairs of folds of the skin of the ventral surface of the body.

Most of these extraordinarily diversified organs are clearly secondarily acquired structures ; it is possible that they all are, and that external gills, as was suggested by Balfour for Elasmobranchs, are to be regarded as embryonal respiratory organs acquired by the larvæ and of no ancestral value. The point however cannot be considered settled, for on this view the external gills of Elasmobranchs and Amphibians would be independently acquired and not homologous structures, a view contradicted by the close agreement in their relations in the two groups, as well as by the absence of any real break between external and internal gills in Amphibians.

It is well known that the frog and the newt differ greatly in important points of their development. The two-layered condition of the epiblast in the frog is a marked point of difference, which involves further changes in the mode of formation of the nervous system and sense organs. The kidneys and their ducts differ considerably in their development in the two forms, as do also the blood-vessels. Concerning the early development of the blood-vessels, there are considerable differences even between allied species of frogs. In *Rana esculenta* Maurer finds that there is at first in each branchial arch a single vessel or aortic arch, running directly from the heart to the aorta : from the cardiac end of this aortic arch a vessel grows out into the gill as the afferent branchial vessel, the original aortic arch losing its connection with the heart, and becoming the efferent branchial vessel. Afferent and efferent branchial vessels become connected by capillaries in the gill, and the course of the circulation, so long as gill-breathing is maintained, is from the heart through the truncus arteriosus to the afferent branchial vessel, then through the gill capillaries to the efferent branchial vessel, and then on to the aorta. When the pulmonary circulation is thoroughly established the branchial circulation is cut off by the efferent vessel reacquiring its connection with the heart, when the blood naturally takes the direct passage along it to the aorta, and so escapes the gill capillaries.

In *Rana temporaria* the mode of development is very different : the afferent and efferent vessels arise in each arch independently and almost simultaneously ; the afferent vessel soon acquires connection with the heart, but unlike *R. esculenta*, the efferent vessel has no connection with the heart until the gills are about to atrophy. In other words the continuous aortic arch, from heart to aorta, is present in *R. esculenta* prior to the development of the gills ; it becomes interrupted while the gills are in functional use, but is re-established when these begin to atrophy. In *R. temporaria*, on the other hand, there is no continuous aortic arch until the gills begin to atrophy.

The difference is an important one, for it is a matter of considerable morphological interest to determine whether the continuous aortic arch is primitive for vertebrates—*i.e.*, whether it existed prior to the development of gills. This point could be practically settled if we could decide which of the two frogs, *R. esculenta* and *R. temporaria*, has most correctly preserved its ancestral history in this respect. About this there can be little doubt. The development of the vessels in the newts, a less modified group than the frogs, agrees with that of *R. esculenta*, and interesting confirmation is afforded by a single aberrant specimen of *R. temporaria*, in which Mr. Bles and myself found the vessels developing after the type of *R. esculenta*—*i.e.*, in which a complete aortic arch was present before the gills were formed. We are therefore justified in concluding that as regards the development of the branchial blood-vessels, *R. esculenta* has retained a primitive ancestral character which is lost in *R. temporaria* ; and it is interesting to note that were our knowledge of the development of amphibians confined to the common frog, the most likely form to be studied, we should in all probability have been led to wrong conclusions concerning the ancestral condition of the blood-vessels in a point of considerable importance.

A matter which at present is attracting much attention is the question of degeneration. Natural selection, though consistent with and capable of leading to steady upward progress and improvement, by no means involves such progress as a necessary consequence. All it says is that those animals will, in each generation, have the best chance of survival which are most in harmony with their environment, and such animals will not necessarily be those which are ideally the best or most perfect.

If you go into a shop to purchase an umbrella, the one you select is by no means necessarily that which most nearly approaches ideal perfection, but the one which best hits off the mean between your idea of what an umbrella should be and the amount of money you are prepared to give for it : the one in fact that is on the whole best suited to the circumstances of the case or the environment for the time being. It might well happen that you had a violent antipathy to a crooked handle, or else were determined to have a catch of a particular kind to secure the ribs, and this might lead to the selection—*i.e.*, the survival—of an article that in other and even in more important respects was manifestly inferior to the average.

So is it also with animals : the survival of a

form that is ideally inferior is very possible. To animals living in profound darkness the possession of eyes is of no advantage, and forms devoid of eyes would not merely lose nothing thereby, but would actually gain, inasmuch as they would escape the dangers that might arise from injury to a delicate and complicated organ. In extreme cases, as in animals leading a parasitic existence, the conditions of life may be such as to render locomotor, digestive, sensory, and other organs entirely useless; and in such cases those forms will be best in harmony with their surroundings which avoid the waste of energy resulting from the formation and maintenance of these organs.

Animals which have in this way fallen from the high estate of their forefathers, which have lost organs or systems which their progenitors possessed, are commonly called degenerate. The principle of degeneration, recognised by Darwin as a possible, and under certain conditions a necessary consequence of his theory of natural selection, has been since advocated strongly by Dohrn, and later by Lankester in an Evening Discourse delivered before the Association at the Sheffield Meeting in 1879. Both Dohrn and Lankester suggested that degeneration occurred much more widely than was generally recognised.

In animals which are parasitic when adult, but free swimming in their early stages, as in the case of the Rhizocephala whose life-history was so admirably worked out by Fritz Müller, degeneration is clear enough. So also is it in the case of the solitary Ascidians, in which the larva is a free swimming animal with a notochord, an elongated tubular nervous system, and sense organs, while the adult is fixed, devoid of the swimming tail, with no notochord, and with a greatly reduced nervous system and aborted sense organs. In such cases the animal when adult is, as regards the totality of its organisation, at a distinctly lower morphological level, is less highly differentiated than it is when young, and during individual development there is actual retrograde development of important systems and organs.

About such cases there is no doubt; but we are asked to extend the idea of degeneration much more widely. It is urged that we ought not to demand direct embryological evidence before accepting a group as degenerate. We are reminded of the tendency to abbreviation or to complete omission of ancestral stages of which we have quoted examples above; and it is suggested that if such larval stages were omitted in all the members of a group we should have no direct evidence of degeneration in a group that might really be in an extremely degenerate condition. Supposing for instance the free larval stages of the solitary Ascidians were suppressed, say through the acquisition of food yolk, then it is urged that the degenerate condition of the group might easily escape detection. The supposition is by no means extravagant; food yolk varies greatly in amount in allied animals, and cases like Hylodes, or amongst Ascidians Pyrosoma, show how readily a mere increase in the amount of food yolk in the egg may lead to the omission of important ancestral stages.

The question then arises whether it is not possible, or even probable, that animals which now show no indication of degeneration in their development are in reality highly degenerate, and whether it is not legitimate to suppose such degeneration to have occurred in the case of animals whose affinities are obscure or difficult to determine. It is more especially with regard to the lower vertebrates that this argument has been employed; and at the present day zoologists of authority, relying on it, do not hesitate to speak of such forms as Amphioxus and the Cyclostomes as degenerate animals, as wolves in sheep's clothing, animals whose simplicity is acquired and deceptive rather than real and ancestral. I cannot but think that cases such as these should be regarded with some jealousy. There is at present a tendency to invoke degeneration rather freely as a talisman to extricate us from morphological difficulties; and an inclination to accept such suggestions, at any rate provisionally, without requiring satisfactory evidence in their support.

Degeneration of which there is direct embryological evidence stands on a very different footing from suspected degeneration, for which no direct evidence is forthcoming; and in the latter case the burden of proof undoubtedly rests with those who assume its existence. The alleged instances among the lower vertebrates must be regarded particularly closely, because in their case the suggestion of degeneration is admittedly put forward as a means of escape from difficulties arising through theoretical views concerning the relation between vertebrates and invertebrates. Amphioxus itself, so far as I can see, shows in its development no sign of degeneration, except possibly with regard to the anterior gut diverticula, whose ultimate fate is not altogether clear. With regard to the earlier stages of development, concerning which, thanks to the patient investigations of Kowalevsky and Hatschek, our knowledge is precise, there is no animal known to us in which the sequence of events is simpler or more straightforward. Its various organs and systems are formed in what is recognised as a primitive manner; and the development of each is a steady upward progress towards the adult condition. Food yolk, the great cause of distortion in development, is almost absent, and there is not the slightest indication of the former possession of a larger quantity. Concerning the later stages our knowledge is incomplete, but so much as has been ascertained gives no support to the suggestion of general degeneration.

Our knowledge of the conditions leading to degeneration is undoubtedly incomplete, but it must be noticed that the conditions usually associated with degeneration do not occur. Amphioxus is not parasitic, is not attached when adult, and shows no evidence of having formerly possessed food yolk in quantity sufficient to have led to the omission of important ancestral stages. Its small size, as compared with other vertebrates, is one of the very few points that can be referred to as possibly indicating degeneration, and will be considered more fully at a later point in my address.

A consideration of much less importance, but deserving of mention, is that in its mode of life Amphioxus not merely differs as already noticed from those groups of animals which we know to be degenerate, but agrees with some at any rate of those which there is reason to regard as primitive or persistent types. Amphioxus, like Balanoglossus, Lingula, Dentalium, and Limulus, is marine, and occurs in shallow water, usually with a sandy bottom, and, like the three smaller of these genera, it lives habitually buried almost completely in the sand, into which it burrows with great rapidity.

I do not wish to speak dogmatically. I merely wish to protest against a too ready assumption of degeneration ; and to repeat that so far as I can see, Amphioxus has not yet, either in its development, in its structure, or in its habits, been shown to present characters that suggest, still less that prove, the occurrence in it of general or extensive degeneration. In a sense, all the higher animals are degenerate ; that is they can be shown to possess certain organs in a less highly developed condition than their ancestors, or even in a rudimentary state. Thus a crab as compared with a lobster is degenerate in the matter of its tail, a horse as compared with Hipparion in regard to its outer toes ; but it is neither customary nor advisable to speak of a crab as a degenerate animal compared to a lobster; to do so would be misleading. An animal should only be spoken of as degenerate when the retrograde development is well marked, and has affected not one or two organs only, but the totality of its organisation.

It is impossible to draw a sharp line in such cases, and to limit precisely the use of the term degeneration. It must be borne in mind that no animal is at the top of the tree in all respects. Man himself is primitive as regards the number of his toes, and degenerate in respect to his ear muscles ; and between two animals even of the same group it may be impossible to decide which of the two is to be called the higher and which the lower form. Thus to compare an oyster with a mussel: the oyster is more primitive than the mussel as regards the position of the ventricle of the heart and its relations to the alimentary canal ; but is more modified in having but a single adductor muscle, and almost certainly degenerate in being devoid of a foot.

Care must also be taken to avoid speaking of an animal as degenerate in regard to a particular organ merely because that organ is less fully developed than in allied animals. An organ is not degenerate unless its present possessor has it in a less perfect condition than its ancestors had. A man is not degenerate in the matter of the length of his neck as compared with a giraffe, nor as compared with an elephant in respect of the size of his front teeth, for neither elephant nor giraffe enters into the pedigree of man. A man is however degenerate, whoever his ancestors may have been, in regard to his ear muscles; for he possesses these in a rudimentary and functionless condition, which can only be explained by descent from some better equipped progenitor.

Closely connected with the question of degeneration is that of the size of animals, and its bearing on their structure and development—a problem noticed by many writers, but which has perhaps not yet received the attention it merits.

If we are right in interpreting the eggs of Metazoa as representing the unicellular or protozoon stage in their ancestry, then the small size of the egg may be viewed as recapitulatory. But the gradual increase in size of the embryo, and its growth up to the adult condition, can only be regarded as representing in a most general way, if at all, the actual or even the relative sizes of the intermediate ancestral stages of the pedigree.

It is quite true that animals belonging to the lower groups are, as a general rule, of smaller size than those of higher grade; and also that the giants are met with among the highest members of each division. Cephalopoda are the highest molluscs, and the largest cephalopods greatly exceed in size any other members of the group; decapods are at once the highest and the largest crustaceans; and whales, the hugest animals that exist, or so far as we know, that ever have existed, belong to the highest group of all, the mammalia. It would be easy to quote exceptions, but the general rule obtains admittedly. However, although there may be, and probably is, a general parallelism between the increase in size from the egg to the adult, and the historical increase in size during the passage from lower to higher forms ; yet no one could maintain that the sizes of embryos represent at all correctly those of the ancestors ; that for instance the earliest birds were animals the size of a chick embryo at a time when avian characters first declare themselves, or that the ancestral series in all cases presented a steady progression in respect of actual magnitude.

In the lower animals—*e.g.*, in Orbitolites—the actual size of the several ancestral stages is probably correctly recapitulated during the growth of the adult ; and it is very possible that it is so also in such forms as the solitary sponges. In higher animals, except in the early stages of those forms which are practically devoid of food yolk, and which hatch as pelagic larvæ, this certainly does not obtain. This is clear enough, but is worth pointing out, for if as most certainly is the case the embryos of animals are actually smaller than the ancestral forms they represent, it is possible that the smallness of the embryo may have had some influence on its organisation, and be responsible for some of the modifications in the ancestral history ; and more especially for the disappearance of ancestral organs in free swimming larvæ.

In adult animals the relation between size and structure has been very clearly pointed out by Herbert Spencer. Increased size involves by itself increased complexity of structure; the determining consideration being that while the surface area of the body increases as the squares of the linear dimensions, the mass of the body increases as their cubes. If for example we imagine two animals of similar shape and proportions, but of different size; for the sake of simplicity, we may suppose them to be spherical, and that the diameter of one is twice that of the other; then the larger one will have four times the extent of surface of the smaller, but eight times its mass or bulk : and it is quite possible that while the extent of surface, or skin, in the smaller animal might suffice for the necessary respiratory and excretory interchanges, it would be altogether insufficient in the larger animal, in which increased extent of surface must be provided by foldings of the skin, as in the form of gills. To take an actual instance; Limapontia is a minute nudibranchiate, or sea-slug, about the sixth of an inch in length ; it has a smooth body, totally devoid of respiratory processes, while forms allied to it, but of larger size, have their extent of surface increased by branching processes, which often take the form of specialised gills. This is a peculiarly instructive case, because Limapontia in its early developmental stages possesses a large spirally coiled shell, and shows other evidence of descent from forms with specialised breathing organs. We are certainly right in associating the absence of respiratory organs in the adult with the small size of the animal ; and comparison with allied forms suggests very strongly that there has been in its pedigree an actual reduction of size, which has led to the degeneration of the respiratory organs.

This is an important conclusion: it is a well-known fact that the smaller members of a group are as a rule more simply organised than the larger members, especially with regard to their respiratory and circulatory systems; but if we are right in concluding that reduction in size may be an actual cause of simplification or degeneration in structure, then we must be on our guard against assuming hastily that these smaller and simpler animals are necessarily primitive in regard to the groups to which they belong. It is possible for instance that the simplification or even absence of respiratory organs seen in Pauropus, in the Thysanura, and in other small Tracheata, may be a secondary character, acquired through reduction of size.

An interesting illustration of the law discussed above is afforded by the brains of mammals; it has been noticed by many anatomists that the extent of convolution, or folding of the surface of the cerebral hemispheres in mammals, is related not to the degree of intelligence of the animal, but to its actual size, a beaver having an almost smooth brain and a cow a highly complicated one. Jelgersma, and independently of him Professor Fitzgerald,* have explained this as due to the necessity of preserving the due proportion between the outer layer of grey matter or cortex, which is approximately uniform in thickness, and the central mass of white matter.

* *Cf. Nature*, June 5, 1890, p. 125.

But for the foldings of the surface the proportion of white matter to grey matter would be far higher in a large than in a small brain.

It must not be forgotten on the other hand, that many zoologists hold the view, in favour of which the evidence is steadily increasing, that the primitive or ancestral members of each group were of small size. Thus Fürbringer remarks with regard to birds that on the whole small birds show more primitive and simpler conditions of structure than the larger members of the same group. He expresses the opinion that the first birds were probably smaller than Archæapteryx, and notes that reptiles and mammals also show in their earlier and smaller types more primitive features than do their larger descendants. Finally, Fürbringer concludes that "it is therefore the study of the smaller members within given groups of animals which promises the best results as to their phylogeny."

Again, one of the most striking points with regard to the pedigree of the horse, as agreed on by palæontologists, is the progressive reduction in size which we meet with as we pass backwards in time from stage to stage. The Pliocene Hipparion was smaller than the existing horse, in fact about the size of a donkey; the Miocene Mesohippus about equalled a sheep; while Eohippus, from the Lower Eocene deposits, was no larger than a fox. Not only is there good reason for holding that as a rule larger animals are descended from ancestors of smaller size, but there is also much evidence to show that increase in size beyond certain limits is disadvantageous, and may lead to destruction rather than to survival. It has happened more than once in the history of the world, and in more than one group of animals, that gigantic stature has been attained immediately before extinction of the group, a final and tremendous effort to secure survival, but a despairing and unsuccessful one. The Ichthyosauri, Plesiosauri, and other extinct reptilian groups, the Moas, and the huge extinct Edentates, are well-known examples, to which before long will be added the elephants and the whales, and it may be iron-clads as well. The whole question of the influence of size is of the greatest possible interest and importance, and it is greatly to be hoped that it will not be permitted to remain in its present uncertain and unsatisfactory condition.

It may be suggested that Amphioxus is an animal which has undergone reduction in size, and that its structural simplicity may, like that of Limapontia, be due in part at least to this reduction. Such evidence as we have tells against this suggestion ; the first system to undergo degeneration in consequence of a reduction in size is the respiratory, and the respiratory organs of Amphioxus, though very simple, are also for a vertebrate unusually extensive.

We have now considered the more important of the influences which are recognised as affecting developmental history in such a way as to render the recapitulation of ancestral stages less complete than it might otherwise be, which tend to prevent ontogeny from correctly repeating the phylogenetic history. It may at this point reasonably be asked whether there is any way of distinguishing the palingenetic history from the later cenogenetic modifications grafted on to it ; any test by which we can determine whether a given larval character is or is not ancestral. Most assuredly there is no one rule, no single test that will apply in all cases ; but there are certain considerations which will help us, and which should be kept in view.

A character that is of general occurrence among the members of a group, both high and low, may reasonably be regarded as having strong claims to ancestral rank ; claims that are greatly strengthened if it occurs at corresponding developmental periods in all cases ; and still more if it occurs equally in forms that hatch early as free larvæ, and in forms with large eggs, which develop directly into the adult. As examples of such characters may be cited the mode of formation and relations of the notochord, and of the gill clefts of vertebrates, which satisfy all the conditions mentioned. Characters that are transitory in certain groups, but retained throughout life in allied groups, may with tolerable certainty be regarded as ancestral for the former ; for instance the symmetrical position of the eyes in young flat fish, the spiral shell of the young limpet, the superficial positions of the madreporite in Elasipodous Holothurians, or the suckerless condition of the ambulacral feet in many Echinoderms.

A more important consideration is that if the developmental changes are to be interpreted as a correct record of ancestral history, then the several stages must be possible ones, the history must be one that could actually have occurred—*i.e.*, the several steps of the history as reconstructed must form a series, all the stages of which are practicable ones. Natural selection explains the actual structure of a complex organ as having been acquired by the preservation of a series of stages, each a distinct if slight advance on the stage immediately preceding it, an advance so distinct as to confer on its possessor an appreciable advantage in the struggle for existence. It is not enough that the ultimate stage should be more advantageous than the initial or earlier condition, but each intermediate stage must also be a distinct advance. If then the development of an organ is strictly recapitulatory, it should present to us a series of stages, each of which is not merely functional, but a distinct advance on the stage immediately preceding it. Intermediate stages—*e.g.*, the solid œsophagus of the tadpole—which are not and could not be functional, can form no part of an ancestral series; a consideration well expressed by Sedgwick* thus : " Any phylogenetic hypothesis which presents difficulties from a physiological standpoint must be regarded as very provisional indeed."

A good example of an embryological series fulfilling these conditions is afforded by the development of the eye in the higher Cephalopoda. The earliest stage consists in the depression of a

* Sedgwick, "On the Early Development of the Anterior Part of the Wolffian Duct and Body in the Chick," *Quarterly Journal of Microscopical Science*, vol. xxi. 1881, p. 456.

slightly modified patch of skin ; round the edge of the patch the epidermis becomes raised up as a rim ; this gradually grows inwards from all sides, so that the depressed patch now forms a pit, communicating with the exterior through a small hole or mouth. By further growth the mouth of the pit becomes still more narrowed, and ultimately completely closed, so that the pit becomes converted into a closed sac or vesicle ; at the point at which final closure occurs formation of cuticle takes place, which projects as a small transparent drop into the cavity of the sac ; by formation of concentric layers of cuticle this drop becomes enlarged into the spherical transparent lens of the eye, and the development is completed by histological changes in the inner wall of the vesicle, which convert it into the retina, and by the formation of folds of skin around the eye, which become the iris and the eyelids respectively.

Each stage in this developmental history is a distinct advance, physiologically, on the preceding stage, and furthermore each stage is retained at the present day as the permanent condition of the eye in some member of the group Mollusca. The earliest stage, in which the eye is merely a slightly depressed and slightly modified patch of skin, represents the simplest condition of the Molluscan eye, and is retained throughout life in Solen. The stage in which the eye is a pit, with widely open mouth, is retained in the limpet ; it is a distinct advance on the former, as through the greater depression the sensory cells are less exposed to accidental injury. The narrowing of the mouth of the pit in the next stage is a simple change, but a very important step forwards. Up to this point the eye has served to distinguish light from darkness, but the formation of an image has been impossible. Now, owing to the smallness of the aperture, and the pigmentation of the walls of the pit, which accompanies the change, light from any one part of an object can only fall on one particular part of the inner wall of the pit or retina, and so an image, though a dim one, is formed. This type of eye is permanently retained in the Nautilus. The closing of the mouth of the pit by a transparent membrane will not affect the optical properties of the eye, and will be a gain, as it will prevent the entrance of foreign bodies into the cavity of the eye. The formation of the lens by deposit of cuticle is the next step. The gain here is increased distinctness and increased brightness of the image, for the lens will focus the rays of light more sharply on the retina, and will allow a greater quantity of light, a larger pencil of rays from each part of the object, to reach the corresponding part of the retina. The eye is now in the condition in which it remains throughout life in the snail and other gasteropods. Finally the formation of the folds of skin known as iris and eyelids provide for the better protection of the eye, and is a clear advance on the somewhat clumsy method of withdrawal seen in the snail.

The development of the vertebrate liver is another good but simpler example. The most primitive form of the liver is that of Amphioxus, in which it is present as a simple saccular diverticulum of the intestinal canal, with its wall consisting of a single layer of cells, and with bloodvessels on its outer surface. The earliest stage in the formation of the liver in higher vertebrates—the frog, for instance—is practically identical with this. In the frog the next stage consists in folding of the wall of the sac, which increases the efficiency of the organ by increasing the extent of surface in contact with bloodvessels. The adult condition is attained simply by a continuance of this process ; the foldings of the wall becoming more and more complicated, but the essential structure remaining the same—a single layer of epithelial cells in contact on one side with bloodvessels, and bounding on the other directly or indirectly the cavity of the alimentary canal.

It is not always possible to point out the particular advantage gained at each step even when a complete developmental series is known to us, but in such cases, as for instance in Orbitolites, our difficulties arise chiefly from ignorance of the particular conditions that confer advantage in the struggle for existence in the case of the forms we are dealing with.

The early larval stages in the development of animals, and more especially those that are marine and pelagic in habit, have naturally attracted much attention, since in the absence, probably inevitable, of satisfactory palæontological evidence, they afford us the sole available clue to the determination of the mutual relations of the large groups of animals, or of the points at which these diverged from one another.

In attempting to interpret these early ontogenetic stages as actual ancestral forms, beyond which development at one time did not proceed, we must keep clearly in view the various disturbing causes which tend to falsify the ancestral record; such as the influence of food yolk, or of habitat, and the tendency of diminution in size to give rise to simplification of structure, a point of importance if it be granted that these free larvæ are of smaller size than the ancestral forms to which they correspond. If on the other hand, in spite of these powerful modifying causes, we do find a particular larval form occurring widely and in groups not very closely akin, then we certainly are justified in attaching great importance to it, and in regarding it as having strong claims to be accepted as ancestral for these groups.

Concerning these larval forms, and their possible ancestral significance, our knowledge has made no great advance since the publication of Balfour's memorable chapter on this subject; and I propose merely to allude briefly to a few of the more striking instances. The earliest, the most widely spread, and the most famous of larval forms is the gastrula, which occurs in a simple or in a modified form in some members of each of the large animal groups. It is generally admitted that its significance is the same in all cases, and the evidence is very strong in favour of regarding it as a stage ancestral for all Metazoa. The difficulty arising from its varying mode of development in different forms is however still unsolved, and embryologists are not yet agreed whether the invaginate or delaminate form is the more primitive. In favour of the former is its much wider occurrence; in favour of the latter the fact that it is easy to picture a series of stages leading gradually from a unicellular protozoon to a blastula, a diblastula, and ultimately a gastrula, each stage being a distinct advance, both morphological and physiological, on the preceding stage; while in the case of the invaginate gastrula it is not easy to imagine any advantage resulting from a flattening or slight pitting in of one part of the surface, sufficient to lead to its preservation and further development.

Of larval forms later than the gastrula, the most important by far is the Pilidium larva, from which it is possible, as Balfour has shown, that the slightly later Echinoderm larva, as well as the widely spread Trochosphere larva, may both be derived. Balfour concludes that the larval forms of all Cœlomata, excluding the crustacea and vertebrates, may be derived from one common type, which is most nearly represented now by the Pilidium larva and which "was an organism something like a Medusa, with a radial symmetry." The tendency of recent phylogenetic speculations is to accept this in full, and to regard as the ancestor of Turbellarians and of all higher forms, a jelly-fish or Ctenophoran, which in place of swimming freely has taken to crawling on the sea-bottom.

Of the two groups excluded above, the Crustacea and the Vertebrata, the interest of the former centres in the much discussed problem of the significance of the Nauplius larva. There is now a fairly general agreement that the primitive crustacea were types akin to the phyllopods—*i.e.*, forms with elongated and many-segmented bodies, and a large number of pairs of similar appendages. If this is correct, then the explanation of the Nauplius stage must be afforded by the phyllopods themselves, and it is no use looking beyond this group for it. A Nauplius larva occurs in other crustacea merely because they have inherited from their phyllopod ancestors the tendency to develop such a stage, and it is quite legitimate to hold that higher crustaceans are descended from phyllopods, and that the Nauplius represents in more or less modified form an earlier ancestor of the phyllopods themselves.

As to the Nauplius itself the first thing to note is that though an early larval form, it cannot be a very primitive form, for it is already an unmistakable crustacean ; the absence of cilia, the formation of a cuticular investment, the presence of jointed schizopodous limbs, together with other anatomical characters, proving this point conclusively. It follows therefore either that the earlier and more primitive stages are entirely omitted in the development of crustacea, or else that the Nauplius represents such an early ancestral stage with crustacean characters which properly belong to a later stage, thrown back upon it and precociously developed.   The latter explanation is the one usually adopted ; but before the question can be finally decided more accurate observations than we at present possess are needed concerning the stages intermediate between the egg and the Nauplius.   The absence of a heart in the Nauplius may reasonably be associated with the small size of the larva.

Concerning the larval forms of vertebrates, it is only in Amphioxus and the Ascidians that the earliest larval stages are free-living, independent animals.   In both groups the most characteristic larval stage is that in which a notochord is present, and a neural tube, open in front, and communicating behind through a neurenteric canal with the digestive cavity, which has no other opening to the exterior. This is a very early stage, both in Amphioxus and Ascidians ; but so far as we know, it cannot be compared with any invertebrate larva.   It is customary, in discussions on the affinities of vertebrates, to absolutely ignore the vertebrate larval forms, and to assume that their peculiarities are due to precocious development of vertebrate characteristics.   It may turn out that this view of the matter is correct ; but it has certainly not yet been proved to be so, and the development of both Amphioxus and Ascidians is so direct and straightforward that evidence of some kind may reasonably be required before accepting the doctrine that this development is entirely deceptive with regard to the ancestry of vertebrates.

Zoologists have not quite made up their minds

what to do with Amphioxus : apparently the most guileless of creatures, many view it with the utmost suspicion, and not merely refuse to accept its mute protestations of innocence, but regard and speak of it as the most artful of deceivers. Few questions at the present day are in greater need of authoritative settlement.

That ontogeny really is a repetition of phylogeny must I think be admitted, in spite of the numerous and various ways in which the ancestral history may be distorted during actual development. Before leaving the subject, it is worth while inquiring whether any explanation can be found of recapitulation. A complete answer can certainly not be given at present, but a partial one may perhaps be obtained.   Darwin himself suggested that the clue might be found in the consideration that at whatever age a variation first appears in the parent, it tends to reappear at a corresponding age in the offspring, but this must be regarded rather as a statement of the fundamental fact of embryology than as an explanation of it.   It is probably safe to assume that animals would not recapitulate unless they were compelled to do so : that there must be some constraining influence at work, forcing them to repeat more or less closely the ancestral stages.   It is impossible, for instance, to conceive what advantage it can be to a reptilian or mammalian embryo to develop gill clefts which are never used, and which disappear at a slightly later stage ; or how it can benefit a whale, that in its embryonic condition it should possess teeth which never cut the gum, and which are lost before birth. Moreover, the history of development in different animals or groups of animals offers to us, as we have seen, a series of ingenious, determined, varied, but more or less unsuccessful efforts to escape from the necessity of recapitulating, and to substitute for the ancestral process a more direct method. A further consideration of importance is that recapitulation is not seen in all forms of development, but only in sexual development ; or at least only in development from the egg. In the several forms of asexual development, of which budding is the most frequent and most familiar, there is no repetition of ancestral phases ; neither is there in cases of regeneration of lost parts, such as the tentacle of a snail, the arm of a starfish, or the tail of a lizard ; in such regeneration it is not a larval tentacle, or arm, or tail, that is produced, but an adult one.

The most striking point about the development of the higher animals is that they all alike commence as eggs. Looking more closely at the egg and the conditions of its development, two facts impress us as of special importance : first, the egg is a single cell, and therefore represents morphologically the Protozoon, or earliest ancestral phase ; secondly, the egg, before it can develop, must be fertilised by a spermatozoon, just as the stimulus of fertilisation by the pollen grain is necessary before the ovum of a plant will commence to develop into the plant-embryo.

The advantage of cross-fertilisation in increasing the vigour of the offspring is well known, and in plants devices of the most varied and even extra-ordinary kind are adopted to ensure that such cross-fertilisation occurs.   The essence of the act of cross-fertilisation, which is already established among Protozoa, consists in combination of the nuclei of two cells, male and female, derived from different individuals.   The nature of the process is of such a kind that two individual cells are alone concerned in it; and it may I think be reasonably argued that the reason why animals commence their existence as eggs—*i.e.*, as single cells—is because it is in this way only that the advantage of cross-fertilisation can be secured, an advantage admittedly of the greatest importance, and to secure which natural selection would operate powerfully.

The occurrence of parthenogenesis, either occa-sionally or normally, in certain groups is not I think a serious objection to this view.   There are very strong reasons for holding that partheno-genetic development is a modified form, derived from the sexual method.   Moreover, the view advanced above does not require that cross-fertilisa-tion should be essential to individual development, but merely that it should be in the highest degree advantageous to the species, and hence leaves room for the occurrence, exceptionally, of parthenogenetic development.

If it be objected that this is laying too much stress on sexual reproduction, and on the advantage of cross-fertilisation, then it may be pointed out in reply that sexual reproduction is the character-istic and essential mode of multiplication among

Metazoa ; that it occurs in all Metazoa, and that when asexual reproduction, as by budding, &c., occurs, this merely alternates with the sexual process which sooner or later becomes essential. If the fundamental importance of sexual reproduction to the welfare of the species be granted, and if it be further admitted that Metazoa are descended from Protozoa, then we see that there is really a constraining force of a most powerful nature compelling every animal to commence its life-history in the unicellular condition, the only condition in which the advantage of cross-fertilisation can be obtained—*i.e.*, constraining every animal to begin its development at its earliest ancestral stage, at the very bottom of its genealogical tree.

On this view the actual development of any animal is strictly limited at both ends ; it must commence as an egg, and it must end in the likeness of the parent. The problem of recapitulation becomes thereby greatly narrowed ; all that remains being to explain why the intermediate stages in the actual development should repeat the intermediate stages of the ancestral history. Although narrowed in this way, the problem still remains one of extreme difficulty.

It is a consequence of the Theory of Natural Selection that identity of structure involves community of descent : a given result can only be arrived at through a given sequence of events : the same morphological goal cannot be reached by two independent paths. A negro and a white man have had common ancestors in the past ;

and it is through the long-continued action of selection and environment that the two types have been gradually evolved. You cannot turn a white man into a negro merely by sending him to live in Africa: to create a negro the whole ancestral history would have to be repeated; and it may be that it is for the same reason that the embryo must repeat or recapitulate its ancestral history in order to reach the adult goal. I am not sure that we can at present get much further; but the above considerations give opportunity for brief notice of what is perhaps the most noteworthy of recent embryological papers, Kleinenberg's remarkable monograph on Lopadorhynchus.

Kleinenberg directs special attention to what is known to evolutionists as the difficulty with regard to the origin of new organs, which is to the effect that although natural selection is competent to account for any amount of modification in an organ after it has attained a certain size, and become of functional importance, yet that it cannot account for the earliest stages in the formation of an organ before it has become large enough or sufficiently developed to be of real use. The difficulty is a serious one; it is carefully considered by Mr. Darwin, and met completely in certain cases; but as Kleinenberg correctly states, no general explanation has been offered with regard to such instances.

As such general explanation Kleinenberg proposes his theory of the development of organs by substitution. He points out that any modification of an organ or tissue must involve modification, at least in functional activity, of other organs. He then continues by urging that one organ may replace or be substituted for another, the replacing organ being in no way derived morphologically from the replaced or preceding organ, but having a genetic relation to it of this kind: that it can only arise in an organism so constituted, and is dependent on the prior existence of the replaced organ, which supplies the necessary stimulus for its formation. As an example he takes the axial skeleton of vertebrates. The notochord, formed by change of function from the wall of the digestive canal, is the sole skeleton of the lowest vertebrates, and the earliest developmental phase in all the higher forms. The notochord gives rise directly to no other organ, but is gradually replaced by other and unlike structures by substitution. The notochord is an intermediate organ, and the cartilaginous skeleton which replaces it is only intelligible through the previous existence of the notochord; while, in its turn, the cartilaginous skeleton gives way, being replaced, through substitution, by the bony skeleton.

The successive phases in the evolution of weapons might be quoted as an illustration of Kleinenberg's theory. The bow and arrow are a better weapon than a stick or stone; they are used for the same purpose, and the importance or need for a better weapon led to the replacement of the sling by the bow. The bow does not arise by further develop-

ment or increasing perfection of the sling; it is
an entirely new weapon, towards the formation
of which the older and more primitive weapons
have acted as a stimulus, and which has replaced
these latter by substitution, while the substitution
at a later date of firearms for the bow and arrow
is merely a further instance of the same principle.

It is too early yet to realise the full significance
of Kleinenberg's most suggestive theory; but if it
be really true that each historic stage in the evolution of an organ is necessary as a stimulus to the
development of the next succeeding stage, then it
becomes clear why animals are constrained to recapitulate.   Kleinenberg suggests further that the
extraordinary persistence in embryonic life of
organs which are rudimentary and functionless in
the adult may also be explained by his theory, the
presence of such organs in the embryo being indispensable as a stimulus to the development of the
permanent structures of the adult.   It would be
easy to point out difficulties in the way of the
theory. The omission of historic stages in the
actual ontogenetic development, of which almost
all groups of animals supply striking examples, is
one of the most serious; for if these stages are
necessary as stimuli for the succeeding stages,
then their omission requires explanation; while if
such stimuli are not necessary, the theory would
appear to need revision.   Such objections may
however prove to be less serious than they appear
at first sight; and in any case Kleinenberg's
theory may be welcomed as an important and

original contribution, which deserves—indeed demands—the fullest and most careful consideration from all morphologists, and which acquires special interest from the explanation it offers of recapitulation as a mechanical process, through which alone it is possible for an embryo to attain the adult structure.

That recapitulation does actually occur, that the several stages in the development of an animal are inseparably linked with and determined by its ancestral history, must be accepted. "To take any other view is to admit that the structure of animals and the history of their development form a mere snare to entrap our judgment." Embryology however is not to be regarded as a master-key that is to open the gates of knowledge and remove all obstacles from our path without further trouble on our part; it is rather to be viewed and treated as a delicate and complicated instrument, the proper handling of which requires the utmost nicety of balance and adjustment, and which, unless employed with the greatest skill and judgment, may yield false instead of true results.

Embryology is indeed a most powerful and efficient aid, but it will not, and cannot, provide us with an immediate or complete answer to the great riddle of life. Complications, distortions, innumerable and bewildering, confront us at every step, and the progress of knowledge has so far served rather to increase the number and magnitude of these pitfalls than to teach us how to avoid them. Still there is no cause for despair—far from it.

If our difficulties are increasing, so also are our means of grappling with them ; if the goal appears harder to reach than we thought, on the other hand its position is far better defined, and the means of approach, the lines of attack, are more clearly recognised.   One thing above all is apparent—that embryologists must not work single-handed, and must not be satisfied with an acquaintance, however exact, with animals from the side of development only ; for embryos have this in common with maps, that too close and too exclusive a study of them is apt to disturb a man's reasoning power.

Embryology is a means, not an end.   Our ambition is to explain in what manner and by what stages the present structure of animals has been attained.   Towards this embryology affords most potent aid ; but the eloquent protest of the great anatomist of Heidelberg must be laid to heart, and it must not be forgotten that it is through comparative anatomy that its power to help is derived.   What would it profit us, as Gegenbaur justly asks, to know that the higher vertebrates when embryos, have slits in their throats, unless through comparative anatomy we were acquainted with forms now existing in which these slits are structures essential to existence ? Anatomy defines the goal, tells us of the things that have to be explained ; embryology offers a means, otherwise denied to us, of attaining it. Comparative anatomy and palæontology must be studied most earnestly by those who would turn the lessons of embryology to best account, and it must never be forgotten that it is to men like Johannes Müller, Stannius, Cuvier, and John Hunter —the men to whom our exact knowledge of comparative anatomy is due—that we owe also the possibility of a science of embryology.

Printed by BALLANTYNE, HANSON & Co.
London & Edinburgh

A SELECTION FROM DAVID NUTT'S LIST OF PUBLICATIONS

POETRY

WILLIAM ERNEST HENLEY

A BOOK OF VERSES. In Hospital, Rhymes and Rhythms — Life and Death (Echoes) — Bric-à-Brac: Ballads, Rondels, Sonnets, Quatorzains, and Rondeaus. xii., 175 pages, 16mo. 1893. Etched Title-page Vignette of the Old Infirmary, Edinburgh, by W. HOLE, A.R.S.A. Fourth Edition. Cloth, 5s. net.

Mr. R. L. Stevenson says at the close of his Christmas Article (*Scribner*, 1888): "From a recent book of verse, where there is more than one such beautiful manly poem, I take this memorial piece; it says better than I can what I love to think."

The Spectator says "the author is a genuine poet."

LONDON VOLUNTARIES. Being the Second Edition of the "Song of the Sword." 1893. 16mo, 130 pages. Cloth, top gilt, 5s. net.

**** *This Second Edition has been enlarged by the inclusion of "Arabian Nights' Entertainment," and Epilogue "Something is Dead."*

LYRA HEROICA. An Anthology selected from the best English Verse of the Sixteenth, Seventeenth, Eighteenth, and Nineteenth Centuries. Library (Third) Edition. Crown 8vo, xviii., 362 pages. Cloth, uncut edges, stamped cover, 3s. 6d. ; or, School (Second) Edition. 12mo, cloth, 2s.

**** *Unanimously recommended by organs of every shade of opinion, critical and political, as the best Anthology of Heroic Verse in the language.*

BLISS CARMAN

LOW TIDE ON GRAND PRÉ. Poems. 1893. Small 4to, 116 pages. Cloth, 5s. net.

Academy.—"All these Acadian lyrics are dominated by an overmastering sense of beauty, and permeated with a love of nature, for which there is no epithet so apt as the' much misused and hackneyed word intense."

CHARLES SAYLE

MUSA CONSOLATRIX. Poems. 1893. 12mo, 130 pages. Wrapper. 3s. 6d.

H. D. RAWNSLEY

IDYLLS AND LYRICS OF THE NILE. 1894. 12mo, 148 pages. Cloth.

CRITICISM

WILLIAM ERNEST HENLEY

VIEWS AND REVIEWS. Essays in Appreciation. Literature. Second Edition. 1893. 16mo, xii., 228 pages. Cloth, top gilt, 5s. net.

Spectator.—" One of the most remarkable volumes of literary criticism —in more senses than one it is the most striking—that have appeared for years."

Athenæum.—" Attracts and delights the reader."

JOSEPH JACOBS

GEORGE ELIOT; MATTHEW ARNOLD; BROWNING; NEWMAN; Essays and Reviews from the *Athenæum.* 16mo. 1891. xxiv., 152 pages. Cloth, 2s. 6d.

Spectator.—" Full of suggestion."
Literary World.—" As important as it is interesting."
Pall Mall Gazette.—" Scholarly and moderate in tone and broad in view."

TENNYSON: and, IN MEMORIAM. 16mo. 1892. 108 pages. Cloth, 2s.

Spectator.—" A thoughtful and kindly critic."
Anti-Jacobin.—" Exceptionally well written, and the work of a clear, acute, and independent mind."

GEORGE MOORE

IMPRESSIONS AND OPINIONS. (Balzac, Turguenieff, Verlaine, Ibsen, Mummer Worship, &c). 16mo, 346 pages, Cloth. 1891. 5s.

National Observer.—" Packed full of ideas."
Literary World.—" One of the freshest and most interesting volumes of criticism that have appeared for some time."

G. S. STREET

MINIATURES AND MOODS. 16mo. 1893. vii., 113 pages. Cloth, 3s. 6d.

National Observer.—" In its charmingly foppish fashion a decided success."

W. C. BROWNELL.

FRENCH TRAITS. 12mo, 400 pages. Cloth, uncut, 7s.

**** *The most suggestive and penetrating study of the social and moral ideas of French Society in the English language.*

Athenæum.—" We doubt whether so thoughtful, so valuable a page of international criticism has appeared since M. Taine's ' Notes on England.' "

FRENCH ART. Crown 8vo. 1892. 248 pages. Cloth, 6s.

Athenæum.—" Rare perspicacity of judgment and clearness of expression."

GIFT BOOKS FOR THE YOUNG

JOSEPH JACOBS

THE FAIRY TALES OF THE BRITISH EMPIRE.
Collected and Edited from printed sources and oral tradition.
With Notes exhibiting the sources, parallels, and literary history of
each tale. Profusely illustrated with full page-plates, head and
tail pieces, cuts in the text, and initials, by J. D. BATTEN. Square
crown 8vo. Each volume, upwards of 270 pages, sumptuously
printed on special paper, with wide margins, in specially designed
cloth cover, 6s.

Already Issued

ENGLISH FAIRY TALES. 1890. CELTIC FAIRY TALES. 1891.
INDIAN FAIRY TALES. 1892. MORE ENGLISH FAIRY TALES.
1893.

**** *The laudatory press notices are too numerous to quote from. The
Series has unanimously been recognised as one of the best ever issued.*

OSCAR WILDE

THE HAPPY PRINCE, AND OTHER TALES. 116
pages, small 4to. Old-faced type, on cream-laid paper with wide
margins, Japanese vellum cover printed in red and black. With
Three full-page Plates and Eleven Vignettes by WALTER CRANE
and JACOMB HOOD. Second Edition. Price 3s. 6d.

Athenæum.—"The gift of writing fairy tales is rare, and Mr. Oscar
Wilde shows that he possesses it in a rare degree."

DOLLIE RADFORD

SONGS FOR SOMEBODY. With designs by G. M.
BRADLEY. Square 8vo. 32 pages printed in monotint, and 6
pages printed in colours, by EDMUND EVANS. With specially
designed cover, printed in colours. 3s. 6d.

**** *In addition to the ordinary issue, a few copies have been struck off
on the finest Japanese vellum, with the cover design stamped in gold.
The price of these is 15s. net.*

Sylvia's Journal.—"A most delightful little book for children."

FOLK-LORE

G. L. GOMME

A DICTIONARY OF BRITISH FOLK-LORE. Part I.
—The Traditional Games of England, Scotland, and Ireland, with
Tunes, Singing-rhymes, and methods of playing according to the
variants extant and recorded in different parts of the kingdom.
Vol. I.—Accroshay—Nuts in May. Demy 8vo, xx., 433 pages.
Numerous Illustrations. Cloth, 12s. 6d. net.

(Vol. II. *Christmas* 1894.)

MISS L. M. GARNETT

THE WOMEN OF TURKEY AND THEIR FOLK-LORE. Complete Edition, with Ethnological and Sociological Appendices, by J. S. STUART-GLENNIE. Two Vols., large 8vo, (1100 pages). 1890-91. £1 6s. 6d. ; or, Text Edition in One Volume (1000 pages), 10s. 6d.

*** *The standard English work on the Folk-lore of the Balkan Peninsula and the Levant.*

G. L. GRINNELL

GRINNELL'S PAWNEE HERO STORIES AND FOLK-TALES—GRINNELL'S BLACKFOOT LODGE TALES Two Vols. 8vo. 1893. (445 and 310 pages). Each 7s. 6d.

*** *Mr. Grinnell lived many years among the Prairie Indians, and his two volumes are the most compact and faithful account of their Mythology, Legendary History, and Ceremonial Customs.*

ALFRED NUTT

STUDIES OF THE LEGEND OF THE HOLY GRAIL, with special reference to the Hypothesis of its Celtic Origin. 8vo. 1888. 300 pages. 10s. 6d.

*** *The only English work on this branch of the Arthurian Romance.*

DR. DOUGLAS HYDE

BESIDE THE FIRE. Irish Folk-Tales, Collected, Edited, and Translated by Dr. DOUGLAS HYDE. With Additional Notes by ALFRED NUTT. Crown 8vo, 260 pages. 1891. 7s. 6d.

ALICE MORSE EARLE

CUSTOMS AND FASHIONS IN OLD NEW ENG-LAND. 12mo, 320 pages. Cloth, uncut, gilt top. 7s. 6d.

CONTENTS :—Child Life—Courtship and Marriage—Domestic Service—Home Interiors—Table Plenishings—Larder Supplies—Drinks and Drinkers—Travel, Tavern, and Turnpike—Holidays and Festivals—Sports and Diversions—Books and Bookmakers—Artifices of Handsomeness—Raiment and Vesture—Doctors and Patients—Funeral and Burial.

*** *A mine of information for the Student of English over-sea manners and speech in the 17th and 18th centuries. .*

KUNO MEYER

THE VISION OF MacCONGLINNE. A 12th Century Irish Wonder Tale. Edited and Translated by KUNO MEYER. With Literary Introduction by W. WOLLNER. Crown 8vo. 1892. liv. and 212 pages. Cloth, 10s. 6d.

*** *A most picturesque and spirited Rabelaisian tale dealing with a supernatural land of plenty. Equally important to the Irish philologist and to the student of mediæval legend.*